FRANZISCA'S BOX

SANDRA PEREZ GLUSCHANKOFF

Cover Art:
Michelle Crocker
http://mlcdesigns4you.weebly.com/

Publisher's Note:
This is a work of fiction. All names, characters, places, and
events are the work of the author's imagination.
Any resemblance to real persons, places, or events is
coincidental.

Solstice Publishing - www.solsticepublishing.com

Franzisca's Box

A novel by

Sandra Perez Gluschankoff

Dedication

To my Abuela Bibi who came to me in a dream and along
brought this story.

Part I

Chapter One

"*Your* abuela *is dead.*" The fateful news delivered by the voice of my estranged mother chased me all the way back to the home I had shared with Abuela, my grandmother, for the past twenty years. I had always entered the house through the garage and continued straight into the kitchen where the scent of a freshly baked pie, dark Turkish coffee along with the warm embrace of my grandmother awaited me. A rising fear of confronting the empty kitchen devoid of its familiar scents and its elegant hostess gave me pause. I felt like a coward, guilty for having let her die alone. I stepped down off the porch and filled my lungs with fresh air, taking in the beauty of the place we had called home. I turned to take a look at the hills sprouting with new green and yellow plant life and I was filled with happy memories. Abuela had loved this place and it was here where she had taught me to see the intricate magic of nature. This was the best time of the year, when the dead moldering vegetation of winter dissolved back into the ground, giving way to tender, sweet pastures that readied themselves to welcome the spring does and their fawns. I laughed inwardly at the irony of the scenery in front of me. I was witnessing life at its pinnacle, while death, my abuela's death, was what had brought me back to face it.

The short walk around the property grounds led me up to the front steps of the house. There was no use in delaying the inevitable any longer, so gathering strength I did not feel, I pushed the key into the lock before the enormity of the task ahead would send me reeling back into the shelter of the open fields.

My footsteps echoed through the silent house, making me feel like a trespasser. The objects Abuela had carefully selected to become part of her fortress now glowered at me for interrupting their mourning. I was not the only one feeling empty. This home, the place she had reigned, had lost its queen.

I followed the yellow glow of light that emanated from Abuela's study. For the past two decades, the warm glow of her brass lamp had become a testament to her solid presence, acting as a beacon, a safe path to her, and to her love.

I hesitated at the study's threshold, but the familiar light lured me in. Always the optimist, I glanced around the room and met the grieving silence along with Abuela's empty leather recliner with a feeling of disbelief. The cream chiffon drapes that framed the windows were drawn, rejecting the intrusion of natural light and the view of her favorite alpine roses. The cord connecting Abuela's old-fashioned, black rotary phone to its jack lay unplugged on the wood floor, reluctant to receive calls. Gone was the pile of pending files that she kept on top of her sixteenth-century, Spanish, cherry-wood desk, as if she had attended to the last of their details before she saw fit to stash them away. Everything around her study lay in a state of disturbing order. And everything pointed to an intruder placed in the center of her large desk. It was an unfamiliar letter-sized box that immediately stole all of my attention. The box was made of wood, clearly weathered by the passing of time and splotched with water stains around the edges. A sheet of Abuela's personalized stationary, folded in half, rested atop the box with my name scrawled across it. The brass desk-lamp stood strategically poised over the tattered container, its golden light illuminating the box, leaving no doubt that she had staged its delivery. All this mystery around a beat-up box made no sense, such as my last conversation with Abuela had made no sense to me at all at the time.

Roughly twenty-four-hours ago, my day had started like any other ordinary day since we began filming what I secretly called, *The Italian Nightmare*. With only four hours of sleep and legs hairier than Jane of the Jungle, I woke up that morning in Siena, Italy, wishing for the movie I was currently producing to be over and done with so I could fly back home to Solvang, California.

With the flavor of the rosemary-raisin bun I had eaten earlier that morning still lingering in my mouth, I pondered over the one commitment awaiting me in Solvang: breakfast with Abuela at her favorite pancake house.

"Sofia."

I lifted my eyes from my laptop to find my assistant waving my ringing cell phone in the air.

She did not say who the caller was. I knew the call was from Abuela. No one ever called me on that number while I was working on location, but general rules did not apply to her. Still, she had never called me in the middle of the day.

Abuela had been everything to me; grandmother, mother, teacher, friend. Ours was a relationship in which unspoken love said more than any of the secrets she had never shared with me. Even at a distance, when my career had taken me away, we had always stayed connected. She was my last phone call before going to sleep regardless of which time zone I was in at that time. As much as I tried to argue against disrupting her sleeping pattern, she would not have it any other way.

With still twelve hours to go to our next phone call, I had found this mid-morning communication uncharacteristically strange.

"Everything okay, Abuela?"

For the first time in thirty years, without preambles, she dove straight into a subject we tended to skirt around.

"Sofia, are you happy?" she asked.

No one had ever asked me that question before, especially not her. Before answering, I looked around the set, felt a pull in my lower back that had nagged me for the past two weeks and visualized my unshaven legs.

"Yes, I am happy."

After a prolonged silence, she came back on the line sounding a bit hoarse as though she had been crying. "I love you, Sofia."

Her urgent declaration had come as a shock. For Abuela the word love was not spoken freely. Her conception of love was a raw, unrestrained surrender of oneself to another, a responsibility, a lifetime commitment. I knew she loved me, but why had she the need to assert it now?

"Abuela, are you all right?" I asked. My chest had tightened with concern.

"Never better," she said, regaining her steady commanding voice.

The conversation continued without any mention of the sudden pronouncement of her feelings and with my assurance that I would be back home in time for our rescheduled breakfast the following Sunday, even if I was dead on my feet.

Standing alone in her study, the irony of the metaphor undid me. One of us was indeed dead. My eyes slid over the darkened order of the room then went back to the box staring insolently back at me from the center of the desk. It wasn't an ordinary box. Its battered state spoke of safely kept secrets, hardship, survival. There was only one character in my life that had tempered all of those experiences and more. With that in mind, the events of the last twenty-four-hours were gradually falling into place. I thought back on the last conversation I had with Abuela. The way in which she had pronounced the words *I Love You,* brought back long buried childhood memories. Her words hinted to a time when we had shared a love for stories, fantasy, adventure. To Franzisca, the make-believe heroine she had introduced me to during my early childhood years. The fearless adventurer who could do it all, the fictional character I had secretly admired all of my life. The brave woman I've always aspired to be.

I remembered looking around the disheveled state of my rented apartment in Sienna, wondering if I had become who I had dreamt of being. Wondering if I was really happy. I shrugged. Was there a real answer to such an existentialist question? I saw my life as sliced in two. One part was infused with unlimited possibilities alongside Franzisca and her adventures. The other was limited by my fears, my skeptical thoughts on happy endings and my repudiation of everything Franzisca stood for.

Perhaps it had been the piled-up exhaustion throughout the production of *The Italian Nightmare* that had me fervently wishing that I could be embraced again by those stories that used to bring me so much warmth and comfort. Stories I ejected from my life because regardless of how much Abuela loved me, I had learned the hard way that fairytales only belonged in books. The most important question that nagged me with a big question mark was, *why now*? Why did I want to claim Franzisca back? The answer was simple. I missed Abuela terribly; moreover, I missed the connection we shared when we were both immersed in the land of Franzisca.

I couldn't wait for another minute to disclose my feelings to her, in the same way she had done it earlier in the day. I knew that if there was a way to tell her how much I loved her, it was by allowing Franzisca back into my life. I reached for my phone and in that instant the caller ID on my phone's screen blinked with an incoming call from Abuela, as if she had anticipated my need to reach her. I picked up the call on the third ring, "What's up, Abuela?" I said in my best American girl slang. I knew how she despised that commonly used greeting, but I meant to humor her. I was expecting to hear her usual response of, *"nothing is up other than air,"* but instead the voice on the other end was Marcela's, my mother, announcing my abuela's death. Phone in hand and unable to utter a word after she broke the news, all I could think of was my missed opportunity and of Abuela's insistence to never let a moment slip by.

The golden light shining upon the box granted me a glimmer of hope as I recalled a promise I made to Abuela when I was a little girl. With all my might, I pressed my hands on the box and prayed for another opportunity. Perhaps there was still one last chance for me to tell her how much I loved her.

Chapter Two

I reached for the sheet of stationary resting atop the box and stared at Abuela's perfectly rounded longhand. *Sofia.* Had my name been the last word she ever wrote, or had she carefully planned this farewell for a long time?

I held the folded piece of paper to my chest and turned to look out the study's window upon the green valley while the brief conversation with Marcela replayed in my mind. "You'll get a call from her attorney," she said without pause after the announcement of Abuela's passing. It felt like hours before the first word rolled off my tongue.

"How?"

"In her sleep," she said, unemotionally as though reading an obituary from the morning's newspaper.

I heard a hint of relief in Marcela, and for a moment I resented her. Not because she did not sound grief-stricken for the death of the woman that bore her, but because I feared I would have reacted in the same fashion should I had gotten the news of her death. Things with Claudia Lazar, my grandmother, Abuela, as I had called her my whole life, were different from the non-existent relationship I had with Marcela, my mother.

I had become the center of my grandmother's life the moment Marcela had turned her gaze away when the nurse presented me to her. Still, I acknowledge her to be the vessel that carried me for a little over seven months. Of my father I knew close to nothing.

I remembered coming home from preschool, barely four years old, carrying a pencil holder I had made out of an empty can of peas and had embellished with rainbow sparkles. It was a father's day gift. Filled with emotion, I ran into my mother's bedroom demanding to meet my father at once and deliver the shiny can to him. My determination was cut short when I stumbled over one of Marcela's half-packed suitcases and I was hit with the sad realization that she was, once more, leaving for another one of her impromptu one-way-ticket trips.

"This is for my papá." Like any other four-year-old, I held out my hideous creation with infinite pride.

"You don't have one," my mother spat while sorting through a pile of scarves.

"My teacher says we all have one."

"Well, go and tell your teacher that yours walked away the moment he knew you were to be born."

He had walked away and it was my fault. That much was clear for my young ears.

I sensed Abuela standing only a few feet from me listening to my mother's rushed explanation. "Can I see that, Sofia?" came the voice that had swaddled me from the moment I entered this world.

Within seconds I was in Abuela's arms and the pencil holder proudly displayed on her desk.

If I had learned anything about Marcela throughout the years was that she never lied. When I reached the age of seventeen, Abuela confirmed Marcela's story and handed me a photograph of the man who fathered me along with his updated information in the event I felt compelled to contact him.

True to Marcela's word, my father, a pseudo revolutionary with the likes of the Che Guevara, had run away the minute he learned about the impending bundle of joy. The matter of my surname and paternity was a transaction sealed at a corner café in Buenos Aires—my birthplace—between Abuela's lawyer and my father. For a fee, high enough to enable him to pursue his political dreams at the unavoidable end of the military regime in my birth country, he waved his right to ever approach my mother or me.

During my first ten years of life, the three of us lived together in a big *finca,* a large property, in San Rafael, Mendoza, an Argentinean province crowned by the Cordillera de Los Andes, where I saw little of Marcela and a lot of my abuela. By the time I was seven years old, I resigned myself to call my mother by her given name and I also ceased to beg her to attend the yearly school plays, where regardless of voice and drama lessons, I was repeatedly cast as the second tree to the left.

Marcela, I was soon to realize, was a repeat offender of sorts. Her crimes were not punishable with the force of the law. She paid for them with her heart. Twice a year, as if complying with a religious mandate, she fell blindly in love and would follow the object of her new obsession to the ends of the earth. Her love affairs lasted the length of a season. Then, she would arrive at our front door heartbroken and spent.

Her retreat into Abuela's house followed the pattern of an addict checking back into rehab after falling off the wagon. Her time with us was mostly spent behind closed doors and would extend anywhere from thirty days to three months. Then one day, unexpectedly, she would emerge as beautiful as ever ready to spring back into the world, ready to give love another chance.

Marcela's yo-yo lifestyle came to an end the week after I turned ten when she announced her indefinite departure. She had finally found her calling and decided to fulfill her dream by studying art in Florence, Italy.

The news of her leaving was acknowledged by Abuela with a slight nod as though her imminent pronouncement had been a mere formality. I, on the other hand, was held captive of a deafening emptiness. A wave of nausea rose up in my throat, my eyes watered, and the feeling of being kicked in the pit of my stomach hit me. I was about to be physically abandoned by my mother for good. I took one last look at Marcela, nodded—a gesture learned from Abuela—turned on my heels and headed to my room with my head held high and my heart broken.

Throughout the following years, my relationship with Marcela had become somewhat mechanical. We would meet for the sake of family business purposes only. We would address each other with a slight nod, and then after the customary signing of legal documents, the only reason for the awkward meetings, we would part as strangers until the next round of legal paperwork would bring us together in the same room once again.

***

Within minutes of Marcela's call, Carl, Abuela's attorney, rang me. Without skipping a beat and as if the conversation had been rehearsed many times over, he communicated to me that the matter of the estate had been settled over a year ago. My eyes swept through the detailed order of the study once again and the succession of events since Abuela's death lined up in my mind like the beat-sheet of a shooting script. Abuela's unusual disclosure of raw feelings. My mother's call from Abuela's phone to make sure I would answer immediately. Carl's communication afterward. The light that had been left on in the study to guide me to the box. I felt like I had walked onto a hot set, a production ready to roll. I had to give it to Abuela, she had been a clever woman and what a better way to grab my attention than to turn the task at hand as if it were another day at the office. If only… But, no, there were no re-takes, edits to be done on a scene or an alternate ending to what had happened. The weight of reality lay heavily in my hands in the form Abuela's last message. The words *forgive me* were written in the center of the page. I read it and reread it trying to decipher the message behind her words. What did I have to forgive her for? For dying? For leaving me alone?

Carl's footsteps along the foyer announced that the first of my two scheduled meetings upon my return had arrived. I folded Abuela's strange note and slid it in the back pocket of my jeans. The box would have to wait.

When Carl walked into the study, I noticed his bewilderment at the sight of the box lying under the lamplight. He acknowledged my presence with a muttered formal greeting then set his battered briefcase on the desk. His eyes stealing glances at the box at every opportunity he had.

"You are to finish the story," Carl said, as if we were in the midst of an ongoing conversation. He piled up documents on the desk and shifted through others until he found the one he was looking for. "This was her last wish." He placed the document face-up on the desk. "She is not to be laid to rest until you can see it through her eyes."

I lifted my eyes from his quick, small hands and stared at him. "Wait a second, Carl." I put my hand up halting his hasty, deliberate moves.

"First of all I don't have the slightest clue which story you're talking about. And, what do you mean when you say that she is not to be buried until I see it through her eyes? See what through her eyes?"

He stared back at me blankly, then his eyes fell on the box. I realized then that the contents of the box were probably as foreign to him as they were to me. I began to pace the length of the office. Whatever Abuela placed in the box was meant for me only. It was to be our last shared moment and possibly the answer to all my questions.

"Why?" I asked.

My question was met by the metallic click of his hard-shelled briefcase and the shuffling of his small feet. I believe that it was a sense of duty and silent adoration of Abuela that caused him to turn around and address me directly. "She told me that you were going to ask all these questions. She also said that you had always wanted to know."

I was still in her office when night crept over the grounds and filtered through the wood shutters that covered the windows, leaving the desk lamp as the only source of light in the entire manor.

The weight of the small box felt heavy in my hands. During my hours of musing over the ridiculousness of her request, I arrived at one conclusion: I could not refuse her last wish. Due to Abuela's inheritance, I had enough money to last me two lifetimes and time was at my disposal.

Per her request, I had taken a break and wouldn't start my next project for another six months. I laughed at that. The old vixen had everything planned out, even my hiatus. I contemplated the box I held in my hands, and perhaps due to exhaustion or sheer resignation; I surrendered to whatever awaited to be exhumed from its depths.

I sank down in Abuela's leather armchair and tried to relax in an attempt to summon her spirit. A minute later, I opened my eyes, who was I kidding? I did not know how to relax, a fact confirmed by my yoga instructor when she grew tired of watching me check my emails on my phone during *shavasana*. I leaned my head back on the cushioned headrest and a whiff of old leather and Abuela's signature fragrance breathed out. All right, I thought, I might not have the skills of a medium to connect with Abuela, but I had the feeling she still lingered in the room, as watchful as ever, to see if I would follow her wishes.

"Okay, Abuela, it's showtime." The lid to the box was stuck; I had to yank it open. The only content in the box, a single, loose, scribbled page escaped from its tight confinement and swayed down to the floor. Abuela's rounded longhand covered the page. I had only to read the first written line, to know it to be the beginning of a familiar story. One I had heard long before I condemned Franzisca to be a lie. I remembered the story well. As a young child I had named it *The Boy She Found*.

This had been the first Franzisca story Abuela ever told me. Many times, I came back to it and exhausted Abuela with my questions. In my heart, I knew this to be the beginning of Franzisca, the story that shaped her, the heart that breathed life to the many other stories that preceded or followed.

Like any little girl, I had loved happy endings and judging by Franzisca's many ordeals she was in a sore need of a happily ever after. Even though she was fierce and always managed to walk out of danger unharmed and victorious, I sensed loneliness in her. Unlike me, she did not have anybody to tuck her into a warm bed at night, tell her stories or bake her pies. Her life was one of relentless fighting and sacrifice. The moment Abuela finished telling me this story, the one she left for me in the box, I knew I couldn't close my eyes before plotting a joyous conclusion for Franzisca. My fairytale brain pointed toward only one direction: I had to reunite Franzisca with her one true love, with the boy she found and lost.

Little did I know that twenty-six years later my invented happily ever after would become the furthest from a child's fantasy and the closest to Franzisca's real story. In my hands I held *The Boy She Found*, a heartfelt declaration of love. The one story that had marked the moment when Franzisca had to choose between love and war. *The Boy She Found* had always struck me as the most unusual tale for the likes of Franzisca, especially when coming from Abuela's lips. Abuela, the bearer of the most beautiful violet-blue eyes, did not dwell on matters of the heart. She was a lover of facts and even in her storytelling, heroic action overshadowed passionate love. Yet there was sometimes an inherent message of passion amidst the devastation of Franzisca's life. One that Abuela had deemed important enough to leave behind as her last words for me.

My eyes fell on the written page again. Suddenly, I was four years old and I was being trusted with a secret disguised as a bedtime story.

Chapter Three

I had fallen asleep on Abuela's big leather armchair, with the story clutched in my hands. The sun fought its way through the half-closed shutters to my closed eyelids. Any other day, I would have welcomed the morning warmth on my face for it had always brought me comfort. I felt too sad to feel comfort, so I delayed opening my eyes, reluctant to acknowledge Abuela's absence and the love she took with her.

After much procrastination, I pushed myself up and out of the armchair. I needed to ready myself for my second and last scheduled meeting, the part of my life I had yet to come to terms with: Marcela Lazar, my estranged mother. It would not be long before she would see fit to waltz into Abuela's house.

Conscious of my frayed state, I made my way to the area of the house I called my own—the east-wing—to wash my face and brush my teeth. I looked down at my crumpled shirt and realized that a change of clothes wouldn't hurt, too.

My private space, which was built like a separate apartment with a sitting room, office, bathroom and private entrance through the pool area, looked exactly the way I had left it three months ago before work took me to Italy. My pile of *to read* books sat on the coffee table right next to the couch, a chenille throw sprawled on the back of my favorite chair, my perfectly made bed looked sorely tempting. Not now, I thought as I shed my clothes on my bedroom floor; Marcela would be arriving soon.

After I splashed cold water on my face, I stared at my dead tired reflection in the mirror for a long time. Brown, brown, and brown. Brown, wavy hair... well, not completely brown but tinted with some natural golden streaks as though sun-kissed. Brown eyes, almond shaped with some green and yellow specks in them, I guessed they came from my father's side of the family. And olive skin, gorgeously tanned during the summer months and yellowish-green during winter, a real treat. On a scale from one to ten, I didn't score that bad. Besides, from the outside, my life looked picture perfect. I was quite accomplished, an up-and-coming young film producer, barely thirty years old, with a bright future ahead of me, and to add to the tempting package, I was sitting on a fortune now.

But I was alone.

As I studied my features in the mirror, I caught a glimpse of the little girl I once was and I relived the day I exiled Franzisca and all her stories from my life. It was the day after my mother left me for good. I remembered standing for hours in front of Abuela's full-length mirror searching for clues for my mother's rejection. What if my eyes were too large, my nose too long, and my hair too frizzy? Tears clouded my vision that day, my image blurred. I rubbed my eyes furiously. If I was to be strong, if I was to grow up, any remainders of my childhood had to be buried away. When my vision cleared, the image staring back at me from the mirror looked taller than the little girl who stood trapped within the frame of the mirror only minutes before. There was one more thing left to do; I had to let Franzisca go. I was angry, hurt. I didn't want Franzisca or Abuela to come to my rescue. Even at that young age I understood that if I surrendered into Abuela's arms it would undoubtedly reel me back into feeling, and on that day I learned that it hurt too much to feel.

Determined to part from the fantasy world that swept me into sleep every night and kept me day dreaming during my every waking moment, I turned my back on Abuela and pulled the covers up to my chin when she walked into my bedroom to fulfill our nightly routine. "Turn the light off, Abuela. I'm sleepy." I feigned tiredness.

"You're never too tired for Franzisca, Sofia. She has a great story for you tonight, a funny one."

I sat up and regarded her with eyes filled with reproof.

"Take Franzisca with you, Abuela. I'm done believing in your made up stories." That night, Abuela's retreat from my room was silent, yet I could swear I heard something in her break.

Now, faced with my image after another heartbreaking event, a bolt of guilt suddenly struck me. From the beginning of my days, she strove to spare me from pain. She sheltered me from my mother's rejection and handed me Franzisca's stories so that I could dream and believe that anything was possible.

"And then I shut you out," I said to the memory of the magic Abuela had created on those long ago nights. "I have nothing to forgive you for, Abuela. It is me who begs for your forgiveness. Only me"

With Abuela dead, my window of opportunity to fix the past was closed. If I could only go back in time and revisit the one afternoon when I had the chance to change the course of Abuela's life. But a ten-year-old, living in a land engulfed in a cloud of pink–a visual effect, literally caused by the hundreds of apricot trees present in the orchard at the finca—all I could think of were fairy tales.

The more I replayed that one last afternoon at the finca, the more clearly I saw the first of many cracks in Franzisca's stories. A crack from where fictional characters had stepped out to threaten Abuela's safety. I remembered feeling the waning warmth of the retreating sun on my back, as I skipped up to house all the way from the foot of the pebbled creek where our property line ended. With my mind still immersed in the message I believed the rocks by the creek had revealed for me, I stumbled upon a man I'd never seen before. He steadied both my shoulders with his big hands. I felt more winded by shock than by the actual encounter, it took me a moment to regain my breath. The man smiled down at me with eyes as warm and rich as Turkish coffee grounds. His face showed lines of a life well lived and his dark hair was threaded with silver strands. The big hands that had prevented my fall felt protective.

I stepped away from him; I rapidly scanned the porch for Abuela. She stood there, silently, watching us. Her hand was clutched to her chest, which rose and fell with every breath she took.

"Who are you?" I asked, arms akimbo, sensing he was the cause of Abuela's obvious unrest.

"I'm a friend of your abuela's," he said. His eyes sparked with humor. His speech carried a foreign lilt and I wondered if he was one of the many hopefuls who came to Abuela in search for a link to their past lives.

"So," I said, while making circles with the tip of my black patent Mary Janes in the gravel, I dropped my hands to my sides. "Did you find what you were looking for? Did my abuela help you find that special person from your past?"

The man kneeled down instead of addressing me from his full height. "And what do you know about the past, child?"

My head snapped at being addressed as a child. "Sofia," I said, trying hard to sound older than my ten years. "My name is Sofia."

"Of course it is." His eyes shot to Abuela where she stood on the porch. "It was my mother's name. And a beautiful name at that."

"So, do you want to know what I know?" I asked impatiently.

"Go ahead, Sofia. I'm listening." He sat back on his haunches mindless of the hem of his coat resting on the dusty ground.

I sat down on the ground at once, I crossed my legs, picked up a twig from between the pebbles beneath my feet and I tried to sound as businesslike as possible. "Well, I'm Abuela's assistant when she does all her history research and stuff. And I know how a lot of people lost things in the war. Not only things, but also family and friends."

He nodded and chose a twig from among the small rocks to draw patterns on the ground himself.

I wiped my hands on my soiled summer dress and fixed my brown eyes on his. "But they all have something that reminds them of how things were before the war, a box with old stuff in it, a coin, a piece of ribbon or something. Do you have one?"

He squinted at me.

"Something from before," I said, matter of fact.

He broke eye contact with me and once again, he looked up at Abuela.

I'm positive I saw Abuela, swallowing hard as her chest heaved with a muted sob.

The man looked at me with sadness. His eyes no longer shone rich and warm. They glazed over with the sheen of unshed tears.

He reached into his shirt and pulled out a brass key that dangled at the end of a leather cord. Without pulling it off his neck, he let me examine it. The key was the oddest-looking key I've ever seen in my life. It was long, with two asymmetric teeth and a bow in the shape of an alpine rose. The flower was familiar to me because Abuela kept a small patch of those same flowers, which bloomed beautifully, with pinkish-red colored bells, over the summer months. Seeing that key with the rose on its head took away all my chattering.

I looked at the key, then I looked into his eyes again, and in that moment, he silently confirmed what I knew. On the gravel road leading up to our house in Mendoza, I witnessed the first of Franzisca's stories become reality. There were only two keys in the whole wide world with that description. They were Franzisca's keys. She had kept one and the other she gave to The Boy She Found.

"You are him. You are The Boy She Found," I said, unable to peel my eyes away from the key.

He squinted.

"You are in the story, in Franzisca's story. She gave you the key before she left the cave. It was her promise to find you, don't you remember?"

He smiled. "It's been a while, sometimes I forget things. Perhaps you can refresh my memory."

"It happened after she stepped out of the ring of fire. She was very sad because she had lost everything, but then she found you, she found the boy and he made her happy all over again," I rushed through.

"So, if she was happy, why did she leave him?"

"Because of the ogres that had started the fire. She had to fight them, to stop them from hurting more people. But before she left, she gave him, *you*, the key. She had two identical ones, you see? She kept one, and the other…" I said, pointing to the key dangling from his leather cord. "Do you remember now?"

He nodded silently.

"So if you are here with the key, why isn't Franzisca with you?"

The man with the beautiful eyes shrugged. "I thought that by now Franzisca would've been done fighting and ready to come back to me."

"Did Abuela help you find her? Did she find Franzisca?"

He reached out for my hands and spoke to me with a mixture of tenderness and heartache. "No. She did not. She couldn't find her. Not yet. But, perhaps you, her assistant, could one day find her for me."

His eyes were pleading and in that moment, I knew I was to be his last hope. More than ever, I felt the responsibility to make a happily ever after happen for Franzisca.

"I promise," I assured him. "I'll find her."

I had never questioned Abuela about the man holding Franzisca's key, or about the sudden change in our lives right after his departure from the finca that afternoon twenty years ago.

I had always wanted to know, however, I had never bothered to ask. I rushed to my room and emptied the contents of my hobo-bag on the floor. I reached for my notepad and pen, and I scribbled the only solid clue I had for the beginning of the story Abuela wanted me to see through her eyes: Franzisca and The Boy She Found. A good title for a movie, I thought.

I tapped the pen over the words I had written, while I internally kicked myself for wasting the many opportunities I had over the years to ask Abuela directly about his mysterious visit.

With one last look in the mirror, I gave up on efforts to improve my appearance. Within minutes, Marcela would arrive. "It'll have to do," I said to the tired face looking back at me.

Chapter Four

Marcela Lazar clasped and unclasped her oversized Swiss watch before deciding against wearing it. She looked tired, she concluded as she glimpsed her image in the mirror. The past couple of days had been more difficult than she had imagined. And there was still a harder challenge ahead: Sofia.

Marcela had lost her mother for the second time in her life. The first time she had been fifteen years old and she had lost her mother as a result of her own desperate actions. She had wanted to help, to wipe away her pain, to make everything all right for her *mamá*. But she had failed.

From that moment on, Marcela's life became a succession of one desperate act after another, destroying everything in her path.

Years of pursuing second—and third—chances had given Marcela an outlet for her unsteady emotions. As an artist, the touch of brush on canvas had replaced her insatiable thirst for male acceptance misguidedly sought through a succession of transient lovers. But the splash of colors that mirrored her life and dreams, ceased to soothe her anguish the moment her mother exhaled her last breath.

The time to face Sofia, her estranged daughter, was upon her and she hadn't the faintest idea of how to do it. Although she seemed indifferent to Sofia, Marcela had kept a silent vigil from the moment she walked away from her daughter's life. Proud of the woman Sofia had become and of her rising success, Marcela found herself searching the internet every morning for the latest news on her daughter's career. Perhaps it had been all for the best. If Marcela would have stayed in Sofia's life the results would have been different, tragic. She shrugged at the thought with resignation. Resentment was bound to be directed her way regardless.

The decision to give up her daughter was not a conscious decision at first. Marcela had secretly fantasized about motherhood and about having someone that belonged solely to her. Someone untouched, without a past. But Sofia's troubled birth had proven once again Marcela's tendency to destroy those whom she loved most.

"Talk to her," Claudia had said. Marcela's heart constricted at the sight of the little scrap of life struggling to survive in the neonatal wing of the hospital. She reached out to touch the top of the incubator that kept her baby alive, but no words came, only tears. Heavy, with the lingering pangs of afterbirth, she flew down the hospital corridors back to her room.

For the next three days, Marcela followed the improvements of the baby from afar. The baby girl, which had yet to be named, was released from intensive care when her lungs released their first sound wail.

"She will be all right, Marcelita. Just listen to her," her mother said.

Then, the baby opened her eyes and stared at Claudia with the deep gaze of an old soul. "Sofia," Claudia whispered. She turned to Marcela. "Sofia."

Marcela nodded, not in approval of the name her daughter was to carry her whole life, but of the decision she had come to.

Sofia was to be Marcela's offering to her mother. A way to repay Claudia for the horror she had brought into their lives. It was evident that with her first cry, Sofia brought light back into her mother's eyes. With Sofia's birth Marcela saw a glimpse into her long path to redemption, and before extinguishing it with yet another impulsive act, she understood that she must cut ties with her daughter even if it was the most painful thing she had to do.

That was to change when her mother paid her a visit a year ago.

Marcela was carefully selecting pieces among her latest paintings in her studio in Florence for an upcoming exhibit in Paris. The darkness reflected in her art served as a constant reminder of the consequences of her past actions. Since leaving Argentina, when Sofia was only ten years old, she had entertained suicide and had acted upon it a number of times to end the pain that ruled over her. She desperately wanted to erase the sordid images that tortured her since she found out the truth about her, about her mother.

The hinges of the front door of her studio protested announcing a visitor. She made a mental note to oil it later and not for the first time. A familiar scent of roses wafted through the room. She needed not turn to recognize the identity of the newcomer. It was her mother. The moment she saw Claudia, Marcela knew her mother was dying.

"How long?" was all she said.

"Six months. A year at most," said Claudia, standing as strong and straight as ever.

"You are here because of Sofia." At the time it pained Marcela to admit it, but they both knew that the opportunity to make amends did not belong in their lifetime.

Claudia nodded. Marcela stepped away from her paintings and turned on her electric kettle. Her concoction of choice was herbal tea, far from the bitter Turkish coffee her mother favored. She prepared only one cup anticipating her mother's refusal to swallow what she called tepid water.

"It is time she knows," Claudia said.

"Are you asking me to tell her?" Marcela wanted to kick herself for showing fear in front of her mother.

"No. It's my obligation to inform you that she will finally know… everything."

A sudden chill crept up Marcela's spine, and she suddenly wished to be fifteen years old again, to be able to change the outcome of her life.

Claudia walked to the wall where a handful of Marcela's paintings waited to be wrapped and transported to the exhibit the next day. Claudia picked one up and held it at arm's length.

"You didn't have to leave." The words were spoken to the dark colors in the paintings, but they pierced Marcela's heart.

"But I didn't stop you because I wanted you back. I wanted my Marcelita back. I thought that the distance would help you see things clearly, that I never blamed you for anything. That you were not responsible for the events in my life. That all I had for you was love... always." Claudia set the painting back down and stared deeply into her daughter's tearful light-blue eyes.

"I was selfish, and my decision not to stop you caused a great deal of pain to Sofia, but I did not have the heart to stop you."

Marcela's hand shook as she lifted her steaming tea to her lips. The hot contents of her teacup spilled, staining the front of her jeans.

"Damn it!" she cried out not letting go of the scalding cup, forcing physical pain to conceal her rattled emotions.

Claudia closed the gap between them, took the cup from her daughter's hand, and hugged her like she never had before. "Forgive me, Marcelita. I love you so much," she whispered.

The moment only lasted a few fleeting seconds, but it was long enough to make both women feel regret.

When Marcela looked up, the door to her studio was slowly swinging back on its whining hinges. "I love you, too, Mamá," she whispered back. All there was left from her mother's last goodbye was the memory of her warm embrace and the sound of retreating footsteps on the cobblestone street.

That was then. Now, with Claudia gone the link that connected her to Sofia was broken. When she set out to visit Sofia at the Solvang ranch that morning, she had done it out of instinct. She needed her daughter as she had never needed anyone before. She craved Sofia's presence. She still remembered the pressure of Sofia's pudgy little fingers on her face when as a little girl she had demanded Marcela's attention. A painful pang shook Marcela to the core. She had never felt so alone, and she was determined to end her misery and reach out to her daughter with the truth.

However, as she donned herself in her fashionable peasant tunic and jeans, her resolve was swallowed by her fear. What was she to say to Sofia? I'm so sorry for your loss? Forgive me for leaving you? I love you? I never meant to hurt you? Yes, those were the words she burned to say to her daughter, but after her pure declaration of love and regret there was a story of war and murder, she was not ready to face or disclose yet. The jangling sound of her many gold bangles reminded her of the real reason why she drove straight from her apartment in Los Angeles to Solvang that morning. She was there to buy time. Although her mother had not asked that of her, she would honor her mother's last wish to let the truth out finally. Claudia's death had become Marcela's chance to show Sofia the role Franzisca had played in her own life. Before the fairytale, before all the secrets, before all the blood and darkness that had tainted her paintings and her life. But to tell Sofia a thirty-six-year-old story, she had to find words, not shapes or colors. And she was not ready.

Marcela stepped out of her car, looked up to the house and sensed a shadow behind the living room shutters. She shook her head sideways and rolled her eyes the way she used to do as a teenager.

"Ay, Mamá, stop worrying, we'll be fine… perhaps not today, but we'll be fine." For the first time in thirty-six years she shared a loving smile with her mother, even if it was with her ghost.

Chapter Five

Abuela taught me that the simple things made even the most reluctant of foes weaken.

"Many treaties that changed the course of history were sealed over a rich cup of coffee and a fresh slice of pie. It makes people feel welcome, Sofia. There's nothing like knowing you've arrived at a place that feels and smells like home. Think safety," she had said, accentuating each of her words while she kneaded some buttery dough.

"*Let them eat cake*; famous last words," was my answer to Abuela's philosophy.

"The problem with Marie Antoinette, Sofia, was that she did not bake." The matter was closed; back to the pie.

Alongside Abuela, I had learned to bake pies, probably my only skill in the kitchen, but I had not had the time to bake before Marcela arrived that morning. Still, I managed to brew a pot of tea, since Marcela was not a coffee drinker, and challenging Abuela's bake goods philosophy, I arranged on a platter some fruit filled cookies from a local bakery. When Marcela called early that morning to confirm that she was on her way up the coast I couldn't fathom any reason behind her sudden visit, other than money. To my understanding, the attorney had met with her the day before he met with me and the details of Abuela's inheritance were settled. I didn't know how the assets were divided or if I was the sole recipient of the inheritance. In all honesty, I never bothered to inquire how much Abuela's net worth was. When I asked the attorney about Marcela's portion, he suggested—in that ill manner of his, that it was confidential and if I really wanted to know I should ask Marcela myself.

To avoid any confrontations, I decided to divide the inheritance in half as soon as I hung up the phone with her earlier that morning. Beyond paperwork related to Abuela's investments, there had been nothing else between us in over twenty years. Without business matters as our liaison only two things could happen: We could count this as our last encounter or as our first of many to come. The jury was still out and I was still hoping.

By the time I had arranged the cups, saucers, teapot and cookie platter on a tray, Marcela was waiting in the anteroom, arms wrapped around her middle, examining her surroundings in that skeptical manner of hers that entitled her to come and go as she pleased. My assumption as to why she had come was cut short before I set the tray on a nearby marble buffet table.

"I know you're wondering why I'm here." She squared her shoulders. "I'm here to bury her. I made a couple of phone calls yesterday and bought a lot by a large old tree at the local cemetery."

Hearing Marcela talking about Abuela, as though she was no more than a broken object to be disposed of, hurt. I looked back at her with disdain, letting her know I did not ask for her opinion in the matter. Not accustomed to being challenged by me, she paused momentarily, then continued on the subject. "She will never know, Sofia. And what difference does it make? She's dead."

I kept a calm demeanor, and while I poured steaming tea in the cups, I dissected each one of her moves. Her hands struggled to unzip her oversized designer bag. Her finger moved nervously inside it searching for her pack of cigarettes, laboriously breathing, as if her life depended on that long paper tube filled with tobacco. Her lips pressed firmly around the cigarette's butt with hunger, a spark flew into the air when she struck the match. After her first deep inhalation of smoke, she looked steadier, supported by an object that would burn to ashes within minutes.

"I'm sure Carl already told you that you are off the hook. Abuela entrusted her fate to me."

I stiffened my spine ready to fight her off. "Thanks for your concern, but I'm a big girl and I've done without you my whole life. I can handle this."

A cloud of white smoke veiled her expression, but not fast enough to conceal her distraught state. After a few deep puffs, she put-out the half-smoked cigarette in one of the teacups. This time she was choked with pain.

"You were lucky, Sofia." She regarded me with her ice-blue gaze. "You had the best of both worlds. A grandmother to spoil you rotten and the best of mothers anyone could ever ask for. One I could never have measured up to." Her fingers fumbled again inside her bag searching for a second cigarette, but the pack was empty. "I often wonder what it would have been like to have a normal family, you know? Like the ones in the storybooks…with a mother and a father, grandparents…" It was the first time I heard her say the word father. All I knew about him was that he had died before she was born. There were no pictures of him and his name had never been spoken.

I watched her closely, trying to understand what she was getting at. She smiled sadly, reached for a cookie, and crushed it until there was nothing left of it other than crumbs. She shrugged and looked at me. "I often wonder if the outcome of my life… your Abuela's life would've been any different."

In a few words, she summarized her crushed dreams of a different life, surrounded by the unconditional love of a proper family and without me. Her words stung. After years of continuous disappointments, I secretly held onto the hope that one day she would break down; apologize for the heartache she had caused me.

Still, I wanted to be the bigger person and cross the abyss that stood between us. For a moment, I envisioned myself with my arms wrapped around her. But my body was not accustomed to hers. I stood rooted to the hardwood floors and my words died on my tongue before I could articulate the faintest sound. I looked over at the tea tray, now spoiled with a floating cigarette and a crumbled cookie.

"Was it because of the store bought cookies?" I said, more to myself than to Marcela.

"What?"

"I have a million things to do, so…" I gestured toward the door.

Marcela adjusted the straps of her bag over her shoulder and took a step toward the door. She paused for a moment, shook her head and her gaze dropped to the floor as if all of a sudden she had found the pattern on the hardwood floors interesting. Then she looked at me over her shoulder. Her voice regained strength and her eyes shone with what looked like fear. "Think about it, Sofia. You don't have to do what she asked. As they say, ignorance is bliss."

I knew this day to be our last meeting, so I chanced the two questions that had burned in me for many years. "Why did you leave me? Why do you hate me?" I spewed the words with anger. Her eyes locked with mine. I was caught completely off guard. I was accustomed to her avoidance. I could count on the fingers of one hand the times she had looked at me in the eye, that was the second time.

"You were better off without me, Sofia," she said, with a mix of shame and sincerity. "And hate? You haven't lived through hate, Sofia." She shook her head. "I hope you never do."

She held my gaze for a few more seconds and I sensed her need to say more. It must have been the jiggling of her many bracelets when she readjusted the straps of her bag over her shoulders what brought her back to her senses.

In a flicker of a moment, her defenses were back up and the faint connection I had felt flowing between us, vanished. Instead of following her instinct, she did the only thing she knew how to do well, leave. Once more, I watched her shape disappear along the long corridors of the house.

After Marcela left, it took me longer than usual to emerge from the familiar feeling of disappointment. In her primal way she expressed her true sentiments for me. I mattered to her, but not enough to reveal her side of the story or the fears that clearly assailed her. Not enough to be welcomed into her own world of secrets.

I went back to Abuela's study to review the many legal documents the lawyer had left on the desk the day before. Throughout her life, she had acquired many properties; she had interests in business ventures and had become an avid art collector. She was also a philanthropist. Abuela was actively involved in every children's charity organization known to man. I knew that her investments and properties were carefully administered by her financial advisors, and from an early age, I had attended each one of the quarterly meetings she had held with her staff. But the charity work was done by her personally and I was committed to continuing her work.

With that decision made, I flipped over some of the legal documents, separated them into piles according to their relevance. I set aside a document mentioning three properties in Europe, which were now in my name. I was not aware of their existence, and attached a memo so I would remember to call Carl about it at a later date. Buried under the mound of papers, I found a picture of the two of us taken on my first day of school the day after we arrived in Solvang two decades before. The faces in the picture spoke a thousand words. My childlike features were contorted with noticeable displeasure. I was scared, I did not speak the language, and I missed my home in Argentina. I studied her face in the picture not for the first time, yet I noticed something different now. In that picture Abuela looked far from the unscratched and victorious woman I always thought her to be. The heavy burden of time suddenly showed in the lines around her eyes, in her forced smile, in the way she looked beyond the photographer as if she were waiting for something, for someone.

It was the same facial expression she bore the day she stood on the porch when the man with the key sat on the dusty road and asked me to help him find Franzisca. She looked pained, as if she knew his visit would mark the sudden end of an era and the beginning of a new one. Franzisca had lived in that way. She moved from one battle to the next and she never looked back.

I thought about Abuela and her lonely life. I could picture her walking away from a life of love to accomplish some stubbornly set goal. She had been that way, once her mind was made up, nothing could deter her from her objective. I had never seen her cry, but the memory of her standing on the porch that afternoon at the finca told me that she must have cried her whole life for the boy and the man, she had loved and lost.

On that long-lost warm afternoon, after the man with the key turned to leave, I ran to her and held her hand until the dust from the gravel road swallowed his car. Then, while she still stood rooted to the porch, I invited Abuela to do the only thing I knew to ease her pain.

"Should we bake a pie, Abuela?" Perhaps, if we would walk into the house and bake, if we could lose ourselves into our private world, then the man with the key would be forgotten.

"It's time for us to go," she simply said.

"Go where?" Fear gripped me the minute I saw her eyes wander from the road. She had moved on, and just like Franzisca she was ready to leave.

"To a new place, to make new adventures."

"You mean stories. Like Franzisca." I saw fit to bring Franzisca back into the picture if only briefly. Perhaps if I would accept her back into my life Abuela would forget all the nonsense about leaving. But no, her mind was made up.

For a moment, I wondered if the man had been real, if the key he held was real, or if the whole thing had been a figment of the imagination of a ten-year-old intent on living through impossible tales. I looked up at Abuela and she still held that pained expression in her eyes, an acknowledgement of the events both of the past and of those which were about to unfold. Our imminent departure from the place I loved, from my home, made me want to punish her for her one-sided decision, so I blurted out the words I knew would hurt her deeply. "I hate you and I hate Franzisca. I never want to be like any of you."

She acknowledged my outburst with her signature nod, then turned toward the house. "Come on Sofia, there's much to be done."

After that day, we never spoke of Franzisca again. Nor did we speak a word, for over twenty hours, until Abuela sat under the portico of our new house in Solvang.

I stood feet from her, my arms stubbornly crossed around my chest, looking away from her.

"I heard that the drama teacher at your new school is looking for a girl just like you for their new play."

I couldn't hold it anymore and the strain of tears I had held for the last day broke loose. She patted the spot next to her, inviting me to sit. I complied out of tiredness and resignation. It was her love that embraced me when my head rested on her chest. She kissed my wet cheeks and ran her fingers through my disheveled hair. Gradually my hiccups ceased and my breathing found a normal pace. She must have been exhausted, but what she did next was her way of showing me that I had nothing to fear, that as long as we were together we were a family no matter where in the world.

"Come to the kitchen, Sofia. We'll bake a pie."

All was forgotten as she enveloped both of us in a mush of eggs, flour and butter. Baking was another method of her storytelling and on many occasions I wondered about the memories she infused into the folds of buttery dough she so carefully kneaded. In the kitchen she would cease to be the powerful woman the world came to know. In the heart of the home, she was an ordinary grandmother. One who sits in a rocking chair and knits. The grandmother, with cinnamon scented hands, who told fantastic stories. I never realized until now, that our journeys through mounds of fruit preserves and dough were her other ways of letting me peek into her private world.

She said you had always wanted to know. The words of Carl, the attorney, hung suspended in the air. Of course I wanted to know, but not like this. Not with her gone. I wanted to know about her and her past. I wanted to know about her relationship with her mother and mine. I wanted to know about the man with the key.

I pushed all those thoughts aside. Needing to get out of the house I headed to the pancake house that Abuela and I went on Sundays for breakfast.

I walked into the restaurant feeling naked without her by my side. The waitress who waited on us every Sunday threw her arms around me and wept as she expressed her condolences. I assured her of my well-being while handing her a tissue and made my way quickly to our regular table by the window.

Tiny syrupy fingerprints showed on the window next to my seat. For a fleeting moment, the thought of a naughty child sitting by that window took my mind off what had tormented me from the moment I learned of Abuela's death. I felt sad of course, but mostly guilty.

Abuela had sounded oddly disappointed when I told her about my delayed return and insisted that they might not have her favorite table available the following Sunday. I dismissed her worries, telling her that the table was permanently reserved for her. I knew I was right, and I went as far as to call her unreasonable before the line suddenly went dead.

For once, we were both right. The table was awaiting her. However, little did I know that I was to sit down to a plateful of Dutch pancakes sprinkled with lemon zest and powdered sugar opposite her empty chair. The empty space opposite me stood as a painful reminder that Abuela would not be accompanying me to my upcoming premiere, the way she had since my first film. The hard reality was enough to make me lose my appetite. I put the fork down and washed down the taste of grief with bitter black coffee.

That night, for the second time in two decades, I wished for the comfort of one of Franzisca's many stories. I knew that sleep would not come, only troubled memories. I was tempted to reach into the box Abuela left behind and reread the story nestled inside. But I didn't want to read a story; I wanted Abuela to tell me one.

I tucked the blankets under my chin, closed my eyes and tried to summon her voice in my head. With a heavy heart I realized I couldn't hear her.

"Thanks so much, universe," I yelled. "What else are you going to take away from me, my memory of her?" I was not very sure about the many stages of grief, but in my case anger had taken over them all. With Abuela gone, there was only one thing left to do, I had to exhume all the stories I had buried when I was ten-years-old.

'Okay, Franzisca, Claudia, Abuela, whoever you are, bring it on. I'm ready."

Instead of closing my eyes to envision what I wanted out of every story, a trick Abuela taught me years ago, I kept my eyes fully open. The time to imagine scenarios was over, now I had to discover the truth. I sat up in bed, reached for the pen and pad I always kept on my nightstand.

As I set pen to paper, the voice of a woman, one I had never heard before, took over. The fresh energy in her lilt denoted a young age, yet it was tainted with an edge of caution. This woman could have been tender in age but her voice projected the burden of many lives lived. She did not need an introduction. I knew her to be Franzisca the moment she brought to life, with the weight of her emotions, a story I had heard more than twenty years ago. I could see her clearly, as clear as ever. There she was, standing at the mouth of a dusty cave, shaking. In her hands she cupped an odd-shaped key and as she looked back longingly at the sleeping young man she had left behind. I heard her mouth the words, *"You hold the other half of my heart."* It was the force of her anguish that pushed my pen as the first page of a love-story that had yet to be told found its way along my blank writing pad. When all the details of the story were safely written the pen slipped out of my fingers as if on its own accord. I stared at it in shock while faded images of the young woman fought to cross the border of fiction into reality.

Thus began the first of many nights of writing and stories, of unraveling and remembering.

Chapter Six

Every story involving Franzisca always went back to *The Boy She Found*. Assuming, as I already had, that Franzisca's stories were far from bedtime tales but a PG version of Abuela's life prior to becoming the woman I came to know, I couldn't help but feel stupid. Since the age of ten, I had succeeded in controlling and anticipating most of the events in my life. I did not like surprises, I had had my share of them and my history showed I did not handle them well.

Now, I was faced with the biggest revelation since our sudden move from Argentina to North America. It was becoming obvious that my life had run parallel to a dimension unbeknownst to me; a secluded spot where Abuela had weaved a life of her own. It would have been so much easier for her to let me into her secrets over our pancakes on Sunday mornings. But, if my intuition served me right after yet another restless night, there was not enough syrup in that pancake house to sweeten Abuela's history.

I paced around the house holding the small box along with the notepad I had written on the night before. Since the first day, when I had read the story of The Boy she Found, I tried hard not to reconcile a fictional character like Franzisca with my real, flesh and bone Abuela. It pained me to know that not even in the fairy tale version of her life she had gone back to the man she loved.

I avoided Abuela's bedroom since my return from Italy. Finally, with box in hand, I gathered the courage to enter her most private sanctuary in the house. The room greeted me with Abuela's familiar scent and an overwhelming silence that whispered, "you've always wanted to know…"

"I did, I do," I said to the empty space. Ever since I was a child I suspected her of keeping mementos that had meaning to her, hidden somewhere where my little hands could not reach when I would sneak into her closet to pilfer different garments to play dress up. Indeed, when I was younger I would wait for Abuela to slip out of the house and search under her bed, inside her drawers and in all the pockets of her coats for clues to the many questions I never asked and the many answers I knew she would never give me.

This time, my search produced an immediate result the moment I opened her nightstand drawer. Right there before my eyes a piece of history faced me. After years of fruitlessly looking for clues to Abuela's past life, I couldn't bring myself to reach for it. I looked around and I sensed without a doubt that many other treasures were at the reach of my fingertips. However, I was no longer a child and my curiosity had been dampened with the fear of the unknown and the consequences they might bring into the controlled life I had created for myself. "One at a time," I told myself. I closed my fists and flexed my fingers a few times before retrieving an old sepia colored picture of a little girl against a thick line of trees. I brought the picture closer to my eyes and dissected each detail of the girl's face, her pudgy little fingers, the stance of her legs, the sway of her coat, the cloth doll she held in her left arm. I searched within the faded look of the girl's eyes for a hint of those violet-blue eyes that had watched over me all my life, but all I could see was the face of a frightened little girl.

After downing three glasses of my favorite Pinot Noir, countless fruit filled cookies, and several hours of musing over the details of the picture, I felt irritated with myself. I should have paid more attention to her ludicrous request, no, her demand, the day she phoned me a year ago while I was on location scouting in Sienna . I should have known something was amiss, especially when she had put trees and my name in the same sentence.

"Abuela, can I call you later? I'm in the middle of something here," I said, distracted by the two beauties in front of me: The villa I had just walked into and the Italian man serving as my location scout.

"No. I need an answer now," she said.

I smiled at the Adonis ready to walk me through the villa. "It'll be just a second."

He smiled back and stepped away to give me privacy.

"Abuela," I hushed. "How could all the gorgeous men in the world end up in just one country?"

"Keep your legs crossed and your eyes open, Sofia."

"Abuela," I exclaimed, surprised by her bluntness.

She laughed, and then went straight into discussing the planting of a new variety of apricot trees for her orchard, a matter I had no knowledge of whatsoever. "I need you to pick the new trees," she said, as if it had been an ongoing conversation between us.

"The trees? Abuela, you know I can't even keep a plastic plant alive. What is this all about?" I had learned to not beat around the bush when talking to her.

"I'm giving you a whole year to plan around it. After you're done with your movie, I want you home. Six months. Then you can go back to all those made up stories you create for a living."

A year-to-date of that phone call had passed and here I was with six full months solely for Abuela and her project, except that I had lost her and the only trees to speak of were not related to her apricot orchard but to the old picture I held in my hands.

I wanted that little girl in the picture to be my Abuela, but after contemplating it for a long time, I discarded the possibility. I stashed the picture in what I officially declared to be Franzisca's box and without any reasonable explanation, I thought of Margaret.

Margaret, an elegant British woman in her seventies with coiffed hair and perfect skin was an auntie of sorts in our made up family. Ever since I could remember, she had been Abuela's confidant and right hand. I hadn't spoken to her since the morning of Abuela's passing. She had insisted on accompanying me to the States to help me sort through the mounds of paperwork she knew I was expected to handle. I declined her offer thinking her too grief-stricken.

I met Margaret on my first trip to England when I was four years old at the eighteenth century manor Abuela had acquired to turn into her headquarters when she was in Europe. The house, located in Belgravia, a district of west London, had belonged to a German dignitary right before World War I, and had been vacated the moment the Germans invaded Belgium after declaring war on France. Through the two Great Wars and onwards, the house changed hands several times failing to find its rightful owner, until the day the run-down manor came under Abuela's radar.

Following her usual modus operandi, she dug out the original blueprint for the manor. She then summoned the top architects and engineers responsible for restoring the majority of London's Georgian manors. After painstakingly attending to each one of its original details, the house in Belgravia experienced its rebirth three centuries forward.

Margaret was waiting for us on the driveway by the entrance of the house with a few members of the household staff. The minute we stepped out of the car she welcomed us with a genuine smile. "Claudia," she greeted Abuela in her clipped British accent. "Sofia," she added looking at me with tenderness. "Oh my, how much you've grown!" She spoke to me in Spanish accented English.

Apparently we had met before. I couldn't remember.

"Did you have a good flight, my girl?"

I stared at the new character in my life without uttering a word while Abuela responded with a smile of her own. Then I witnessed something I've never seen Abuela do with anybody except with me. She hugged Margaret affectionately.

"I expect all is well with you, Margaret," she said.

Margaret responded with a reassuring nod.

Young as I was, I sensed the subliminal understanding that flowed between Margaret and Abuela; I took an instant liking for the woman. She must have felt the same way about me because on our way into the house, she held her hand out for me and I took it without hesitation. The picture was completed when the fragrance of Turkish coffee and freshly baked pie greeted us on our way into the kitchen. I felt at home and right then decided to adopt Margaret as one of us.

Because of our close bond, I had asked the attorney to refrain from calling her. It was my duty to inform Margaret of her dear friend's death. It was a family matter and Margaret was family. Thinking back on our conversation I failed to notice, at that time, the composure in Margaret when I delivered the news. Her stoic attitude had nothing to do with her British blood, I now understood, but rather with the fact that she already knew of Abuela's imminent death.

Of course, she knew. I only needed to relive our last encounter to understand her words for the warning they held of the events to come.

Two nights before my mother called me with the news, I dined with Margaret at a little family-owned restaurant we both loved in Florence. She had flown in to get the latest gossip on the drama unfolding on set and to make sure I wasn't suffering too much abuse under the leading actress' legendary bad temper. We shared a lovely meal and Margaret burst out laughing at the many anecdotes I held in my repertoire.

When we parted she cupped her hands around my face. "I'll see you soon, then?" It wasn't a question. It was a confirmation.

"Oh, Margaret, I don't think so," I said while placing my hand on one of hers acknowledging her kind gesture. "*The Italian Nightmare* might be almost over, but I expect to have a string of meetings by the time I head back." I stifled a chuckle, "I wonder how I would explain that to Abuela. I'm supposed to be free, to help her with some–" I thought for a moment, "I don't know, with one of her many projects, who knows what she has up her sleeve now."

Margaret nodded and patted my face lightly again and looked at me in the eye. "You'll manage."

Of course I'll manage, I thought. I had always managed, but someone could have dropped me a hint of what was to come, even a smoke signal would have been nice. Instead, a whole lot of plotting had gone on behind my back by the two women I trusted the most. I suspected that Abuela had not wanted to disrupt my most important project yet with such a tragic forecast. Still, I wished she had let me decide how to handle the matter of her death for myself.

I felt like dismissing the nine-hour time zone difference with London and call Margaret in the middle of the night with my endless list of questions? Why didn't you tell me? Who's the girl in this picture? Who was the man with the key?

"There's always tomorrow," I said to Franzisca's box as I laid it on Abuela's desk.

For a few minutes, I entertained the idea of going into town to walk off my frustration, or drown it in the custard of a big fat éclair. The now empty platter of fruit-filled cookies I had been nibbling on the whole day, reminded me that a walk among the property's trees would have a more soothing effect and be much healthier than the giant éclair I planned to drown my despair in.

With my notebook and pen, lest any important memory would decide to pop-up, I stepped outside anxious to catch the sunset illuminating the trees. The clash of green, peach, and gold was spectacular, heavenly. Dawn and dusk were Abuela's private hours with her orchard. She would sit among the trees and after contemplating the beauty surrounding her she would close her eyes as in prayer. I wondered if nature had been Abuela's deity. Perhaps, for I had no knowledge of her religious preferences. God was not embedded in her speech. We had never attended church for Easter or Christmas, we did not have a Buddha sitting on our front lawn, and not once did we fast on the Day of Atonement. I blamed the extensive research she conducted on Bible stories for the lack of religion in our lives. Sure enough, by the time she was done stripping off any traces of divine influence on the biblical characters humanity worshiped, they were no more than regular folks capable of performing amazing deeds based solely on the strength of their will and sacrifice, and not by the fruit of celestial miracles.

We did have traditions of our own, though. We rejoiced in the birth of the new apricots when we lived back in our finca, making dozens of jars of preserves. Jars of which our nearby neighbors waited for expectantly, a tradition we continued at the Solvang ranch.

We also welcomed the change of seasons by inviting local artists into our home. On the 20th day of every quarter, our home was filled with the composition of new music, the first lines of literary creations and freshly colored paintings.

I never tired of observing the way our eccentric celebrations brought forth a different person in Abuela. Her response to the intoxicating effects of music, words and color was almost primitive. Her barriers came down, and only those who knew her well, if such a person existed, could recognize a glint in her eyes. The shift in her went beyond the enjoyment of the arts. It was as if she had suddenly been released from a self-imposed prison, and for a few hours every three months, she would allow herself to step into a much yearned life. To me, those precious moments were answers to the vast silence that was her past. Beneath her unguarded smile, I would catch a glimpse of the little girl she had been. A cherished girl who twirled and laughed until her sides hurt, until she fell down exhausted and drunk with happiness.

The smile the memories of our life together brought to my lips faded abruptly when the matter of Abuela's burial surfaced. How was I supposed to plan a burial for a person without a God? Cremation was the first thought that came to mind, but I rejected it immediately. I knew in my heart I could never subject Abuela to such fate. She had never spoken about it out loud, but her aversion to fire was clear. Every day she routinely checked and double-checked the stoves and heater pilots before leaving the house and before retiring for the night. She never mentioned the reason for her obsessive behavior and I just took it as one more of her peculiarities. However, since her death I learned not to take anything at face value when it came to Abuela. Thinking back on the many stories she told me as a child there was one that involved Franzisca and a ring of fire. In it, Franzisca had lost everything dear to her in a devastating fire. The line between fact and fiction blurred again and if I was to untangle the riddle before me I had to find solid proof that Franzisca's stories mirrored Abuela's life. I jotted down all this new information that had come to me and trudged back to the house with a firm decision. Abuela would not have a funeral. She would have hated the idea of gloom and hushed voices. Her farewell would be a celebration of all the things she cherished in life. As for the arrangements for her body, it was still an enigma to be solved.

Back in the house, engulfed with more emotions than I had ever felt, I headed to the bathroom ready for a relaxing bath. While shedding my clothes on the floor as I waited for the water in the bathtub fill up, I thought about Margaret again and the role she played in my life.

Before slipping into the water, I reached for my phone and dialed Margaret's private line at the house in Belgravia. Judging by the time in London, Margaret would be up and ready to start her very predictable schedule.

She woke up every morning at five, took a shower and got dressed in one of her many skirt suits, fit to attend a session at the House of Lords or tea with the Queen if the occasion ever arose. Then, she had a breakfast of toast, poached egg and black tea with milk, in complete silence. Her breakfast was never finished until after she had meticulously washed her own dishes, a chore she never imposed on the cleaning staff at the house. Clean and fed, she cloistered herself in her office until lunchtime where she went about her duties, which consisted of managing all of Abuela's affairs in Europe. She never took lunch at the house. Margaret had a group of contemporaries, all women, some of which she gathered with every day at noon and they ate together.

I was certain of Margaret following her daily routine, considering that all of Abuela's enterprises would continue even after her death with me as their executor.

The phone rang once before her voice came through the line.

"Margaret, do you remember the first time we got on the tube?"

"Mind the gap," she answered. "Of course, my girl, like a parrot you echoed the irritating warning at every station and then you kept repeating those three silly words throughout the day. Mind the gap, mind the gap. Claudia and I were so relieved when you finally fell asleep that night."

Her comment had managed to make me laugh for the first time since I got the news of Abuela's death. "In my defense," I said, "they were my first three words in English."

"What of it, Sofia?" she asked, knowing there was more to my question than recounting my first underground experience in London.

"That day," I said, choosing my words carefully, "when we got back to the house you pulled that big old English-Spanish dictionary of yours and you read me the exact meaning of the word *gap*."

As if reading it from the dictionary, Margaret recited the words. "Hole, void. Do you still have it?"

"Sitting on my nightstand." That old dictionary had been the most precious gift Margaret had given me through the years. After our move to America I made it a habit to sit after dinner with the heavy tome on my lap to learn new words. Gradually, I acquired a vast vocabulary and a corner of my brain became like a dictionary I could resort to when I was in need of a word.

Now, I could picture the pages in my grey matter flipping at full speed until the word *gap* stood out as if highlighted in neon lights. Margaret only stated the most commonly known meaning of the word, yet, the depth of the thesaurus working overtime in my brain enlightened me to the further significance of the word. "It is also a way, a pass, a bridge."

I heard Margaret sigh on the other side of the line.

"You did not ring me at five in the morning to discuss the full meaning of a word."

"You're the gap," I said.

"The hole or the bridge?"

"It's up to you to decide, Margaret. I have all these questions about Abuela, about this man, I don't know, the list goes on and on. You were her best friend, her only friend, the only person with enough information to help me fill in the abyss that is her story."

"I wish that to be true, my girl. There are things she took to the grave. Answers I will never get."

Through the line, I heard the doorbell ring. "Who's at the house at this hour, Margaret?"

"It must be Evelyn, my new assistant." I sensed a hint of relief in Margaret's voice.

"Wait, Margaret, before you go there's one more thing I want to ask you. What do you know about a little stuffed doll?"

"Sofia, my sweetie, you've always had an aversion to dolls. Have you had a change of heart, now?"

"No, the sight of them still creeps me out. It's a doll I found in an old photograph Abuela kept in the drawer of her nightstand. It's not just the doll, you see? There's a little girl holding it. The picture is really old."

The line went silent and for a moment, I thought the call had dropped. It was the insistent faint sound of the doorbell on Margaret's side that told me otherwise.

I must go, now," she said. Without another word, she was off the phone.

Chapter Seven

The next morning, I woke up earlier than usual thinking of Margaret's reaction to my question about the doll. If all the mystery surrounding Abuela since her dead had taught me anything valuable was to not leave a single stone unturned until I found the truth. I needed to talk to Margaret and judging by the time in London, I could still catch her at the house in Belgravia.

The phone rang seven times before the answering machine picked up. The same was the case for her phone at her private residence in Covent Garden. The house was a souvenir from a short-lived marriage, to which she sometimes retired at the end of the day.

I decided against leaving messages, hung up immediately in both instances and dialed Margaret's cell phone as a last resort. The call went straight to voice mail. I assumed her to be on the tube, where the reception was beyond poor, or on her way to one of her afternoon errands then I suddenly remembered it was Monday, the day she religiously kept a hair appointment for the past twenty-five years. Later, I thought, and moved onward with my day.

Since my arrival in Solvang, the phone rang consistently from nine to five as though paying respects for my grandmother's passing was to be done only during business hours. Leaving all sarcasm aside it was natural for neighbors, friends, and other people who had been associated with her to call and express their sympathy. But the calls were not a mere formality. Every single one of the callers had a story to tell about how she had changed their lives, how she had saved them. I was familiar with some of their accounts as a result of my years serving as her *assistant*. I relived the hours I sat silently in a corner of her office, witnessing how Abuela helped them untangle their deepest memories buried by shock and grief. In many cases, the memories came back with names and places they had long forgotten. And just like magic, that name or that place usually ignited the process of reconstructing their way back to concealed identities, long-lost friends or family.

The phone calls, while overwhelming, brought with them comfort. Abuela had lived a life of meaning and all the people she linked back together during her eighty-odd years were a testament to it. What I couldn't come to terms with were the customary flower offerings people were compelled to send to the family of the departed. It had been only a few days since Abuela's death and the house already reeked of rotten carnation petals. While opening every window in the living room, I wondered if the ritual of amassing enormous amounts of decaying vegetation was meant to signify the smell of death.

After answering the multitude of conciliatory phone calls, I realized that not once had I asked any of the callers how they came to know about Abuela or her work. *If you never ask how will you ever know*, it was one of her famous lines. "Not that it had ever worked with you, *mi querida Abuela.*"

Abuela had been impenetrable, a marble statue, surely no one knew any secret details of her life, yet I did not allow that fact to discourage me. Armed with my notepad, I got ready to write down what I was sure to be helpful information from *the sympathizers*.

"So, how did you hear about my grandmother and her work? Did you know her from before?" My questions were met mostly with similar answers. No, they had never met her before. None of them had grown up with her or knew anybody that had, and ultimately they learned of her through word of mouth.

Thanks for nothing.

When the seventeenth-century wall clock, the one that Abuela had had shipped all the way from Switzerland, struck the seventeenth hour, I knew my job of accepting condolences was done for the day. I also realized that the day had gone by without news from Margaret. It was three a.m. in London; I decided that the call would have to wait until later that night.

My back was stiff from sitting for so many hours. Other than taking calls, I hadn't done much else in the past few days except reading through mounds of paperwork, signing legal documents, inspecting the contents of the many safe deposit boxes Abuela kept in the house and in banks across town and adjusting to a world without her.

I grabbed an apple from the fruit bowl on the center of the kitchen island, the one Abuela made sure it was always stocked with seasonal fruit, picked up Franzisca's box from the couch in the sitting room of my private wing and made my way outdoors.

The sun was still high, but it was hiding behind some thick clouds. I hugged myself against the cool breeze and tilted my face up, I could smell it in the air, rain was on its way. I sank my teeth into the apple, sat on the ground and rested my sore back against a tree trunk, opened the box and took out the picture I had found the day before. I stared at the picture as if it was the first time I had seen it. At that moment, under the shade of the tree, I felt profoundly certain I was finally seeing Abuela as a little girl. That thought lingered in my mind for about ten seconds before dismissing it as too easy. Knowing Abuela, anything in the photo could have been a clue or not; the little girl, the house, or even a minuscule squirrel standing in the background. I knew better than to trust first impressions. No, that little girl could not be her nor the barely noticeable house in the background her residence.

Indeed, discovering the identity of the girl was not a trail I had considered following at that moment. It would have been like looking for a needle in a haystack; a job that could have taken me years and most likely with little or no success.

Against my better judgment, I decided to do a little research on the mysterious photo.

I ran back into the house, made some hot tea and settled in front of the computer. I focused on the picture and narrowed on the house, which seemed like the right place to start. The type of construction and the size of the estate was not one commonly seen in America. As a film producer, scouting for locations was part of my job, and I knew just the web page where I could get information about a house like the one in the picture.

After a lengthy internet search, the results put the manor to be European, somewhere east of the Atlantic Ocean. Focusing my attention on the rest of the details in the picture, I set the house on the backburner and moved on to the next possible clue. I narrowed in on the little girl again. Perhaps the clothes she wore could shed some light. Luckily, I knew the right person for the job. Dana, the last Costume Designer I worked with, was an expert in period costumes. We had become good friends during the shooting of *The Italian Nightmare.* It looked like another call was in order.

"Did you get my message? I heard about your grandma through the grapevine, Sof. I'm sorry, girl," Dana said, with honest sentiment. "I must say, I sensed there was something going on with you." Dana swore by her psychic abilities.

"Thanks, Dana. Sorry for not returning your call. It's been pretty crazy since I got home."

"Whatever you need, Sof—" Dana's unfinished sentence caught in a sob. "Just name it."

"Actually, yes, you might be able to help me with something." I quickly filled her in on the details of the photograph.

"If I drive up the coast now, I'll be there in time for dinner," Dana said. "See you at our favorite joint at seven."

We met at a local brewery, a place we both liked for their beer selection and French onion soup. Taking advantage of the mild evening, we sat outdoors. After a nice dinner, a cup of coffee and a shared slice of my favorite chocolate cake, I had the first tangible lead to step into Abuela's mystery.

"You gotta be kidding me," Dana cried as she inspected the picture closely. "A Norah Wellington," she finished in awe.

Finally, I thought, a name for the girl, "Is that who the girl is, is that Norah Wellington?"

"Not the girl, genius." Dana pointed at the doll in the picture. "The doll. The doll is a Norah Wellington."

It took Dana less than a minute to recognize the picture as being taken sometime after World War I, most likely during World War II. I sat amazed while Dana pointed to the doll the girl proudly held in the crook of her arm as one of the determining factors as to when the picture was taken. A collector of rare dolls herself, she easily spotted the one in the picture as a Norah Wellingtons cloth doll.

According to the expert sitting across the table, which kept turning the picture amazed at her finding, the doll was one of Norah's early sailors made in her factory located in Wellington, a small town in England.

"The sailor dolls," Dana explained, "were made intentionally to be distributed on several cruise lines and sold at the ships' gift shops as souvenirs." Her eyes moved slightly up, her right eyebrow arched upwards. "Sof, you'll meet a tall dark stranger."

"I take it that we're not talking about the doll anymore." Dana was the most unexpected character.

"Not even close." She grinned.

I frowned. "Are you seeing my future again?"

"More like your present."

"Uh?"

"Don't turn around," she said, holding my hands. "At least not yet." A smile cut across her lips.

"What is it?" I asked alarmingly.

"Two tables from the door. Over six feet of yumminess with the most wonderful caramel color eyes only for you." Dana was close to drooling. "Uh, and those jeans."

I shrugged losing all interest. "He probably saw me on some magazine cover. The publicity has been good—trust me—but also a flytrap for wannabe actors and writers. Everywhere I turn, I bump into someone who has either written the next best movie or wants to be in it."

"I'd take my chances with this one. He looks like a badass," Dana said, eyeing whoever the man was.

There had been a considerable amount of press with this last movie and my face made it to the cover of some of the most popular magazines under the heading *Powerful, Beautiful, and Single*. I didn't care for the first two words, which did not depict me at all. But when I read *Single* all my short-lived, disastrous relationships flashed before my eyes and got me thinking if that was to be my lot in life. Abuela had been a very powerful woman and in my eyes the most beautiful one too. But she had also been single, and when her time came, she died alone.

After Dana left, I stayed at the restaurant answering some emails on my smart phone while finishing my third cup of coffee. My curiosity peaked and I glanced sideways toward the direction the handsome man had been standing, but all I got was a perfect view of him leaving—his white shirt hugging his broad shoulders.

"You've got to get a grip," I muttered between clenched teeth, thinking of my foolish reaction.

Focusing back on the picture, I narrowed on the ragdoll. Dana's full report on the doll had set me back to the starting line. How on earth was I to find the one ship this doll had been sold on? Impossible, I thought, absolutely impossible.

The weather took a sudden turn and I drove back home under a light drizzle with my thoughts still wandering around the images in the picture. And as much as hated to admit it, I was also thinking about the man with that glorious behind, those broad shoulders and that wavy chestnut hair.

A giggle escaped my lips while I negotiated through the narrow road leading up to the ranch as I couldn't help but place the faceless stranger at the restaurant as the perfect character for the romantic fantasy of my early teens.

The smile on my face faded when faced with that empty monster of a house. I'd have to get used to it…

I entered through the back entrance and chose the dark hallways of my rooms where no lights were ever waiting for me. Before I had the chance to drop my bag on the couch and leave Franzisca's box on the coffee table, the phone began to ring. Margaret. It had to be her.

When I picked up the phone, it was her on the other end. The connection was bad, crackling and fading out but before the line went dead, she assured me that we would talk again in two days' time. She said she was travelling, taking care of some unfinished details. I was certain there were countless details in need of attention, especially now with Abuela gone. I made a mental note to talk to her about it and take on some of the load.

Waiting a few more days until I could grill Margaret with questions was nothing compared to the many years I had waited for answers. I dropped my oversized bag with all its dead weight on the couch, kicked off my shoes and as I headed to the kitchenette that was adjacent the sitting area, the phone rang again. It had to be Margaret.

The lady was too conscientious to allow a bad phone connection to come between her and years of propriety.

Without saying hello, I continued the conversation as if we had never been disconnected. "It's all right, Lady Margaret." I teased her. "Word of your ill behavior will never reach Buckingham Palace." I expected her laughter in return as she always did when I teased about her secretly being a member of the royal family. A void of silence lingered on the other side of the line. I assumed the connection was bad again and rambled on. "Don't worry Margaret," I said to the empty line, "call me back when you have all five bars lit up." Time and time again I had explained to Margaret about the importance of the bars on her cell phone screen, to which she always shook her head in defiance of the rules of wireless communication towers. "I never had any of these problems with good old fashioned phone booths before you forced me into this ridiculous contraption."

To which I always replied, "I know Margaret, but can you fit one of those in your purse?" This point usually ended the argument.

I was about to end the communication when the raspy voice of a man spoke my name.

There were only a handful of people who knew the number of my private landline, and the stranger on the other side of the line was not one of them.

The man called my name again.

"Yes, who's this?"

"She saved my life," he went on, ignoring my question. "She saved many of us..." His accent was thick and foreign.

"I don't know what you are talking about—"

He cut me off. "She was a woman of many faces. No one knew who she really was. But, I did. I could see through her from the moment I met her."

"I thank you for the call, sir." Didn't he respect the normal hours for condolences like the rest of the callers? This man was not a *sympathizer*. He lacked the compassion I grew used to hearing from the many callers paying their respects. He was cold, unemotional.

"It took me years to put the whole story together, who she was before the war, and who she became after. She looked so high and mighty the first time I saw her wrapped in that white coat. Times were hard. We all did what we had to do to survive. As much as I hated her from the moment I met her I knew she would fight hard to come out a survivor in the war. It must have not been easy playing the whore to the likes of Baron Lupescu and who knows how many others while playing the Samaritan in the eyes of war victims. Everything has a price and hers was high. Her money, the money you now hold in your hands it's stained with blood." A silence lingered and I could hear his heavy breathing. "Yes, she saved many of us, but only to save herself."

I was conscious of having lost the grip on the phone when the raspy voice vanished from the line. The next thing I knew I was hunching over the toilet bowl, violently sick and completely empty.

Chapter Eight

After Alex died Daniel sat by his side, wondering what was next for him. From an early age, he had learned about death and Alex's death had not come to him as a shock. The man was old, of delicate health in his later years, and deep inside, he had carried a broken heart, which was bound to give up without a moment's notice. It was perhaps because of the latter that Daniel could not stop the tears from dampening his face. He had contributed to Alex's grief and for that he felt responsible. With the brush of his fingers, Daniel tidied a snowy white lock on Alex's forehead. Once, his head had been covered by a wealth of rich-brown waves that had matched the depths of his eyes and the resonance of his baritone laughter. Daniel remembered those days, and with bitterness he remembered the day Alex's eyes lost their luster and his laugh muted forever.

Daniel's hand trailed down the length of Alex's right arm. His skin now soft and saggy had once been coppery brown and had housed strong muscles. A cattle and horse rancher, Alex had worked hand in hand with the ranch hands he employed from dusk till dawn ever since Daniel could remember. His caress stopped at Alex's hand. The old man's fist was clamped with rigor mortis. But as he freed each one of Alex's fingers from the body's natural reflexes to death, a crumpled note Alex held clutched in his hand, fell on the white sheets of the deathbed.

Through teary eyes, Daniel stared at the note and cursed at the irony of life and death. How could a handful of simple words reveal the essence of the man he thought he would never get to know? And why now? Why when Daniel was denied of further explanations, of one last heart to heart chat? "At least you left me with this," Daniel whispered to Alex's still form. At least he had something to hold on to, Daniel thought. Even if it was a weathered piece of paper that held the key to every unfinished sentence Alex had spoken just days before his death.

Daniel wished he could give the old man the love he had withheld from him. But his remorse had come too late. He read and reread the note Alex had held so fiercely to until his last breath, committed to memory the last name he whispered and wiped away his tears, a sign that his humanity was not completely lost. In that moment he vowed to bring this lonely man, he had so unjustly condemned as a young boy, together with his past.

His days as a Mossad counterterrorist agent were over. Daniel had handed in his resignation months before Alex died. His initial mission, the one he had devoted himself almost two decades ago, when fresh out of high school, had garnered him many personal victories. Every time an attack was intercepted, a terrorist was caught, or a bomb deactivated, he felt vindicated. However, the thrill lasted only until he lay trapped by the resentment that had pushed him away from Argentina and out of the life of the only family he knew.

The walls within him started to crumble almost a year ago on the morning of his thirty-fourth birthday. Daniel had stood on the balcony of his small flat in Rechavia, Jerusalem, enjoying the most wonderful views of the Old City while drinking his black coffee. The walls of this city had withstood centuries of wars and had harbored more different cultures than any other place in the world. Yet, amid its tireless role, its gleaming stones stood proud, undefeated, forgiving. He yearned to become what Jerusalem was, but he was not made of stone, he was a man. He struggled with the defeat brought by his inability to forgive, and as time went by, he feared his resentment would transform him into a soulless stone.

"At least there's some fear left in me," he said to himself. But his soul-searching was interrupted by an urgent summon from the Mossad's headquarters. An hour later, he was on a plane to Argentina, a country he had vowed never to return to.

As the plane took off, he surveyed the file he held in his hands. His mission was to intercept the resurgence of the Iranian terrorist cell that had attacked the core of the Argentinean Jewish Community in 1994. Daniel pulled out a file and studied the list of names and pictures of the individuals he was to pursue. Amongst the major conspirators was a wide range of politicians including former Argentinean President Saul Carlos Menem and several businessmen with close ties to the Iranian government. Methodically, Daniel replaced the file back into the briefcase and pulled out a second file, one he had personally requested before leaving Israel.

Daniel opened the file and studied the face of the woman that took over the center of the first page. Her name was Claudia Lazar. For over half a century, Mossad had been on her trail. The octogenarian philanthropist, of unknown past or origin, had been under Mossad's scope for decades suspected of being a Nazi collaborator during World War II. Many anonymous tips fed the agency with loose- end information about Lazar immigrating to Argentina before Hitler's downfall under a bogus name, and since the murder of Israeli Olympians during the games of Munich in 1977, Claudia Lazar was on a list of possible terrorists' financers. After years of hitting one brick wall after another, Mossad had grown cold on her trail. Daniel believed the woman to be guilty of all those charges and more. Before boarding the plane he swore to his superior that he would see Claudia Lazar prosecuted even if he had to do it on her deathbed.

Being back in Argentina brought back ghosts Daniel thought he had buried. He became careless with his work and before his personal life could come between his mission and his impeccable record, he presented his resignation. On the same day, he got in his car and drove back to a place he should have never run from in the first place. The moment he walked into Alex's house, they both clung to each other and cried endless tears of forgiveness. Nothing else mattered for Daniel; he was back home with the one man that had done nothing wrong other than love him with all his heart.

Once a military man always a military man, Daniel saw the stages of his life as missions. It was this mission that had made him resign from his post. It was because of this mission that he had tracked down Sofia Lazar to Solvang, California. It was his need for answers that had made him follow her all the way to a restaurant and now to her ranch. It was for the same reason that he would forgo the meeting with Margaret, Claudia Lazar's right-hand. If there was something clear in Daniel's mind, it was that neither a spoiled Hollywood brat nor an old lady with a lame excuse would stand in the way of completing what he considered, singlehandedly, the most important mission of his life. Besides honoring the promise he made to Alex when he died, it was finally time to confront the person responsible for ruining his life as well as his grandfather's.

Sitting at a brewery in Solvang, California, six months later, staring at Sofia Lazar had not been on his list of even the remotest of possibilities. The moment she walked into the restaurant that evening; Daniel's years of training as an intelligence agent were washed-up at the sight of her. He had set out to crush Sofia Lazar with the detailed report he had gathered throughout the years about her grandmother. His evidence was weak, his informant anonymous. Daniel shook his head, he did not care about any of that, all he wanted was the truth, closure, and Sofia could be his ticket to finally getting there.

He was anxious to corner her, play with her mind with the same tactics used to extract information from criminals. His thoughts came to a halt when her easy laughter breezed through him. What had her crime been? There wasn't a reasonable answer that would satisfy him. She was guilty of nothing.

Daniel drank the coffee the waiter had just set on the table. Not the best coffee he had tasted, he thought with his second gulp, still the warm concoction felt soothing as it trickled down his throat.

Sofia had said something to the woman sitting opposite her and they both laughed again. The other woman bent over something they were both dissecting in the middle of the table. In that moment, he had a full view of her face. She was prettier than the pictures he saw of her on the recent magazine covers and online articles. Strain showed in the dark circles around her eyes. Her face was void of makeup, her hair a tumble of untidy curls. He did not think her shabby. In his line of work, he had learned to recognize that specific profile and Sofia Lazar fit it perfectly. She was in mourning.

A conflicting surge of compassion rose up within him and all he wanted to do was to jump out of his seat and tell her that everything would be all right. That she was not to blame for the sins of her ancestors and that he was here to protect her not to harm her.

He finished the last of his coffee and laughed at the burst of sudden emotion he had not felt possible only hours before.

***

That evening, after getting his first sight of Sofia, he walked back to his hotel thinking about the people that had affected his life. Alex was dead. He was gone. The man had been a dry piece of burnt toast, but it was Daniel that had made him that way. He had held back his love from the old man and for that he felt indebted. Then, he thought about Claudia Lazar, a woman he never met.

Before Alex's death, Claudia Lazar's ghostly path had turned her into the mystery he swore to see unraveled even if it took him all of his life to do it. In his mind she was guilty of every charge she was ever suspected of and of a murder case he had yet to solve. However, Daniel's dilemma began the moment Alex died, the moment when Claudia Lazar ceased to be a picture in a file and a suspect on a list. Suddenly, Claudia Lazar became a real woman.

If he would not have found the note and later the envelope in which it was sent to Alex, Daniel and Sofia would have never crossed paths. Even though the envelope did not have a return address, the one detail that helped him track down the origin of the anonymous missive was the stamp from the local Solvang's post office. The note was written on an ancient looking sheet of parchment, a detail that sent him to meet the few antiquarians and antique shops around the small town. It was in the first shop he walked into where a name he never imagined to be connected with stood up to challenge him.

Mrs. Larsen, the frumpy storeowner took a quick look at the unique stationary of the note he carried. "This is Claudia Lazar's parchment," she confirmed with an assertive nod. Then to validate her knowledge, she retrieved, from a drawer under the cash register, a thank-you note written on the same kind of parchment. "It is her trademark paper for personal missives. Not everyone in town gets one of these." She beamed with pride.

Still unable to digest the information he had garnered earlier in the day, Daniel stared at the dimly lit Lazar Ranch, wondering how the connection between Alex and the Lazar woman had gone under his radar. The pain that still gnawed inside his chest like a festering wound had blinded him. He had done all the right things, hadn't he? He worked tirelessly to hunt down terrorists, to save lives hoping to heal his own wounds in the process. He reveled in the victory of his missions and tried hard to transfer that sense of satisfaction to his personal life. But the sour taste in his mouth and the constant feeling of uneasiness refused to leave him. The salve to mend his heart had not come into his life as yet. He had experienced brief moments of joy, when involved in frivolous relationships he had mistaken as meaningful. But they had all ended abruptly when he found himself unable to open up, to trust, to love.

Daniel stepped out of his car and walked slowly to the main entrance of the house. He looked down at the envelope and wondered if his complicated story would not land him in jail under suspicion of stalking Sofia Lazar. The lady was somewhat famous and he had known Americans to call 911 for no reason.

Whatever was about to happen he was certain would forever change his and Sofia's life as they knew it. He shrugged, faced the moonlit sky. "You'll get what's yours, old man. Just give me time."

Chapter Nine

Right up until the moment I received that unsettling phone call, I had been the picture of composure. I hadn't suffered a meltdown and had not allowed myself to cry. I knew I needed to. All of that changed the moment I crawled out of the bathroom and reached for the only bottle of alcohol I had. Sitting on the marble and glass built-in minibar in my sitting room was a fifty-year-old, single malt Irish whisky, a reminder of a steamy two week romance with an Irish Director of Photography.

The whisky proved to be the same thing as a torch in a bottle. The first gulp took my breath away, and in that moment, I questioned my choice in men. What kind of man gifts his lover with alcohol? Toasting to yet another poor choice in men, I forced myself to down three consecutive glasses barely breathing in between. With a fire burning down my esophagus and gripping the neck of the bottle tight, I made my way to Abuela's room. On unsteady steps, crying and sniffling uncontrollably, I made it to her bed and I threw myself on it, dramatically. Her scent was still on her pillows, her comforter and on her neatly tucked bed. I slid out of the bed, forced down some more alcohol, tottered back and yanked off the bed covers.

"She's dead!" I yelled at the bed, at her room, at myself. Next, I moved to her walk-in closet, which was as big as a college dorm room. The lights, soothing and golden, went off as soon as I stepped in; falling on Abuela's immaculately arranged clothing collection. Everything was hung by season, color, and length. I was familiar with most of her clothes; shopping was among the long list of things we enjoyed doing together. I touched the sleeves of the blouses she wore perhaps no more than twice, reminiscing when we bought them and the moments we shared during each one of those shopping sprees. While burying my nose in the collar of a royal blue silk shirt I had insisted she should buy because it made her violet-blue eyes sparkle, I decided to stop beating myself up, as I had been for days, about my overlooking of Abuela's character and what lay beneath it. During my thirty years there had been countless moments when she could have opened up to me and told me real stories instead of fictionalized tales about a girl named Franzisca.

"You can't hide from me anymore, Abuela." I pulled down the last row of blouses as if by doing so I could tear her bare. And there, hidden in the back of her closet, was a bulging dark grey silk garment bag I had never seen before. The whisky bottle slid from my fingers and bounced on the closet floor. Just like the picture left in her nightstand drawer, I knew this to be another treasure she had purposely placed for me. I inched toward it and with utmost care I pulled down the metal zipper. The heavy grey silk parted, out wafted the stench of mothballs. The bag fell open to reveal a white vintage wool coat.

The coat was knee-length, princess style, with a slight A-line flare and soft pleats. The front was lined by triple rows of diamond-cut crystal buttons. I traced the lines of collar and sleeves, the coat felt soft to the touch, cashmere most likely. I had never been much into fashion, but according to the many historical documentaries I've seen and the many books I've read, the style was one worn by women during the 1940's. The discovery of this garment in Abuela's closet sobered me temporarily. Slightly steadier, I slid my arms into the coat. The cream-colored silk was yellowed with time, yet it still enveloped me with a cool soothing caress. One by one, I fastened the row of crystal buttons running from neck to mid-thigh. The coat felt snug around my waist and reached slightly above my knees. Without a backward glance at the mirrored walls in the closet, I walked out of her room and into to her study, the last place I had used my laptop.

The first time I saw her wrapped in that white coat... The words of the mysterious caller pounded inside my chest with my every breath. I turned on my laptop and typed in the name Baron Lupescu.

The search came back in less than a second with the most unsavory of results. Lupescu, Baron Mihail Lupescu, to be more precise, had been a senior member of the Iron Guard—the Romanian Nationalist Party—and had acted as a Nazi ally during World War II. I scrolled down the page and found no records of a wife or children.

A black and white caption showed the baron months before he had been swallowed up by a crack in the earth. He had small precise features and a narrow frame. He looked fair-skinned, blond, and with light colored eyes, the typical image of an Aryan. The article describing the Romanian fascist continued below the picture. There was no record of his imprisonment or death. Some sources cited he was suspected to have died during the murderous operation in Iasi, the north of Romania, in which he was one of the leading officers. Others speculated his disappearance to be linked with another Nazi criminal living happily under a bogus identity in South America. Most likely in Argentina or Paraguay, countries that had welcomed Nazi war criminals with open arms in exchange for substantial amounts of gold that had been stolen from their war victims. But as far as mentioning heirs or women in his life, the query came back empty.

I had vast knowledge about the adoption of new identities after the war. During my many hours of sitting in the shadows of Abuela's study, watching her interviewing World War II survivors, I witnessed resurgences of hidden pasts and forgotten names. It was common for many of them to dig out whatever scraps they kept from their life before the war. Some of them had done it to shield themselves from the uncertainty of their future in an unknown land. Others, preferred to migrate into a fantasy life in an attempt to conceal the grief that never left them when reminded of their past. Many of them did it to avoid public embarrassment or judgment for all the actions they dreamt of taking to stop the carnage they witnessed, but were too weak to act upon them.

However, I had never encountered the other side of the ghosts of war, the aggressors' side. I was well aware of Nazi hunters making their way to South America pursuing justice. As my search intensified I found a report stating that over nine-thousand Nazi criminals were admitted in South America during the last months of World War II all the way up until 1950. The shocking numbers kept popping up on my computer screen. Of those nine-thousand Nazi criminals, five-thousand of them were admitted into Argentina under President Peron. During Peron's first term which ran from 1946 to 1952, the government sold ten-thousand blank Argentine passports to an organization set up to protect former SS men in the event of defeat.

The information I had read so far about Lupescu, named him as another fervent Nationalist, one more Nazi collaborator during World War II. His participation did not show to have been greater than many of the other pawns Hitler's regime controlled across Europe.

I slumped in Abuela's armchair when a sudden realization hit me. *Forgive me,* were her last words to me. She wanted to be forgiven for the truth she knew would surface once she was dead. Her past as a mistress of a Nazi and a Nazi sympathizer. Her blood money. The monster she had once been.

I reached for Franzisca's box, opened it, and retrieved the note she had left addressed to me. *Forgive me.*

"What you're asking me to do is very hard, *Abuela.* How can I forgive you for a lifetime of lies?" I crumpled the note in my hand while holding back tears. "How can I forgive you for not being her, for not being Franzisca?"

None of it made sense. Abuela could not have been more than twenty-years old when the war ended. But age had never stopped women from using their bodies in desperate times. Yet, what I had a hard time wrapping my mind around was her travelling from Argentina to Europe during those perilous years to join the Nazis. It just did not make sense.

Nausea and a migraine headache shot through my body. I had discovered during my college years that hard alcohol had that immediate effect on me. I closed my eyes and willed it to be gone. Too late, the damage was done. I struggled to stand up, falling back on the chair time and time again. Determination won out and I succeeded to wobble around the desk and out of the study.

A loud ring, what seemed to be the doorbell, threatened to split my skull in two. "Go away!" I yelled, aggravating the sickening headache that had rapidly spread down my nape and shoulders. The invasive ring penetrated my skin and took residence upon my pounding head unending its painful sound. To prevent my head from exploding I had to get away from it.

Doing my best to remember the layout of the house and the direction to my private wing, I plastered myself over the walls as much for support as for guidance. During the blind journey to my rooms, I knocked down vases, tripped on valuable pieces of art, and came in contact with paintings that grudgingly aimed for my head with the corner of their frames before falling noisily on the limestone floors.

In a way, I welcomed each blow I received from the household's inanimate residents with the hopes they could drive out what the alcohol could not. Vivid in my mind was the strange phone call, Baron Lupescu, his empty eyes,

Franzisca, Abuela and all her lies, and the man in the white shirt from earlier in the evening.

The events of the day along with an insistent pounding on my head chased me to my bathroom. I wanted to soak my aching body in a soothing bath, to shut out the outside world and relegate the events of the past few days as a nightmare.

I went down on my knees, and on all fours, I crawled to the bathtub. With eyes closed I let the warm water run in the tub. I needed to relax; a bath always worked. Suddenly I felt the asphyxiating weight of the coat wrapped around me. I struggled out of it, almost yanking each crystal button out of its eyelet. It was the last button; the one at hip level that gave me the most trouble. Desperate to be rid of it, I pulled the coat open. The stubborn crystal button shot up in the air at the same time that I heard the lining of the coat rip. I felt the weight of an object wrapped in soft fabric fall on the tip of my toes. I bent down and picked it up. My fingers traced its shape over the silk bag. I knew what it was. It was proof that not all was a lie. Not all of this was fantasy. I closed my fist around the wrapped object and let the damaged coat and the rest of my clothes pool at my feet. Free of the weight of the coat and what it represented, I filled my lungs with air and I allowed my eyes to adjust to the dimness of the bathroom. Moonlight came through the wooden plantation shutters. Before sinking into the bathtub, I opened the bathroom windows. A cool breeze washed over me. The soothing effect combined with the warm water embraced me.

Through blurry eyes, I followed a house spider dangling from a corner of the ceiling. I found the meticulous weaving of its web fascinating. The movements were mechanical, premeditated, designed to trap its prey.

Suddenly my body felt light, levitating, until it reached the spider web from where I hung suspended. Immobile. Watching.

Stories rushed into my head with the force of a hurricane. A flash of white in the window pulled me out of my trance. Even though I had not seen his face, I was certain it to be the man from the brewery. Was he here to save me from the story? Or was he here to sink me even deeper into the unknown? None of it mattered. Abuela won. Her voice, in the same way she had talked to me countless times when I was a child, penetrated the silent room. I must have passed out dozing deep into the enchantment. Gradually her voice faded into the voice of a little girl. A melody from an era of innocence, mixed with giggles and breathless joy.

***

Vienna 1928

"Franzisca! Franzisca!" came her mother's worried call. Franzisca giggled knowing fully well she was being naughty. Anna, her mother, was flushed, out of breath, running frantically through the woods searching for her young daughter. Her racing heart slowed down when she saw Franzisca's little brown boots behind a thick old tree. She should not have worried so much; Franzisca was barely two and after a day of sun and fresh air her almost never-ending energy was finally waning.

It was near dinnertime and she knew her disapproving parents would not tolerate a dirty little girl at their table. They already thought her daughter dirty with the kind of filth impossible to scrub off even with the most scalding bath. Franzisca was the product of an unacceptable relationship and her birth was beneath the Schultz's standards.

Anna Schultz was guilty of no more than love. She had fallen for Asil, a good boy from a good family, but penniless. Her parents knew of their friendship, and they never objected to it. In fact, they made allowances for Asil, the son of a prominent Turkish Jewish couple destitute by the winds of war, now under the domestic employ of Anna's family.

But those allowances were terminated the moment the furtive looks between Asil and Anna had obviously passed the barrier of friendship and ventured into a territory heavily charged with sensuality, curiosity, and yes; love. Their connection had been magical, and from the moment they laid eyes on each other, Asil and Anna became inseparable, until a fever two years later claimed him from her.

Before his death, she had never experienced pain or loss. After his death, all she experienced was pain, loss and the constant reminder of her precarious condition. Asil had left this world, but he left behind a part of himself. Six months later the emptiness left by Asil's sudden death was replaced with the arrival of Franzisca. A beautiful olive-skinned baby girl, with thick raven hair and the rarest of violet-blue eyes.

The moment Asil's parents attempted to claim her as their own flesh and blood they were immediately banished from the Schultz's grounds.

At seventeen, Anna felt her life had gone full circle. She had loved and had been loved, and now she bore the responsibility of motherhood.

True to her prediction Franzisca's short legs tired and the little girl sat under a tree playing with dried autumn leaves. Anna made her way to her daughter and sat next to her. Franzisca held a number of crunched brown leaves in one hand, and a small package in the other. Without resistance the little girl surrendered her find to her mother. The package had Franzisca's name written on it and without unwrapping it, Anna knew its content. They were *The Keys*.

Asil had described the odd-looking brass objects to Anna many times before. They had been in the possession of his family for centuries and had been passed on from firstborn to firstborn. Nobody knew what those keys had once opened, but he thought them to be possessed of magic. Asil had seen them only once before their departure from Istanbul when his father retrieved them from a safe they had in their house. The keys looked almost identical and had their bows shaped in the form of an alpine rose.

Anna remembered that warm afternoon, one of the last ones she spent with her beloved Asil under the shade of the trees. She had rested her head on Asil's lap while his elegant hands had softly caressed her blond curls. In the past year his voice had become deep, manly, a fact that made his storytelling abilities all the more attractive.

"The keys," he said to her, "will open the gates to a kingdom where you will forever be my queen and I will forever be your subject. That is my dream. This is my vow to you."

Anna sat up and met his eyes. "You could never be my subject, Asil, because you already own my heart, and I'm yours."

Their first kiss started clumsily. They bumped noses and laughed nervously at the proximity of their breaths. When their giggles died down, they rested their foreheads upon each other's. Anna took the initiative and softly traced the contour of Asil's face. He wasn't laughing any longer. Her touch was as smooth as the apricot skins he so hungrily sank his teeth in every morning and he could only guess at her being as satisfying and ripe as the flesh of his favorite fruit. He covered her hand with his and they slowly traveled over the terrain of her body. Their hands discovered hidden ticklish places, their difference in bone structure, and the shape of their desire. Linked by a newly found familiarity, their bodies melted together under the brush of their lips and the blending of their souls. Never before and never again would they love so deeply. For soon after, he would depart for eternity and she would die until revived within the warmth of his arms.

***

Anna placed the keys safely in her pocket and patted them reassuringly. She knew that Asil's parents had left them there hoping Anna would find them and pass them on to Franzisca, Asil's firstborn. Perhaps she would not have to endure a life under her disapproving parents any longer. She would soon leave on a journey to regain her freedom and provide her daughter with a dignified life. The keys in her possession opened the doors to a life Asil had dreamt of. If he believed in its existence, she believed in it too. She would look hard for the right lock that would open the gates to Asil's kingdom.

Satisfied with her decision she held out a hand for Franzisca.

"Come on, my little Turkish doll. We have company for dinner tonight." Anna's stomach turned at the thought of Baron Lupescu and his conceited son.

The younger Lupescu had cold, empty eyes and he never tired of letting them crawl all over her.

Chapter Ten

The last time Daniel had run with his heart in his mouth was during his first secret operation as a Mossad Agent. He still felt the way fear had gripped his gut. It wasn't his life he was afraid for, it was the unknown. Back from his first mission he swore never to be hostage of that sense of vulnerability ever again. Thus, he mastered his mind to disassociate from his emotions. Daniel was a man of logic, numbers, facts. He learned to approach each subsequent operation like a math problem, with a jumble of creative possibilities to achieve one infallible result. None of that worked when he thought of Sofia Lazar in mortal danger.

Daniel arrived at the ranch, no more than two hours after Sofia left the brewery. After much procrastination and soul searching—a behavior he was not comfortable with—Daniel walked up to the house. Encouraged by lights going on and off in different areas of the house, a sign that Sofia Lazar was home and awake, he rang the doorbell a couple of times to no avail.

When he realized it was nearing on midnight, he knew he should have waited for the morning to face her and that nothing would change between now and eight in the morning except for his feelings. He was under a rare spell of vulnerability thrust upon him by the note he held in his hand. How could it be that a simple sentence could bulldoze the walls he so carefully built up around him throughout the years? The hell with propriety, he decided, now was the time.

Cheated by the shadows of the night, he had failed to notice the overly large size of the house. At close range, his engineering mind at work, told him the house to be a structure of roughly twenty-five thousand square feet. All of this for a spoiled thirty-year old who barely reached up to his chin? Daniel whistled under his breath. Well, perhaps she was not as lonely as the media portrayed her to be. That thought bothered him slightly. His years as an intelligence agent pushed that thought away immediately. He was not here for a woman. He was here for the old man Alex and for himself.

After ringing the bell a few more times, he thought he heard a faint voice coming from the innards of the house. Expected to be greeted by Sofia Lazar, he straightened his clothes, ran his fingers through his wavy mass of hair, and cleared his throat as if he was about to sing the national anthem at the Super Bowl. After minutes of waiting by the door his calls remained unanswered. Before retreating back to his car and the hotel room, he chanced one last look around the perimeter of the house.

The house was lined with wall to wall windows to provide the inhabitants with endless views of the Santa Ynez Valley. It was obvious that whoever was in charge of closing up the house for the night had forgone his responsibilities to protect the privacy of the residents. Or perhaps Sofia, the only person living in the house at the moment, had requested it this way. Whichever the reason, it had worked to his advantaged. The transparency of clean glass afforded him a full view of the inside. The house looked desolated, but the sound of clear sobs, her sobs, echoed in the still night. He was invading her privacy and for that he felt like a bastard. He should leave, let her cry her heart out and come back in the morning. But it was the anguish of her cries, the way he imagined her body rattling with each new bout of sorrow that kept him from leaving. And then do what? he asked himself; slam her with facts until she bleeds. No, he decided, tomorrow it'd be as good as today.

The clatter of fallen objects and broken glass gainsaid his resolve. Daniel stood in alarm and looked through the window. Sofia, he thought. There were a handful of possibilities as to what had happened inside. One of them was of Sofia being attacked by an intruder, another one besides him. And why not? The gate to the property stood wide open when he drove in and the cottages, structures he assumed to be the homes of the permanent workers at the ranch, lay eerie dark as if unoccupied. Could it be that Sofia Lazar was alone on this gigantic breadth of land? Concerns about her lack of safety were materializing and right under his nose, someone may have slipped unnoticed onto the property.

Infused with adrenaline, he chose not to dwell on it; Daniel was a man of action. He needed to gain immediate access to the house.

He tried several entrances leading to different areas of the house. They were all locked. Daniel ran around the length of the house until he found access through an open door to what looked like separate living quarters, a private apartment off the pool area. As quietly as he could, he slipped into the house and walked straight into the living room. A trail of fallen objects and paintings led him to where the supposed struggle had started. One by one, he inspected every room, closet, and alcove in the silent house. There were no signs of Sofia or of that of an intruder. He traced his steps back to the open entrance. The intruder, Daniel, suspected could be hiding in that area. The thought of Sofia Lazar in danger turned his blood to ice. He rushed though the private apartment. Everything looked in order, until he heard the sound of cascading water. The door to the bathroom was locked. Daniel rammed against the bathroom door and in one blow, he brought it down. The floors were flooded with water overflowing from the bathtub. Daniel's heart stopped when under the warm light of the full moon he spotted Sofia Lazar sinking into the water, unconscious and a hairsbreadth from drowning.

He scooped her out of the tub. Instinctively, he pressed her wet goose-fleshed body to his.

Sofia's eyelids fluttered and for a fleeting moment, she looked into his eyes. "You are here to save me, then," she said before her eyes closed again.

Chapter Eleven

I was aware of not being alone. The house was strangely silent. The rays of sun intruding on my extremely sensitive eyes and the neon numbers on my alarm clock made it clear it was past noontime. My hair was stuck to my face and I smelled like a distillery. Images of the night before played through my jumbled mind.

I bolted up in bed not certain how I had gotten there or changed into the stained sweatpants and frayed zip-up hoodie I had on. My bladder felt full and my mouth pasty. I was desperately thirsty. Water! I thought. My eyes dropped to the floor and it was water that I saw.

The floor was sodden and I could see water damage on the hardwood floor and the entrance to the bathroom. One by one, the events blended together with the swiftness of a movie trailer. Dinner with Dana at the brewery, the man in the white shirt, Margaret's phone call, the mysterious phone call after that, my drinking binge, Abuela, the man from the brewery again. Other than a spell of nausea, a stabbing headache, and the remnants of the biggest flood since Noah, there were no signs of any additional damage I might have caused during the aftermath of my overindulgence.

I scraped my hair out of my face when my fingers encountered a rather large, painful bump. Gingerly I traced its contour. It was the size of a Spanish olive. I did a quick check over the rest of my body and found several scrapes on my legs and arms; some of them in the process of turning into unappealing bruises. I slumped back on my pillows wondering if my lack of recollection, the water damage, and the injuries on my body were enough to attend an AA meeting. I could picture myself standing in front of a group of sympathetic faces while stating: "Hi, my name is Sofia. I purposely got drunk to reject the fact that I might be the granddaughter of a Nazi whore."

The smell of coffee permeated through the house confirming my suspicions; I wasn't alone. I had given the house staff the week off because I needed to be alone. Perhaps one of them came back taking pity on my poor cooking skills and my tendency to eat burnt food.

The flash of a white shirt, one I thought I had seen during the night spurred me into action. With heavy limbs and armed with the baseball bat I kept under my bed, I crept out of my room. The feeling of my bare feet on the cold, damp floors sent a shiver up my spine, which did nothing to diminish the uneasiness for what I might encounter.

I noticed several vases missing and a few paintings with dented frames. I reached for the throbbing bump on my forehead, a vivid explanation for the missing and damaged items. By the look of things, someone—without a doubt now, one of the household staff—had taken the time to clean up my mess. The trail of semi-destruction took me back to the study, forcing me to retrace my steps. My computer, Abuela's last note, and Franzisca's box lay on the desk.

To gain understanding of what had caused the flood the night before, I made my way back to my quarters. Other than water, there was nothing to indicate what had happened. The coat I would have sworn to have left discarded on the floor was not there. Even the fastidious spider I had spotted on the corner of the ceiling the night before was gone. Perhaps, I had imagined the whole thing, the phone call, the spider, my levitation, the girl Franzisca, her mother Anna, the young Lupescu ...

Then I remembered the object I picked up from the tiled floor after I ripped the coat open. I switched the baseball bat to my left hand and stared at my right palm.

Indeed, a faint mark of something that had dug into my skin was still there. My eyes fell on my bed, then on my pillow. I always slept with my right hand tucked under my pillow. Flexing the fingers on my right hand as if I could make them memorize their actions of the night before, I reached for the pillow. There it was. A small, red silk sack safekeeping the core of Abuela's untold story.

"You are up," came a deep baritone voice behind me.

I literally jumped at those words and put away the bag in my hoodie's pocket. I spun around to face the potential murderer in my house—steadying myself from the dizziness that threatened to knock me down. I stood ready to strike the intruder with the baseball bat I held in my sweaty hands.

The man in the white shirt stood holding a mug with steaming coffee in each hand. He did his best to bite back the smile forming across his lips.

"Stay there," I warned him in. "I'm known for my homeruns." What was I saying? I had never played baseball, I didn't like baseball. Nevertheless, I walked to my nightstand, never taking my eyes off my supposed attacker and stood by the phone. I eyed him, then the phone. If I let my guard down, he could jump me.

"Who are you? What do you want? How did you get in?" I asked, lowering the bat and aiming it at him as if it were a broadsword.

He grinned as if the whole scene was funny. "May I set one of the cups down? It's for you."

"Don't move." I hated my evident fear.

He ignored my order and proceeded to sip from one of the mugs. Then while keeping his caramel colored eyes on me—how could I notice that detail at this time—he set the other mug on the floor.

"It's been a long night, Sofia, and I believe you could benefit as much as I from a strong cup of coffee."

There was something in his speech I recognized as familiar. It was a barely unintelligible lilt. He was foreign and English was not his first language. Having never gotten rid of my own accent completely, I knew a thing or two about foreigners.

With his booted foot, he pushed the mug toward me. Coffee sounded like something I couldn't resist. The white shirt guy looked harmless, if one did not look at the size of his biceps or the width of his shoulders. Against my better judgment, with my eyes glued to his face and the baseball bat slightly shaking in my left hand, I bent down to pick up the proffered mug, took a quick sip, and set it back down.

"What sort of person stays in this huge place all alone, with a door unlocked?"

He was angry. I was about to explain myself when I realized I was being reprimanded by an intruder.

"Are you for real? This is my house and you—" My words were cut off by yet another of his angry bursts.

"And to top it all off, you were wasted, *borracha*, like a sailor, and what does the lady decide to do?" he asked the walls, the lamp, the nightstand as if he were addressing a jury. His calm demeanor abandoned him. Were he a dragon, fire would have flowed out of his mouth instead of words. "She takes a bath." At the lack of response from the room, his attention rounded back to me. "One more second, Sofia, and you would have drowned."

He advanced toward me; both my hands were back around the neck of the baseball bat. "Are you trying to kill yourself or are you just…" He dropped his arms to the sides. I must have looked scared. "Listen," the edge of anger gone, "I just want—Sofia, we must talk."

Everything about him was unsettling, his deep voice, his eyes, the perfect definition of his jaw and chin, but mostly the fact that he could say my name as though he had known me all of my life.

I looked down at the clothes I was wearing. "You put me in these clothes."

He nodded.

"You were at the restaurant last night. You've been following me." My eyes traveled to the window. "I saw your reflection in the window... You are stalking me."

He didn't respond this time.

"Who are you?" I insisted, my tone guarded.

He took a step backward, resumed drinking his coffee.

"I planned never to meet you. It wasn't you I wanted... but I believe you could use my help right now." He raised his eyes to meet mine, "I could use yours, too."

His last statement raised a red flag. Of course! This guy was another hopeful taking desperate measures to make it to Tinseltown. Good looking, over six feet of stature, sculpted... I was doing it again. Focus, Sofia!

"What is it that you have? The best screenplay ever written, or do you think you are the next Clark Gable? I thank you for saving my life, your worries about my safety are appreciated, and the coffee, it's actually really good." I nodded toward my mug. I was the picture of arrogance. "If you don't leave my house right this second, I'm calling 911." I freed one hand from the baseball bat and picked up the phone.

He looked at me nonchalantly while sipping his coffee. He stared at me for a moment, his wheels turning. When he had reached his decision, he crossed his arms over his chest. The man became unreadable and a wave of fear washed over me. I knew I had to act, call the police or run. Instead, I asked him, "Who are you? What do you want?"

"My name is Daniel Alcaly. I'm here to collect a debt," he declared, his eyes as cold as ice.

My eyes travelled through him until they stopped on a naked spot on his chest. What I saw there, barely peeking out of the opening of his shirt was all I needed to strike this stranger out of the threat list and add him as one more piece of the puzzle Abuela had left behind.

I put the phone down, crossed my arms over my chest, jutted my chin out, and could not suppress a grin from stretching across my lips.

Chapter Twelve

"Show me your I.D. Anything that shows that you are who you say you are," I blurted out.

Daniel pulled out his wallet and slid it on the floor toward me. I picked it up and flipped it open. He had several I.D. cards and driver licenses from a number of European countries, Israel and Argentina, and an access card from the Technion, the technological University in Haifa, Israel, with his professional title of Mechanical Engineer. Although varied, his identification cards were consistent with one thing, the name Daniel Alcaly was on all of them. Still I couldn't help myself and when I tossed his wallet back to him, I raised an eyebrow and with a smirk I said, "Bond. James Bond."

He responded with a smile of his own. "Something of that sort, yes."

I studied him for a while longer still deciding what to do with this intruder. By the dark hollows under his eyes, I could tell that he had spent a rough night. His angry declaration about my brainless, drunken binge and consequent actions shook me. I could have died. To someone who did not know me, Daniel Alcaly being one, I must have been the picture of depression with suicidal tendencies. I needed this man to trust me. The object looped through the worn leather cord I had just glimpsed under his shirt, looked as real as the one I had seen twenty years ago hanging around another man's neck. Daniel Alcaly could very well be connected to the man who enlisted me to find Franzisca all those years ago. The nagging doubt was enough to help me reach a temporary decision. Daniel Alcaly was staying… for now.

"I hardly ever drink," I stated, using a strategy to clear my name first. "I do enjoy the occasional glass of red wine, but I don't do well with hard liquor. It makes me sick as soon as I smell it."

He raised his eyebrows. He had witnessed the results of my bad relationship with whisky and had been the one to clean up after me.

"Thank you," I mumbled, utterly embarrassed.

He did not respond to my explanation or apology. Instead, he tilted the mug in his hand.

"I think we could both use some more coffee." He looked at me, examining me from head to toe. For the first time that morning, I felt self-conscious about my rumpled, wretched state. I did not need a mirror to confirm it. His face said it all.

"In your case, plain toast would do."

He turned on his heels and I was left to follow in his wake like a little puppy.

When we reached the kitchen, a sensible breakfast was prepared. The man, Daniel, looked comfortable around knives, plates, and coffee makers. He struck me as the strong, silent type. I sensed there was more to his presence in Solvang than the *debt* he claimed he intended to collect. In the meantime, I decided to nurse my hangover with more coffee while I silently scrutinized his character. It was a trait, which had served me well when discerning between truth and fiction in a business filled with daydreamers. Daniel's movements were precise. He wore a frown on his face, a crease between his brows as if in constant worry or suspicion. My thorough inspection of the man in my kitchen was suddenly interrupted when a wave of nausea nearly overwhelmed me. I had to close my eyes for a moment. The smell of toast filled my nostrils.

"Breathe in," he said.

When I opened my eyes, the toast was neatly served on a plate on the table. Daniel leaned against the island. His coffee mug was suspended halfway to his lips; he stared out the kitchen window toward the rows of green trees, which would soon be festooned with juicy, sweet apricots. His hand completed the journey up and he sipped his coffee slowly, giving me space.

I sat down heavily at the table and forced down a few bites of toast. We could have stretched the silence for days, but I had a long list of things to do and Daniel Alcaly had become the first item on my to-do list I needed to take care of that morning. I wanted to hear what he had to say.

"Say what you have to say, Mr. Alcaly." I didn't mean to sound rude, but I did. After all the guy had apparently not only saved me from drowning, he also had toasted a piece of bread to perfection to help me recover from a horrible hangover. Still my senses were on high alert and it showed in my actions and my speech. There was something about his calm demeanor as he stood with his back turned to me that reminded me of a pressure cooker. The guy could explode without a moment's notice and I could be the recipient of his ire.

"Sofia," he said again with that unnerving familiarity, his caramel colored eyes showing no emotion. "It is clear that you don't trust me, nor should you. Are you sure you want to hear what I came here to tell you?"

"You are right." I stood by the table and grasped its edge lest I fell. "I don't trust you. I don't know you." I shook my head. *Awkward,* was the right word to describe my feelings while standing across from this man.

"Yet, you decided against calling the police. Why? What makes you think I will not hurt you?" He kept his distance, waiting to be invited into my space, even though he had already barged into my house uninvited.

I sat back down, motioned him over to the chair opposite me. "You saved me from drowning, and made me breakfast to kill me later... who are you, the witch from Hansel and Gretel?" I looked into his eyes. "You have five minutes of my time." I wasn't expecting him to jump at my command. In fact, I was not surprised when he leisurely walked to the coffee machine and helped himself to another cup. He lifted the pot, asking me silently if I wanted a refill. I nodded faintly. So far we had communicated civilly through sign language.

After he set both mugs on the table, he sat back on the chair opposite me.

"Beautiful view you have from here." His eyes moved back to the window. "Do you cook?"

"Mr. Acaly—"

"Daniel, call me Daniel." His smile was frank.

"Mr. Alcaly." If he meant to baffle me, he succeeded. "You have five minutes to explain yourself and you chose to waste them in small talk?"

"Doña Lola, she was our cook back in Buenos Aires. The kitchen had these…" His arms stretched out wide. "Big windows, not as big as these ones, but she loved to look out into the fields. I would stand by her side, she had a bench for me, and a bowl too, so I could help her."

The smile was still on his lips and it touched his eyes with innocence, like those of a child.

"We watched the world from there and a lot of cows, too. Doña Lola loved to make up stories while she prepared homemade gnocchi, or quince *pastelitos.* We made up stories about everything we saw through the windows. Cow stories, gaucho stories…" He shook his head faintly.

"And why do I need to know all these details about your windows?"

"Have you ever seen the person you love the most suffer?" The smile was gone.

My mind travelled back to that day at the finca in Mendoza. The day of the man with the key. The one day I witnessed Abuela's carefully arranged world rattle around her.

"It was through those windows that I saw the real face of the man I owe my life to. The man I intend to give back everything that was taken from him." Daniel stared at me hard. He meant every word. "I was about sixteen, too old for Doña Lola's stories, but I still visited her in the kitchen every chance I got. That day, the kitchen was empty; I think the old woman was sick with a sore throat. Funny how the weather turned that day from a warm afternoon to a miserable cold and rainy evening. I saw his car driving up the gravel road. He stopped and got out of the car in the middle of the torrential rain. In a matter of seconds he was drenched, but he didn't care. He just stood there looking; maybe thinking, or waiting for something."

He paused there. I saw him swallow and I knew the way he felt. I had seen Abuela doing exactly the same thing on our last afternoon at the finca. I had the urge to reach across the table and place my hand atop his. Tell him that I understood his pain, that children were not responsible for the unhappiness of adults, but I sat rooted to the chair and decided to attack him with sarcasm, my weapon of choice.

"So explain to me how I fit in this story of yours about this man and the windows, and what do I have to do with that debt you've come to collect. Last time I checked all my payments were all up to date and I did not have a Daniel Alcaly on my list of creditors."

"It's not your debt, you're right. Like I said before, It wasn't you who I was looking for. It was your grandmother, Claudia Lazar."

"She doesn't owe anything to anybody. Especially not to you." At that moment, my eagerness to confirm my suspicions about what Daniel Alcaly held under his shirt dissipated. I stood up abruptly in a way that made the table rattle. Both coffees sloshed in their cups and spilled over. "We're done talking, Mr. Alcaly."

Daniel sat on his chair ignoring my dismissal and continued talking. "When I came to find you yesterday, to talk with you, I had other things in mind. Those things changed after I scooped you out of the water."

My cheeks burned. "You mean after seeing me completely naked?"

"Not a bad view, I must say." He reached for my hand before I had the chance to walk away. "Please, Sofia."

His touch was as unsettling as the rest of him. I did not reject it; I analyzed it. Just like his eyes and his half smiles there was caution in the way he conducted himself.

"Tell me again, who are you and why are you here?" I slid my hand from his and stood back.

"All right," he said. He stood and paced toward the opposite side of the kitchen, then he looked at me. "You want to know? Here it goes. I know you've been making enquiries about Claudia Lazar, your grandmother, Abuela, as you used to call her."

I was taken aback by the information this complete stranger had about my recent activity and my private life. I kept my eyes on him, waiting for more. My overextended silence gave him permission to move forward.

"Like they say in this country, Sofia, you are on a wild goose chase."

"Since you seem to know so much, go ahead, enlighten me."

"There are no records in Argentina of a Claudia Lazar, at least not one matching your abuela. She wasn't born there or anywhere, she never entered the country legally or illegally. There are no traces of a birth certificate with her name on it." He shook his head faintly. "She never existed."

I had never questioned Abuela about her birthplace. To me her Argentinean nationality was a given. She had never spoken of any other birthplace and showed no hints of a foreign accent in her speech. Abuela was a polyglot. I loved to tease her and tell her that she could run for president of the Tower of Babel. With her fluency in many languages, she could have easily disguised herself as a national of many countries if language and accent was to be the decisive factor.

I did not want to give Daniel Alcaly the satisfaction of confirming the information he had given me. Other than her California driver's license and American passport, Abuela's name was nowhere to be found on any other official document. Since the day I discovered the three properties transferred to me from an undisclosed corporation, I had placed many calls to Abuela's attorney, and I wasn't surprised when his secretary called me back stating that he was out of the country and out of reach. I now suspected both excuses to be lies. His lips were sealed.

It struck me now that I had never seen Abuela's birth certificate or anything with the name Claudia Lazar that could state her origins. Since her death, I had gone through every drawer, cabinet and closet, but found no clues. The same thing happened when I opened the deposit boxes she held around town at different banks. I discovered pieces of jewelry I'd never seen her wear, my birth certificate, vaccination chart, and school transcripts. Nothing confirming her name.

I wanted to hear nothing else from Daniel Alcaly at that moment. My heart raced with the urgency to prove everybody wrong. Claudia Lazar had existed; she was my abuela.

I rushed to my room, picked up my oversized bag, then walked briskly to the foyer, opened the front door and ran out to my car.

"Sofia!"

I did not stop at his command. I got in the car and turned on the engine. I caught a glimpse of myself in the rear view mirror. I looked like I just ran away from an asylum where they did not provide hairbrushes to their patients. I did not care; looks were the least of my worries when my very existence depended upon the validity of a name.

Before I shifted the car in reverse, my door flew open. Daniel's towering figure loomed over; he stared at me in disbelief.

"Where are you going?" We were back on his terms.

I was determined to prove him and the mysterious caller wrong and for that, I needed factual confirmation that what I knew to be true my whole life was still true. Where to go for official documents? I thought. "The Argentinean Consulate in Los Angeles," I said, matter of fact.

He let out a suppressed laugh. "Move over, I'll drive."

Chapter Thirteen

Daniel kept his eyes on the road. A sudden rainstorm broke over us as soon as we made our way down the 101 Freeway. Rain came down in sheets. He kept his attention on the red taillights of the cars that were constantly breaking ahead of us. It was true what they said about Southern California drivers; the moment a drop falls from the sky, the whole network of freeways gets washed out by panic.

Back at the ranch, I had gotten into the car clueless as to what to do next. Daniel's revelations were as startling as he thought they would be. This whole *Where in The World is Waldo* game Abuela left for me to resolve was bound to be full of mysteries. I was keen to follow it, in truth I was intrigued. The unsettling part of it was the possibility of having lived a lie my whole life.

When Daniel relegated me to the passenger seat I was silently grateful. My head had not ceased pounding since the night before and on top of that, I needed time to plan what I was to do once I reached the Consulate and how to approach the matter of the key with Daniel. He did not strike me as the chatty type. Moreover, I did not feel in the right frame of mind to trudge down that path yet. If there was one thing I was sure of was that this stranger was after the same thing I was. What were his reasons? I was yet to find out.

The thick tension growing between Daniel and me was partially relieved by the sounds inside of the car. Our quiet breaths, the swish of the windshield wipers, and the drumming of raindrops on the hood; acted as a dark intro to a dramatic scene if translated in film language. To my right, the ocean, dark as lead, crashed onto the shore as if intent on swallowing anything that dared to stand up against it.

I replayed the last few hours since meeting Daniel while focusing on the depth of the car's headlights on the wet road. I did not believe his first statement of having never planned to meet me. I suspected the opposite. Daniel's type did not act on impulse the way I would. Behind his boy next-door façade, Daniel was a calculating man.

"This drive to the consulate is useless, Sofia and you know it."

"It seems that you know a lot more than I do, Bond. Go ahead say what you've come to say."

Daniel shifted in his seat and glanced my way. "Ask your mother. She's bound to know more than the clerk at the consulate." His words hit my stomach with the searing coldness of ice bullets.

"So this is what it's all about. You're in with my mother," I seethed in between teeth. "Stop the car. Stop the damn car."

With an impassive look in his eyes, he sped out of the lane and drove the car into a rest area off the freeway. I gripped the edge of my seat and held my breath until Daniel maneuvered the car and brought it to a sudden stop at the edge of a steep rocky cliff.

On any other day, the view from this point, where the ocean meets the infinite blue of the sky, would be breathtaking. But today, the muddy cliff set against the raging ocean seemed like the ideal setting for murder. I jumped out of the car before he shifted into park, and headed in the opposite direction. I needed fresh air, or rain in this case, to clear my muddled head. I felt so stupid. I should have seen it coming. Thinking back on the brief meeting with Marcela, things had gone too easy. She made no demands and for a moment, I had the impression that she cared about me. I heard Daniel following me above the sound of the crashing waves. I was drenched, frustrated. I stopped.

He wiped the rain off his face with his hand and then he ran his fingers through his wet hair. "In case you haven't noticed, it's raining."

"I won't hold it against you, Alcaly, the woman seems to be a man magnet. You're her type," I emphasized, sensing the anger brewing in him, "younger than her, good looking." I appraised him up and down, "hard in all the right places, but most importantly, you're disposable."

Daniel's anger was noticeable. I took a step backward but he was faster than me. He grabbed my arms. I felt my feet leave the ground as he pulled me within a hairsbreadth of his face and crushed my fading smile with an angry kiss. He settled me back down, his eyes never leaving me. "Let me make something very clear, Sofia. I'm my own man."

Still hostage of his stare, I tottered back. My first impulse was to slap him, but I was too stunned to move or utter a word. If he meant to shut me up, he had succeeded, and Oh, boy! The man could definitely kiss. It took a couple of full breaths to get my wits back under rein. "Let's make something else very clear, Alcaly. The reason why I'm putting up with this whole nonsense with you has nothing to do with the macho-overbearing attitude you just displayed, but because I want something from you. You're using me and I'm using you. And by the way, don't you ever do that to me again."

"Point taken," he said. "The kiss, I won't apologize for." A smile cut across his lips, "nor I can promise I won't do it again. But I owe you a fresh start." He put out his hand. "I'm Daniel Alcaly and for the past few months I've been looking forward to meeting you."

I don't know what made me trust him at that precise moment but I took his hand and shook it.

"Sofia Lazar, I've never planned to meet you and I won't lie, somewhere between the restaurant last night and now, I might have fantasized of kissing you."

He looked startled at my words.

I walked to the car without a backward glance, my lips still stinging from his kiss. "Did anybody ever tell you that you look at lot like your grandfather?" I said out loud.

He didn't see that one coming. Daniel Alcaly stood perplexed, and I felt vindicated. "Do you still want to drive me down to the consulate, Bond?"

Back in the shelter of the car, we sat in complete silence with our attention glued on the choppy ocean. According to the clock in the car, the consulate would close in another three hours. In the downpour, I'd be lucky to make it before they closed.

Before I could voice my concern, Daniel turned the key in the ignition and drove the car back onto the freeway. The two-and-a-half hour car ride to the consulate passed without incident and felt like it lasted an eternity. We drove in silence.

When we pulled up in front of the consulate, I was the first to break the heavy silence between us.

"I'd better go. They'll be closing in twenty minutes." I tried hard to avoid looking at him, but it was impossible. His eyes bore into mine. I saw resignation.

"I'll be waiting for you in the *café* down the street."

Daniel handed me the car keys and like a good Argentinean, he kissed me on my cheek. His kiss was quick and a mere formality, far from the angry, passionate kiss he gave me in the rain. In Argentina that one kiss on the cheek was as common as saying *chau* when parting, or eating *asado* with friends and family on Sundays. However customary his kiss was, the feel of his lips on my skin lingered long after he walked down the street.

A car blasted its horn reminding me why I stood on Wilshire Boulevard under the most ridiculous rain I had ever experienced in Southern California. I jaywalked against bad tempered Angelino drivers who did not care about my urgency to make it into the consulate before closing time.

There were still a few people filling out forms and waiting for their names to be called when I walked into the consulate. I felt welcomed by the sounds of a language that had once meant home to me. I rarely spoke Spanish anymore and the times I did it were never with a fellow national. There was something about the lilt in their speech and the body language of the people at the consulate that suddenly made me feel homesick for the finca in Mendoza.

That was it, the title to the *finca*. I remembered retrieving it from one of the safe deposit boxes the day before and leaving it in my purse. I rummaged into the depths of my bag and pulled out the only legal document I had found with Abuela's name on it. I made my way to the help desk to initiate my inquiry. The woman behind it, was middle aged, dressed in the latest European fashion, with tanned skin, and perfect golden highlights in her hair. An Argentinean through and through. The kind of woman that would never be caught in sweats and flip-flops in the supermarket line. Her full attention was on the document lying on the desk before her. After several minutes of standing in front of her, I cleared my throat in case she hadn't noticed me or the line growing behind me. With an arched eyebrow, she finally addressed me. I ran my fingers through my hair, realizing for the first time how awful I must have looked. I was conscious of still looking sick and greenish, and that I had walked out of the house in the miss-matched clothes Daniel had changed me into. In addition to that, I was soaked to the bone.

"Do you have a question?" she inquired. Public employees! I had forgotten how intimidating these people could be. At my hesitation, she sighed and looked at her coworker sitting right behind her and shook her head. "We close in twenty minutes."

I squared my shoulders and thrust the finca's deed under her nose.

After a brief glance she said, "I'm not psychic, *querida*. You have to tell me why you are here." She eyed the line forming behind me.

I pushed the title closer to her. "Could you... can you look her up? My abuela, Claudia Lazar."

The woman squinted at me, then back at the title. I must have looked the picture of distress because she stepped from behind her post and walked around to the reception area. "We do not keep records on every *Argentino* that immigrates to The United States. We deal with passports, documents, that sort of thing." She handed the title back to me.

I pushed the document into her hands. "You have to tell me that the name on this title is real. That she existed. That Claudia Lazar was her name." I felt my face dampen with tears. Dozens of eyes stared at me. I heard a familiar voice behind me followed by a comforting arm around my shoulders.

"I promise you, Sofia, we'll get to the bottom of this." Daniel slid his hand into mine and led me out of the consulate.

The rain had stopped and the weather had turned unusually cold. I had never felt so tired. All I wanted was for my abuela to hold me, tell me that it had all been a bad dream. But that was not possible, because every step I had taken after her death made me sink deeper and deeper into the web of mysteries she had left behind.

I held on to Daniel's hand as if he were my lifeline. I let him drag me into a small restaurant near the consulate.

He procured us a table at the far end of the room and I heard him place an order with the waiter.

"I hope you like tomato soup. I think you could do with something warm." He spread butter on a piece of bread and placed it on a plate next to me. "Eat."

I obeyed and sank my teeth into the buttery bread. I was hungry. Daniel left a second piece of bread on my plate. He finished eating his and placed the finca title on the table. "I guess you'll be needing this."

I rubbed my hands together cleaning any bread crumbs left in between my fingers and reached for the title. I read Abuela's name over and over again. "Earlier today you said you were looking forward to meeting me? What are you after?"

His eyes were guarded, devoid of all traces of macho confidence this time. "You told me I looked like my grandfather. How do you know how my grandfather might look like or if I even have one? "

The waiter set two bowls of steaming soup in front of us and a fresh basket of bread.

"I asked you first." The exchange between us no longer held its previous tension. I spooned some of the rich red, creamy soup into my mouth and was delighted by its delicious flavor. "Great choice on the soup by the way."

He spooned some for himself and nodded. "Not bad."

Daniel left the spoon in his bowl and propped his elbows on the table, one hand cradling a fist.

"I came across her name before, Lazar. Claudia Lazar."

"You and thousands of others. My abuela was a well-known figure. A historian, researcher, philanthropist. More of a celebrity than I could ever be."

"Her name was on a list. Unidentified Nazi collaborators." He spread his palms wide. "Financing terrorist cells to conduce attacks, like the one on the A.M.I.A. in 1994, call it the Argentinean Jewish Federation if you will. Not for the first time Nazis financed an Arab terrorist group," he continued, casually. "I'm sure you are familiar with the Munich massacre in the 1972 Olympics. Black September, the Palestinian terrorist cell, was aided by a German Nazi group. The strongest evidence points toward the Iranian government, anyway."

Up until then I had enjoyed every spoonful of my soup. I was even planning on ordering a second bowl. But the accusation Daniel so casually threw in between the bread basket and the soup made my breath catch in my throat and for a few seconds I forgot to breathe. I let the spoon drop in the bowl with an audible clank. "My abuela, on a list of terrorists, what did she do? Blow up The Mechanical Engineering Union? Is that why a mechanical engineer is after her? Surely you've got your wires crossed, Mr. Alcaly. Or your fuses blown. I don't know mechanical terms so take your pick."

The bridge we had crossed when he saved me from crumbling at the consulate collapsed the moment he named my abuela a Nazi. A growing fear gripped my chest. Only hours before I had gotten that unsettling phone call. The name Lupescu and the other horrible things that resentful man on the other end of the line had filled my head with were not far from what Daniel was saying to me. Now Daniel was taking the subject even further. Beyond being a Nazi whore, Abuela was also a Nazi collaborator responsible for financing terrorist activities.

"No, she did not blow up any engineer union. Yes, I'm a mechanical engineer and a—"

"And a fool who's playing secret agent and wasting my time!"

"Sofia, all joking aside I am a former Israeli Intelligence agent, Mossad, who's been after Claudia Lazar's trail for years. And no, I'm not playing games," he responded, trying to keep his temper reined in.

A heavy silence stretched between us. "You must understand the conflicting feelings I have toward Claudia

Lazar. On the one hand, there are no records of her place of birth, past, or entry into the country—not under that name or any name. Just a vast fortune tied to her. All of it dated sometime during the 1940s. She's believed to be one of the many Nazis that got the carte blanche into Argentina from Peron right after the second war."

I had no idea what he was talking about. I had left Argentina as a child, I knew of President Peron only by name and by the information I read on the internet the day before. The 1940s only meant World War II to me and all the people I met throughout my years of witnessing Abuela helping them find themselves through their pain. It couldn't be. She devoted her life to make it right for all of them. To help them find their way home. She could never have collaborated with criminals. Never! I rummaged in the corners of my memory for any hint of truth to Daniel's allegations. I went even further into the stories Abuela drew me into every night, Franzisca stories. No. It wasn't possible for Abuela or Franzisca to hate to the point of murder. Never. Unless her post-war actions were an attempt to ease her guilt. A way to achieve redemption. Exactly what that anonymous caller claimed Abuela to be.

I couldn't help but sneer, but my hands were clammy and my heart was racing. "You're surely mistaken; if you knew anything about my grandmother..." My voice shook involuntarily.

I knew I had to leave to stop the storm of information about to crash on me. I would have done so if my legs would have agreed with the commands of my rational brain. Glued to the chair, as if by a spell, I was forced to listen to what Daniel had to say.

I felt nauseous. My face must have shown every bit of it because next thing I knew, Daniel was standing next to me pushing a glass of water into my shaking hands. I pushed it away spilling the liquid on the tabletop.

I stood up and faced him. "What-do-you-want? Now that Abuela is dead, are you after me then, Agent Alcaly? Do you find me suspicious, too?" I hated showing how affected I felt. Still, I stood in front of him unable to hide the tears that were brimming in my eyes. 'You don't know a thing about any of us."

"There's one thing I know. I know none of it is true."

I stared at him, my confusion growing.

Daniel reached under his shirt and pulled out the key he sheltered there. It was the same key from that long gone afternoon, from my dream, from Franzisca's story. I held my breath and gripped the silky red sack I had put away in my pocket after retrieving it from under my pillow.

Before I could blink away my tears, he gently placed a written sheet of paper on the only clean spot remaining on the table.

"Alex, my grandfather, held this in his hands when he died six months ago." His eyes travelled from the note to me and I could see his own sadness taking hold of his controlled demeanor. "And the name *Franzisca* took his last breath away."

Chapter Fourteen

Sofia stared at the note on the table and once again a silence charged with tension stretched between them. Daniel decided to sit back and observe her reaction. It was this note that had brought them to this point. It would be her willingness to show him her cards and authenticate the missive as her grandmother's that would see them through this next phase together.

Things had not worked out the way Daniel had envisioned. He had sought out Sofia with the sole purpose of extracting information. Daniel never got emotionally involved while on a mission; he never cared for the needs of his suspects. By now, he should have walked away from her and planned his next move.

From the moment he fished Sofia out of the bathtub, and saw the contents of the red bag she had gripped so tightly even while she was passed out, he had done nothing else but watch out for her wellbeing. He had made her breakfast for crying out loud, driven her to Los Angeles—after her previous state of inebriation, and like a father would do for a child, he had buttered her bread—twice!

He was losing it, and for a woman who had threatened to bash his head in with a baseball bat. But the kiss had been worth it, he relished in the memory. On the other hand, her blunt, candid way compelled him to open up in a way he had never done with any other woman before. Perhaps it was because the woman sitting across the table from him, twirling a spoon in a congealed cup of tomato soup, felt real. Her nearness made his fingers tingle with the need to touch her, not to let her go. For a moment, he pondered if that was the way Alex, his grandfather, had felt about Franzisca, a woman who at this point was nothing but a name he whispered with his last breath of life.

When he had found Sofia close to drowning the night before, he had counted on a damsel in distress he could rescue from a crisis. A few minutes after being on the receiving end of her hot temper, Daniel changed his opinion of her. Sofia was not that. She was in a crisis and obviously in distress, but she was not the kind of person waiting to be rescued. All right, he concluded, that was just fine with him; he did not cope well with needy people, especially women. But if he was not to rescue her, at least he wanted her to let him in. His feelings caught him by surprise for he never thought he would *feel* something when faced with a Lazar.

For most of his adult life, Daniel had devoted his free time to getting to the bottom of the one event that had eternally labeled his father as a murderer. The only accounts of that fateful night came from the vague and delusional memory of a former *Montonero*—an old acquaintance of his father from the time of the Argentinean guerrilla—a man who had lost his marbles in a military torture chamber. He claimed the person responsible for Armendariz's death had been a young girl he had sold a grenade to and not Isaac, Daniel's father. Names flew out of the crazy man's mouth tangled with ramblings about his days as an activist and his months as a political prisoner. The name Lazar was one among many.

Daniel did not believe in accidents or coincidences. Even though the envelope which had carried that note for his grandfather lacked remittance, it was obvious that the sender did not want to be completely anonymous, but that she wanted to be found.

He looked across the table and saw Sofia finally reaching for the note. Another thought occurred to him. The sender gambled with the chance that Daniel would never get to see her alive. The sender of the note meant for

Daniel to seek Sofia. She had carefully staged this scenario before her death. Daniel understood that in this he was not the master of his own destiny.

With Claudia Lazar dead, her daughter Marcela was his next stop. A chill ran through his spine at the thought of meeting her face to face. But he had decided to bypass that meeting for now and let the game he had been called into playing reveal the answers of his own tragic story.

The course of Daniel's life had changed, six months after his birth, with the death of general Armendariz.

Isaac, his father, was accused of Armendariz's murder and of participating in the planning of a series of bombings that were responsible for the deaths of several military officials during the last years of Argentina's military government in the early nineteen eighties. Even this late in the regime, the military still hunted their insurgents and Daniel's family became a deadly target.

Alex, his grandfather, was a man of sizable wealth, a rancher in the outskirts of Buenos Aires, known for his charitable heart and his impartiality to every presidency, democratic or not. His money and influence bought him enough time to smuggle his only son, his daughter-in-law and their two older children out of Argentina into Israel. But the hasty escape would have been deadly for Daniel, his youngest grandson. Afflicted by every childhood illness known to man, little Daniel struggled to thrive. It was questionable that the baby would survive under normal circumstances and Alex was not about to play with the weak life of his tiny grandson. A decision Daniel never forgave his grandfather for.

When Daniel presented his resignation to the Mossad he had promised to leave that chapter of his life behind, and to reconnect with his grandfather.

During his short time with Alex, Daniel learned much about the man's life. Alex spoke freely about his time before immigrating to Argentina. He spoke about his mother, his brother, and the many borders he had to cross before boarding a ship to take him far away from war and persecution. Not once did the old man talk about the woman who gave birth to Isaac, Daniel's father. Not once did the old man talk about love. Not until the name Franzisca slipped between his lips in a final whisper. A call between lovers, a voice that was to be heard beyond the restraints of corporeal existence.

Daniel regarded Sofia from across the table. Her eyes were downcast, studying the note closely. He thought her beautiful. The kind of woman he wouldn't mind getting to know. She was obviously a savvy businesswoman, and according to the several interviews he had read, she also possessed a sense of humor. She had gotten under his skin with all her flaws, her klutzy drunkenness and the sincerity of her loss. He wanted to kiss her again. Damn the woman!

"This was hers." Sofia's confirmation pulled him out of his thoughts. Her fingers caressed the edges of the paper. "Abuela was a nut for everything ancient. She once had a paper forensic recreate the original vellum used in 1452 for the Gutenberg Bible. She searched high and low until she finally found a collector of rare books in France willing to sell his copy. There are only a handful of complete Gutenberg Bibles written in vellum in the world today." She raised her eyes to Daniel, a corner of her mouth arched upwards. "So, I own one now."

"Mrs. Larsen, the owner of the antique shop told me about it. She even showed me a missive she had gotten from your grandma written on the same paper as this note." They were dancing around the subject. Both of them avoiding the contents of the note.

"Of course, Miss Larsen, the poor spinster probably provided you with every tidbit of information about us, and would have probably volunteered a kidney should you needed it, just to keep you in her store a while longer."

Daniel laughed. "You do have a sense of humor, you know?"

Sofia rolled her eyes. "Bond, if you think I'm funny you need to get out more." The humor subsided; the tension was back in place.

"The note was mailed from your local post office, that's how I found you," he said.

Sofia pushed the note to Daniel. "The paper is hers, I won't argue that. But the words... she would've never said that to anybody, least of all write it for the words could never be erased. Abuela would never write this," Sofia concluded. However, thinking of the story, *The Boy She Found*, and now thinking of Franzisca and Alex in the tunnel, she knew that Franzisca would.

The words escaped her mouth before Sofia could stop them. "I met him, Alex, your grandfather when I was a little girl. It was probably a few days before you saw him through your kitchen window. He had come to our place in Mendoza. Just like you are doing it now, he came looking for her, for Franzisca." Sofia's eyes met his. "I knew who he was even though I never asked for his name. He belonged to a story my abuela told me once, he was a character in it. It was a love story."

Daniel felt his throat constrict with growing emotion. "After that weeklong trip, Alex never wore the key again. I suspected something had gone terribly wrong. You see, he had never taken that damn key of his neck before."

Daniel looked at Sofia, questioning if she could explain what had happened on that day. She remained silent.

Daniel traced the edges of the key with his thumb and index fingers." On the day he died, after twenty years, I found the key around his neck again."

"He had your eyes and your smile... And I made a promise to him." Sofia retrieved the red bag from her pocket and slowly emptied the contents on the table. Looped through a silver chain it was the twin of Daniel's key. "I promised him I would help him…"

"Find Franzisca," Daniel finished for her. "Well, it seems we are both guilty of the same promise. I say we start looking for her." Daniel left a few bills on the table, stood up and reached for Sofia's hand. "Ready?"

She took hold of Daniel's hand and looked at him. "If not now, when," she said to him.

Daniel recognized the phrase once written by Hillel a famous Jewish religious leader back in the Babylonian times somewhere around 100 BCE.

If I am not for myself, who will be for me?
And when I am for myself, what am I?
And if not now, when?

There was a truth ringing in Hillel's phrase. He was here on a mission. Was he doing this for Alex or for himself? Would the answers be his undoing? Would Sofia be the one for him? Whatever the outcome, he thought, *let the games begin.*

Daniel nodded. "It is now, then."

Chapter Fifteen

As a result of the nature of my work, I was used to late nights and little sleep. But the emotional toll of the last days had put a new kind of strain on my body, greater than any of the most challenging of my productions. When people think of filmmaking, they fast-forward to the glamour of red carpets and champagne-infused after-parties. What they don't think of is the amount of physical and mental work behind the make-believe world of movies. It wasn't until my first production that I really appreciated God's creation. In only six days He put together the biggest production ever seen without cast or crew. Genius!

When I sat at the wheel, with my hand on the stick shift, I could savor the soothing effects of the upcoming warm shower and uninterrupted night of sleep in between my fresh sheets. Daniel looked at me with furrowed brows. "I would feel better if you'd let me drive." He was obviously dubious about trusting his life to a driver that had yawned five consecutive times in less than ten seconds.

"Not a chance, Bond. It's a free country; you can drive back with me, or catch a train back to Solvang. I think the last one leaves in a couple of hours." I was bone tired; perhaps driving was not the best idea. But I needed to focus on the work ahead and driving at night had helped me organize my thoughts in the past. My producer's mind was already spinning its wheels calculating the amount of planning it would take to time travel into our grandparents' youth. Before starting any kind of work together we had to exchange as much information as we could about each other, our lives with our grandparents, and any details that might help shed light on their story, before determining if they had ever shared a past beyond the keys.

We had been together for the best part of the last twenty-four hours. By now, I had already concluded that Daniel Alcaly was far from a serial killer, celebrity stalker, or rapist. Still, the matter of sharing the ride back with him demanded effort, an element in short supply at that point of the evening. Regardless of his wants, I was determined to keep my eyes on the road, my thoughts to myself, and my mouth shut. One way or another, the ghosts from the past would still be there in the morning when I could see through them in the light of a new day.

Behind his impenetrable mood, he too must have been weighing his options. He mumbled something under his breath. It must have been in Hebrew, the words sounded very foreign to me. He let his full weight slide into the passenger seat, and with a deep scowl on his face, we left Los Angeles under a storm and smog-charged sky.

The drive back to Solvang was a reprise of our drive down to Los Angeles. Tiredness was gradually weighing heavily on my lids and I wondered if his deafening stillness was his way of turning my exhaustion against me to earn the command of the car. I would fight fire with fire.

"Pay your fare with conversation, Bond. Tell me, what makes an Argentinean cattle rancher, turn Mossad agent?"

He stiffened in his seat. I had hit a nerve throwing out the window any chance of casual conversation.

"There are events that change the course of our lives, Sofia. I spent years trying to right wrongs the way I saw fit. My family—my parents and siblings—died in a terrorist attack in Israel. I had to see justice done, even if I had never met them."

"You've never met your family?"

"No. I was a weak baby. They didn't think I was going to make it, so Alex decided to keep me. My family had to escape the country before the military got to them.

My father was wrongly accused for the murder of a General." Daniel shifted in his seat.

The flow of information was much more than I had expected. I was ready for a story of cowboys and Indians, not for a full confession of his life's tragedy.

"Wrongly accused?" I felt like a parrot repeating each one of his last words. I couldn't help it. I wanted to know more.

"Everything points to people of influence. The safety of a family was exchanged for my family's extradition."

"I'm sorry."

"It is not your fault, Sofia."

I was afraid to dig any deeper into his personal life. Yet his response struck me as odd. Of course, I was not to blame for his loss. Up until twenty hours ago, we did not know of each other's existence. I had to ask. "So, did you? Did you avenge them?"

"When I made *alyah*, when I immigrated to Israel, I saw the bigger picture, much larger than the loss of my family." He paused for a moment. "Revenge wasn't taking me anywhere other than to my own destruction."

"That sounds like a lot of therapy, Bond." He was giving me free rein to take my pick of questions, but only briefly, I could see the portal closing.

"What made you change?" All of a sudden, I wanted to know him better, deeper. I wanted the drive to be endless, forget about the secrets of the past our grandparents left us and live the present.

His eyes bore into mine. "I witnessed my abuelo Alex die, longing for what could've been. I don't want to die like that. I don't want to live like he did."

His words touched the very core of my being. I pulled the car over into the emergency lane, turned the engine off, and unbuckled my seat belt. Before I knew what I was doing, my arms were thrown around his neck. I did not want to die like that either, nor live the lonely life Abuela had.

His returned embrace was immediate, borderline desperate. We clung to each other with a silent promise to live life at its fullest. My eyes closed momentarily, taking in his scent, the feel of his arms around me. I gave in. The prospect of driving one more mile against the blinding lights felt exhausting. As if reading my thoughts, Daniel pulled gently away from me, stepped out of the car and I slid into the passenger seat.

"I'll wake you when we get there," he said, cradling me to his side.

I fell asleep with the warmth of his arm around me, much better, I thought, than my clean, cold sheets.

***

"We're here." His nudge was as soft as his voice. I blinked a couple of times until my eyesight cleared to the starry night.

"It's like living in a planetarium. It surprises you every night with a different show." He stared into the beauty of the night thoroughly enjoying the view.

I looked at him then I focused back on the glittery night. Yes." I yawned lazily. "Beautiful."

His smile suddenly wiped off his face. His head turned sharply toward the house. I swiveled in my seat and followed the direction of his gaze. There was a light in the house. "I don't remember leaving any lights on."

"Stay here," Daniel commanded. The soldier in him suddenly alert. His face filled with determination. His eyes on the target.

He stepped out of the car and I followed against his advice. I couldn't sit and wait for the military debriefing.

A red car was parked on the circular driveway. "Daniel." My loud voice echoed in the quiet night.

The way he regarded me with his scowl made me wish never to confront him in battle. "Don't kill me just yet. It is Margaret. She's home." I pointed to the car.

***

Margaret paced the foyer. Where on earth was this child? She had called Sofia earlier in the day to announce her arrival in Solvang, but both phones, her cellular and private home line, had gone unanswered. That was completely out of character for Sofia. The girl lived through that palm-size device and unless something really awful had happened to her, the only other logical explanation would be that she was forced to give it up at gunpoint.

She had hated lying to Sofia when they spoke last, but she was not ready to answer questions yet. Margaret had planned this trip ahead of time, even before Claudia's death. She predicted Sofia would refuse her offer for any kind of help after learning of Claudia's passing. She had also predicted Marcela's first attempt to reconcile with her daughter would fail, even before Marcela had phoned her in complete misery after the disastrous meeting with Sofia. However, Margaret had not travelled to California to help Sofia sort through paperwork or to console Marcela. Their journey as mother and daughter was yet to come full circle and for that to happen they would have to allow forgiveness to act as their only mediator, a road she hoped they would walk through together.

Still, a fierce sense a responsibility had driven Margaret to take this trip. The idea of disclosing the truth of Claudia's past to Sofia had been Margaret's. Claudia mulled over the notion for months, but could never bring herself to face her granddaughter. Margaret loved Claudia with her whole heart. She had been a sister to her, a friend, the only family she had ever known. Claudia had been headstrong and that had led her to make many mistakes at the expense of her own happiness. Margaret could clearly see how the same pattern was wrecking Marcela's and

Sofia's lives, the two girls she loved as if they were her own. Only the truth would prevent them from following Claudia's self-destructing path.

"There's more to the past than my personal history, Margaret." The lines of worry on Claudia's face spoke of the tangled web her life had become. "You have to promise me you will not interfere. I will tell Sofia… everything. But in my own way. In my own time."

Claudia's time had come and gone. She had privately predicted this would happen, but she was not concerned. Everything would eventually be revealed, in its due course, as part of a plan. It wasn't up to Margaret to disclose the truth to Sofia. She would never betray her late friend, but from the moment Sofia mentioned the old picture, the doll, and the little girl, she felt she must act upon her own unfinished business lest her own time would run out. Little did she know that in forcing Claudia to come clean with her granddaughter, her longtime friend would leave an open path to the questions that had burned in Margaret all her life. But before meeting with Sofia, she had planned to help Claudia settle old scores with another major player in the story. The meeting with the young man, that resembled his grandfather greatly, had been among Claudia's last requests.

"I've been expecting him for six months, now. I thought he would come and do away with me before the cancer," Claudia had said to Margaret over a video communication days before her death. "I just want you to tell him how sorry I am for what happened to him. Please, tell him not to make Sofia pay for my crimes."

With the help of a private-eye Claudia had used in the past, Margaret had finally gotten a hold of him. The young man was in California, too close for comfort, Margaret thought. He had been reluctant when she asked to meet with him, which was probably the reason why she was not surprised when he had not showed at the appointed time and place. He had also failed to meet with Marcela. It didn't take a rocket scientist to know that he had chosen Sofia as his target. Margaret would not stop him; however she would make sure of Sofia's safety.

Margaret had the keys and access codes to all the homes Claudia owned. Before letting herself in, she rang the bell a few times, hoping Sofia would answer, but the door had gone unanswered just like her phones had.

Claudia's absence was felt the moment Margaret closed the door behind her. There was an echo ringing in the empty space waiting to be filled with her bustling energy. She couldn't blame Sofia for not being there. With Claudia's absence the house seemed to have lost interest in being a home.

After noticing Sofia's car was not in the garage, Margaret set off toward Sofia's private suites, skipping the main house entirely. When she opened the door, the apartment smelled like wet dog. The floorboards were stained with water, the result of a small flood, she suspected. The bed looked slept in and the bed-sheets were folded outwards, in the way Sofia always laid them out whenever she left her bed.

Margaret's hair stood on end when she noticed Sofia's bathroom door splintered at the edges, as if someone had forced an entry. She tried to control her anxiety until she tripped over a white coat. Margaret lifted the coat in her arms. She held it to her cheek. She had seen Claudia wearing that coat more than a half century ago. In it she had looked regal, a different person. Perhaps it was a distorted memory. The smile on the woman that wore the coat was so unlike Claudia's. The woman in the white coat never allowed her smile to reach her eyes. She was cold and had walked past Margaret as if she had never seen her before in her life. Yet the coat was now in her arms. She had wanted that woman not to be Claudia, but the white, wool garment in her possession confirmed otherwise.

Margaret's exploration of Sofia's last actions before leaving took her to the main wing of the residence. Judging by the path of destruction from Sofia's room to the rest of the house, the girl had experienced some type of rough awakening. Cracks were visible on several pieces of art in the living room, some were missing and a few of the wood frames from the valuable paintings were chipped. Claudia's room appeared to be the starting point of the subsequent mayhem. The bed was stripped of its linens, an empty bottle of whisky lay on the closet floor and every single drawer and article of clothing was strewn across the room as if by scattering them out, some shred of truth could be squeezed out of them.

Claudia's office was untouched. The laptop and Sofia's prized cellphone indicated that she had been there. Margaret turned on the laptop and the screen came alive with some interesting information.

Margaret closed the laptop having seen enough and headed for the kitchen. There would be a lot to talk about whenever Sofia came back. Pie and coffee were in order.

Chapter Sixteen

I was not surprised to find Margaret sitting in the armchair by the door. I wasn't surprised either by the aroma of lemon pie, my favorite, floating in the air. Margaret had come to me with a purpose and it was a family tradition to digest bitter truths with sweet pies.

I shared an emotional embrace with her. There was no need for words just yet. We clung to each other until our bodies ceased trembling with emotion.

Margaret pulled away, then raised her eyes and looked past me. With a nod, she acknowledged Daniel, who had stood in the background allowing us privacy. I reached for Margaret's hand. "Margaret, this is Daniel Alcaly. He's been… he has…" I ran out of words. How was I to explain to Margaret the way I had met him?

"We met at a brewery yesterday evening," Daniel said, saving me from recounting the embarrassing truth.

I looked from one to the other. There was recognition in the way they exchanged polite smiles. A pregnant silence hung heavily across the foyer as Margaret dissected Daniel as if he were a dead frog in biology class.

"The pie is fresh out of the oven. Coffee or tea with it?" she finally said, evidently satisfied with the DNA results of the specimen in front of her.

"I'd better go. It's been a long day," Daniel said. He raked his wavy hair with his fingers and then stuffed his hands in the front pockets of his jeans.

"I insist that you stay, Mr. Alcaly," Margaret ordered. "Pie and story time are traditions in the Lazar home. And we all love a good story, don't we?" she finished, one eyebrow arched in defiant invitation.

"Then coffee sounds great, thanks," said Daniel.

I was drained, but I had not missed the strange vibe that flowed between them. My first thought was of Margaret's overprotective demeanor toward me. However, there was more to it and I was determined to find out before this impromptu dessert party was over.

Margaret's gait, as elegant as her accent, took her toward the heart of the house. It was clear who would be calling the shots. We sat in silence at the kitchen table. Margaret served three cups of coffee in elegant porcelain cups and served three slices of pie on matching plates. She had something up her sleeve.

For the first half hour we made small talk about apricots and the upcoming pruning of trees—a subject I knew very little of—about the weather, and about the pie. There was so much I wanted to ask her. I noticed Daniel making himself inconspicuous at the kitchen table. His moves were quiet, his breathing virtually inaudible. However, his presence was hard to ignore.

Since I had taken possession of Franzisca's box, I never went anywhere without it nor had I shared its contents with anybody. I reached into my oversized bag, pulled it out and placed it on the table. Daniel, who had been silent since we sat down, shifted in his seat to take a better look. Margaret on the other hand, did not seem fazed by the closed box. She smiled encouragingly. It was apparent she expected what was to come.

I opened the box and retrieved the picture of the little girl with the cloth doll. The box, which had originally held one written sheet of paper, suddenly surprised me with the number of stories I had added to it since then. The box had acted as a magnet attracting the bits and pieces of information I had stumbled upon ever since I had read the first lines scribbled in Abuela's handwriting.

I placed the picture next to the box and waited. With trembling hands, Margaret's long fingers hovered over the picture clearly afraid to touch it and disturb the images in it. She looked up at me, her eyes glistening with tears. "Oh, God." Her hands motioned toward the picture "May I…" Her voice broke. She lifted the picture for closer inspection.

"Do you know who that little girl was?" I risked asking.

"Is." Her tears now flowed unrestrained. "Is."

And then, without the need of fictionalized characters, Margaret closed her eyes and told us a true story.

***

A wave of conflicting memories invaded Margaret as soon as her eyelashes rested atop her cheekbones. But this time, unlike the weeks preceding this trip, she did not pursue the safety of the light, and kept her eyes shut. It was time she revisited the event that had triggered her becoming Margaret.

Her silence had been sworn more than sixty years before when she was only a little girl. But her tender age had nothing to do with the years her soul had accumulated during her short life. Perhaps it had to do with the distress all survivors of war suffer. She had been amongst a group of thirty-five fortunate children who have fallen under the protection of an anonymous philanthropist.

It had happened during the second year of World War II when Margaret was a girl of six. Streets, sewage tunnels and abandoned buildings had become her temporary housing during the war-years. Margaret learned survival skills and to hide like a rodent during the daylight. She was not certain of the reasons that drove her to live in hiding, but the memory of her parents' glazed eyes, as they lay dead after being shot in the head, caused her to avoid being seen by anybody in uniform.

Since the death of her parents, the butchery on the streets had diminished significantly. The soldiers sporting the interlaced crosses on their jackets became a common sight in her town, especially around the oil refineries. On many nights, when she was scared and hungry she had made her way back to where she thought her home was. But when she approached the main gate of the property, visions of guns and death pushed her back into the darkness, back to the safety and the anonymity of homelessness.

However terrifying the Nazi occupation had been in her town, Margaret had found a certain balance to her survival. The intense questioning the citizens of Ploesti had been subjected to during the first year of the war had ceased soon after her parents were murdered. She noticed that most men, the ones she knew as neighbors or local business owners, were no longer in the vicinity and she wondered if they, just like her parents, had breathed their last breath down the cold barrel of a pistol.

The lack of adults made for a large amount of unattended children, which at one time or another moved together as a swarm of bees only to shoot in different directions at the slightest sign of danger.

When caught, children were forced to work in the oil refineries managed by the Nazi soldiers. The activities inside the refineries were a mystery to her. Yet, the results of being swallowed by those grim buildings stayed branded on the faces of their young prisoners. Some of the kids, who only days before had been on the run with her, were now gradually turning grey behind the barbwires surrounding the forced labor camp. Margaret was too young to understand the concepts of freedom and oppression, but she was old enough to notice the path of death, a one-way road, the imprisoned kids were set upon.

The refineries had become a target for continuous bombings. It was said that the Germans milked the depths of Ploesti to help finance their dream of worldwide domination. With each blast, the interest the Nazis had in the town waned. The cash cow Ploesti represented during the first years of the war became a trap where high-ranking Nazi officials lost their lives; burning in the fires of the hell they created. As the production of the rigs stopped, the number of people imprisoned diminished. Soot-faced zombies in striped pajamas became the latest sight along the deserted streets of Ploesti. The Nazis did not waste bullets on the escapees; the smoke and tar inhalation took care of their dirty work for them. After a few steps into a desperate freedom, the former prisoners met their untimely death by natural asphyxiation.

Although tender in age and ignorant to the mechanics of war, Margaret noticed that the appearance of the enemy had changed over the years. No longer were the neatly dressed soldiers wandering the streets of Ploesti. Instead, a new breed of bearded savages roamed the shell-shocked industrial town. Much like the Germans, the newest invaders, the Bolsheviks, were bent on mayhem. Both spawns of similar evil, sought out murder as a way to leave their imprint and manifest their domination. However, there was a noticeable difference between the two. While the Nazis conducted their operations in a cold and organized manner, turning their massacres into business transactions, the Russians behaved like butchers. Their trail was bloody and dirty.

The day she was discovered, she was huddled, with two other children, in the bowels of an abandoned aqueduct in the outskirts of Ploesti, Romania.

There were three things about herself that Margaret did not remember. One was her name. She had no recollection of her given name. She remembered her mother's panic-stricken face and her last attempt to call for her. However, every time Margaret tried to put a sound to the last word formed on her mother's lips, all she heard was the deafening explosion of the gunshot that silenced her. The next thing she did not remember was how to talk. Since the day she became an orphan, nobody ever addressed her directly again. She understood the tongue of the local people, the foul sound of the iron invaders; however, she could not articulate a single word.

The third thing she did not know was what she looked like.

Not until the day before she was found did she discover her face for the first time. Right before the earth swallowed the ball of fire that illuminated the city, the children made their way to the Teleajen River to try their chances at catching anything edible from the riverbank. It was customary for fishermen to take pity on the little souls that roamed the docks as if sleepwalking, and before retiring for the evening, they would toss them a few scraps of fish.

A storm had hit the vast river the previous week, and after succumbing to its natural course, the waters became once again a silver mirror. Margaret was among a group of children who inched hopefully toward the docks scouting for food. The sight of a lone fisherman cleaning his dinghy sent the group of starving children running his way. Margaret was ahead of the pack when she hit a rock with her naked toes. The impact sent her flying a hairsbreadth from plunging in the river. Suddenly her face was confronted by a pair of hollow dark circles that fixed her with shock. She blinked a few times, fighting tears ready to slide down her face. The pain shooting through her toes was unbearable, but the curiosity at the image that floated on the face of the river was enough to make her forget about it. The vision staring back at her from the water remained still while she did her best not to breathe. Then, she wrinkled her nose and arched her eyebrows. The silver image mimicked her actions without skipping a beat. Margaret suddenly forgot about the nagging hunger clawing at the inside of her stomach. Instead, she smiled at a reflection that accepted her with the same smile. Move by move, she discovered the contours of her face, the mechanics of her facial joints and the many funny things she could do with them. For a brief moment, her mind was free of war, and in the watery mirror, she relived her short life before everything was lost. Filled with memories of happier times, that evening, Margaret snuggled next to her wretched companions and fell into a deep slumber.

When they heard heavy footsteps approaching the large sewer pipe where they had decided to spend the night, two of the children took off running. She and a few others were too tired to flee and slept beyond the allowed depth for survival. There was a soft knock on the outer wall of the tunnel. Resigned, Margaret and the other children crawled out. She was worn out, and if surrendering meant going back to the warm embrace of her parents that had kept her safe during one the best dreams she had in years, so be it.

What she encountered outside out of the pipe was far from fear. A soft hand reached out and took hold of hers and from that day forward, Margaret was never alone again.

Chapter Seventeen

"So, this is you in the picture. This little girl, it's you?" I said, with a hint of disappointment.

"Yes. That's me after months of proper nutrition and daily baths," she said, with a mild laugh. "Were you hoping it would be Claudia?"

I stifled a yawn and my eyes watered as I nodded in assent.

Margaret's hands were no longer trembling. She placed the picture next to the box; still, her eyes never left the photograph. She nodded; a longing smile brightened her face. "I remember the day this picture was taken." Her fingers traced the image of the doll. "The doll had been left on my bed that morning. The doll and the new outfit. It was a sign that we were to leave the house for a new life."

Daniel got up and cleared the dirty dishes trying to disappear behind the sound of water as he washed the plates and served us a second round of coffee. He placed our cups on the table and leaned back against the kitchen sink.

"If you're not too tired to listen to the ramblings of an old lady…" The invitation was extended to Daniel as Margaret turned to him. "There are some more stories I've been burning to tell you."

The second half of Margaret's story time did not begin until she was satisfied with having served us a second course of the late night snack. Adding to the weariness of my body, which kept accumulating, my throat closed with nerves and anticipation. The need for constant nourishment might have had something to do with the war years, I pondered, when presented with a golden grilled cheese and a cup of tea dabbed with a drop of milk. Eating at that point of the day seemed like an ambitious project to take on.

"Eat and drink while it's hot. You're nothing but skin and bones, my girl." She looked at Daniel for support. He looked as tired as I was. For the third time that day, Daniel rearranged the food on my plate. He cut my sandwich in four portions, as if the smaller sizes would make eating more bearable. Then, he took a hearty bite of his own and nodded my way. "Eat."

Pleased to see our jaws in motion, Margaret relaxed in the chair with her tea cup and smiled. "How long will it be before you'll ask about my connection with Mr. Alcaly, Sofia?"

"I thought you'd never ask, Margaret," I said, in the same playful manner she had addressed me. "So, spill it out. What's up between you two?"

Margaret smiled. "It's what's between the two of you. If I'm not mistaken, by now, you're both in possession of a key. Your grandparent's keys."

I reached under my sweatshirt and slid out the silver chain that held my key. Daniel followed suit. We set them on opposite sides of the table. At a first glance they appeared to be no more than two awkwardly shaped pieces of brass. My first impulse was to push them side by side, to see how those oddly shaped teeth looked when brought together. Yet I refrained from acting, afraid I'd open a portal to a secret dimension.

"I haven't seen the key for many, many years," Margaret continued, fully expecting that none of us would risk interrupting the flow of the much needed revelation. "Yes, I've seen the one key before," she said, picking up the one I had found in the red sack. "Franzisca's."

Margaret, placed it back on the table, joined the keys together, and smiled. "She always carried one of them dangling from a chain around her neck. I used to play with it before falling asleep at night. That is when she was around. She disappeared for days, weeks at a time, and I was always afraid she would never return."

Margaret held them up and toyed with them with her hands, and in that moment I could see the little girl she once was. "Even though I had never seen them together, I knew about the existence of a second key. She referred to the keys as the only things that could open the lock to her heart. The keys were the keepers of her secrets. Of that private space where she could go to safely and hide the parts of her that would make her vulnerable for the road ahead."

We waited with baited breath for Margaret to continue. Daniel's eyes were as expectant as mine if not more. Under my lashes, I studied him. Daniel Alcaly, Mossad agent, mechanical engineer, cattle rancher who had come into my life with a plan. His initial mission had been to barge in, extract information, and leave. However, the look on his face resembled what I always imagined James Bond would look like when faced with the revelation that he was a fictional character at the mercy of his creator. Daniel Alcaly may have lost control of his well-planned mission the minute he walked into my life. The more he chose to stay in it, the more he would lose control of his initial objective and be driven by the plans of those who had raised us. As I feared before, this joining of keys, this joining of two strangers was intended to crack open the gates to an era of silence.

"One night," Margaret spoke up again as if emerging from the yellow pages of some long forgotten storybook, "she came back to the house. It had been her longest absence. Months I would say. It was late and dark, her cheeks were as cold as ice, but her heart was warm. I had never known what love looked like, because I had forgotten about it during my time on the streets, but by the flush on her face and the dreamy look in her eyes, I could tell it was a feeling different from hunger or cold, it was love." Margaret took hold of one of the starched napkins she had set earlier on the table and ran her fingers along its folds. "That was the night she told me about Alex, the special man who held the other key, the keeper of her heart." She raised her eyes from the keys, leaving the memories behind. "I never saw her again after that night. Not until thirty years later, when she sought me out. It was the day I met Marcela, your mother."

Daniel cleared his throat and drank the last of his tea. "You've always known about me, about my grandfather, about the key. What else do you know?"

Margaret stared into Daniel's eyes. "I wish I had all the answers to your questions, Daniel. When we met after all those years, Claudia recounted what I believe were fragments of their story during the war."

Margaret slid her hands across the table and reached for mine. Her grasp was strong and I felt her need for support as much as her need to tell me the truth.

"I really hoped," she said. "I really hoped she went first. I wanted her to die before me."

My eyes searched hers questioningly. She wanted Abuela dead that much was clear, but the cruelty of her statement made me ask the obvious. I tried to pull my hands from hers, but she held on strongly. Why, Margaret? Why did you want her dead?"

She looked down at our linked hands, and a tear slid down her face landing on the table to form a perfect, clear, round dot. "I wanted Claudia dead." Her eyes were swimming in tears now, but she still faced me daringly. "I wanted her dead before she could kill whatever there was left of Franzisca."

Part II

Chapter Eighteen

Bucharest January, 20 1941

Her birthday had come and gone unnoticed by everyone except for her. She did not want to complain, but preparing four meals a day for the past week at the residence of Baron Mihail R. Lupescu was not what she had envisioned as a way to celebrate her seventeenth birthday. Yet, there was nothing she could have done differently about it. Anna, her mother, had fallen ill the week before with a burning fever and hacking cough fits that rattled the tiny cold room they occupied at the apartment complex that was once a hotel.

Anna's health had plummeted two weeks ago, the day Lupescu had turned her body into a mass of bruises and cuts. Franzisca had seen her mother battered before. She had cleaned her cuts and had fed her sweet tea with a spoon because Anna's lips had been too torn to close around the rim of a cup. This latest beating, the worst so far, was never discussed in their one-room kingdom. Franzisca did not have to ask. She knew Lupescu to be the one delivering the blows.

She turned to look at her mother one more time. The bruises refused to leave her beautiful face, however, for some strange reason Anna looked at peace.

"I can't leave you like this, Mama. There are others at the palace who can take over your duties. I must stay with you." Franzisca could not find in her heart to leave.

"But nobody makes pies as good as you," Anna answered weakly. "Go Franzisca, I'll be fine."

Franzisca knew they couldn't afford to lose the only job they had. With war spreading all over Europe, a job, even if under Lupescu was a thing to keep.

Against her will, Franzisca made arrangements to leave her mother under the watchful eyes of a neighbor who had promised to stop by at least once to make sure Anna ate.

"I love you, Mama," Franzisca said, with a knot in her throat.

"I left a present for you at the big house in the room we sleep in sometimes. Promise me you won't open it until tomorrow." Anna regained some strength, her request became serious.

"Why tomorrow, Mama? My birthday is today." Franzisca was puzzled.

Anna slid a silver chain with Asil's keys from her neck and summoned her to the cot. Franzisca knelt by her mother and in one slow, painful motion Anna slid the chain over Franzisca head.

Franzisca looked at her mother in shock. "No, Mama, I can't. It's the only thing you have left of *Tată*." Franzisca tried to take the chain off but Anna stopped her.

She cupped Franzisca's face with her feverish hands and kissed her fiercely on her forehead. "You are what I have left of him. Always in my heart." Anna swallowed her tears. "I love you, my Turkish doll."

Franzisca stood up. With a last glance at her mother lying on the narrow cot next to a gas stove in the far end of the room, she set out to fulfill her mother's obligations at the baron's palace.

Franzisca had known the baron for most of her life, fifteen years to be exact. The events of those years were scorched into her soul. The way her life had been before bending at the service of Baron Lupescu and what had brought her and her mother Anna to him. Franzisca despised Lupescu with every fiber of her being. She knew him for who he really was: A rabid anti-Semite, a thief, a murderer, and her mother's torturer.

For the Romanians, Mihail Lupescu, was a symbol of national pride. He was member of the Romanian nobility, the scion of a long line of landowners and politicians. To enhance his celebrity status in the eyes of his people, he had been called to serve in the ministry of foreign affairs after the abdication of King Caroll II in 1940. Lupescu, a Nazi sympathizer, shook hands on an alliance on November 23, 1940, with the German minister of Foreign Affairs. It consisted of a pact with Nazi-Germany—between Adolf Hitler and the Romanian fascist Prime Minister, General Ion Antonescu—officially allying Romania with Germany, Italy, and Japan. Franzisca knew Lupescu's anti-Semitism to be selective. He abhorred Jews and shared the Nazi sentiment of holding them responsible for the economic downfall of Europe, yet he could not go a day without her mother, the Jewess Anna Schultz.

***

Mihail Lupescu paced his study like a caged animal. His face twitched nervously, his fists curled and uncurled at the side of his body. In a rage of fury, he reached his desk in two quick strides, grabbed a brass paperweight shaped like a lion and hurled it against a wall. Just as the paperweight made contact with the wall, his chauffer walked into the study unannounced. He stared at the crater made by the heavy brass lion.

"She is still bedridden, *domnul meu*. It is her daughter, Franzisca, taking her place again." The chauffer, an intimidating mass of muscle, spoke to Lupescu with caution. There was no telling what the baron would do after hearing the latest update on his whore. The chauffer waited by the door.

Lupescu looked through the chauffer as if he were a mere piece of glass. Two weeks had passed since he had availed himself of Anna and his body burned for her. He resumed his relentless walk around his study.

"Did that filthy bastard say when her mother would return?" Mihail Lupescu asked in a sotto voice.

The chauffer recognized the threatening tone; he braced himself for the upcoming storm. "She wouldn't say, *domnul meu*. It seems that the Jewess is very ill. She hasn't recovered since the last..." Too late the chauffer realized he had hit a nerve.

Baron Lupescu was a slim man that stood five foot eleven, with fine blonde hair, soft hands, and delicate facial features. In a flash, he lashed out at the chauffer with the wrath of a titan. His fists, which only minutes before had been tight by his sides, were now delivering left and right blows on the chauffer's face. The chauffer hunched his shoulders before the raining blows and took the punishment. He saw it coming the moment the whore Anna had failed to report to work.

"See that she comes to me tonight!" Lupescu turned his heaving back to the abused chauffer dismissing him.

"Yes, *domnul meu*."

The door closed behind the chauffer. Lupescu looked at the wall clock in his office. Very soon the streets would turn to chaos. Big events were about to unfold and Lupescu felt afraid without her. She was *his* Anna and had been his since the first time he laid eyes on her. He needed her now and knew that he could not wait until the evening to see her. Why? He questioned himself over and over again. I am Baron Lupescu. I could have any woman of my choosing. Why does this filthy Jewess torture my body, my soul? Why do I love her so? The very thought of her left him revolted and at loss at the same time. And for that alone she would pay.

Mihail Lupescu met Anna when she was a girl of twelve and he was barely fourteen. In those days, Anna was a golden princess, the daughter of one of the most prominent Jewish families in Vienna. Mihail's father, Baron Lupescu, was a patron of the arts and in Stephan

Schultz, Anna's father, he found the perfect partner to pursue his passion for all things cultural. With Lupescu's name and Shultz's money, the pair created the most spectacular events at the Opera House in Vienna, always followed by five course dinners at the Schultz's mansion. Having previously made generous donations to the Schultz-Lupescu Foundation for the Arts, the honored guests had the privilege to shake hands with the most prominent musicians, painters and dancers from all across Europe. It was at one of those lavish events that young Lupescu saw Anna. Up until his first meeting with the Schultzes, Mihail had never seen a Jew up close before. He experienced a sudden shock at the instant attraction he felt for her instead of the repulsion he had anticipated.

One of the many tutors Mihail had for his aristocratic education was responsible for revealing to the young Lupescu the inner workings of The Iron Guard, a right wing school of thought pioneered by Corneliu Zelea Codreanu. The Iron Guard was deeply rooted in the Orthodox Christian Church and was built on the grounds of ultra-nationalism and anti-communism.

Mihail's first encounter with Codreanu happened at the Faculty of Theology at the University of Bucharest. Because of Mihail's nobility, Codreanu had singled him out and had touted him as the future of the Iron Guard. Under Cordrenau's wing, the young Lupescu rose above his father's frivolous cultural endeavors. Young Mihail became a key contributor to the creation of the ideology of *State Anti-Semitism,* which promoted economic and racial anti-Semitism, and violence against all Jews.

Mihail hated Jews and the mixed emotions he felt when in Anna's presence were not welcome in his tormented mind. His groin tightened at the sight of her porcelain-skin. Her big, blue eyes always downcast when in his presence, purposely ignoring him. He had sworn to himself that the day would come when he would make her look him in the eye while he released himself inside of her. His sexual fantasies about Anna involved a great deal of submission and punishment.

Lupescu looked down at his fisted hands and opened them slowly. He could still feel the touch of her skin on his. A sudden sob choked him. If she wouldn't love him at least she would fear him. But not even the most severe of beating could break Anna. She despised him.

Mihail's prayers were answered the day Anna showed up with her bastard daughter at his doorstep, months after the murder of her parents at the hand of the Austrian-Christian Socialists. Besides that dark-skinned daughter of hers, Anna had been left destitute after her parents' death. Baron Lupescu, Mihail's father, had gained full control of Anna's fortune after he declared under oath, with forged documents in hand in front of a carefully selected anti-Semitic council, to be the rightful owner of the Shultz's fortune.

As ruthless as the Lupescu line was, Mihail's father, did not hesitate to take Anna and little Franzisca under his roof. He also provided them with false identities and hired Anna as a house servant.

For two whole years, he watched her as she dutifully fulfilled her chores around the house. Never a smile or a glimpse from her was spared his way, contributing to the mounting fury of his desire. Mihail, a calculating and cold young man, had secretly set a date and a time to ambush her. But his plan was foiled when his family made a sudden move up north due to a dispute regarding his father's agricultural lands, a problem he had to see to personally.

Although frustrated and hungry for a taste of her, Mihail had no other choice than to accompany his father on the voyage that would formally place him as the head of the family business.

Stuck in the north for longer than was planned, Mihail cursed his luck at the sudden death of his useless father. For the next ten years, Mihail fought off the encroaching Bolshevik presence on his agricultural lands. With the winds of war at Europe's threshold, a secret non-aggression pact between Russia and Germany was in the works. Mihail's lands were directly affected by this treaty when Nazis and Soviets sliced territories of Romania, Poland, Lithuania, Latvia, Estonia and Finland like pies, forestalling future political and economic arrangements once the war was won. In the end, Mihail left his lands to the mercy of the Soviets and made his way back to Bucharest with the vision of the beautiful Anna in his mind.

A line of servants stood in the foyer awaiting the new master. Three playful dachshunds jumped around Mihail's calves. Mihail's eyes traveled over each and every one of the women who stood with their eyes downcast and their knees trembling. Mihail's features changed from controlled to displeased. A playful dachshund that had settled at his feet was suddenly sent flying with the force of Mihail's furious kick when he noticed Anna gone.

That first night back in Bucharest, Mihail tossed and turned as his obsession with Anna dealt him another sleepless night. All those years had done nothing more than engorge his twisted desire for her.

The very next morning, he had his chauffer search for her. Finding her had been easy. Even though she still carried false documentation, she had chosen to settle in the Jewish quarters. Mihail cursed her stubbornness. Once more he wondered why she had left the Lupescus for the uncertainty Jews faced on the streets of Romania. The answer to that made Mihail's blood boil. Anna had thrown herself into the arms of yet another filthy Jew. One who had filled her head with dreams of a Jewish Nation, had warmed her bed, and had gotten her with child. Her Jew lover got what he deserved when he was executed in the streets by members of the Iron Guard after he and five other members of a resistance group were dragged out of a secret meeting. The news of her lover's death sent Anna into early labor, which produced a stillborn child.

Disgust was what Mihail felt when she finally stood before him. He sat behind his desk taking in the new appearance of the woman that had robbed him of sleep. Her eyes, always downcast, looked tired yet still shone sapphire blue. Her lips, although cracked and dry, still stirred a desire in him, but her wasted body did not. She was not the beautiful Anna he had dreamed of all those years. At twenty-eight she looked twice her age.

Nevertheless his desire to subdue her, to corner her, to have her on her knees begging for survival was stronger than ever. She had wounded him with the kind of pain that had seared his body. He had loved her from the first time he had seen her, but every time he had been close to her she had regarded him as less than a flea-ridden dog.

A tear escaped Lupescu's eye the moment a faint rasp on the door announced the arrival of his tea. Every morning, when his wall clock struck the tenth hour, he consumed a cup of tea with a drop of Cognac. His heart raced with the anticipation of seeing Anna through the door. His desires were crushed when her dark-skinned bastard, the only person Anna ever looked at with unconditional love, deposited the tea tray on his desk. Unlike Anna, her bastard never refrained from looking straight at him. Violet-blue eyes, cold, calculating, vindictive eyes.

Chapter Nineteen

Anna shifted on her cot thinking she hadn't felt this tired in a very long time. It wasn't her stubborn cold or the dark bruises covering the length of her body that weighted her down. For the first time in almost eighteen years she did not feel like fighting anymore.

Anna looked down at her wasted body and laughed. Less than two decades ago, she had been nothing short of royalty. The bare walls around her, the coarse blanket on her, and her rough callused hands were a clear indication that her days as a Jewish princess belonged to another life, to another Anna.

Anna swung her legs to the side of the cot. With effort, she stood up. Taking small steps, stopping every few paces to catch her breath, she surveyed the room she had turned into a home for her daughter. Franzisca had grown into a strong, young woman, the kind of woman Anna wished she could have been, but perhaps in another life, she thought, as she sat heavily back on her cot. For now, she was happy at the outcome of her latest fight. She did not matter anymore. The important thing was that Franzisca would not have to endure what Anna had.

Thirteen years ago, Anna thought herself free of Mihail Lupescu. The north had swallowed him in a bitter dispute with his neighbors and Bucharest was all the better without him. During the years of his absence, she had let go of much of her anger and moved on. She had even given love a second chance. Within these four walls, that now felt as tight as a coffin, she had raised her beautiful daughter, taught her how to behave as an aristocrat and how to stay true to her convictions. Franzisca was her masterpiece, and for that, Anna felt at peace.

The respite from Lupescu lasted ten years. Then, the odious man had come back for Anna with a vengeance. Stupid man, he had no idea what she had in store for him.

When Anna had made the conscious decision to go back into his employment, she did it out of love for Franzisca. A month of no work had driven her and her fourteen-year-old daughter to the edge of starvation. It was all Lupescu's doing. Since his return to Bucharest, Lupescu had Anna fired from her current job and unemployable for any other.

The uneasy feeling the young Lupescu radiated still lingered every time she thought of him. As a young man, he had rejoiced in inflicting pain. He skinned stray cats, broke birds' necks, and was known to light occasional fires in the servants' quarters. Her skin prickled at the memory of his ever-stalking stare. If it would have only been her life on the line, Anna would have turned down his offer. But her daughter's violet-blue eyes sunken above the hollow of her cheekbones, and the certainty that Lupescu would find a way to crush her, drove her to return to his palace.

On the drive to the Lupescu estate Anna traveled backward fifteen years in time to the day her life took a dramatic turn. She had been playing hide and seek with Franzisca in the woods when her birth-home was raided. From behind a tree she witnessed her mother being stripped down to her underwear in front of a squadron of sardonic anti-Semitic youths. Anna heard them yell, *"with compliments of the baron,"* before they shot her mother in the back of her head as she tried to make a run for her life. Anna's father was forced to dress in his best tuxedo before being tied to the back of the beat up Renault van, the vehicle the mob had used to drive onto the Schultz's land. Her father was dragged off the property screaming, crying and cursing. His cry filled the air through the expanse of woods and lands, but they were not as loud as the gunshot that silenced him. Too late, Anna noticed Franzisca had seen it all.

Her parent's last cries for mercy reverberated in Anna's head. So were the words of the thug that had shot her mother, *with compliments of the baron.* Lupescu was behind her parents' murder. He had always panted after their fortune and in that moment, she knew she had lost it all.

Anna and Franzisca spent that night hiding in Asil's old room. Since Asil's parents were discharged from the Schultzes service when Franzisca was born, the cottage had been vacant for two years. Her family had experienced a hard time finding Jewish help. Nationalist, anti-Semitic groups were sprouting all across Germany and Austria making Jewish crossing over the European borders increasingly dangerous.

The vacant cottage had become Anna's safe heaven. She usually made her way to the rodent infested abode late at night to cry out the mounting humiliation her parents put her and Franzisca through, calling her a whore, and her precious daughter a bastard. During those nights while her sobs echoed through the empty house, she wished her parents dead. When she was spent from crying and the cottage sat silent, she could hear Asil, soothing her, telling her that she needed to keep going for the sake of their daughter. And so she did.

Anna planned to leave her parents' home eventually. She hid all of her savings, some of the silver that magically disappeared from her mother's cutlery service and warm clothes for her and Franzisca, within the cottage's old brick oven. When she wished her parents dead, she had not really meant it. As odious as they were to her and her baby, her parents represented security. Under the roof of her paternal home, she was Anna Schultz, and even though unwanted by her grandparents, Franzisca was a Schultz too. That was Anna's security blanket. In the meantime, they would not want for anything, and Franzisca was secured an education and a certain standing in society. She also knew that if she decided against leaving, in a few years' time Anna's indiscretion would have been forgotten, she would have entered a loveless marriage, and become a mirror of her own mother.

None of that would ever happen now. God had granted her wish. Her parents were dead and she was alone with Franzisca and free to leave.

For one last time, she lay down on Asil's bed and begged for his guidance, and for the first time in two years silence was her only response. Her first thought was that it was his way of punishing her for wishing for her parents' death. But Anna was a logical person and knew that her parents' murder had been the work of greed sealed with the name of Baron Lupescu.

Before dawn broke, she bundled up Franzisca in Asil's old blanket, gathered her hidden savings and clothes, and snuck out of her birthplace with her sights set on England, where her cousins lived. Her meager savings took them as far as Bulgaria. Stranded and facing the harshness of winter, she worked as a housemaid for the better part of a year. Finally, after saving enough money for another passage, she reached Romania in hopes of finding a Jewish Agency that would take pity of her situation and help her reach England. At that time, the Jewish Agency was flooded with families desperate to leave the country and to get as far away from the impending Bolshevik threat that was quickly spreading through its neighboring countries. When her turn arrived, her story was not believable enough, and she had no documents to back it up. The agency had exhausted its resources, and even if her story would have been believable, there was nothing they could have done for her. Penniless and hungry, she knew she would hate herself for the rest of her life when she made the decision to beg the treacherous Lupescu for help. But when it came to saving her daughter from starvation and a life in the streets, pride was not an option. At least they would have two meals a day and a place to sleep.

As the years went by in the baron's household, her spirits were crushed. She no longer yearned for England or the security of her old life. She could not even remember what her old life had been like. Her only truth lay in the violet-blue eyes of her daughter, filled with love and hunger, staring at her from the other end of the grim room they called home. Franzisca made any sacrifice worthwhile. Before leaving the room and letting the chauffer drive her to the gates of hell, Anna formed a plan in her head. It might take years, she thought; but she would see it through.

Anna stood in Lupescu's study ready to surrender her dignity in exchange for the protection of her daughter. In return, she gave him what he had fantasized about for most of his life; she looked at him in the eye, and submitted her body to the lust that had inflamed him over the past decade.

Anna grew numb to the constant rape she suffered under him and their relationship developed into one of sadomasochism. She had learned to play his sadistic games, to deliberately drive him to agonizing pain when she would refuse to look him in the eye, to make him feel worthy of her attention. Anna regarded the black and blue marks he inflicted upon her as no more than stepping stones, triumphs, which drove her closer to her prized goal. There was no saving her. Lupescu had ruined her forever, corrupted her until she was as sick as he was. But there was Franzisca.

Anna's carefully crafted plan was finally materialized during one of those sessions of tormenting lust. Mihail fell down on his knees panting from the exertion of beating her and pleading. Anna, bedraggled and shaky, leaned against the wall. Despite her hair covering most of her face, hair that was matted with the stickiness of blood that seeped from the blows she had received, her triumphant smile was visible.

"Look at me, whore! Look at me!" he cried, broken with ire and desperation. Anna took a few unstable steps toward him and stood above his submissive form. He raised his hopeful eyes to hers. But she was not done with him yet. Her face was turned toward a mahogany desk that sat in the corner of the room. A rich burgundy velvet drape lined the window behind it, dressing the room with a hint of nobility. However, there was nothing noble about a grown man sobbing on his knees, begging to be acknowledged by battered woman, dressed in blood, with little pride left.

"Anna, please. Love me," Lupescu wept.

"Sign the document," Anna ordered.

On hands and knees, Mihail reached the desk. A document Anna had scribbled the day she entered in his service was there waiting for his seal to make it official. Before signing it, he searched her eyes, but found no more than a stony expression looking through him as if he did not exist. He could not bear the pain any longer. He finally signed and stamped with his family crest a document that would keep Franzisca forever safe.

Once he put the pen down, Anna locked her eyes with his.

Her job was done.

***

Franzisca looked out the back door before she stepped out onto the streets with a smile. "Great," she muttered. There were still a few hours left before her birthday was over.

Marietta, the head maid, who loved Franzisca as a granddaughter, had sent her home early with a lemon cake to celebrate her birthday and with a pot of soup to nurse Anna's cold. Franzisca brushed a kiss on Marietta's cheek, and loaded down as she was with food, rushed out of the palace and ran the whole way through the icy streets to their building.

Franzisca wanted to leave the baron's service at once. Anna had told her about their cousins in England. There had to be a way to contact them, to reach England before the Iron Guard's revolt would unfold. The revolt, Franzisca thought, her gut tight with the weight of knowledge. What could a seventeen-year-old Jewish servant do about it? She pushed the worry aside and decided to tell her mother everything she had heard during the past week while she had waited on Lupescu and other officials at the big house. "The big house," Franzisca exclaimed with dismay. She felt like stomping her feet on the cobblestone street like a child. She had completely forgotten about the present her mother left for her. She wanted to open it today, even though Anna had been very specific about opening it tomorrow morning. "It'll have to be tomorrow, then."

When Franzisca approached the corner of the pension, she saw a large crowd gathered around it. Over the dozens of heads that blocked her vision, she saw a cloud of black smoke rise above the building. The pot of soup crashed to the street. Her world stood still. She did not hear the screaming around her nor did she feel hands that pulled her backward as the building exploded.

Chapter Twenty

There were voices, and footsteps, and an overpowering stench of fear. When the smoke cleared, all that was left was a steaming pile of rubble. Her mother was gone. At that moment Franzisca swore revenge on everybody that had made her mother suffer, starting with Lupescu.

Franzisca was pulled into a bottomless darkness. A state she had been in since she had seen the rubble atop her mother's remains. There was no day or night. No pain, or emotion, only darkness. Somebody had pressed a canteen with water to her lips and her mouth had responded instinctively out of a sense of survival. Up until that day, she had never considered the workings of the human body. She could envision her throat, straining to swallow the water, as an independent entity. Her lips shut in a straight line, when her body no longer required hydration. Her face turned away from eyes that sought to find hers. Her body had become fragmented, a puzzle in disarray, and the pieces were floating in front of her eyes like the ashes from the fire, detaching her from the life she knew.

Before her world had turned black, Franzisca considered herself one with nature. She felt connected to the warmth of the sun, to the twinkling stars, and to the dark curtain of the night. Franzisca was one with the leaves of the trees and with the flying birds. She had been all those things because of her mother and the lessons she had taught her had allowed her to be. Her mother was gone, and now everything was dark.

Not until she tried to move, did she notice the dust beneath her feet. Strong, unfamiliar arms held her back when her body tried to spring forward and without resistance, she fell back within them.

"You must stay here," the voice belonging to the arms whispered. A male voice, rough, yet soothing. The voice that had been leading her through this newly found blind landscape of her life.

"We are safe here... for now." He shifted and readjusted her frame against his.

There was possessiveness in the way he held her. There were others among them, she noticed. She also noticed that he held her fiercely, as if to prevent anything from harming her any further.

"They say a fire started on the ground floor... I saw you outside by the building... Your mother? Was it?" He paused, then swallowed hard. "My Nicu,—the old baker... I left for only five minutes. He was hungry and I had promised him sausage. Five minutes..." his words faded away at the realization of the old man's fate.

Suddenly Franzisca's chest trembled, but instead of the anguished wail she expected to release she broke into a hysterical laugh. The young man covered her mouth with both his hands and shook his head no.

She looked in his eyes and saw herself in them. He was scared, lonely, and grieving. All he had left was her shaky frame to hold onto. She stopped laughing.

Franzisca's eyes wandered off his face and scrutinized her surroundings. She had no recollection how she had gotten there, but it was a cavernous, narrow tunnel that they had sought shelter in.

No longer restrained by the stranger's embrace, Franzisca crawled around the tunnel. The other occupants regarded her with suspicion. Crouched as they were, their heads touched the roof of the tunnel. Franzisca was terrified of tight, close spaces and a sudden need for fresh air gripped her chest. She couldn't breathe. She needed to get out of there or she would die.

The young man, that only minutes ago had been comforting her, noticed her panic brewing. He quickly crawled to her, gathered her back in his arms, restraining her flailing limbs.

"Shh, breathe, just breathe."

Franzisca became aware of the young man's presence once more. He had been shielding her from the others. They had regarded her with distrust. Nobody knew of her origins and as far as they had observed in the past, Franzisca and her mother kept to themselves, away from the other Jews in the neighborhood. Franzisca had heard the hurtful rumors about her mother before. The hateful stares of all those hiding in the same tunnel with her confirmed that they thought of Anna as nothing more than Baron Lupescu's whore.

The young man holding her turned her to face him. "Look at me," he whispered. He took her hands in his and looked at her in the eye. "My name is Alex." He breathed between the pocket of air that separated their faces. "We will get out of this tunnel, I promise. We will get out of here."

The sound of gunshots, explosions, screams and broken glass penetrated the thick walls of their hideout. Alex read her expression and keeping his soothing way, he spoke to her as though he were speaking to a scared child.

"There are raids on every corner of Bucharest. Neighbors are denouncing neighbors..." For a second he lost his composure and Franzisca did not want to hear another word. She knew what Alex's words implied.

During the past few days while she worked in Lupescu's home, a parade of high-ranking Iron Guard officials and their Nazi counterparts had held secret meetings in Lupescu's study. Thinking Franzisca ignorant of the German language, she had been assigned to serve them during those meetings. While she silently poured dozens of cups of tea, Franzisca kept her senses alert and assimilated every word. Their plan was to overthrow Antonescu from power for his reluctance to support the actions that the Iron Guard employed to strip the Romanian Jews of all of their possessions. A process called Romanianization, which intended to divest the Romanian Jewish population of their property, was aggravated by the Iron Guard's method of robbery and torture. Antonescu had no sympathy for the Jews and agreed with the appropriation of their belongings. However, a proud Romanian at heart, he had trouble reconciling himself with the sadistic methods of the Iron Guard. Antonescu stressed that the expropriation should happen gradually, through an orderly implementation of anti-Semitic laws.

Many Iron Guard officials, Baron Lupescu among them, considered Antonescu's response arrogant and thought him soft-handed toward the Jewish population, especially in a time when Jews were deprived of sanctuary throughout Europe.

The meetings in Lupescu's study outlined a plan to create a revolution targeting the Jewish population so that Hitler's wrath would not be turned toward Romania. Antonescu's downfall was not only logical but necessary to safeguard Romania from a Nazi invasion. The destruction of Antonescu's government, in way of revolution, was to be seen as a mob attack on the Jewish quarters, based on claims by the Iron Guard that Jews were in support of the communists. Therefore, the devious plan called pogrom, was to be seen as a side effect of the revolution and not as the parallel attack that it really was. In that way, Antonescu, would not be able to anticipate the rise to power of his enemies.

With every gunshot, every broken glass and every scream of terror, Franzisca felt the traitor. For a full week, while she played servant to Lupescu and his cronies, she had thought to reveal their secretes to her mother. The fear of her mother's actions in the face of this news stopped her from confessing what she heard. She had known about the Iron Guard's plan to use the Jewish population as bait. She had known of their plans to assert their power by openly displaying on the streets their undying anti-Semitic sentiment for the eyes of the Nazis, and the end of Antonescu's reign.

She should have died when the pension exploded and not her mother. She should have been punished for her own cowardice. Now, thousands of deaths would forever rot in the depths of her conscience.

Once again, she retreated into the remoteness of her disconnected body. With every explosion, flashes of her life with her mother burned in her brain like the fires that devastated the Jewish Quarters around Bucharest. *Shot*, her grandmother murdered. *Shot*, her grandfather's deathly silence. *Shot*, their escape on a farmers' hay cart. *Shot*, her mother's body for a piece of bread. *Shot*, Lupescu's preying eyes. *Shot*, Anna covered in black and blue. *Shot*, death.

The last deafening shot echoed up her spine filling her with determination. The sounds of gunfire in her head would not cease until she personally saw the last of the dead avenged.

Chapter Twenty-One

Solvang, CA, March 2013

We sat at the kitchen table for hours piecing together ghost stories and forgotten memories.

Absentmindedly, I kept joining and separating the keys. There was more to Abuela's secret than her name before the war. Looking over at Daniel I guessed that all of our lives would have been different if only Abuela would have lived the love story I always envisioned the girl from the tunnel must have lived. If only…

Daniel must have picked up on my thoughts because we both regarded Margaret with a questioning stare. At that moment, I understood he was just as much at a loss as I was. Yet he was still hiding something. Time, I thought, give him time.

Margaret stood up and paced around the kitchen for a moment. She stopped at the marble buffet and rearranged the position of the silver candelabra.

"You see," she said, as she moved the candelabra from one end of the table to the other and back to its original place. "I only met Daniel's grandfather a little over a year ago. Right after Claudia was diagnosed with cancer."

"And you never thought I had the right to know my abuela had cancer? That I was about to lose her?"

"She wouldn't hear a word of it, Sofia. She didn't want her death to be an obstacle in your career. Your daily phone calls and your enthusiasm about your latest movie and future projects kept her happy till her last day." Margaret sounded genuinely sorry for keeping Abuela's condition from me.

Right around the time of the diagnosis of her terminal illness, we had been sharing one of our customary pancake breakfasts at her favorite spot in Solvang. On that Sunday, Abuela had been unusually chatty and had shown a heightened interest in the projects I had lined up for the year. I suspected something was amiss, but out of fear, I decided to push it to the back of my mind. Then as the year went on, I had been so busy that I hadn't stopped to think about her sudden visits on set twice. She looked tired, thinner. I attributed the changes I noticed in her to her advanced age and to my own blurry vision after several sleepless nights. Not once had I asked after her health. Abuela was strong, invincible. Nothing could ever be wrong with her. Except that she was dying, and I was too afraid to see it.

"But she asked you to find Alex Alcaly. She wanted you to tell him." I was trying to find reason in Abuela's machinations before her death.

She turned, hands poised on the edge of the marble tabletop. "No. She never asked me to find him nor did she ever know I went to see him. Like I said, I only met him a year ago. I tracked him down. I wanted to inform him about Claudia's condition. I loved your grandmother, Sofia. She saved my life. If I could only give her a happy memory to take away with her. If I could only bring them back together." As if walking on a cloud, Margaret floated back to us and sat down.

"What did he say to you when you told him she was dying." My throat closed.

"He was dying too, Sofia," Daniel responded.

Margaret nodded. "Yes, Alex Alcaly looked frail… but a smile illuminated his face when I told him about Claudia. He told me that their time to be together was finally near. That this time he would not let her go."

I couldn't fight the tears anymore so I let them fall. Daniel grasped my hand. I was grateful for his presence. He looked as affected as I was without the tears. The grip of his hand spoke of his own need for support. Men's emotions are underrated. One look at Daniel Alcaly was enough to understand why most fairytales, which include a great deal of love, were written by men.

"When I met Franzisca again forty years ago." Margaret closed her eyes and shook her head, "she was a different person. No longer the young woman I knew, she had adopted a new name, Claudia, which was not surprising for those who had immigrated during or after the war. Myself, I never knew what my real name was. I guess I must have intentionally left it behind with all the gory memories of the day when my life changed forever. Fortunately, I was saved. I spent the worst years of the war in a safe environment with plenty of others, children, who had suffered their own losses during the war." Margaret focused on the joined keys. Her fingers inched toward them until she finally brushed them with her fingertips.

"She never talked about her ordeal, Franzisca, *your abuela*. For the most part, she was a loner. The changes in her went beyond the name. She had grown stern and suspicious. The light I saw in her eyes the day she confided in me the meaning of the keys, was gone. I don't remember what made me look toward her neck, but my hands moved instinctively, as they had done so many times when I was a little girl and she sat by my cot telling me stories until I would finally fall asleep. I reached for the silver chain, but it wasn't there. Then I knew what had changed her." Margaret's smile was sad. "She had lost him."

Silence fell upon the kitchen table once more. Each one of us huddled back into our thoughts. I looked at Daniel, still trying to figure out his participation in my grandmother's life or mine. It was obvious he was here to represent the one man Abuela had loved. I wondered what secrets he harbored. I studied him a while longer. Daniel was not the kind of man I was usually attracted to. I had followed a pattern of falling for self-absorbed, emotionally unavailable men that would guarantee a short stay in my life. That was the way I wanted it. My heart had been broken several times since childhood. I was in the fifth grade when I suffered my first romantic disappointment. It was after a heart to heart talk with Abuela that I learned to save the joys and pains of love for only one.

"Margaret," I called out, catching everybody's attention, "do you remember the first time I fell in love? If I remember well you were with us at the finca."

I noticed Daniel interest in the matter at once, for he sat up on his chair and stared in my direction.

"How could I forget," said Margaret. "That day you cried all the way home from school."

"You know it." We shared a brief laugh. "What you don't know is what happened next. I believe you left for the afternoon on an errand or something."

"It's possible," Margaret concurred.

"Well, Abuela allowed my tears to run their course, then, she cut a generous slice of a pie she had browning in the oven, and in between bites, I asked her if she had ever been in love. She was my world. She knew everything. For sure she knew about love, too." I looked at my audience. They waited expectantly for me to cut to the chase. I wasn't going to rush through it. It was important for Daniel to hear the whole of it. "Her response took a while. My ten-year-old mind already understood that love had to be more complicated than I had anticipated if Abuela had to think on it. Then she confessed to have never been in love."

I saw Daniel flinch as if someone had just slapped him, but he didn't question me, so I continued. "I looked at her as if she had grown a second head. She smiled back at me and said that Franzisca had once fallen in love, deeply, with the kind of love that never died." My heart ached for Abuela now more than ever, I had to pause.

"She did love him, then," Daniel asserted.

"She forever loved the only man who ever owned the one key to her heart." I could still see her as if she were sitting in front of me. Her hand hovering over that space close to her heart and then resting it back immediately on the smooth surface of the table.

"If she would have only admitted it to him, to my grandfather," Daniel shook his head slowly showing every bit of the sorrow I felt.

"She never stopped dreaming of him, you know? She loved him," I said to no one in particular.

I traced the worn edges of Franzisca's box. Whatever stories lay stashed in it, whatever stories I had written down on my notebook out of memory and out of fantasy, they had become the truth about her life. I opened the box and the image of Abuela lying like an ice sculpture in a frigid mortuary chamber suddenly disappeared. The person waiting to be buried at the end of my discoveries was not Claudia Lazar, that woman had been nothing more than a facade. I finally began to acknowledge that I had been raised by Franzisca. Every lesson I had ever learned, every truth I had ever known came out of Franzisca's lips. Franzisca's story or Abuela's life was tainted with vengeance, war, and loss. But that was not what had changed her into the secretive woman I came to know. What had torn her was a failed love story.

My heart broke for her and in that moment I forgave her for all the lies and for the horrible things she might have done during the war years. At thirty years old, I had yet to find out what love was. Through her stories all she had meant to do was show me what she had done for love.

I looked up from the box and found Daniel staring at me. "Why didn't he love her back? Why didn't he come for her? Why did he have to wait until his last breath to call out her name? Why?"

His faced showed the tiredness of sleepless nights. He too had been fighting ghosts and half-truths from the moment he set out to find me. He reached for the picture of young Margaret.

"Alex... my grandfather... during his last days, he spoke of a woman and of the love they shared. He never said her name, but I could see the pain in his eyes every time a memory claimed him." Daniel let a breath of a laugh escape his lips. "He told me not to be an idiot like him and to hold on to that one person that feels right from the beginning."

His eyes were charged with emotion. He left the picture on the table, folded his hands firmly around mine, gathering strength to say his next words. "He fought hard to have her, to get to her. But she wouldn't listen. She wouldn't let go of the past."

Chapter Twenty-Two

Bucharest, February 1941

For two weeks, they skirted the shadows. Hiding during the day and looking for food and shelter at night. Franzisca kept quiet except when asked if she was cold or hungry. Alex knew how to take care of himself, even take care of others. When he lived back home, he had done so with his younger brother and his mother.

Alex himself was the product of a mistake. His mother, an educated young Jewish woman of means, did the one thing that would free her forever from her controlling parents—she got pregnant. Both she and the family's dairy boy, an ignorant rogue, with calloused hands and arrogant beauty, were kicked off her parents' land as soon as she was found vomiting with morning sickness. She thought herself in love, and with nothing more than the clothes on their backs, they moved into an abandoned shed, the only home Alex ever knew.

The lust they shared lasted until Alex grew big within his mother's womb and the dairy boy became repulsed by his young lover's swollen body. It was then that the drunkenness and the beatings started.

Wasted by a life of abuse next to a man she grew to hate, Alex's mother, Sofia, swore she would see her son grow into a sensible, well-educated man. She found strength, in that sacred place mothers have only for their children, and instructed Alex in everything her tutors had once taught her. By the age of six, Alex knew all his letters and had discovered the secret messages within the language of numbers. For the most part, he was a happy child, sweet, and loving, except when his father was around. It was then that Alex's eyes flickered with what his mother recognized as unadulterated loathing.

A large rat squirmed between Alex's boots. He kicked the disgusting rodent away. His sharp move disturbed Franzisca momentarily. He looked down at her. She was asleep in his arms. Her sleep, although troubled, freed her of the pain that furrowed her beautiful features. Franzisca shifted in his arms and mumbled something unintelligible. He tucked a wild tendril of her raven hair behind her ear. "Sleep, *inima mea*," he whispered. His words took him by surprise. When had she become his heart? It did not matter, he decided while contemplating her thick, dark eyelashes atop her high cheekbones. He looked at the hands that held her and all he saw were the hands of the man he despised the most. In that moment, he vowed never to hurt her.

Three years ago, the day Alex retaliated and beat his father senseless; he knew it was time to leave his birth-home. Before departing on the first of many one-way journeys, he pleaded with his mother's estranged family to take her and his little brother in. His grandparents cried tears of joy and shame at the sight of their daughter and her scrawny offspring. Alex remembered looking into his grandfather's remorseful light blue eyes. Yet he could not find it in his heart to forgive him.

Leaving the only two people he loved under the care of family and servants, Alex, a young man of seventeen, looked forward to an uncertain future. He wanted to put some distance between himself and the brute that had fathered him. He wanted to leave that life behind and claim one for his own in the big city.

Bucharest was beyond anything he had imagined. Accustomed to open space and wide expanses of green, the closeness and filth of the city left him gasping for fresh air. Slowly, as he grew accustomed to the fast moving pace of the city, Alex felt his lungs expand and his feet became grounded; it was time to start the rest of his life.

***

The cries of a small child, quickly silenced by a female soothing hush, set Alex in high alert reminding him of his precarious situation. He was a survivor and so far, regardless of his rough beginnings, luck had been on his side. No, he corrected himself, the outcome of his life in Bucharest had nothing to do with luck, but with the kindness of a man he had not yet mourned, Old Nicu.

The beatings he suffered under the fist of his father, for the sole crime of being bright, finally paid off, when two days after his arrival in Bucharest, he walked into a bakery looking for a job. The storekeeper, a good-natured man, with a full head of snowy white hair and rosy cheeks, was struggling through a ledger presented to him by a flour supplier. The supplier argued aggressively, threatening the future of the old man's business unless a demanded sum was paid off on the spot. The flour merchant, a skilled dramatist, used the body language of a street vendor, raising his voice to emphasize the injustice he claimed to be a victim of.

To Alex, it looked obvious that the supplier was taking advantage of a man who knew nothing of numbers, an honest man that ran his business through trust and the power of a handshake.

Flexing his fingers, Alex restrained himself from interfering and stood in a corner waiting for the old man to sort out his affairs with the shady merchant. Before he knew it, he stepped forward and took the ledger from him and pointed out the intentional inconsistencies with the merchant's arithmetic. The baker listened to Alex with interest and did not interfere until the flour merchant left the bakery, fuming for being caught out in his dishonesty. A revelation which resulted in the gentle baker coming out ahead with a five-week supply flour.

Flushed with the excitement of having used his skills openly without the fear of being thrashed for it, Alex missed the bewilderment on the old man's face.

"What's your name, *baiatu*?"

Alex turned to the baker. He was not used to be addressed kindly by another man and was wary, almost afraid of the man's reaction. Previous experience had taught him to keep his eyes down and make a run for it to save his skin before a rock-hard fist smashed into the side of his head.

The baker walked around the counter and chose a golden loaf from a rack. He cut it lengthwise and smeared both sides with creamy butter.

Alex's mouth watered at the scent of freshly baked bread. In the two days since his arrival in Bucharest, he had barely eaten a morsel, and the rumbling in his stomach was a testament to his desperate hunger.

"Tea?" the baker asked.

Alex lifted his eyes and found the baker busy pouring steaming water into two cups. Alex could only nod and driven by hunger he cautiously approached the counter.

"Eat, *baiatu*. Perhaps after you fill your empty stomach you might remember your name."

"*Merci*," babbled Alex. Summoning his best manners, he slowly drank his cup of tea and ate the loaf of bread to the last crumb. After wiping his mouth with a clean linen napkin, Alex was ready to talk.

"Alex… Alex Alcaly, sir."

The old baker smiled broadly and showed a full set of brown teeth. "Alex Alcaly, how long have you been in Bucharest?"

"Two days, sir." Alex looked back at the baker.

"Do you know, *baiatu*? That trickster you just sent away cursing has been emptying my pockets for a long time." The old man smiled. "Thank you."

Apart from his mother and younger brother, Alex had never been shown any kindness in all of his seventeen years. He felt a lump forming in his throat, and knew it to be a new sort of emotion.

"You're welcome, sir," was all he said. His heart sank knowing his last coin would not cover the meal he ate. Alex looked at the baker, his eyes pleading. "Please, sir. Do not call the police."

The baker frowned. "Are you in trouble, *baiatu*? Have you stolen? Are you a Jew?"

In his mind Alex answered the questions in order, *"perhaps, no, yes,"* while his eyes travelled guiltily toward the remnants of his finished snack.

The old baker laughed heartily and patted Alex's back. "All my employees get to taste my bread, especially my new bookkeeper."

Alex could not believe his luck. Within a couple of days of arriving in Bucharest, he had secured a job with a decent pay and a place to live. The old baker, Nicu, was his name, a childless widower, lived in a room a couple of blocks from the bakery on *Strada Micsunele*. The building was a former four-story hotel, abandoned by its Jewish owners when the Iron Guard strengthened its grip on its anti-Jewish policies.

Nicu assigned Alex the small gas stove, located in a corner at the far end of the room, and all cooking duties; in exchange for a pallet and a soft mattress. Once again, Alex gave silent thanks to his beloved mother. It wasn't until that moment when he was faced with chunks of sheep, raw vegetables and raw beans that he understood his mother's purpose behind teaching him to cook. She had raised Alex to be an independent man. She had raised him to leave.

Alex's days were filled with his duties at the bakery, which included the handling of the books, and the upkeep of their room back at the hotel. He quickly noticed that Nicu's memory was failing, and took it upon himself to learn as much of the trade as possible.

Over two steaming plates of *mamaliga* topped with Mama Sofia's sweet and sour tomato sauce, Alex laid out to Nicu his proposal to expand Nicu's rudimentary business. There were rumors of another big war coming and their future was as uncertain as everybody else's in the city. Alex's plan, to build a wealthier clientele, would guarantee Nicu some extra savings for the troubled times ahead. Besides his own plans for the future, Alex saw the need to provide for the old man, a thought he kept to himself. Without a family to look after him, and when he no longer could care for himself, Alex would become Nicu's caregiver. He considered Nicu the grandfather he always dreamt of and never had, therefore, he would provide for this good natured man as if he were his own flesh.

When Alex was done explaining Nicu his expansion project, Nicu wiped his mouth, slurped his tea, and with a smile that reached his eyes said words Alex had never imagined a grown man to say, and never to him. "I prayed for a son all my life. I'm old and soon I will not remember who I am, but still... *baiatu meu,* my boy, you came."

The next morning Alex went out into the streets of Bucharest to set his plan in motion. With a dozen loaves of bread and an assortment of pastries, he knocked on the backdoors of the most prominent households. After letting the main cooks sample his bake goods, Alex returned to the bakery with five new accounts, and the memory of seeing the most beautiful girl in the world. The girl he now held protectively in his arms.

It was at the last door he knocked on, at the Lupescu palace, where Anna Schultz, the Lupescu's head cook, took pity on Alex's cold, red face and sat him down for a cup of hot tea and some of her own pastries. The apricot Danish he bit into melted in his mouth. There was no way he could sell his breads to *Doamna* Anna Schultz, her pastries were superb. They made small talk, and although he did not press on the purpose of his visit, he left behind his last samples as a way to thank her for her kindness.

Before Anna Schultz closed the door, she looked at him with curiosity. "You are the new boy living with old Nicu, aren't you?"

Alex, taken by surprise, searched her face for some recognition.

"My daughter and I live on the first floor. Sometimes, that is…when we are not needed here." Anna looked down as if she regretted sharing so much personal information with a stranger. "Give old Nicu my warm regards." She ran back to the oven and retrieved a golden meat pie. She covered it with a dishtowel and gave it to Alex. "Take good care of him."

Alex's eyes met hers and opened his mouth to thank her, when a young maid of perhaps fifteen, with the brightest violet-blue eyes and flawless olive skin appeared at the far end of the kitchen. Before he could utter a word or get another glimpse of that beautiful girl, the door closed on his face.

It had been two years since the first time he laid eyes on Franzisca. And for two years he had watched her from afar, trying to gather the courage to speak to her.

Now, this rare young woman slept in his arms wrestling demons in her dreams. He caressed her hair and made shushing sounds to help her relax. She did.

Before they fell asleep at dawn, he thought about their predicament. They were dirty, hungry, and cold. Nicu had died in the explosion along with Anna Schultz, Franzisca's mother. He allowed himself a brief moment of happiness, in a city devastated by violence, and took comfort that her slight frame rested against his chest. It was her warmth that allowed him to escape into a sweet slumber where anything was possible.

In his dreams, he held her in his arms, for he had loved her from the moment he saw her. But in his dreams, there was no war, no death, nor heartache.

"You hold the other half of my heart," Franzisca's whisper penetrated his dream.

His eyes sprung open and he found that she wasn't lying in the hollow of his arms anymore, the way she had when the sun crept into the sky. She was gone and without her to care for, to love, to hold, he felt naked, empty. The only evidence that her presence had been more than a dream was the key left behind in the spot where her body had lain. The words that had permeated his sleep, now echoed in his mind as he held the key in his hand, *"You hold the other half of my heart"*

She wasn't a dream, then.

Chapter Twenty-Three

Peeling herself out of Alex's arms was the second hardest thing she had to go through in her life and they both happened in the span of two weeks. In that brief time after the explosion, she had grown accustomed to the shelter of his arms, the warmth of his breath, and the reassurance of his beating heart. He had brought her back to life, even though she did not feel worthy of living. When Franzisca woke up that morning with the taste of dust in her mouth, the weight of the world fell on her shoulders once again. That day, while she watched Alex sleep, she planned the rest of her life. She would never forget their time together. Alex had gotten under her skin with his sweet reassuring smile, with the warmth of his rich, brown eyes, with his protective embrace. She would forever reminisce their time in the tunnels as a time tainted with dirt and fear; but mostly with an inexplicable feeling of what she suspected to be love. It was because of the new feeling sprouting within her that she had to leave. She deserved to serve a self-imposed sentence, a life sentence, to make up for her silence and cowardice that had caused the lives of so many. With those decisions in mind, her body retreated back into the same numb state she had experienced right after the blast, yet the pull of his body kept jolting her into the possibility of another life. One where she would be forgiven and could live happily ever after, like the princesses of her favorite fairy tales had lived when in their lovers' arms. God! The thought was heady, intoxicating, and she could easily drown in the idea of their own happily ever after.

Before slipping from Alex's loving hold, she hardened her resolve. Perhaps, Franzisca thought, perhaps when my job is done, I would be worthy of a tale as sweet as the ones I dreamt of before this tragedy. That was when the idea of the keys came to mind. Franzisca looked at the two pieces and how well the fit together. The shape of the entwined keys gave her hope. Just like the keys, she and Alex would always belong to each other. Whatever roadblocks lay ahead, ultimately they would come back together. She swore it. Looking back at Alex's sleeping form, she unclasped the chain holding the keys and broke them apart. Then she left one next to Alex's open palm.

The tightness in her chest returned and she gasped for air. She had the need to run and free herself from the good that had befallen her out of tragedy. She had to leave Alex at once.

When she crawled out of the tunnel, daylight blinded her. No longer sheltered by the anonymity of darkness, she prayed for the success of her plan. She would make her way back into the heart of the Lupescu estate, and replace her mother's role in Lupescu's life.

In truth, she needed not hide. Her time as a fugitive with Alex had started as a way to mourn her loss, then it had turned into a time to plan revenge. Without notice, during those two weeks she was sure she had discovered love.

Franzisca was a Jew. Both her mother and father were born and raised Jewish and although never part of a community, Anna made sure of Francisca's education as a Jewess. Whenever possible they lit *Shabbat* candles. In between flour fights and plenty of laughs, they braided *challah* bread for the holidays' blessings. Whenever Anna was not needed overnight at the Lupescu manor, she loved to snuggle in bed with Franzisca and read through the *Siddur*. The prayer book was not used in their home as a religious tool, but as the basis to elaborate the many stories of the Bible Anna loved to read to Franzisca. In the privacy of their one room kingdom, Franzisca became the recipient of the most wonderful gift from her mother. Anna enlightened her daughter with everything she had been taught during her time as the daughter of the most powerful Jewish family in Austria, plus the lessons she learned from love, motherhood, and survival.

Franzisca knew the story of her mother and father inside out. She also knew the treason the Schultzes had suffered at the hands of the Lupescus, thus she never comprehended the sickening relationship Anna had with the baron.

Two weeks before the blast, Anna had dragged her battered body through the door of their room, and collapsed on the floor before she reached the bed. The rage Franzisca experienced that day had never left her. Her mother had sacrificed her body and soul to see Franzisca settled. She knew that much. As she tended to her mother's wounds, Franzisca tried to stay level headed. Something good had to come out of tragedy. It was one of the many lessons Anna had instilled in her daughter since the moment Franzisca could read her first letters.

Once her mother was settled in her cot and asleep, Franzisca looked around her. Although, Anna did her best to make the grim living quarters a wonderland in the eyes of a young Franzisca. She was no longer a child; she could see their lives for what they were. They were outcasts within their community for eating from the hand of a powerful anti-Semite. They were pariahs outside the make believe world they had created for themselves. A world where there was no room for dreams beyond the constricting space of their meager four-walled palace.

Franzisca understood her mother's fearless approach to life. The day Anna had watched her parents being humiliated and then shot, her body had lost the ability to feel. The day Anna stood at Lupescu's mercy she became resolute to pursue one thing: Justice. Never mind her perishing in the process. Death would reach her nevertheless.

After the last severe beating, Franzisca stood vigil over her mother's bed. "No," she had whispered, careful not to wake her. "You will not die, Mama." Franzisca knelt by the bed and softly stroked Anna's forehead. "We'll get out of here, I promise, and we'll live happily ever after in that palace you and *Tată* dreamt of."

It had been over three weeks since she had made that empty promise to her mother. Anna was dead. She had been blown into a million pieces and Franzisca did not even have her mother's remains so that she could lay her to rest in lush, green grounds where she was meant to live free.

Franzisca's determination to see her mother's plan through intensified with each step she took toward the Lupescu mansion.

Nobody paid her heed when she slipped through the back door and into the kitchen. Word of Anna's fateful passing had reached the baron, and according to Marietta, who by now had settled Franzisca in front of a steaming cup of tea and a plate of corned beef and cabbage, the news had kept him withdrawn behind the closed door of his study for a week. Only when Nazi and Romanian officials summoned him for an urgent business on the eighth day of his confinement, did the baron step out. He looked haggard and reeked of alcohol and vomit. Within an hour, with the assistance of his valet, Baron Lupescu was brought back to his usual carefully groomed self.

Franzisca felt a surge of pleasure at the baron's torment and without noticing, she spoke up for the first time since crossing the threshold, "in time, there will be nothing but darkness for him."

"It's your grief talking, *fata meu*," Marietta patted Franzisca's shoulder. "You'll stay here with us, the baron is away, and the streets are not safe for a young girl like you."

The news of Lupescu's absence from Bucharest was known to Franzisca before she had set foot on the grounds of the estate. The word was still on the streets and it was the only subject of conversation between housewives and food vendors. The terror created by the Legionaries—the members of the Iron Guard in Bucharest, in a double attempt to overthrow Antonescu while blaming the Jewish population for the revolution—had failed.

The short-lived revolution claimed the lives of one hundred and twenty five Jews and thirty soldiers, but the effort to wrest power from the hands of Ion Antonescu, was in vain. On the third day of the pogrom, Antonescu, with a pact with Hitler up his sleeve, and heavily supported by the Romanian military, ordered his opponents crushed. In a matter of hours under the leadership of General Ilie Şteflea, the Iron Guard met a crumbling defeat. The nationalist movement which sought to ally with Hitler and rule Romania was quickly disbanded when nine-thousand of its members were arrested and the movement destroyed.

In the case of Lupescu, his aristocratic status granted him a choice. He could claim loyalty to Antonescu or follow the fate of the now imprisoned Legionaries. Hungry for power and determined to keep his fortune as well as his name in the highest spheres of government, Lupescu did not hesitate to turn coat. However, his presence in Bucharest could have enticed those who had escaped the force of Antonescu's command, to rekindle yet another attempt to take over Romania, a risk the government was not willing to take.

Within an hour, Lupescu was in his car heading toward Iasi, where he was to become the leader of a joint Romanian-Nazi operation in the northern region of Romania.

Franzisca was sick with loathing for Lupescu, but just like her mother, she learned to desensitize her emotions to perform her duties without complaint. She wished she could be that strong when it came to remembering Alex and the weeks she had spent in his arms. Franzisca had allowed herself a moment of grief, even a few tears. But those tears receded at the thought of the twin key she had left in his possession. That was to be their promise, she knew he would understand when he woke up and found her gone. The key was the only thing she had to give that would assure Alex of her undying love for him. She had given him half her heart. The key was her promise to find him and forever be together at the end of her journey, however long it might be.

Marietta was still blabbering when Franzisca wiped her hands on a white linen napkin. She pushed her wooden chair back, thanked the old woman for her attentions, and walked out of the kitchen without a backward glance.

She headed toward the servants' quarters to a room she had shared with her mother during their overnight stays at the palace. The morning of the blast, on Franzisca's seventeenth birthday, her mother had mentioned a present left for her in that room. Pain ripped Franzisca heart in half once again. Did her mother know that was to be their last day together? Everything pointed to a long-planned farewell, the passing down of the keys, and the request to not open the gift until the day after her birthday.

The gas stove, Franzisca thought. No, Franzisca rejected the notion of her mother leaving her alone willingly, or of her mother initiating the fire that killed not only herself but so many others.

When Franzisca entered the room, she saw a plain, rectangular box made of dark wood sitting in the middle of the bed she had slept in on many occasions. She sat down on the bed and contemplated the box. She imagined Anna placing it there on her last day in the service of Lupescu, the night he had beaten Anna within an inch of her life.

Franzisca lay down, curled around the box and buried her nose on the thin comforter. "Tell me, Mama," she cried silently, "why did you do it? Why did you leave me?" She fell into a dreamless sleep.

Hours later Franzisca woke up stiff with cold. Her tears had shed no answers. A gas lamp and a few matches sat on a small three-legged table at one side of the bed. Franzisca had always relished the spark of matches and the first explosion of light when they were lit. In her mind, light symbolized new beginnings, discoveries. She struck a match to the lamp; the warm light illuminated the box on the bed. It was time to open it.

When she lifted the lid, a single folded sheet of paper lay in the box. Maybe her mother left a letter for her? More than anything Franzisca yearned for Anna's wise words, for her guidance.

It was a document written in her mother's hand. At the bottom of the page, Lupescu's signature and family crest were stamped. Franzisca thought the flickering light of the lamp deceived her. She reread the document and word by word, the last actions of her mother started to make sense. Word by word, Franzisca realized her mother's long planned revenge. Before she folded the document into a small square and stashed it in her brassiere, Franzisca read it one last time. The document stated Franzisca was the sole heir to the Lupescu barony.

Franzisca let out a small laugh. Upon his death, she was to be the recipient of all his lands and wealth. The fortune she was being granted, a document signed in a moment of weakness driven by a perverted passion, was none other than the fortune the older Lupescu had stolen from Franzisca's grandparents, the day she and her mother witnessed their execution while hiding among the trees.

Franzisca made her way to the room at the far end of the first floor, Lupescu's study; the room where her mother had suffered rape and corporal punishment. The room where Lupescu kept each one of the titles and documents that had made his vast fortune and soon would make Franzisca's.

When her mother had forced Franzisca to commit to memory the three-digit combination that opened Lupescu's safe, she had thought Anna delusional. When the safe clicked open, she silently apologized to her mother and examined the contents. Buried within the depths of the safe, she found thirty-five blank passports originated in *Republica Argentina*, and a roll of documents. She took her time to read them. In her hands she held three titles for the properties her family, the Shultzes, had owned across Europe before their murder. She laughed silently. At her fingertips, she had all she needed to right every wrong done to her mother and her family. Tucked away in her brassiere she had Lupescu's handwritten promise to her mother, a useless piece of paper, unless Franzisca could figure out a way to validate it in the eyes of the law.

Franzisca knew she had to act fast and disappear before Lupescu came back to Bucharest. One by one she put the documents back in the safe and closed it. It was too much to take in all at once and she did not feel ready. Not yet.

Chapter Twenty-Four

Solvang, CA, March 2013

As much as I wanted to stay up and wring out every last piece of information Margaret was willing to give us, the night was growing old. Margaret retired to bed first with the promise of more talk the following morning. We hugged for a long time. Knowing how she worried about me, I assured her I was fine and that I would be in bed within five minutes. Then in that manner of hers, in which she always seemed to be imparting orders to a battalion, she commanded Daniel to stay in one of the guest rooms in the main house. "I don't need to be worrying about you driving this late at night, Daniel."

The comment was deviously directed at me. Margaret anticipated I would object to his stay, so she used the oldest trick in the book and blackmailed me with her peace of mind. "Sofia, please take care of the details." I knew better than to argue, so I nodded and with that she disappeared behind her door.

The main house had seven bedrooms. Abuela's bedroom and the one I had occupied during my teenage years were housed in a separate quarter. The remaining five bedrooms were lined along a hallway off the family room. Marcela was appointed one of the bedrooms, although she had never stayed in it, and one was Margaret's. The rest of the rooms were always ready to accommodate the many guests we hosted throughout the years.

I led Daniel to a bedroom at the end of the hallway. It had a lovely view of the gardens and hills. The room smelled of fresh linen and I was happy to see that even without Abuela the house was still kept immaculate; not a speck of dust in sight.

I pointed to a door. "That door opens to a full bathroom. There are clean towels under the sink."

Daniel had not uttered a word since recounting the story about Alex. He stood by the doorway staring out the window. It was dark outside. Still, through the windowpanes, the twinkling stars were visible. After everything we had gone through during the day, his nearness still made me nervous. "Now that you know for sure who Franzisca was, I guess your job here is done."

His gaze travelled from the window and rested on me. "You don't have to stay. Margaret will get over it when she wakes up. I just didn't have the strength to argue with her."

Daniel ran his fingers through his hair, another one of his habits I had noticed, and sat down on the bed. "What now?" His question was raw.

I had no idea what was next for us. Every muscle in my body hurt and my eyes were begging for sleep. But I did not want to be alone in my room. For some inexplicable reason I wanted to be with Daniel.

I walked over to the bed and sat down next to him. For a second time in a day, I allowed my impulses to act on my behalf. I gently pushed him on the bed and snuggled next to him. He gathered me in his arms, enveloped me in his warmth, and supported me with the solidity of his body. I felt safe in Daniel's arms and for the first time since Abuela's death, I let my guard down and surrendered.

"Now." I inhaled deeply. "We sleep."

The initial warmth that had driven me to surrender my body to rest was gradually replaced by a different need. I closed my eyes tight to erase the images of his body next to mine. The solid, male body, *his* body pressed against me was a reality. He buried his nose in my hair, "Sofia," he whispered.

I knew what would follow if I would not put an end to it. But my response to Daniel went beyond physical attraction. He was the connection to my past, and he was next to me, protective and immediate. I did not want to dwell about the feelings, perhaps regret, that would invade me come morning. I wanted for once to stop thinking and to start feeling.

I moved my head slightly to give him access to explore the length of my neck. Ever since his impulsive kiss earlier that day, I had yearned for another taste of him. This time though, his touch was different. His lips were soft and teasing and continued the job he had started that morning. He meant to make every kiss last, he meant to make me beg for more. And I realized that I wanted more.

I disengaged from his embrace and turned to face him. I rubbed the spot between his brows that was often creased in a frown. I leaned forward, kissed it, then I ran my fingers through his mass of brown wavy hair. At my touch, he closed his eyes and sucked in a tight breath.

"Sofia," he whispered again. He pulled me into his arms and we rolled together on the bed, his body hovered over mine. Our lips met halfway. A caressing touch, an exchange of breaths. Our kiss deepened, our tongues entwined in a tender mating dance. My fingers worked the buttons of his shirt until all I could touch and feel were his taut arms and torso. I explored the planes of his chest, the ridges of his abdomen, and downwards toward his groin. I kissed his neck and the place where his key had rested on his chest. His weight pressed down on me and I ran my hand between us, I could feel him growing hard at my touch.

"Not yet," he said. Daniel pulled my hands up over my head and unzipped my hoodie the same one he had dressed me in after he had scooped me out of the bathtub the night before. His long fingers stroked my bare breasts.

"Next time, I'll show you where I keep my bras," I said, breathless. His fingers slid under the waistband of my sweatpants and his warm hands on my bare buttocks reminded me that I wasn't wearing any panties either. "They are in the drawer next to where I keep my panties."

"I have no need for them." He smiled as he slid my sweatpants off and threw them on the floor. His mouth closed hungrily over my nipples. I was not a novice in bed by any means and had had my share of lovers, but the sensations my body was experiencing at Daniel's touch were intoxicating. When his hands travelled from my buttocks to the length of my legs and up to the slippery cleft between them, I could barely breathe. His movements were precise, controlled, aimed to memorize every inch of my body.

"Daniel," I cried. I needed to feel all of him over me and inside me. "Your pants. Take them off."

With one hand he freed himself of the restraints of his pants. He was hard and ready for me, but he would not let me touch him. He turned me on my stomach and while he explored the length of my back with soft kisses, he mumbled unintelligible words against my skin making me shiver with the warmth of his breath. "Daniel, please," I begged.

He turned me on my back to face him. He was propped on his elbows, and I lay caged below his body. His breath was ragged, his eyes glistened with want. But he just looked at me. "I don't want just to have sex with you, Sofia. I want to make love to you. I want you like I've never wanted a woman before." His declaration was heart stopping. He just didn't want to sleep with me. Well, he did and his hard shaft throbbing between my legs was a testament to it. But, besides that, I had the feeling that he wanted me, all of me. I felt exposed and my hands flew to my chest to cover my naked breasts. It wasn't nakedness what bothered me, but the kind of nakedness I experienced under Daniel's stare made me feel uncomfortable. Uninvited, he had stepped into a territory no other man had ever had access to. I could see my reflection in the mirror of his eyes and I could see what he saw. He had delved into my depths. He had looked into me, through me. Regardless of his findings, he still wanted me.

My first thought was to run away. Prevent him from gaining any more terrain. But I was prey of his caramel-eyes, of his tenderness, of his passion. What had started as a response to the presence of his body had evolved into the surrendering of my whole self to a man I barely knew. As scared as I was I could not deny that I wanted him in the same way he wanted me. Just for a night, bring your defenses down for a night, I told myself. And I did.

I lifted my hands from my breasts and pulled him closer. We kissed again, with our mouths, our hands, and our whole bodies. All inhibitions, doubts, and fears we might have had vanished when he claimed me with his first powerful thrust. We rode the waves of heady pleasure, explored each other's depths, and plunged toward ecstasy with every thrust, every kiss, every cry.

When our heartbeats slowed down, Daniel pulled me close and held me in a possessive grip. "Sofia." My name rolled over his tongue as if he had created it. Too tired to speak, I answered with a moan. "Promise me that when it is all said and done. When we both find the answers we're looking for, you'll still be here, with me, in my arms." He hugged me tighter, for reassurance or perhaps to wake me for a response.

"Daniel, I don't know what's going to happen tomorrow. I don't even know what this means." I knew I was avoiding the subject. I had never promised my heart to any man. Still, the comfort and pleasure I felt with Daniel was disconcerting.

His lips covered mine we kissed deeply, intensely. He was the first to break away. I was left shivering, envisioning a life without Daniel in it.

Other than Abuela and Margaret, I had spent a lifetime developing meaningless love relationships lest I be hurt in the way I was in my earlier years. Suddenly, I found myself in the arms of a man I had just met, and totally out of character for me, the thought of discarding him the way I had done it with others, felt strangely painful. Yet, I could not give him the answer he demanded. I started to get out of bed but he stopped me and pulled me back into his arms. "Not tonight," he said. I buried my head into the nest of his shoulder. My last thought before drifting into sleep was tomorrow.

When I woke the next morning, I found Daniel's embrace replaced by a thick throw. He was standing by the window, watching the day being born. His hair was wet; some drops ran down his bare back. My eyes traveled down some more. His whole body was in sight except for his nether region, which was wrapped with a bath towel. The red of dawn upon his magnificent figure made him look like a mythological God. I looked at the rumpled bed. The night had been restless and restful.

"Is it always this beautiful in the morning?" Daniel turned around just as I was slipping out of the bed. Guiltily, I held the throw over my body. I was escaping.

He didn't say a word. He just nodded faintly and turned around to watch the sky change colors. "It wasn't just about Franzisca. My being here is personal." He crossed his arms about his chest. I realized that my window of time to share Daniel's private space suddenly closed.

I left the room.

Back in my private wing, I stood under the shower and I lingered under the hot water, unable to scrub Daniel from my skin. When I came of out of the bathroom, he was gone.

**

"You are a lot like her, you know?" Margaret sat at the kitchen table, searched my eyes under my downcast lashes.

I shrugged slightly. The night spent with Daniel had gone beyond a night of great sex. For the first time, I had felt truly embraced, cherished by a man. I hadn't repelled his closeness the morning after the way I had with others. On the contrary, the contact of his skin felt natural against mine as if we had been designed to be together. But I waved my sentimental thought immediately. "I can't add him to the equation, Margaret. Things are already too complicated as they are."

"You can't think of life as an equation, my girl." She reached for my hands, "I loved your grandmother like a sister would. But you, I love you as if you were my own. I would hate to see you follow your grandmother's footsteps and grow proud, stubborn, lonely. It's all right to let go. Give love a chance. Give yourself a chance."

"Who said anything about love?" I replied defensively. "If I'm like anybody, I'm like Marcela. A slut that jumps in bed with a man I barely know."

Margaret tugged at my hand demanding my attention. "I will not allow you to speak ill of your mother, do you hear me, Sofia? She's not a slut nor are you." Margaret's hold softened so did her tone. "Some things are obvious, my girl, and the look on your face speaks more than a thousand words. It might not be love yet. It might never be love if you don't let yourself find out."

"Love at first sight belongs in romantic stories, Margaret."

"And who said you are not to live one?" Margaret let go of my hands and reached into the pocket of her cardigan. Her hand closed on an object. I saw the leather cord before she opened her palm. It was Daniel's key.

"He left it with me while you were busy scrubbing away your feelings." She placed the key on the table, waiting for me to take it. "Like I told you last night, I lost contact with Claudia, Franzisca—your abuela, for more than thirty years. War and time, do for a fact change people, trust me, I know. But what I found beneath the armor she chose to shield herself was a deep anguish, very different from any scars wartime leaves behind." Margaret tapped the key lightly. "The keys were never back together, as a whole, and just like them your abuela was never whole again. Every now and then, when she thought nobody was watching her, she would bring her hands to the place where her key was supposed to be, she would close her eyes and mourn for what had slipped out of her life."

I stared at the key and weighed the truth of Margaret's words. Before the night I spent with Daniel, I had decided not to repeat history and choose a different path for myself. Perhaps that was why a moment of forced spontaneity landed me in bed with Daniel. Maybe it was what made me savor the intimacy like I had never done before. The chance to fantasize about a what if.

"I'm scared, Margaret." I finally met her eyes. "I'm scared to find out horrible things about Abuela. I'm scared of love. I'm scared of becoming the hopeful girl I was before I decided hope did not fit in the life of someone like me."

Margaret pushed the key toward me. "Hope won't kill you."

***

Back at his hotel room, Daniel threw his suitcase on the bed. He stuffed it with the few items he had put away in the closet. He was furious at himself. How could he fall for someone like Sofia Lazar? The more he thought about it the less sense it made. Well, not really. He paused to gather his composure, yet every time he tried, he was assaulted by her smile, her scent, the feel of her body beneath his, by the way she had cried out his name over and over again. He pulled the zipper of his suitcase harder than necessary, grinding its teeth together in the process, now the zipper was stuck. "Damn!" He flung the suitcase across the room, denting the freshly painted wall.

A knock on the door interrupted his urge to slam his fist into it and run it through the cracked wall. His fist was still closed and trembling when the knock came a second time. He ran his fingers through his hair and sucked in a breath. It was probably housekeeping. He needed privacy, a few more minutes to master his frustration before heading out the door. He was an idiot. What was it about this woman that made him act out on things that only happened in romantic movies or books? A man like him did not hold a woman to his chest and asked her to stay with him forever.

He felt suddenly lost. Finding Sofia and solving the riddle of his grandfather's past had been a welcome project for a man who had not known how to wake up in the morning without a mission. But missions were accomplished only when staying emotionally detached from them. The slightest personal involvement jeopardized the outcome of any operation. Yes, leaving Solvang and distancing himself from Sofia Lazar was his only option if he meant to accomplish anything else. Besides unveiling the identity of Franzisca, there was still the matter of his family, which he had been willing to forgo only for Sofia. But she had rejected him. Out of sight, out of mind. End of story. Onward with his original plan.

And then what was he to make of the words Margaret had said to him before he had left the Lazar house early that morning? She had told him that Claudia Lazar was sorry and to not make Sofia pay for her crimes. She was bluntly asking him to let go of the matter of his dead family. That was something he would not do.

There was a third knock on the door. His breathing had normalized and his fists were not shaking with rage anymore. He needed a few more minutes to finish packing and control his emotions before leaving. Better to answer the door and get rid of whoever it was before they barged into the room with their cart filled with cleaning supplies.

Sofia was standing there when he opened it. She looked as bad as he felt, a fact that gave him a wicked satisfaction.

Daniel did not invite her in. Unaffected, she pushed past him, strolled into the room and sat on the bed.

"Close the door, I'm not leaving." She crossed her legs and then her arms.

"You can stay as long as you want. Check out is at eleven." Daniel left the door open and continued packing.

"What if I told you that you might have not been wrong? That your first hunch about Claudia Lazar might hold some truth? That you're not the first one to think her of as a Nazi collaborator?" Sofia stared at him straight in the eye.

Daniel stuffed the last of his clothes into his suitcase and pressed his palms on it. "What do you want, Sofia?"

She slid off the bed and walked to him. In her hand, she held the key that belonged to Alex. She bent down and placed it on his suitcase.

"I'm not good at this, Daniel. I'm not good at letting anybody in." She bit her lower lip to prevent it from trembling. "Don't go."

Daniel stared at the key. He felt Sofia next to him. For a moment, he stopped thinking about her, her plea, her feelings. Leaving would take him back to a path that he had already traveled. A path of loneliness, devoid of conflict, but without Sofia.

"Live a little," his grandfather had told him one afternoon when they had walked through the pastures of the ranch. "Cry and scream for things you've done and not for things you wished you could've done."

Daniel picked up the key and slid it over his neck. His hands reached for Sofia's face and caressed its contours from her eyebrows to her chin. His fingers traveled down her neck and to the place between her breasts where her key rested.

Not for a moment did she take her eyes from his. When his hand closed around her key Sofia covered it with hers. Their pact was sealed.

"Do you want to tell me about it?" he said.

Chapter Twenty-Five

The Solvang house was transformed into a mini intelligence headquarter immediately. Although no longer Mossad, Daniel kept a tight relationship with ex colleagues. They took interest in helping us trace our grandparents' trail from their time in Bucharest in 1941. Even the toughest of men could not resist the unveiling of a love story marred by war. Especially, when many of them had grown up in families with similar stories of their own.

Tracing the mysterious phone call which had sent me into the drunken state that Daniel had found me in became our priority. The old man, on the other end of the phone, held information that could shed light on the life Franzisca and Alex must have lived during those years. The caller, it turned out, had not been careful about concealing his identity. With the touch of a button on his computer—in the same way I had seen it done in TV detective shows—Daniel retrieved the man's name and address.

"Lukas Blau," he said, walking into Abuela's office waving a paper high in the air.

My head had been buried in my laptop as I had been unsuccessfully trying to find more information about Baron Lupescu and his fate after the war. When I looked up, I got a glimpse of Daniel as an intelligence agent. The man was all business, focused, unemotional. The morning shower and change of clothes had washed away all traces of the passionate man who only hours ago had given me more than a night of great sex.

I leaned back on the chair and narrowed all of my attention on him.

"According to this information," he shook the paper slightly, "and the Simon Wiesenthal Center, Lukas Blau immigrated to Argentina in early 1944."

"Wait a second," I interjected, "why would the Simon Wiesenthal Center have any information on Lukas Blau?" My knowledge about Wiesenthal and his Nazi hunting operation came through the world of movies. In 1982, The Simon Wiesenthal Center produced the Oscar winning documentary *Genocide*, and only ten years ago I watched it for the first time on cable.

Simon Wiesenthal, a Holocaust survivor, made it his life's mission to hunt down Nazi criminals throughout the world after World War II. He had been responsible for tracking down and arresting the notorious mastermind of the Holocaust, Adolf Eichmann—who lived under the name of Ricardo Klemens in Argentina in 1960. The documentary was heart wrenching. Even though I had heard many stories of war survivors, thanks to Abuela's efforts to reunite those who had lost contact with their families during the war years, nothing had prepared me for what I saw: The before and after World War II in the way the documentary depicted it.

My mind flew to Franzisca's stories. In each one of them there was a before and after. Before she became the fighter bent on defeating the ogres that walked the earth. After her fight turned her into a lonely warrior. Gradually, I understood Abuela's plight. The need for a new identity, a new name.

My fear must have shown, for Daniel reached over the desk and placed a comforting hand on mine. "We were never able to tie her to the Nazis. There was a trail once, but it went cold. There was not enough evidence against her."

I swallowed hard. I had so many questions, but couldn't articulate any of them. Daniel took the chair opposite me. "Mossad works hand in hand with the Simon

Wiesenthal Center. Because I'm Argentinean, I was given several missions to dig into some of the concealed identities of Nazi war criminals. Claudia Lazar was a name many of us used to toy with. Although never proven, she was suspected to have slipped into the country sometime after the war was over." Daniel shook his head and frowned. "Whatever she did, she was smart about it. She probably crossed illegally into Argentina from one of the neighboring countries, Brazil, Uruguay, or Paraguay. Tracing her origins was the biggest wall Mossad encountered. Without a documented entry, or witnesses, we had no place to trace her from, no nationality. Nobody knew of her past or much about her at all. Unlike others, who entered the country after the war." A pregnant silence was a clear indication that *others* meant other criminals. "She was never spotted within any of the post war social groups, Nazis or non-Nazi."

That was a true depiction of Abuela's social life. She was a society woman and could be found on the front page of the arts section of the leading national newspapers on a weekly fashion. However, she did not belong to a community. We did not gather with the same people twice and her mingling was merely formal and politely impersonal.

My eyes travelled swiftly through the computer screen as I digested the new information Daniel had disclosed. Suddenly, the name Baroness Irina Lupescu, highlighted at the bottom of a document I had opened, caught my attention.

"What is it, Sofia?"

Aware of Daniel's scrutiny on my every move, I tried hard to hide my surprise and clicked on the name. "No… nothing," I said. I quickly scanned through three documents from 1941 that bore her signature. "So…" My voice wavered. "What made you put her case to rest?"

Daniel looked down before answering. He only needed to rake his fingers through his hair to confirm what I already suspected. Even in death, Abuela's name was still on every list. For a brief moment, his eyes locked on the key lying over my tank top, then on me. "She was my abuelo's Franzisca. That's all the proof I need."

Daniel's cell phone went off. He looked at the screen, "I have to take this," he said, and walked out of the office.

I sent a silent thanks to the caller that had diverted Daniel's attention, and zoomed in to get a better look at the document. There were noticeable darker creases where the paper had been folded over and over again along the years. Water and yellow stains caused the wiry handwriting along the document to fade; it was practically illegible. The documents dated in July of 1941, were the transfer of three property titles from Baron Mihail Lupescu to his wife Baroness Irina Lupescu. The dwellings were in Austria, England, and France. Alarm bells went off in my head. I had seen those properties before. But where? I scrambled through the pile of documents I had reviewed only a few days ago. Among them, I found the document listing three properties that matched the descriptions of the ones on the computer screen. I felt the blood drain from my face. Lukas Blau had spoken the truth. These properties I now owned had belonged to Lupescu and had been secretly transferred to me under an anonymous corporation. There was blood in the fortune I had inherited.

At that moment, Margaret and Daniel walked into the office and I slammed my computer shut.

Daniel studied me with concern. He walked to me and reached for my hand. "Are you feeling all right, Sofia?"

No, I was not all right. I felt like a boulder had just crashed on my head. I squeezed his hand and smiled. "Yes, it's all good. A bit tired."

Daniel frowned slightly, a sign that I could not fool him. His comforting presence made me realize that I could not go ahead with this mission on my own. In a little over two days, we had developed a strange connection, one that could only belong to soul mates. We were linked by more than a shared past or unveiled mysteries. We were united by loneliness and desperate need to hold each other's hand through the uncertain path ahead of us. Still, I had decided to keep this new discovery from him, at least for now, until I could trace a logical link between Baroness Lupescu, Abuela, and me.

Margaret sat on the chair on other side of the desk, looked from me to Daniel, and smiled approvingly. "In or out of the bedroom, I'm happy to see you've come to an agreement."

The mention of the bedroom made me blush instantly. "Shit, Margaret. Could you be a bit more subtle?" The word was out before I could prevent it.

Margaret was used to my sudden use of some unladylike words, especially when I was caught unawares, and she feasted on the notion of my lack of propriety. Still with over-exaggerated mockery, she scowled at me. "We are not on a movie set, Sofia. Watch your language." She turned to Daniel. "Have you ever been on a movie set, Daniel?" Daniel shook his head, bit down a chuckle. "Sailors, the whole lot. And my girl here knows how to keep up."

"Margaret!"

Daniel changed the subject quickly although the smile in his eyes reflected how much he was enjoying my embarrassment. "Have you ever heard the name Lukas Blau?"

Margaret squinted as if she were reading the fine print at the bottom of a cell phone contract. Her hand went up shakily to her temples. Her voice shook, too. "I never heard it. I read it."

Tears welled up Margaret's eyes. I sprang out of my chair and kneeled beside her. "It's all right, Margaret." I looked up at Daniel reprovingly.

"I was the youngest but I picked up reading faster than some of the older kids at the house. We had tutors, you see? They were probably kids themselves, perhaps fifteen or sixteen years old, staying at the house temporarily until they also could be transported."

"Is that how you and Abuela met?"

"Yes. She was already there when I and the other children were taken in. Our rescue, for I could not call it anything else, was somewhat dangerous." At that moment, Margaret had our full attention. She paused to regain composure and let the memories flow. "In the beginning I kept my eyes closed for most of the time. I remember being driven in the back of a car, then taken into a tunnel, all six of us. There were blankets and clothes, although oversized and torn in places, they were clean and dry. The tunnel felt safe. I had my first real meal there after a long time of stealing scraps from street vendors and trash piles."

"Had others been there before you, Margaret?" Daniel asked.

Margaret nodded. "Definitely. Like I said, there were clothes, and food, and makeshift beds. We stayed underground for days, I cannot recall how long, but a week is a good guess. Until one day, we were awakened in the middle of the night and taken out of the tunnel in sacks, big empty flour sacks, I remember them because fine, white dust covered me as soon as I squeezed into one of them, and I sneezed furiously when the flour went up my nostrils." Amid the memory of such traumatic event, Margaret laughed. "One by one, we were carried out of the tunnel and loaded into a wooden cart. We were told to be quiet. We were told to play dead."

"How did you make it out of…?" Up until that moment, I hadn't realized that I did not know Margaret's country of origin.

"Romania," she replied. "We were in Romania. My sack had a few holes from which I could breathe through and also peek out. The cart was hauled by two young men, and our passage was paid in gold coins. Years later, when reliving the escape, it became obvious to me how our route had been carefully planned and our way paid from place to place. From Romania, we crossed into Yugoslavia. It was there when our rocky passage ended. The young men who had taken us all the way to Yugoslavia delivered us into the care of a priest. *Father*, the only name we ever called him, was a middle-aged man. He had a stern, pockmarked face and arms that were made to give warm hugs. He hid us in the basement of the church."

I pictured Margaret as the tiny girl from the picture hungry, cold, and frail. "I can't even start to imagine how scared you must've been."

"Not, really. It might sound ridiculous to you both, but it was the first time I felt safe since my parents were murdered." Margaret was becoming more assertive with every chapter of her story as she conveyed her transition from despair to hope. "There was a solid operation caring for us. Many men and women put their lives in danger to save those whom others had chosen to turn their backs on."

I heard the clatter of teacups on a tray and the cushioned footfalls of one of the kitchen maids bringing in mid-morning refreshments. I stood up and walked to the door to welcome the tray. It gave us all a chance to get up and move around the office for a short while. Margaret served tea in the cups, Daniel passed around a cheese and fruit platter the cook had prepared for us. I scribbled quickly in my notebook important facts of Margaret's accounts to flesh them out in detail later.

"I assume Yugoslavia to be a stopover, am I right? A change of hands to reach the next destination." Daniel was anxious to reach the core of the story.

Holding a few green grapes in her hand, Margaret picked up her story from where she left it. "The food at the church was the best yet. Twice a day, we were given soup or stews, freshly baked bread, and on more than one occasion, we had fruit pies. If we were to be smuggled out as regular children, we had to look the part. We were taken in by families after Sunday mass sometime after our arrival. That morning, we were given better clothes, hats, mittens. It was really cold. We were instructed to behave as if we belonged to our new parents." Margaret flexed her hand as if ready to reach for that hand that took her one step closer to freedom. "The couple that took me in brought me aboard a ship to Italy. Afterward we travelled by train all the way to France and then we crossed the water to England. I never saw any of the other kids who were at the church with me. I don't know what happened to them."

"I think you do know, Margaret." I was thinking about Lukas Blau and the name she read. "You said you read Lukas Blau's name. Where?"

"I always wondered why I was never given one," Margaret went on. "I had the doll and the new clothes. But I was never given a passport. But whoever Lukas Blau is or was, he got one. I read his name on one of the passports Franzisca kept hidden under the floorboards in one of the rooms of the house we stayed at. There was a passport for him and thirty-four others. But none for me."

"I closed my grip a bit tighter on her hand. "Where was that house, Margaret?"

She shook her head slightly, as if seeing something from afar, something remote, resurfacing from the folds of time. "I don't know," she whispered. "I never knew where we were, exactly. Somewhere in England, of course. I was moved shortly after the other children left."

Daniel stood protectively behind Margaret's chair.

"It was a boarding school, a place designed to shape the daughters of society, a school for well-bred ladies. My benefactor was anonymous, of course, but he or she must have cared for me a great deal because I never wanted for anything. After the war, my summers were filled with trips to different parts of the world, always accompanied by a tutor and my closest friends from school. My winters were all about studying, attending concerts, art exhibits. Everywhere I went, I always looked over my shoulder, to see if that person, my benefactor, was ever present. Perhaps watching me from a distance. I never dreamed of misbehaving, in case I would embarrass him." Margaret's hand touched my face softly and smiled. "I never dared say shit in public, my girl."

I placed my hand over hers. "Well, I'm glad you can do it now."

"Shit, indeed!" Margaret said, with a light chuckle. Of course, with her sophisticated accent, the word sounded regal. She inhaled deeply and stood up. With her emotions under control, she smoothed the nonexistent wrinkles on her immaculate skirt and walked firmly to the door. "Eventually, it didn't take a rocket scientist to figure out who my benefactor was." Margaret fixed me with a matter of fact stare.

Of course not. Margaret had been treated to the Claudia Lazar cosmopolitan education program. My mother went through it, I went through it, and so did Franzisca.

According to some of the bedtime stories Abuela told me, Franzisca and her mother lived in a one-room palace where she learned her letters, every rule of society, and most definitely, the art of storytelling.

Margaret nodded, putting that subject to rest. "Lunch will be served at twelve thirty. I expect you both to join me on time."

Before she reached the door I had one last question. "Margaret..."

She did not turn; she just paused for a brief moment.

"Yes," she said. "I remember all thirty-five names as if I still had those passports in front of me."

Chapter Twenty-Six

Bucharest, February 1941

*Y*ou *hold the other half of my heart.*

Even in sleep, Alex had felt every movement that Franzisca made. He refused to open his eyes when she left his side. First, she took away her sweet breath from the cocoon of his shoulder, a place she had rested her head for the last two weeks when sleep claimed her. He felt her slowly sliding out of his arms. Vertebrae, by vertebrae, peeling her body away from his, leaving him naked, cold, and alone. He had known she would leave even before she was aware of it. It was said out loud in her ongoing silence, in the way her eyes focused on the cavernous wall opposite them, or the way she responded to human interaction without engaging herself in it. Franzisca was a ghost with unfinished business, and Alex had been no more than a single step in the many steps she would take on her way to her goal. Was this his reason for not having stopped her from leaving him?

He tried to forget her from the moment she walked out of the cave. These were not the times to form sentimental bonds. She had come into his life when he needed to feel like a savior. He could not save Old Nicu from the explosion, and he had no knowledge of the fate of his mother and brother. But Franzisca had temporarily filled the emptiness caused by his inability to save those he loved. Alex had taken Franzisca into his arms, and she had molded herself into them as if her body was a part of his. They did not speak much during the two weeks they spent together. There was no need to. She needed him as much as he needed her. They found refuge in each other, but as he had come to learn during wartime, refuge is only temporary.

In the beginning, Alex had sought the tunnel as the only place to keep Franzisca safe. He had seen her standing mere steps from the rubble of the building that had crushed her mother to death. He had gotten to her in time, before she could throw herself into the hungry flames, which did not forgive anyone who dared to trespass into their territory. Not even for love.

After the explosion, came the riots, and three days later when the fighting on the streets ceased, all there was left was uncertainty. He did not need to hide. Alex was not for one faction or the other. Though a Jew at heart, he was unmarked by the covenant between Abraham and God. For his ignorant father, circumcision would have diminished his sons' manhood. In his father's mind, a man with a clipped shaft was no man at all.

Alex's identification papers allowed him to move freely through the streets and learn the state of affairs around the city. Some of the people, who had hidden underground, were Jews, others were homeless as a result of the explosion, but most of them decided to go underground out of fear.

During their two weeks in the tunnels, he had become the leader of the pack, not by unanimous vote, but by his innate capability to smell danger, a trait he had developed to avoid as many beatings as he could at the hands of his abusive father. Through his keen eye and ability to engage others in conversation he found out that Jews were no longer the main target of attacks down the streets of Bucharest; still it was wise to remain unnoticed. In groups of two and three, the close community of refugees that had been forcibly created when all hell broke loose, eventually dissipated until there was nobody left for Alex to protect.

Every passing day the void left by Franzisca increased his need for her, which could only be satiated with her physical presence. He quickly erased that thought from his mind. Franzisca was unattainable. Even though they had both experienced loss and had met in a moment of grief and desperation, Franzisca belonged to another class. She had been the daughter of a cook, but there was elegance in her gestures, culture in her speech, intelligence in her eyes. Alex had been graced with a quick mind and a quick mouth. His mother had taught him the basics to becoming a gentleman, yet the brutish nature of the man who fathered him ran through his blood. He feared that in time he would become the man his father was. It was evident in the size of his body, the breadth of his back, the weight of his hands. No, he thought, Franzisca was a woman to be cherished. The memory of the miserable life his mother endured by his father's side was enough for Alex to force himself to forget Franzisca. He closed his fingers into fists swearing never to touch her again with hands, which might betray him and hurt her.

Determined, he rose to his feet ready to start a new chapter in his life. It was the weight of the key that now dangled next to his heart what undid his resolve. Alex closed his fist around it and prayed for strength for he had to let her go. *"You hold the other half of my heart."* Franzisca's parting words echoed in his head.

Alex tried to absorb the essence of her in that old key. He pictured its twin resting next to Franzisca's heart. Alex smiled, and for a moment he allowed himself to fantasize about a future with her.

With only the clothes on his back, without prospects, and a part of Franzisca to remember her by, Alex left the tunnels. As a consequence of the explosion of the building where he lived with Old Nicu, he was now homeless. The only place he could go back to and call home was the bakery.

When he arrived at the storefront, he was not surprised to find it in ruins. The revolt incited by the Legionaries had unleashed a mob of looters bent on destroying Bucharest. Their orders were to raze everything in their path, and as a reward, they could fill their pockets with as much loot as they could carry, after the Iron Guard had taken theirs, of course.

Alex picked up the battered bakery sign he had painted a few months after Old Nicu took him in and wiped it with his hands. *Nicu and Son Bakery Shop,* the sign read. It had taken many attempts to convince the seasoned baker that a sign displaying the nature of his business could increase walk-in clientele.

"But everybody knows me," Old Nicu claimed.

"No, not everybody," Alex answered over and over again. Then he would take Old Nicu to the sidewalk to show him the growing number of German soldiers riding on supply trucks, or in the back of luxury sedans.

"Fine," he said, one morning while slurping his usual scalding tea. He popped a sugar cube in his mouth and slurped some more of the steaming concoction reveling in the simple pleasure of melted sugar. "We will have a sign." Nicu held his arms high and wide, envisioning the lettering hanging above the entrance of the store. "Nicu and Son Bakery Shop," he said, popping another sugar cube in his mouth and smiling merrily. His eyes shone, watery from emotion and the heat emanating from the teacup.

Alex stood motionless. His hands, which had been busy with stacking the different size baking sheets, gripped the edges of the stack he held to the point of pain. He wanted to feel pain to drive away the emotion brewing inside of him. He could deal with pain, he could deal with beatings. He could not deal with kindness. Not from a man proud to call him son.

Nicu had studied him closely. "It is all right, *baiatu meu.*" The old man had stood up from his chair, walked to

Alex and wrapped his arms around him. Alex's grip on the trays weakened and they crashed to the floor. Alex started, but the old man tightened his embrace. "It is all right," he repeated. "It's all right."

Now, with Old Nicu gone, and with only devastation to greet him, he hugged the sign to his chest and wondered if it would ever be all right again.

He stepped into the store. His boots crunched over shattered glass and dirt. The looters had smashed the window of the storefront and by the looks of the many empty flour sacks scattered on the floor, they had done away with the inventory, too.

Alex picked up a couple of empty flour sacks to use as sleeping mats. He cleared some glass from the counter and made his way to the back of the store with the hopes of finding some wood planks and tools to cover the bare window and broken doorway.

When he stepped into the darkened backroom, he was met by a fist to his jaw, followed immediately by another punch to his gut. He fell down on all fours and sucked in a ragged breath before a boot winded him with a forceful kick.

Alex tasted blood in his mouth and bile rose in his throat. He could not afford to be sick, unless he wanted to die. His hard-earned survival skills kicked in. In a heartbeat, he was on his feet. He reached for the attacker's neck and closed his hands around it bent on crushing his windpipe. Strong arms pulled him back, yet he kept his vice grip on the whimpering man.

The hold on his arms slackened, Alex stumbled forward throwing punches into the dark, empty space. He knew they were close, he could hear them, smell them.

A gas lamp flared up lightning up the dark space. He blinked twice before he could focus on the faces in front of him. Three young men, no older than him, thin, ragged, and beneath their armor of fake bravado, scared.

Alex knew their faces. He had seen them lurking around the bakery and the apartment building weeks before the explosion. Old Nicu had taken pity on them and had fed them bread and tea on a couple of occasions.

Alex took a step forward, he was more angry than hurt and the three young men sensed it. They scuttled backward.

"How long have you been here?" His voice boomed across the dimly lit room.

One of them took a small step forward he looked down to the top of his worn boots. "We thought... we didn't know you'd be back. After the explosion..." Alex could hear a hint of apology in his tone.

"I'm back and I don't need rats like you creeping around my store. Out!" As soon as the words left his mouth, Alex knew he did not mean them.

The three young men froze. They had nowhere to go and starved as they were they did not have the strength to take another step.

"You don't have papers." Their silence was all the answer Alex needed. "Family?" Silence again.

Alex nodded. He walked toward the single gas lamp spilling light into the room, took it, and looked around. He needed to think and assess the damage around in the backroom. The three young men stood silently rooted to the floor. Alex saw one of them sway, but was quickly steadied by the other two.

"We didn't steal anything. We're not like that. We liked the old baker, your father," the same young man spoke again.

Those words were Alex's undoing. He believed them. No one who had ever crossed paths with Old Nicu would have harmed him or his property. Anguish gripped his chest at yet another loss in his life.

Alex had lovingly taken care of the old man. Nicu had grown disoriented and lethargic in the weeks preceding the explosion. He had taken to rambling about his adventures during the times of the first big war. He talked of gold, lots of gold smuggled out of Romania into Russia. "We were young and reckless," Old Nicu would recount in moments of clarity. "The gold was never intended to make its way back to Romania. We knew it was never to be seen again."

Nicu had been a soldier of the Romanian Army during King Ferdinand's reign. He was a proud Romanian and loved to talk of the time he served under the King. He had lived through the fall of the Austro-Hungarian Empire, the demise of the Turkish power and Romania's territorial gain of Transylvania, Bessarabia, and small portions of upper Bulgaria. "But those were short-lived victories," he recounted. "The German army gathered its forces and resisted the cross of the Romanian army. It was the Russian Tsar the one who supported our army," he would often say. "For that, we paid a price."

When the German advance into Romania became imminent, King Ferdinand and his government abandoned Bucharest for the North, and as a safety measure, Romanian gold bonds were transferred into Russia. "Most of it," Old Nicu would say cryptically.

"What do you mean, Old Nicu? What happened to the portion of gold that did not make it to Russia, did you keep some of it?" The conversations were usually carried before Old Nicu fell asleep when their room was enveloped by darkness.

"Whatever I have is yours, *baiatu meu*, you're my boy, my son."

The conversations would always end with those words. He would have loved to grow up as Nicu's son. He loved the old man and the old man loved him back unconditionally. He was grateful for the time they had spent together. But loving memories were painful reminders of his loss, so for the second time on that day Alex decided to bury the past.

Three weak, hungry young men stood staring at him and once again, he realized he had become the unnamed leader of a pack of strays. "Food. What we all need is food." They nodded and stood expectant at the promise of sustenance.

"Don't move from your spots," Alex growled as he moved away with the gas lamp in his hands.

Alex walked to the very back of the bakery where the two stone ovens he had once shoved hundreds of bread loaves into stood. Opposite to the ovens—a niche, an aborted third oven, served as the storage for the bakery's tools and baking sheets. Alex set the lamp on the floor. All the tools and trays had been stolen. He cursed under his breath. He had held hopes of resuming business with whatever supplies he could get his hands on. He would worry about that in the morning. His stomach clenched painfully reminding him of priorities.

Alex scanned his surroundings for a sharp object. Next to the wall lay a metal bar. He reached for it, and slowly, careful not to make any loud sounds he worked on a bottom brick. After a few minutes, the brick gave way.

Alex had never gained access to Nicu's secret cache. It had been his private space, one he took pride in. Even with a feeble mind, the old man took care of their emergency food supply. "War might not kill you, but hunger will," were the words Nicu said every time he disappeared into the back to hide the few cans he had secured for their secret stash.

The light of the lamp illuminated the rims of food cans. Alex slipped his hand through the narrow opening and grabbed two cans of beans and two cans of sardines. Food would be scarce until he could figure out a plan. Before he replaced the brick to seal the food storage, Alex brought the lamp closer to the opening to get a better idea of the supplies he would have to rely on until he could find a way of bartering work for food.

The lamp showed him a deeper space than he had imagined. There were cans of beans, sardines, jars of fruit preserve, cans of ravioli Nicu had bought from some Italian soldiers, and some canned meats he had gotten his hands on. A wave of peace fell over Alex and he mouthed a heartfelt thanks to Old Nicu. For the time being he had four mouths to feed, and by the looks of his new dependents, they would not be much help outside of the bakery's walls. Papers, Alex thought. He had to get these boys papers. With one last look at his supplies, he planned on taking care of that in the morning, before, after or during his job search.

Alex tilted his head to the side to get a better view of the contents of the secret niche when he saw a bundle covered with a flour sack. His hopes rose. If he could only bake some bread. The war was in full steam now and the shortage of food demanded anything resembling fresh and out of the oven. He slid his arm through the opening until his shoulder met the edge of the wall. The sack was just beyond his grasp. His arm would not magically stretch so he grabbed the metal bar he had used before and tried his luck again. After much swearing and sweating, the tip of the metal bar snagged the canvas of the flour sack. He pulled it once, and then again. Little by little he brought the sack toward him. The load was heavy. As drained and battered as he was, he could not afford to let flour go unused, it was a precious commodity.

He had other people depending on him now and he vowed to outlive this stupid war. He pulled one last time. The sack was within the reach of his hand. He placed the bar carefully on the floor and grabbed the top of the sack. It was tied with a thin rope. With his fingers, he felt where it wound itself around the mouth of the sack and the sailor's knot that tied it.

He had seen Old Nicu tie all the flower sacks in the same manner. He summoned patience, and searched his memory for the method in which Old Nicu had done the knots. Within minutes, the mouth of the sack was loose. Alex sighed. He reached into the sack. He needed to feel the result of his efforts sifting between his fingers. But nothing flowed in between his fingers. Instead, his hand met hard, cold metal, shaped like bars of soap. He closed his hand around one and brought the object out to the light.

Nicu's ramblings about the missing gold slammed into his brain. Alex held in his hand the glowing truth that not all of it had made it to Russia.

Chapter Twenty-Seven

For nearly two decades, he had been the anonymous man behind the wheel, the one to throw a lethal punch to anybody who dared threaten his master. He was the keeper of secrets. His actions were dictated by his master's irrational temper, by the flicker of his cold eyes and by the mood he sensed in a room.

Lucien Marcus cracked his knuckles, studied his face in the rusted mirror nailed to the wall of the rented rat's nest he now called home and considered his next move carefully. Six months ago, he was reminded of his station in life. He was a servant, dispensable, a nobody.

For two decades, he had worked as Baron Lupescu's chauffer. He was royalty among the servants at the Lupescu's mansion. He was the baron's man. Other men feared him, respected him. He was the wall between Baron Lupescu and the rest of the world. He was his confidant, his lapdog; he was the baron's dirty hand.

He had condoned Lupescu's sadistic personality, his petulance, his relentless tendency to remind Lucien who was master and who was servant. Lucien saw no wrong in Lupescu. He idolized his employer. In his mind, the baron was the future of his country. He rejoiced in Lupescu's message of national pride and would have followed him to the trenches of death. He almost did.

After the Legionaries thwarted uprising, those who had led riots throughout the streets of Bucharest or had a hand in the making of the revolution, were snatched in the middle of night by Antonescu's forces. If not shot in the process of escaping, the detainees were taken to prison to be thoroughly interrogated. Out of those torturous procedures more names were produced. As Lupescu's man, it wouldn't be long before Lucien would follow that fate. He had a family to protect. He could not afford to die.

Lucien braved the danger on the streets, knowing he could be killed, and ran home to collect his family to flee Bucharest before it would be too late. During his time with Lupescu, Lucien was able to put aside a bit of money every year. He dreamt of moving out of the congested city to a small dairy farm. He wanted that freedom for his children. Lucien wanted to live a simple life. Leaving Bucharest would be a good thing, he thought. Even if his wife hated rural life, he hoped she would grow to love it.

Lucien's plans for the future went up in smoke when his wife stood with her arms crossed at their front door and denied him entrance. She wouldn't listen to his frantic plea and laughed in his face for the hundredth time at the mention of the dairy farm. She pushed him toward the direction of the stairs and would not let him say goodbye to their five-year-old twins or to collect a few items of clothing. She declared him a coward, an imbecile for not turning his coat in time to save his family before disgrace fell upon them. She looked at him with disgust and refused to lie for him, hide him, or run away with him.

Lucien was stunned, shriveling with every word out of her mouth. He was known to be violent; however, he could never bring himself to raise a hand to his wife. Home represented a safe haven from the beast he had become. It was the only place he felt human. Before she slammed the door of their apartment in his face, Lucien swore to come back for her and their children. The baron valued him, he whispered, his forehead pressed firmly against the closed door. The baron would reward him for his relentless loyalty, he promised through the interminable wood plank that kept him from what was his. The baron would take his family to safety.

Two days after the revolution was extinguished, Lucien risked coming out of his hiding place to plead his case in front of the baron. He crept into the palace smelling like the rat he felt like and for the first time in his life, his body betrayed him with fear. Before Lucien's words left his mouth, Baron Lupescu stared him down and struck him across the face; cutting his cheek with the ruby ring he wore on his right pinky finger. The chauffer stood stunned for a moment, the recipient of unjustified punishment not for the first time.

Mihail Lupescu was prone to bouts of aggression. Physical abuse was his addiction. His body would tremble akin to a sexual climax when administering pain. However, this time, Lupescu did not seem satisfied with the first drawing of blood or with the subsequent kicks his booted foot delivered repeatedly over the body of Lucien. Amid his groans of pain, he heard the baron speak words slurred with tears and drink.

"Anna. Anna." Her name hung in the air. Lupescu's crazed eyes scanned the empty space for an answer.

"It was too late." Lucien wanted to explain Baron Lupescu what happened. He had followed his orders, but by the time he had gotten to the building…

The baron was deaf with rage. A kick in the ribs took the last of Lucien's breath.

"Useless piece of shit! You failed me. You were to bring her to me. You were to keep her safe. For me!" Lupescu spat on Lucien and flogged him nearly senseless with the horsewhip he often beat Anna with.

Followed by the demented baron, Lucien crawled out of Lupescu's study and made his escape on all fours into the streets like the dog he was.

It took Lucien several weeks to recover from the beating. Every time he drew in a breath, the sharp pain piercing in his chest reminded him of the humiliation he suffered at the hands of Lupescu. Layered with grime and stripped of everything he thought he had, he saw the world through a different lens. At one time or another we all become targets, he thought. He was one now.

Lucien became a lurker in the shadows. He followed Lupescu's every move up until his transfer to the north. He knew he was still a hunted man, but his determination to bring Lupescu down to his knees, break him and make him beg for his life was stronger than his fear of death. The life of an outcast was far from lonely. Several of the men he had met when in the service of Lupescu had suffered his same fate. The men gathered, talked of their banishment from the outside world. Some of them continued to stick fervently to their former cause and continued to plot against the current government.

In Lucien's mind, the love he felt for his country and the admiration he once had for Lupescu, were no more than bitter life lessons. Jews, Nazis, Russians, there were no safe sides to take other than his own. He knew that the time would come when he would crush Lupescu with his bare hands. But he needed more than hatred to get to him. Lupescu thrived on two obsessions, the Jewess Anna and power. His whore was of no use to him now, she was dead. He had seen the building blow up before his eyes when he drove there to drag her back to Lupescu's bed. The only thing he had left to manipulate Lupescu with was power.

His prayers were answered in the form of a young woman he saw walking the streets. He had heard of her subtle inquiries.

Never in a million years had he entertained the Jewess's bastard as a possibility. But then again, she was not any bastard. She was a Schultz.

***

Months passed since Franzisca's return to the Lupescu estate. The usual bustle of household staff was reduced to a minimum as a result of Lupescu's absence. No one questioned Franzisca's stay at the palace. She became just another speck of dust floating through the inactivity of the house.

The two housemaids and the groundskeeper still under Lupescu's employ had watched Franzisca grow up. The child, as they referred to her, needed to eat and have a roof over her head. It was the least they could do for Anna's daughter. It was their way of defying the master they so deeply loathed.

During the daytime, Franzisca kept busy with whatever duties were assigned her: The over-polishing of untouched silver spoons, the airing and dusting of unused rooms, the raking of leaves off the empty manicured gardens. Her moves were paced; her eyes always focused on the object she worked on, her mouth never uttered a word. Days of silence filled her shattered mind. During her sleepless nights, her mind struggled with reality.

She was seventeen years old and alone. Even though life had dealt her a difficult hand, up until her mother's death, she had lived inside of a crystal castle, the creation of her mother's love.

Within their one room kingdom, Franzisca had received the education fit for a monarch. Her mother taught her to read and write in five languages. She had instructed her in fine arts. Franzisca could name famous classical composers after hearing the first sounds of a piece and she could waltz as though she had lived a life of parties. Franzisca was a princess among paupers.

"Time to step out of the castle," Franzisca said to herself, while she looked out of the dining room windows. She suspected a motive behind her mother's relentless efforts in the making of the young woman Franzisca had become thus far. It wasn't for the pleasure of having an educated daughter; Franzisca was meant to reclaim what was hers by right. Did her mother ever pause to think if that was what she wanted?

It did not matter what Franzisca wanted anymore. Guilt would always remind her of the many deaths her silence had caused. She should have died that day with her mother or on the streets like so many others.

Death. She did not fear death. At times she considered it the only solution to relieve the burden she carried.

Every once in a while, when she did not contemplate the advantages of death, Franzisca would trace the contours of the key she carried over her chest and allowed a smile to come to her lips. No, she was certain it wasn't death what she feared. After all they were at war and death was bound to strike without a moment's notice. What she feared the most was to die without having experienced love.

Death. Love. She now understood the unearthly detachment with which her mother endured the physical pain Lupescu had inflicted on her. She had lived her love story and bore a child, as a testament of that love. When at Lupescu's mercy, Anna retreated to that part of herself which was hers and hers alone, a place where Lupescu could never reach with the force of his fist or the sting of his whip. Love had been Anna's safe haven. Love had been Anna's armor.

Death. Love. Duty. Never mind death and love, Franzisca had a duty to fulfill and it would not happen with her staying behind closed doors. From that day forth, Franzisca announced to Marietta, the head maid, she would go to the city for provisions.

Unlike her previous food shopping experiences, Franzisca surveyed the city with eyes of a strategist. It was a battle that she had ahead of her and information and allies were needed. Franzisca learned that the long lines at the doors of food vendors provided a person with the latest updates on the war. Throughout the length of a line, rumors contradicted themselves several times. Rumors came from two types of sources: From those who reveled in delivering false hope or from those intent on spreading paralyzing fear. Putting together the real information was like putting together a puzzle. Franzisca did not mind it. In a way it kept her mind working, decoding the truth behind the many versions of the same story.

It was on the streets where Franzisca heard of the latest advance of Nazi boots into Russia, their victory over Stalin's forces and the news of more deaths.

Word of a pogrom in Iasi, an ethnic cleansing in the north of the country, made its way to Bucharest. Fearful, the Jewish population went back into hiding. There was no way to know how far the arms of the murderous campaign would reach this time. For the first time in many months, the ominous rumors held true. According to the fortunate few who had escaped, the pogrom in Iasi had taken over thirteen thousand Jewish lives. Men, women, and children were shot in the streets by local police or in the courtyards of the police headquarters right after being arrested. Thousands more were packed into freight cars and deported to labor camps in Calarasi and Podull Lloaei—towns located south of Iasi. Merchants that had travelled from the north told of the horror they witnessed and heard. Those transported into the labor camps never made it there alive, dead bodies strewn along the roads attested for that. It wasn't long before Franzisca learned the name of one of the leaders of the campaign; Baron Mihail Lupescu.

Rage flowed through her body and as she stood in line to buy her ration of flour. Death came back to occupy her mind. This time death did not claim her name, it claimed Lupescu's.

She wished nothing more than to stab him in his heart with a knife and see him bleed out slowly. Of course, that was just a fantasy. Lupescu was far from Bucharest and she would be killed before she could confront him, with or without a knife. She forced herself to think beyond bodily harm. The answer lay tucked in her bodice and stashed in Lupescu's safe. But to put that plan in motion she needed help.

It was no secret that the socially awkward Lupescu had used his money and his early rise to power within the Iron Guard to snub peers and sell political positions to the highest bidder. It was also common knowledge that immediately after the failed revolution; Lupescu vomited, without remorse, every name he knew that had plotted against Antonescu. Hundreds of men who served under Lupescu were now sitting in Romanian jails charged with treason. Others ran away. And a significant number of resentful Legionaries were lying low but still free.

Franzisca became an expert eavesdropper. She learned the places where the resentful, defeated rebels met and through their hushed conversation, she knew when the time came, she would be able to gather enough men eager to drive Lupescu to his ruin.

The dislike for Lupescu charged her with further courage to make inquiries. She carried a mental list of the officials that had met with Lupescu before the uprising, and she attempted to trace the whereabouts of those who had fallen out of grace with the Romanian government. Franzisca's subtle questioning was met with deep shrugs and blank faces. The men she sought had either disappeared in jail, or had struck deals with Antonescu in exchange for their life and the keeping of their social and financial positions.

Every day Franzisca learned a new lesson on the streets, different from the instruction she had received from her mother. Franzisca opened her eyes to the way the world was managed. Money talked, power talked. After weeks of wandering the streets without any results, Franzisca learned another lesson and reached a cold hard decision. She needed a man by her side, a powerful man.

When Franzisca went back to the house that afternoon she felt the air inside the residence suffocating. As she slid open each one of the heavy, crimson brocade drapes and pushed the long windows open, she felt like screaming in frustration. How was she to fulfill her duty? Hadn't her mother thought about that before entrusting her with the document she carried tucked in her bodice? Her attempts to find a former associate of Lupescu angry enough to help her had failed. There was nothing else for her to do in that house. She hated its smell, she hated its gloom, she hated its memories.

Marietta and the other housemaid residing in the palace had left for the weekend. Franzisca was left in charge of the house and she had promised Marietta that she would stay within the perimeter of the estate until their return on Monday morning.

After a simple meal of bread and tea in the kitchen, she retired to her room in the servants' quarters. She did not bother to undress, or to get under the covers. Franzisca lay on the bed, with the light off and her eyes open and stared into the darkness. She felt drained, hopeless. Her hand went instinctively to her chest and rested upon the key that hung around her neck. Alex. She thought of him and of her rash decision to leave him. She wanted to feel him close, breathe the same air he did. She wanted to rest her head on Alex's shoulder and sleep within his keep, safe. Alex…

Unable to stand the emptiness of the room and the loneliness of her life, she bolted from the bed and lit the gas lamp she kept on the tiny wooden table next to her bed. Even though he was not the powerful man she needed to accomplish her goal, she had claimed him as hers and that was enough. Her body trembled with the urge to leave the house, to seek out Alex.

Franzisca stuffed her only two articles of clothing and the wooden box Anna left for her into a cloth sack. Holding the gas lamp in her hand, she made her way out of the servant's quarters and into the main house. The night had cooled down and wind tore through the opened windows. The scent of imminent rain flowed through the house and the heavy drapes lashed upon the ghostly covered furniture, an omen of a powerful storm. Franzisca ran toward Lupescu's study. Before pushing the door open, a fierce wind blew her light out, she heard a glass object crash to the floor somewhere to her right.

Franzisca shivered with cold and fear. The wind lashed, lightning struck. She could not stop thinking of the storm as Lupescu's fury for what she was about to do.

Franzisca opened the door of the dark room. The scent of pine and cognac assailed her nostrils and she gagged disgusted with the smell, Lupescu's smell. For a moment, she feared that somehow he had come back and had slipped unnoticed into the house.

A strike of lightning illuminated the room briefly and Franzisca saw that it was empty. Without a second thought, she walked directly to the safe. She knew the code by heart and could open the vault with her eyes closed. Less than a minute later, she slipped her hands in and emptied the contents of the safe. The property titles belonging to her family, the stash of bills, gold coins and the thirty-five blank passports. Touching every object and piece of paper before retrieving it from the safe, she took a quick account of the contents before shoving them into her sack. Anxious to leave, she locked the safe behind her and hurried to the door.

She heard a flint spark, the she saw the quivering shadow projected by the light of the short-lived fire.

"In hurry, *donmisiara* Schultz?"

She did not need turn to know the face behind that voice. His sudden presence startled her. She had thought he had gone to the north, soldiering in a murderous campaign.

She looked over her shoulder, and stared at the man behind the cloud of white cigarette smoke. He had changed somehow.

Franzisca laid her sack on the floor, squared her shoulders and feigning bravery she did not feel, she faced the man hiding in the darkness.

Chapter Twenty-Eight

Solvang, April 2013

Of the thirty-five names Margaret had committed to memory, twenty-two had died within the past three decades, six did not exist, more than likely they lived or had lived under their original identity, four lay in hospice with acute Alzheimer's, leaving us with only one coherent survivor, Lukas Blau.

Throughout our search for what we knew now as the *Treizeci si cinci mic ofiteri*, The Thirty-Five Little Officers, we gathered bits and pieces of a story that had never made it into the history books. Thirty-five children had made it out of Nazi Europe and immigrated into Argentina under passports given only to Nazi war criminals that escaped from Hitler's downfall.

We were lucky to get some of the family members of the *Thirty-Five* on the phone. Their parents or grandparents, in some cases, had told them of their narrow escape from Europe. Some of the descendants speaking on behalf of the saved children referred to the savior as an anonymous Russian aristocrat, or a French baroness, others claimed. Regardless of the title, they always talked of a woman. The most spiritual of them called her a faceless *Moses* able to part the seas and lead an exodus of orphaned Jewish children to safety. Others went as far as calling her a modern day Queen Esther, a Jew in disguise willing to risk her life to save her people. No one knew the real face of that woman except for me.

It had been Franzisca, my abuela, wearing one of her many coats. The story of the thirty-five young officers was one more bedtime story she had once told me. An army of thirty-five little soldiers had walked through water, stepping on the back of grey whales, as they wiggled their bottoms and stuck their tongues out at the frustrated ogres. Ogres that were snapped up by the unforgiving jaws of hungry sharks that set out to chase them.

"Did Franzisca lead the army, Abuela?" I had asked her at the time.

She had smiled absently as if looking back into the story, trying to find the right words for a six-year-old girl. "She couldn't. She stayed behind. She talked to the whales and the sharks, and together with the bravest of the soldiers she had ever come across, they took on the mission to get every little officer across the ocean safely."

"So were the children alone? When they reached the other side of the ocean, when they stepped on the shore, was there anybody to give them pie?" My voice had caught a little at the thought of crossing the ocean without Abuela to hold my hand. I had felt terrified at the notion of waking up one morning without the familiar scent of baked pie and fragrant coffee wafting through the soft glowing corridors of the finca in Mendoza.

"Do you think Franzisca would have left those children alone? Do you think she could have left them without pie and fresh milk for their breakfast?"

For once, she was giving me a hint of how the story might have ended and I took the chance.

"No. You always say that Franzisca was happy when she made other people happy." I said, desperately trying to read some confirmation on Abuela's face.

She nodded and I smiled. My worries dissipated when I imagined Franzisca taking care of the children the way Abuela took care of me.

"When the children set foot on land, a large bird, an eagle," she resumed her story, "led them to a welcome party waiting for them in the heart of the forest. Behind the thicket of trees where the sun speckles the earth with golden dust, the children found chocolate pies, baskets of fruit, and piles of sugar cane, spread all over the green shrubs and wildflowers touched by the colors of the rainbow. As the little soldiers took their places around the banquet, crickets jumped on the lower branches of trees, fined tuned their wings and antennae and performed a light and music show. And before the children got thirsty, cows from nearby towns, marched into the party, to offer warm and creamy milk to the brave little warriors."

As exciting as the reception sounded, I still worried about the children. Abuela noticed my frown and lifted her eyebrows.

"When the party was over, when it was time to go home..." I hesitated.

"When the party was over every little soldier bore cheeks as red as the berries they had eaten, noses as brown as the chocolate in the pies, and milk mustaches over their drunken smiles. The food had filled their bellies and their bodies were ready for rest. They all yawned taking turns; in the way soldiers do, and in that precise moment as if the silent sound of the yawns had worked as a bell, parents and grandparents, with lots of love in their hearts but with no children of their own to give it to, walked into the celebration."

"The moms, dads, grandfathers, and grandmothers stretched their arms out to the exhausted children taking home with them as many as they could gather within the breadth of their arms. Adults and children became family from the moment of their first embrace and all the bad memories of ogres and battles were erased from the children's minds when they got their first good night kiss. That marked the beginning of their new life."

Then Abuela kissed the spot between my brows, which was still furrowed with questions.

"What is it, Sofia?"

"You said Franzisca couldn't lead the little soldiers across the ocean." Abuela nodded. "You said a very brave soldier did." She nodded again, there was caution in her eyes. "Who was that person?"

"Somebody she trusted with all her heart." She kissed me again and tucked the covers around my shoulders. "One day," she said, as if anticipating my next question, "you'll get to see the rest of the story with your own eyes."

I kept this information to myself, knowing that it contained more truth than fiction. I wrote it down in my little book of stories which was gradually growing thick with pieces of the puzzle and tucked it back safely in Franzisca's box.

The filmmaker in me wanted to jump at the story and shock the world's decaying long-term memory with yet another graphic documentary about the Second World War. But I was not on this quest as a filmmaker. Abuela was not a subject I was investigating or wished to expose to the world. My decision to not share my knowledge of where the story was going, at least not yet, was because I wanted to be the first one to get to know the young woman that was hidden under bedtime stories of her own creation. She dedicated those stories to me in the language reserved for children, with tales of larger than life heroes and supernatural creatures more often silly than malevolent. It was always just the two of us when she lay on my bed, head tilted toward mine, legs crossed at the ankles, the words flowing from her mouth painting a picture of bravery. The magic was created in my bedroom, the only place Franzisca felt safe to reveal her secrets. Those stories belonged to us, Franzisca, Abuela, and me. The truth was yet to be discovered.

After my morning shower, I joined Daniel and Margaret at the kitchen table for a quick breakfast. My heart still skipped a beat every time I laid eyes on him. Two weeks had passed since the first time we met. We spent every waking and sleeping moment together and his presence in my life felt as natural as breathing. This way of relating to a man was new to me. Before him, I had my share of casual affairs, which had never lasted more than a full month. I had blamed it on my work, on the guys I dated; I had even held the weather responsible on one occasion. "Blame it on the annoyingly perfect temperatures we have in Southern California," I once told a guy on our third week together after he brought up the words *couple* and *exclusive* all in one sentence, "it makes it easy for a person to want to sleep alone."

With Daniel, it was different. I did not have to explain myself to him. He knew of my limitations, because he suffered the same emotional ailments. We experimented with our mutual boundaries and allowed each other to delve into paths where no one else had had gone before. We talked of our childhood, without finishing sentences. It was in our silences where the scars were visible. We approached our emotions with caution, until words could no longer placate our urgent need to possess each other fully.

My logical mind and natural skepticism rejected the possibility of love. I was convinced that once Daniel and I had accomplished our mission into the past, we would go our separate ways. After all, if the latest studies in behavioral epigenetics were correct, we were both suffering the effects of the traumatic experiences suffered by our ancestors. I tried to convince Margaret of this a week after he became part of our household, when she had attempted to broach the subject about my obviously more than casual involvement with Daniel.

"Here," I said, pointing to an article I had saved under favorites in my computer. "Traumatic experiences in our past, or in our recent ancestors' past, leave molecular scars that adhere to our DNA. You see? It's not my doing but what's contained in my genetic memory."

Margaret nodded, but kept silent. She knew not to interject when I was in the middle of elaborating on a theory.

"If Abuela was in fact the woman Daniel's grandfather loved, it's only natural for us to feel an attraction. But history shows that they were never meant to be. So there, that's how we will end up, too." The conclusion of my theory brought me unexpected pain. I wasn't ready to admit that I wanted Daniel in my life beyond the thirty-day mark.

Margaret listened to each one of my words and did not utter a sound until she was assured I was finished with my theory. She walked to me and reached for my hands in that way of hers when she meant to be heard. "If your DNA theory is right, my girl, you'll love Daniel till the end of your days and you'll carry with you a broken heart."

The matter of Daniel and my feelings toward him had to be put on the back burner before Lukas Blau could suddenly die of old age or a heart attack, taking his despicable secrets to the grave. Blau was not surprised when I called him on the phone or when I demanded an explanation for his horrid accusations.

"I will tell you everything you want to know," he replied calmly, a faint foreign lilt coloring his perfect Castilian Spanish. The line went silent for a prolonged time and I thought we had been disconnected.

"*Señor* Blau, *hola!*" My tone sounding impatient even to me.

His voice came back to the line with that unnerving calm he had displayed on our first communication. "Tea," he said, "tomorrow at five. I assume you already know my address." Without further words, the line went dead.

I looked at the phone in my hand. "The man is impossible." I turned to Daniel who was watching me with curiosity from Abuela's desk.

Daniel rose from the chair, walked to me and took the phone from my hand, and placed it back on its charger.

"Let me guess," he said. "He wants to run the show on his terms and on his turf."

"Tomorrow at five," I moaned, "for tea."

Margaret worked her magic and thirty minutes after my conversation with Blau we were on the way to the airport. Tickets were waiting for us at the gate and fourteen hours later, Daniel and I were back on Argentinean soil.

A car blasted us through the busy streets of Buenos Aires toward Blau's residence in Palermo. The vibe beyond the car's window was contagious. I had the urge to open the door and join in the colorful disorder of one of the most beautiful capital cities in the world. My familiarity with the city, the way people walked and talked on the streets, the dance with death of those who crossed the streets challenging bus drivers and their infernal smoke spitting machines, remained intact in my memory. The vagrant dogs, the sweet smell of peanut pralines sold on street corners. After twenty years of absence, none of that had been washed from my veins and my body itched to become part of the crowd.

Daniel eyed me with understanding. "It never goes away." He slid closer to me. "It's a strange feeling, Sofia. We belong to this place in so many ways and in so many others we have become foreigners."

The car came to a stop at a corner at the entrance of a giant tower of glass and steel, a contemporary statement for high-rise living. According to my notes, Blau lived on the top floor. The guard in the bottom foyer checked our identifications before admitting us. He directed us to an elevator that was for the exclusive use of the residents of the top three floors.

The elevator ride to Blau's apartment was smooth and quick giving me little time to adjust my mind to the meeting ahead. Less than twenty-four hours ago, the man had ordered me to tea at his house at five o'clock the next day as if the six-thousand one hundred miles between me and his teatime were irrelevant.

The elevator reached a silent stop and I felt Daniel's hand cover mine. His gesture was unexpected. Even though Daniel had sat next to me on the plane and in the car, I thought this meeting as one I had to face on my own. The knowledge of Daniel standing by my side, holding my hand, gave me the strength I needed to walk to Blau's front door.

The man who greeted us at the door was far from the nonagenarian I expected to meet. He was tall, of a strong build and was the bearer of a full set of dark hair streaked with silver. He looked slightly taken aback when he noticed I wasn't alone, but he covered his surprise with his booming voice.

"You made it on time." He checked an antique wall clock behind him very similar to the one Abuela bought in Switzerland. "Tea will be served in the greenhouse."

Blau led the way through his spacious and bright apartment. The flat was lined with large windows overlooking the *Rio De La Plata*; the floors were made of white marble. Mirrors were strategically placed to enhance the illusion of endless space; ivies crawled around metal columns like venomous spiders ready to bite.

A large patio at the end of his residence had been turned into a greenhouse. The temperature inside was warm and humid, thick green vegetation and the exotic presence of tiny colorful birds flying from one end to the other added to the tropical atmosphere of the tearoom. The greenhouse resembled a small piece of the rainforest. A glass door divided the homemade rainforest from a sitting area set with wicker lounge chairs. A small bookcase held books on birds, flowers, and all things green, and in the middle of the room, a round glass table was impeccably set with food and refreshments.

"I spent many years in Costa Rica and Brazil doing business." He took what I assumed to be his spot at the table and gestured for us to take a seat.

It wasn't the type of tea I expected. The table had the look of paradise itself. Tropical fruit was served on platters, bowls of nuts and dry figs were scattered over the table. There were two cutting boards with a variety of cheeses and breads, crystal jugs with pink, yellow and orange fruit juices stood between some fruit-filled pastries, and finally, to Blau's right, clashing with such a tropical display, a traditional British tea pot with cups and saucers to match.

"I can't do coffee anymore." Blau touched his abdomen. "Ulcers."

I nodded as if I really cared about the state of his health.

He did his best to play host. He passed around platters of food and his intense stare was his way of saying, *don't be rude, eat!*

We spent the first fifteen minutes in silence, swallowing everything offered at the table. My stomach was in knots as much from nervousness as with the effects of the international flight, which always left me feeling bloated and nauseous. I felt Daniel shift in his seat, a hint to start the conversation. I drained the last of my tea and addressed Blau, who had folded his hands on the table and looked ready to be interrogated.

"This is lovely, Señor Blau," I said, eyeing the remnants of the afternoon delight. "We really appreciate your hospitality."

The smile he gave me was condescending. "She raised you well, with manners, I see. But then she carried herself with that aristocratic air about her. However, you did not come here to compliment me on my ability to entertain." The smile gone, he was all business. "I'm your last resource, as far as I know. The rest of them are all dead or crazy with old age." His eyes shifted from me to Daniel. "I was very sad to hear of your grandfather's passing, Daniel. Alex was a good man. The best man I've ever met throughout my long existence."

It was then when I realized introductions were never made. It was then when I realized that Daniel had looked at Blau with recognition when the man had opened the door. My silent debate was cut short when Blau rested his eyes back on me. "The moment I met her, I decided she did not deserve him. And I made sure she that she could never have him."

Chapter Twenty-Nine

Buenos Aires, April 2013

The food and tea I had ingested swam upstream closer to my throat instead of downstream to my stomach. Blau, a living and breathing Dorian Gray, had just admitted to have intentionally destroyed the link between Abuela and Alex. It was obvious the man stood on more than strong bones and good health. He had functioned on years of bitter hatred.

"I saw you once. I was six or seven," Daniel spoke calmly.

"Right after your family died in that terrorist attack in Israel," Blau confirmed, unfazed to have been recognized.

I wiped drops of cold sweat from my forehead with the back of my hand and rubbed my palms on my thighs. I inched close to my own brewing point, but suppressed my temper for the sake of a glimpse into the past. It was time to put the forks down. It was time to talk. "Señor Blau," I started.

Lukas Blau turned to me, an insincere smile across his lips. Eyes cold and grey as stones. "Lukas, my dear, call me Lukas."

I noticed Daniel raise an eyebrow. He smiled faintly. "But that's not your real name, is it, Blau? Before you came to Argentina, before the passport."

Lukas Blau looked genuinely pleased for once. "Everything you see is make-believe." He turned once again to me. At that moment, I noticed he had trouble turning his head from side to side, which forced him to turn with his torso every time he looked at either one of us in the eye. "She pretended to love him, so she could use him." He turned back to Daniel. "He pretended to forget her, so he could forgive her."

I stood up and the room tilted. My body was reaching its breaking point. "Señor Blau," I resorted to my business pose, the one I had used so many times when I was the only woman in a meeting with the decision makers in Hollywood. "I'm jetlagged, the humidity in the room makes my blood pressure drop, your piece of paradise is as fake as your smile, and I'm tired of riddles. I flew," I glanced at Daniel. "We flew halfway around the continent to get to you. You made first contact, remember? *You* are the one with a thorn in your chest, the one that needs to purge his conscience before dying. Let *me* tell you, you might look unbelievably good for your age, but old age is unforgiving and death will come for you, too." I felt like the dark angel delivering an omen. I closed my eyes. "I can't breathe in here," I said, and left the greenhouse.

I hurried back the direction we had come from and reached the room with the mirrors and windows. I needed fresh air; I opened one of the massive windows. With eyes closed, I inhaled deeply and then made the big mistake of opening my eyes and looking down. There was vast emptiness. For a moment I swayed, my knees weakened, and I surrendered to the pull beckoning me.

I was in Daniel's arms when I regained consciousness moments later. His caramel-colored eyes scanned my face with concern.

"You fainted."

I tried to sit up, but he pushed me back down onto Blau's immaculate white couch. "Give it a few more minutes. You're white as a ghost."

I nodded and managed a smile. "You don't look too hot yourself, Bond."

He stroked my forehead. "You scared me."

Blau's looming figure behind Daniel brought me back to the business at hand. "Help me up," I asked him.

He did as I asked; still he kept a protective hold on me. The room spun for a few seconds, but then came swiftly into focus. Nestled in Daniel's arms nothing mattered much to me anymore. I was ready to let the whole mystery rest. My abuela was the person that I knew, period. She was Claudia Lazar during the day and Franzisca during story time. I loved her with all her eccentricities, her stories, her secrets.

I reached for my bag and walked to the front door, Daniel followed behind me. His footsteps halted and I felt him turn to Blau, who stood stoically in the middle of his glass and steel palace.

"Jakub," Daniel muttered, first to himself as if asserting a memory. I looked at Blau from the corner of my eye. I saw him move slightly forward as if the name Jakub carried a force strong enough to make him lose his stony stance.

"My grandfather... that afternoon at the ranch... he called you Jakub." The cloud of memory lifted from Daniel. "Jakub Berkowicz," Daniel said, waking Jakub Berkowicz from a lifetime of hibernation.

Lukas Blau carried the weight of Jakub Berkowicz all the way to the nearest seat, a white leather and aluminum couch. Both he and his act dropped as he slumped onto the couch.

I was no longer eager to leave. I understood the unpleasantness resulting from this meeting as part of the process of discovery. I had witnessed the unveiling of the past when sitting in the corner of Abuela's study. People were like wrapped boxes. The outer appearance was always neat, free of wrinkles, making it difficult to peel the layers around the box without disturbing the contents. Abuela had taught me to open boxes without a care. "Rip that paper at once. What matters is what's inside. The wrapping is just for show."

The same principle was applied to the many people that came to her in search of a piece of their past. She pulled it from a box of sacred memories they carefully wrapped away within them.

"Jakub Berkowicz," I said, all signs of my exhaustion replaced with adrenaline. "You've already admitted my abuela saved your life. So, why all this hatred?" I looked at Blau. At his advanced age he was still a handsome man and I could only imagine how gorgeous he must have been in his youth. A man never denied by any woman, except for one. "Was it because you couldn't have her?" I was building a theory and was probably wrong.

"No one could have her," he said, looking at me. "Not even Alex. Not even after everything he did for her." He smiled, but this time his smile was tinged with pain.

The story buried in Jakub's own box was fighting its way out. "Of course, I wanted her, even when I wanted her dead, I desired her. Every man that laid eyes on her wanted her and she knew how to play them. Lust was not the reason for my hate." Blau looked out one of the enormous windows that lined the room. Dusk was claiming the clear skies over Buenos Aires.

"Jakub." He tasted the name in his tongue. "Kuba, my mother used to call me no matter how angry I made her... Kuba." A glint of mischief flashed in his eyes and was soon replaced with a veil. "Some call it God's work. The trials of a merciful God." Blau shook his head slowly. "A merciful God, would've never allowed the Holocaust. The God of my childhood prayers, the one that was supposedly watching over me, would have never taken away the four people I loved the most so cruelly." He looked down at his hands and closed his fists. "A merciful God would have kept my brothers alive so I could fulfill my promise. And yet, he kept me alive this long. He let me have all of this. What for?" Blau yelled at his reflection in the mirror opposite him. His voice boomed across the empty rooms of the flat.

Up until now Lukas Blau had made sure Jakub lay buried along with those close to his heart. Meanwhile, until death would claim him, until he could let go of the bitterness anchoring him to a name and a life he despised, Blau lived the endless nightmare of those who had survived war and had never put it behind them.

Blau crossed his arms around his middle. When he looked up, his face was streaked with tears. "I wanted to die, too, but she wouldn't let me. *She*, the woman I held responsible for the loss of my brothers, dictated my fate. *She*, a self-proclaimed savior, decided I should live."

I looked at him with pity. If I were in his place I would have wanted to die, too. "I'm sorry." I did not mean to apologize, but the words escaped my lips.

Lukas Blau looked at me intently. "I'm the one who's sorry, Sofia. My hatred for her drove me to do horrible things. I could not see clearly at the time... I did not know the truth. Too late. I broke them apart." He stood up straight ready to confess his crimes. "I am the one responsible for the tragedy in Franzisca's life. I'm the one who brought a monster back from the dead and ruined your mother's life. "

"My mother?" I whispered.

He turned to Daniel. "They were meant to be together. Because of me the only thing they shared was pain. You can stop searching for answers, Daniel. I am the one responsible for your tragedy, too."

Chapter Thirty

Bucharest, July 1941

With the help of the three young brothers Alex found at the bakery on his first night back, he brought the shop back to some sort of normalcy. In the evening, when the bakery closed its doors for the day, the brothers came out of the hiding spot Alex had assigned for them in the basement and put them to work. They covered the broken window with wooden slats. Alex fixed the lock on the door and secured it with a metal bar. He swept the store clean from the vermin accumulated during his absence. Next, Alex sought his previous suppliers, stocked the shop with overpriced flour, sugar, salt and spices—luxury items in times of war—and trained his three new assistants in the arts of bread making.

The brothers were a tight unit. The residue of trauma was apparent in their eyes, in the way they jerked every time they heard a suspicious sound when out of their hiding place. Signs that were most evident when they slept, when their demons claimed them in haunting sobs and shrieks.

For the most part, the brothers were quiet. Jakub, the oldest and the only one that spoke some Romanian was the bridge between them and Alex. Alex understood a bit of Polish, the language they spoke among themselves, but never dared intrude in their conversations until the night a fight broke out between the brothers.

Breathless, Alex stepped between the flying fists. He pushed all three to different corners of the backroom and warned them. "We'll all be arrested if not killed if we're found, do you understand?"

The youngest of the three set his jaw tight and stared at Jakub. "*Wolność*," he said. Alex got the message. The brothers wanted to break free from the prison in the basement. They wanted freedom.

Troubled, Jakub ordered the brothers back into the basement and remained with Alex in the back of the store.

Jakub shoveled coal in one of the burning ovens and kept his eyes on the growing flames. "They want to join the Russian army. Russians don't care much for Jews. But they won't turn anybody away that would enlist to fight the Germans."

Joining the Russian army would mean death for the brothers. If not killed in combat; they would surely starve or freeze to death. Alex kept his thought to himself and kept kneading dough.

"I can't let that happen," Jakub said. I can't let them die." Jakub propped the shovel against the wall and sat next to it. Alex sat opposite Jakub and waited. The time to learn about their story had come.

The sons of a Jewish banker and a beautiful opera singer, Jakub, shrank with overwhelming pain as he told Alex of their brush with death and of the horrors suffered under Aryan dominance.

"Four Polish policemen stormed into our house followed by a group of German Nazi soldiers." Jakub kept his composure but his broken voice betrayed him. "We were held at gunpoint and they made us watch while each policeman took my mother, they…" He shook his head and cleared his throat. "When they were done with her they held my father down."

Jakub stared at the empty space as if watching the horrifying chapter all over again. "They cut off his manhood and they laughed." Jakub's face was wet with tears. "Then, they poured every bottle of alcohol they could find in the house on them and set them on fire." Jakub looked into Alex's eyes. "They forced us to watch until our parents were nothing more than charred scraps."

The brothers' youth and physical strength, valuable for forced labor at the camps, saved them from the same fate their parents met. The brothers were herded into a boxcar bound to Gross-Rosen, a concentration camp where prisoners were employed primarily as forced laborers in the construction of the camp and in the nearby SS-owned granite quarry.

Once at the camp, the brothers were housed in the same barracks. Jakub, the oldest, spoiled and a rogue by nature, fought the fear that engulfed him from the moment life as he knew it was over. He honored the memory of his beloved parents with a vow to get his brothers and himself out of there alive.

Jakub's senses were at a constant alert. He timed the rounds of the guards, learned their habits, he kept a mental tally of their bathroom breaks. He also memorized the weekly delivery schedules; the food truck, the one carrying prisoners, and the one driving prostitutes in and out of the guards' barracks.

As he planned their escape, most likely within the prostitute's cargo, he made sure his brothers were kept as strong as possible. In the beginning, they refused the watery soup they were given for lunch and the small piece of black bread, sometimes spread with marmalade, a slice of sausage or a small chunk of cheese, the camp provided for dinner. The nagging pain in his stomach and the increasing weakness in his limbs became warning alerts that soon the meager food portions would not be enough to sustain their overworked bodies for long. In his brothers' bodies, he noticed the way the whole camp population was deteriorating. He hated to see how his younger brothers' bones showed under their bruised skin. But mostly, he was scared at the way they had become progressively subdued.

It was time he used his hard-earned unruly reputation for a worthy cause.

On Friday evenings, after the camp was silent for the night, the prostitutes were brought into the soldiers' barracks. Every other Friday, Jakub and his brothers were taken to the makeshift brothel to serve spirits and clean up after the many officers who could not keep their alcohol down. The parties never ended before dawn. Still inebriated, most of the guards would catch an hour or two of sleep before their shift. It was the brothers' responsibility to wake the guards in time to terrorize the whole camp as a result of their hangover.

Week after week Jakub became more acquainted with the prostitutes. Although they never spoke a word, they communicated with their eyes, nods, crumpled, clandestine missives, and infinitesimal hand gestures.

On the Fridays he and his brothers waited on the guards, Jakub watched patiently for a sign.

The time to escape the camp came along with the suggestive wink from one of the prostitutes. That night, after the party was over, they would leave the camp aboard the truck that drove the prostitutes back to the city. On that night, unlike any other, a couple of the girls paid a special visit to the guards standing vigil. They kept them distracted with their pants down around their ankles while the brothers slipped out and into the truck.

Alex admired Jakub for his strength. He had made good on his promise to his parents and had brought his brothers to safety. Alex believed in fate. There was a reason these survivors had stepped into his bakery. There was a reason he had found the treasure on the night he came back to the bakery and not before. Just like Old Nicu saved him, it was his turn to help others, to ensure their survival beyond their escape from a concentration camp. And there were sure to be others in the same situation.

The first glimmer of the new day filtered through the tiny window adjacent to the ovens. The bakery would soon open its doors and the brothers would disappear into the darkness of the basement until the last ray of daylight was swallowed by the black night.

For the first time since meeting Jakub, Alex rested a hand on his shoulder. "Give me a few weeks. I'll see what I can do."

In that subtle way that information is sought when illicit services are needed, Alex inquired about an underground cell that could forge identification papers. For a very high price, Alex was given a couple of leads; however, they had all resulted in dead ends. The anxiety of the brothers grew with every passing day, especially when the news about the massacre in Iasi reached the doors of the bakery.

The events in Iasi had their repercussion on the moral of the people of Bucharest. The traffic slowed to a crawl and so did the supplies Alex needed to keep his business alive. The name of Baron Lupescu was spoken on the streets of Bucharest with menacing impact, bringing back with it the division left among the Romanians after the failed revolt of The Iron Guard.

For Alex the name Lupescu burned him like pure alcohol poured on a raw wound. If he was capable of thrashing a woman the way he had done with Anna Shultz.... Fear gripped him. What if Franzisca had gone back to the Lupescu palace? With Anna dead, there would be no stopping him from subjecting Franzisca to the same treatment.

He had vowed to keep her safe. But, unlike Jakub, he did not make good on his promise. He hated the cowardice that trapped him when he felt her leaving. He should have put his claim on her. He should have behaved like a dominating male and pulled her back into the tunnel by her hair.

He closed the bakery at noon that day and set out toward the Lupescu mansion, the first place in his search to find Franzisca.

The house looked closed down. He knocked on the back door. Someone had to be around to ward off looters from breaking into the mansion.

A gray-haired housekeeper opened the back door for him. She let her tears run free when he asked after Franzisca.

"The child is gone." Her lips trembled. "T'was my fault. We should've never left her alone. The floor was covered with broken glass, drops of blood..." Unable to articulate her fears she shook her head slowly.

Alex stood numb. From the door, he stared at the place in the kitchen where he had his first glimpse of Franzisca two years before. The spot was now empty, shadowed with fragments of his memory and flashes of red. His eyes played tricks on him, he closed them, and when he opened them again the flashes of red had turned into a pool of blood on the white tile. For a fleeting moment, he saw Franzisca lying in it. "She can't be," he mumbled before he fled, breaking into a run leaving the sobbing old woman openmouthed at the door.

Back at the bakery, Alex took down a bottle of Vodka, put it to his lips, and did not release its neck until the last drops burned down his throat. Nothing eased the pain. He slumped in Old Nicu's chair and cried unashamed in front of the three pairs of eyes that watched over him that night. The brothers acted in harmony for the first time in weeks. They followed Jakub's orders without arguments and baked the loaves of bread that were needed to open the store when the clock struck the sixth hour.

With strong cups of coffee, Jakub forced Alex into sobriety. The younger brothers wiped his face with a dampened cloth and got him into a clean shirt. At five thirty in the morning, before dawn broke, there was a rap on the door. The Polish brothers froze with fear halfway through their activities and stared at Alex.

The rasp became a knock and soon the knock became a relentless pounding. Shocked into reality, Alex instructed the brothers to hide in the basement and he went to the front door to see what the loud pounding was all about. By the time he reached the door, the urgent knocks had stopped. Alex removed the metal bar and opened the door to an empty, dark street.

The black hood that fell over his head caught him unawares. So did the blunt object that smacked him full force on the base of his skull sending him into oblivion.

Chapter Thirty-One

In a matter of two weeks, Franzisca went from being a servant in the Lupescu household to sole heir to the barony and the fortune behind it.

Her fateful encounter with Lucien had set her plan in motion. She decided to leave her murder revenge behind and in turn bankrupt Lupescu of every cent of his fortune. The man was powerless without his estate in a country where monarchy was nothing but a romantic memory.

After the initial shock of seeing *his chauffer*, Lucien, in Lupescu's office, Franzisca came straight to business.

"I heard you're down on your luck," she said, defying the intimidation she felt in the presence of this frightening man.

Lucien unfolded his huge frame from the chair to stand mere meters from her. Franzisca fought the urge to step back.

"I heard we might share something in common." Lucien tone was cynical. The man was used to play the cat and mouse game.

"I doubt it," Franzisca replied.

"Lucien. The name is Lucien," he volunteered. "Let's cut to the chase, little girl, and tell me what you were about to do with the things you just stole from the baron's safe."

With a trembling hand, Franzisca reached inside her bodice. The document, signed and sealed by Lupescu, was revealed under the light of the moon that had broken through the thick storm clouds. Lucien bent his head and squinted at it, he barked a hoarse laugh, and bowed to her.

"I'm at your service, Baroness." He lifted his eyes to meet hers. "For a price, of course."

Lucien's price was far from what Franzisca had imagined. She was ready to hand over most of Lupescu's fortune in exchange for his help. She did not care about money. She was in dire need to make amends, to ease her guilt.

"I want to get my family back. I want enough money to buy a dairy farm and dress my wife like a queen." The man, who only minutes ago stood before her resembling a killing machine, looked humble, fragile when he spoke of his family.

Franzisca couldn't help but smile at him. "A dairy farm? I like that."

Lucien was taken aback. For the first time he wasn't mocked at the mention of his dream of a dairy farm.

"A dairy farm you shall have, then," Franzisca pronounced.

"I want it in writing," Lucien pressed.

Franzisca nodded. "For that, I need you to summon Anton Vasile." Franzisca walked around Lupescu's desk and sat down in his chair. Lucien remained standing.

Anton Vasile was on the list Franzisca composed of the many powerful men Lupescu had betrayed. He was also one of three solicitors who had forged documents to turn over the Shultz's fortune to Lupescu in front of a crooked, anti-Semitic judge. Franzisca had searched for all three solicitors. One of them was dead. Another had fled the country the day Antonescu crushed the rebellion, her last hope, Anton Vasile, had been sitting in the Rahova penitentiary under suspicion of treason up until a week ago. Vasile had suffered the same fate many of the Iron Guard loyalists had after Lupescu betrayed them, naming them enemies to Antonescu's regime.

Upon news of his release, Franzisca had tried to contact him. She had knocked on his door and had been turned away every time. Now, with Lucien as her strong man, things would work out differently.

The next morning, Vasile's wife ushered Lucien and Franzisca into the house through the back door. The place looked naked and gloomy. It was clear what had bought Vasile's freedom. The months the solicitor had spent in jail had eaten up his entire savings. Undoubtedly, every last piece of furniture and jewelry went into a government dignitary's pocket in return for his release.

On the other hand, Vasile was too small of a fish to be kept in jail longer. In exchange for his promise of undying loyalty to Antonescu upon his release, he was allowed to keep his main residence and his lawyer's license, a title as useless as his name, for every former Iron Guard rebel had become an exile in his own land.

The penniless solicitor stood arrogantly in his empty office. He scanned Franzisca's document and the property titles she had surrendered to him. When he was done, he returned them to her. She felt a moment's dismay, thinking that the documents might be worthless.

"I advised the baron many times to change the name on the property titles. I drew up several documents for the transfer. But he never got around to doing it." He fixed Franzisca with a stare to make sure she followed his words.

He then pointed at the document Anna had left Franzisca in the wooden box. "That," he said, with a smirk on his face, "that is the death of Lupescu." He looked at Franzisca again. "By his hand and your mother's blood, you are his one and only heir."

"Upon his death," Franzisca remarked.

The solicitor smiled fully for the first time. "Amendments are common in my practice. We must have a witness," he said, looking at Lucien "And I assume you came prepared to pay for my services."

Franzisca looked at the bare walls and empty rooms of Vasile's house and laughed inwardly at the way the wheel of fortune turned. "Call your wife in."

Lucien watched Vasile eye Franzisca dismissively. He didn't like what he saw and acted as he had done so many times before when at Lupescu's service. He stepped forward, grabbed the arrogant lawyer by the front of his shirt, and held him suspended, inches from the floor, so he could have him at eye level. "The baroness called for your wife."

In a matter of seconds, Vasile was back into his empty office with his wife. The woman looked worn and tired. Franzisca almost felt sorry for her, but the memory of her mother, the way she had sacrificed her life to regain what was stolen from her, pushed Franzisca's compassion aside.

"Your husband," she addressed Vasile's wife, "might as well be the pistol that murdered my grandparents, and I hold him equally responsible for the death of my mother." Franzisca spoke calmly. Vasile's wife stood in front of her, eyes glued to the floor. "Everything you owned and the little you still own, the life you had, while my mother sold herself to keep me alive, belongs to me." Vasile's wife's silent sobs racked her thin frame.

"Anton Vasile." He was a worm and a murderer, but he was also her only ally and she needed him. "I come here to offer you a deal. You will never gain riches again on your own. You're a tainted man and Antonescu despises traitors. You disgust me, as I do you, but we are at war, we must play by its rules and use each other."

Franzisca had surprised herself at the way she addressed the man in front of her. She wasn't the Franzisca of the crystal castle that stood in that room. The person denigrating a man and his wife in their own home was the result of the many years of training Anna had given her to reach this critical point. There was no fear in her; she felt empowered.

"You will be in my employ as my solicitor until all of Lupescu's assets are safely away from Romania. Do as I ask and I promise you'll be a rich man again. You will make sure I am the sole recipient of the Lupescu barony and that Mihail Lupescu will never lay claim on my fortune again. I want the country estate to be transferred to Lucien's name. The palace and the oil refinery in Ploesti..." Franzisca though for a brief moment, "keep that in Lupescu's name, I only want what belongs to me. All other properties and bank accounts outside of Romania, which belonged to the Schultz family, will be transferred to my real name, Franzisca Shultz. But first you must make it legal in the eyes of the government and invisible to Lupescu."

Franzisca hated not knowing anything about the world of finances. It made her look weak. "You are a con-artist by nature. You managed to steal from my family without leaving a trace of your crime. You can work your magic again."

"The safest way to protect your assets is for everything to be liquidated into gold and transferred to The Swiss National Bank in Zurich." Vasile was all business. "You don't want anything under your name, *Donmisiara* Shultz. You are a Jew and there's no telling which way the war will go yet. I wouldn't trust the Swiss more that I'd trust the Nazis."

Franzisca nodded. The man was right. "Show me how it's done."

Sitting on the floor of the empty office and warmed by several rounds of tea, Anton Vasile drew a plan to transfer all of the liquid assets of Baron Lupescu, to a secret bank account in Switzerland with Franzisca as the only account holder. Her name would have to be concealed under a phantom company, with her as the undisclosed executor. It was the way the Nazis safeguarded the wealth they stole from their victims, and the Swiss were not too discriminating when it came to filling their vaults.

"Per this document." Vasile held up the signed document that Anna had left for Franzisca "You are as good as a baroness. Lupescu played his cards well and his name is highly regarded in both Nazi and Romanian circles."

Deep in thought, Vasile paused and nodded when he had obviously reached a conclusion. He looked at Franzisca. "For this transaction to work, you must marry him. You must marry Mihail Lupescu."

A chill ran through her body leaving her covered with goose bumps. The notion of marrying the one man she hated, the one she sought to destroy was revolting. But she had to admit that Vasile was right. Her position as Franzisca Shultz was precarious; she needed protection beyond the one Lucien provided. No one should ever know how Baron Lupescu had been stripped of his last penny by three of his enemies, or that the marriage was worthless in the eyes of the law. All that mattered was that until Franzisca could leave Romania, on paper, she was the baron's legal wife, and that she was protected by his name.

"And when he returns?"

"*If* he returns," Vasile remarked. "Word in Rahova is that Lupescu disappeared after the Iasi pogrom. Some say he was mortally wounded. Others claimed the baron was out of his mind. That they had found him wandering through the barracks, naked, crying out the name Anna."

Franzisca felt a sick satisfaction at the knowledge that her mother was still haunting the accursed baron to the point of madness.

"Then," she said, "Baron Mihail Lupescu is as good as dead."

Within an hour, a physician, a former fervent Iron Guard member, was called to the meeting. He had met

Lupescu during their younger years at the Iron Guard meetings at the University and had detested the arrogant bastard at first sight. The man demanded enough gold to leave Romania and without a second thought signed a death certificate that declared Lupescu dead. The cause of death was stated as a self-inflicted gunshot. The body was said to have been found by his faithful chauffer at Lupescu's country manor outside of Bucharest and laid to rest there.

Franzisca was thankful for the ruthless corruption that had resulted from the fall of the Iron Guard. Those who had fallen out of grace with the current government were desperate and would do anything for coin. She was also glad for the heavy gold in her pockets, and as ridiculous as it sounded to her own ears, she was thankful for Lucien.

Lucien had seen to her every need. He was quick to summon to the clandestine meeting several characters he had met during his days in hiding. These were desperate men who would attest to anything they were asked to, from Lupescu's and Franzisca's wedding to the baron's death, all for the price of a train ticket out of Romania.

Once all documents were drawn, Vasile looked at Franzisca inquisitively. "A name; you need a name."

Franzisca searched in the depths of her memory for a story her mother had once told her that might serve her in the future. Dobos, was the family name, Franzisca now remembered. The Dobos family had vanished from Vienna more than two decades ago, when Herr Dobos became the subject of an official inquest involving stolen art objects. No one knew of the Dobos' fate and they were soon forgotten. And the Dobos' daughter's name was... "Irina Dobos," Franzisca said, as if in trance. "The name is Irina Dobos."

Franzisca spent the day in a fog signing forged documents, getting married and becoming a widow all within the matter of an hour.

By the time darkness claimed the skies over Bucharest, Franzisca Shultz had become Baroness Irina Lupescu.

A week after becoming a baroness, Franzisca, Vasile and his wife, with Lucien at the wheel, left Bucharest in Lupescu's 1939 Rolls Royce. With a banner displaying the Lupescu crest and a swastika flag above it, they made their way to the Swiss National bank in Zurich. True to Vasile's word, the Lupescu name, her identification papers and marriage license gave Franzisca and the rest of the passengers in the car sufficient diplomatic immunity to cross borders without being questioned or searched. The car was loaded with gold coins, gold bullion, and jewelry Franzisca was certain had belonged to her grandmother. It took them nearly three days to reach Zurich. Once at their destination, Franzisca secured her gold, Swiss francs and jewels into a secret account the way Vasile had set it up.

With the gold Franzisca paid Vasile for his services, the lawyer decided to stay in Switzerland, at least until the end of the war. He advised Franzisca to do the same.

"Lupescu might turn up alive on any given day. The man is insane. He has disappeared before and has come back every time."

"I won't be in Romania long," Franzisca responded.

Before Vasile went on his way, he turned to her one last time. "In the safe, Lupescu had thirty-six blank passports. A Nazi general sold them to him at the beginning of the war for a small fortune. They are a free way for Nazis to get into Argentina should the Reich fall. Were they still there when you opened the safe?"

Franzisca declined to answer. "Have a good life, Vasile," Franzisca said, and slid into the back seat of the Rolls Royce anxious to return to Bucharest and set the rest of her plan in motion. A gnawing feeling settled in the pit of her stomach. The passports were in her possession, but only thirty-five of them.

Chapter Thirty-Two

Back in Romania, Franzisca settled in a secluded home Vasile had secured for her, before his departure, in the outskirts of Bucharest.

On their first day back, Franzisca dismissed Lucien from her services. She had filled his pockets with enough gold to buy cows and all the dresses that his wife wished. She urged him to go to his family and begin to live the life he yearned for in the country home he now owned. But Lucien was intractable.

"I won't leave you until I know you're safe, Baroness. Until you leave Romania." His response was immediate, out of duty. "Your concern for my family..." Lucien shifted in his frame as if uncomfortable in his clothes. "If I may, Baroness." He chose his words carefully.

"Go ahead, Lucien."

"Your mother, she did not deserve what happened to her. I don't hold with punishment of women and..." Lucien held his tongue. The girl didn't need to hear the details of her mother's ordeal under Lupescu. "I was a coward. I should have helped her." Lucien looked genuinely ashamed.

"Yes, you should have," Franzisca whispered. "I should have helped her, too."

Franzisca and Lucien stared at each other for a long time. Both lost in their thoughts and their own regrets.

"I have already sent for my wife and children," Lucien cut in. "I received word that they are settled in the new home. I'm forever grateful, Baroness."

Franzisca contemplated Lucien and wondered, not for the first time, how such a monster of a man could be so gentle at times.

"Thank you, Lucien. I won't stay in Bucharest for long. But, before I go, I could use your help one last time. I need to find a man. He saved my life. His name is Alex Alcaly."

With a quick bow to Franzisca, Lucien was out of the door and on his way to fulfill the baroness' request.

***

Lucien located Alex Alcaly within an hour of arriving in the city. Everyone he spoke to had only good things to say about the young baker, except for his competitors.

Alcaly was known to sell his baked goods below cost or to give them away to those who were not able to afford them. His charitable actions were viewed by his competitors on and around *Micsunele Strada* as a threat. They had complained to the local authorities, called him a Russian ally, a Jew sympathizer, but time and time again their complaints were dismissed.

For one whole day and night Lucien watched the activity around Alcaly's bakery. The young man opened his store at six in the morning to a long line of customers ready to buy their daily bread. The activity continued all through the day until the doors of the bakery closed at four in the afternoon. Once or twice a day, a policeman walked into the store, stood by the counter and chatted amicably with Alcaly over a cup of tea. The exchange of a bribe with their parting handshake was only visible in the eyes of a man like Lucien who knew what to look for. Alcaly did more than bake in his store, and Lucien would not risk the safety of his new charge to a rebel.

When night spread over the city and the curfew sirens warned the citizens to stay inside until morning, the activity in Alcaly's bakery changed.

Lucien, his ear pressed to the door, overheard three other male voices besides Alcaly's. He shook his head at the young man's carelessness. The other merchants in the area had it in for him, didn't the boy know? It was only a matter of time before heavier bribes outweighed Alcaly's and his days as a baker by day and activist by night would reach a dramatic end.

Exposing his baroness to this irresponsible idiot was dangerous. The young woman had shown strength beyond her years, Lucien admired her for that. For years, he had considered her lower than dirt and always referred to her as The Bastard. Lucien sucked in a ragged breath, and struggled with shame and dishonor. No one was a bigger bastard than he was.

For the first time in twenty years, Lucien regretted the path he had chosen. Too thickheaded for the classroom but rough enough for the streets, Lucien fit into the life of a ruffian. A bloody brawl at a bar where he took down five men within a few minutes, caught the eye of the baron who sat in a shadowy corner. The rest was history.

Lucien had forgotten he was human until six years ago when Mariah came into his life. He never thought a woman could look beyond his brutish appearance and the noticeable bulge between his legs. Mariah did. In the beginning, he had paid for her attentions. She had matched him move for move in the bedroom and never shied away from his bruising touch. In every encounter, she taught him to be gentle, to act beyond his immediate need, to soften his touch into a caress. Lucien felt sick with love for Mariah. Never before had a woman treated him with such kindness or laughed at his silly jokes. Two months after they met, they were married in a small church in the country. The day his twins were born and he held their tiny life in his savage hands, Lucien wept.

Sometimes Lucien flinched at what Mariah's uncertain fate would have been if he had not married her. There were plenty of men like the baron who thrived on the sadistic treatment of women. The memory of Anna Schultz covered in cuts and bruises made him feel less than a man. If he could only undo the past... Instead, he forced himself to think toward the future. The baroness was young and Lucien swore to watch over her like a faithful dog. He was good at it and she needed him.

What to do about this boy? The baroness' voice had quivered slightly when she mentioned his name. Alcaly had saved her life, for that Lucien was grateful. Argh! Against his better judgment, he would fulfill his duty. He would deliver the baker to the baroness, but first he would have a heart to heart with the boy.

***

Hours had passed since Alex had answered the early knock on the door. The bakery shop was silent. Several knocks and loud calls from frustrated customers, demanding their daily bread ration, slipped through the thick walls down to the basement, but Alex was not there to answer them.

Jakub's younger brothers grew restless with every passing hour. Alex's obvious absence had them imagining all sorts of horrors. In their minds, he had abandoned them to their fate. Yes, they agreed with Jakub, Alex had given them protection for months and had risked his own neck to hide three fugitives under his shop. But even the best of men broke under the current dire circumstances. They urged Jakub to let them leave or better yet, leave all together.

Trapped in the basement they felt as enslaved as they had been in the camp. "Don't you see, Kuba?" they pleaded. "If we could get out of here, if we fight with the Russians at least we would be fighting for our freedom. In the meantime, we're trapped in this infernal room, waiting for others to fight for us."

Jakub would not hear a word of it. He knew his brothers resented him and saw him as their jailer. But, it would all be worth in the end. He would see them grow into the fine men his parents intended them to become. He had made that promise while the ghost of his parents still hovered in the room that they were murdered in.

"Alex is a man of his word," Jakub told his brothers. "He will be back before nightfall, you'll see." But Jakub himself was assaulted by ominous visions. Alex could have been arrested by the police. After all, he dealt in the black market to stock up the bakery shop with enough supplies to cater to his customers and that came with a price. Alex's other activities were invisible in the eyes of officials as long as their pockets were lined with coin. Corruption was just another moneymaker during the war and it never surprised Alex, to see a man in uniform come into the shop and demand money for his protection to turn a blind eye to illegal activities, such as the harboring of Jews, they knew Alex was suspected of.

When night fell over Bucharest, Jakub left the bakery intent on finding Alex. Before climbing the stairs to the main floor of the shop he looked at his brothers with threatening eyes. Their argument had escalated to a shouting match, which was followed with physical blows. Jakub's knuckles were raw and stung with the aftermath of the fight with his brothers before he left their basement prison. Never before had he raised a fist against his brothers. Never before had he drawn blood on them. The resentment in their eyes due to his control over them haunted him. Out on the street, when the first rush of fresh air filled his lungs; he understood his brothers' desperation.

***

As the world came into focus Alex felt his skull would explode if he moved his head an inch. Trying to piece together the event that gave him the nauseating pain in the back of his head he suddenly remembered. His first impulse was to jump to his feet and fight, but he found that he was restrained by a tight rope that tied him to a tree. Alex looked up. The sun was above the horizon. It was close to seven in the morning, he guessed.

A rustle of dead leaves came from his left. Alex turned his aching head carefully and was met with a man the size of a house.

"And who the fuck are you?" The man might look like a demon from the underworld, Alex thought, but he was not impressed, he was fathered by one.

Alex's question was answered with a backhanded blow across his face. He knew his head had finally exploded into a million pieces when all he could see was black. A few blinks later, the man was still standing in front of him and Alex's head had somehow remained attached to his neck. The man walked closer to him and knelt to meet him at eye level. He opened his mouth to speak, but then closed his lips firmly. After a couple of more attempts, Alex wondered if the man could speak.

"Can you not speak, man?"

"I will say this once, little shit," the man finally spoke. "I will be watching your every step, following your every move. I don't care if you saved her life. You as much as make the baroness unhappy once and I will rip your head off. Are we clear?"

Alex squinted at the man for two reasons; he couldn't open his eyes fully without feeling excruciating pain and he had no idea what the man was talking about.

"I'm sure you have the wrong man" He frowned. "And as far as a baroness…"Alex was at a total loss.

"Are you Alex Alcaly?" the giant growled

Alex nodded. The giant pulled a knife from beneath his belt and inched closer to Alex. Alex saw his short life flash before his eyes before he realized the man cut the rope loose.

The man pulled a stunned Alex to his feet, straightened his clothes, and even raked his thick fingers through his messy hair. Alex knew he should run, but curiosity got the best of him.

"A baroness?" he asked with a mocking tone.

The man nodded toward a house hidden beneath the trees. "She's waiting for you."

Alex felt the man's iron grip on his shoulder and the tip of the knife at his neck. "Remember what I said."

When they reached the house, a decent size cottage, a middle-aged maid opened the door for them and greeted the big man with a frown on her face. "My Lady is worried sick about you, *domn*. She spent the night pacing around the house thinking you harmed."

A flash of regret softened the big man's menacing scowl. Quick footsteps approached the foyer. Alex looked down at his feet. It was probably the baroness and he was dirty, covered with dry dough and soot, not fit to be in the presence of a monarch.

"Lucien!" a female cried with relief.

The moment Alex looked up to follow the sound of the voice, the footsteps stopped. It could not be. He knew that voice. He had heard it only a few times during his waking hours. He heard it every night in his dreams.

She stood in the shadows of the room. He did not need to see her. He could draw her with his eyes closed. Sense her in a room full of people. Make out her shape in the depth of darkness.

Alex's feet moved forward of their own accord. He forgot to breathe, but came back to his senses when he felt her trembling body in his arms.

They would never remember how long they stood there crying and staring at each other without uttering a single word.

Before retreating silently from the room, Lucien contemplated the picture before him. The baroness was in love, and so was baker boy.

His list of charges was growing.

Chapter Thirty-Three

By the time Alex and Franzisca pulled away from each other, satisfied that neither of them would vanish into thin air if they eased their hold, everybody at the house had left.

Alex stepped away from Franzisca and walked around the house taking in every detail. He hadn't grown up among fine things; he had never slept on a proper bed or eaten out of porcelain dishes, so it was easy for him to discern the ordinary from the sophisticated. There were gilded framed paintings on the walls, plush rugs covering the floors, silver candelabras standing on fine lace table runners. The furniture was made of sturdy dark wood, carved with perfection, and finished to a glowing shine.

Franzisca did not follow him as he made a thorough inspection of the house. She stood exactly where she had the moment she had spotted him across the main room. The initial thrill and relief to have him back, was slowly replaced with self-doubt. She had wanted to find him, to be with him again. They were finally together and under his scrutinizing eye, she feared he would reject her for the choices she had made.

"Baroness," Alex formed the word, a perplexed whisper across the silent room. His eyes rested on Franzisca. She was dressed in finery and adorned with jewelry. The silky raven hair he had run his fingers through when they huddled together in a dusty corner of the tunnel, was now carefully coiffed and held back with gold and pearl combs. She looked older somehow; more unattainable.

"You brought me here." He made no attempts to step any closer to her. Franzisca shivered. The room had suddenly turned cold.

Franzisca kneaded her fingers together searching for the right way to explain the house, the clothes, and the wedding ring around her finger Alex couldn't tear his eyes off.

"Yes," she answered. "I wanted you here."

Alex paced a short circle around the room. Anger trailed behind him. "What for? Are you in need of a baker for your kitchen?" Alex reached under his shirt, grabbed the leather cord holding the key, and tore it clean from his neck in one tug. "Or is it that you found a worthier candidate for your key, *Baroness.*" By now, he was only inches from her. His breathing was ragged, his voice broken with fury. He threw the key at her feet. "Back in the tunnel, you... you..." Alex's body shook with restrained emotion. Who is he?" he demanded sick with jealousy, knowing he had no right.

"Baron Mihail Lupescu. I am his wife, the only beneficiary to the Lupescu barony, and his widow." Franzisca struggled with every one of her words. Everything she had said was the naked truth. It sounded awful to her ears and by the look in Alex's eyes, it had sounded worse to his. She needed to get that part of her life off her chest. She was Lupescu's wife, if only on paper, his heir and hopefully also his widow. She would not lie to Alex, even though she wished she had, for his accusatory glare was unbearable.

"You're worse than a whore." Alex walked past her without a backward glance and reached the front door before she realized he was leaving.

Franzisca ran to the door and blocked his exit. Words were off the table. Alex would not listen. She had to show him she had not sold herself for a title or security to the man she despised the most in the world.

Alex's eyes were moist. "Please, Franzisca..." He shook his head and dropped his arms to his side. "Please."

Franzisca took a step toward Alex and reached for his hands. He stood stone still. She rested her head in the center of his broad chest and inhaled his scent. How much she had missed him! He smelled of yeast, soap, and what she thought was man. One of her hands went up to his chest, rested temporarily there, and then made its way to his face.

Alex did not move, even though she could feel his racing heart.

With her eyes closed, she traced the shape of his face. He had a long straight nose, high cheekbones, a defined jaw, soft lips. Then, she searched for the thin line she remembered so well, an old scar right above his right eye. She thought about his eyes and of the first time she looked into them and had lost herself in their warmth.

Franzisca looked up and found him staring past her into the empty space. She cupped his face with both her hands and forced him to look at her. He did.

"It is me. It is still me," she whispered.

Franzisca stood on the tip of her toes and brushed her lips on his. She had never kissed a man before and knew her kiss was hesitant, clumsy. Alex did not reject her and she braved another kiss. This time she pressed her lips to his and kissed him longer, softly.

Alex inhaled shakily, lifted his hands to hers. "Franzisca," he exhaled.

Alex lowered their hands and drank the sight of her in. Her face was flushed, her violet-blue eyes bright with desire. God, how many times had he dreamt of her looking exactly like this. Here she was, between his body and the door, kissing him. There was no telling what tomorrow might bring for him. They were at war. Today he was alive. Today he was with her. Tomorrow, if he lived to see a tomorrow, he would hold the memory of today.

With thumb and forefinger, Alex slid Franzisca's wedding band off her finger. The ring clanked as it hit the floor. Then, he ran his fingers through the mass of brilliant hair that crowned her head and pulled loose the combs, letting the hair cascade over her shoulders and back.

His mouth found the line of her jaw and kissed her softly. His hands undid the top buttons of her silk shirt until he touched skin. She was so beautiful and when she nodded he knew she was to be his.

Franzisca took his hand and led him to a bedroom at the far end of the house. A giant bed, surrounded by brocade drapes, sat in the center of the room. Alex forced aside thoughts of Franzisca with Lupescu in that bed. Somewhere within the blur of her words, she had said the word widow. He couldn't remember or think straight. His body throbbed for hers, married, widowed, he did not care.

His kiss was far from the gentle nibbling she had done on his lips. His kiss was demanding.

When his tongue claimed hers, Franzisca surrendered completely. It was the first time she had allowed herself to feel something other than guilt and grief since the death of her mother and the Bucharest pogrom. Her body felt light, her senses heightened.

Alex divested her of the fine garments that made her a baroness and between kisses and incoherent words he explored her every inch. His clothes came off in a flurry of nervous giggles.

It was Franzisca's first time seeing a naked man and she took her time examining the shape of his body and his erect penis.

Her playful touch was torture to him. He tried to contain his need to throw her on the bed and thrust deep into the tender spot in between her legs. Alex forced his thoughts to loaves of bread and sacks of flour. By the time he had figured out how much flour he would need to supply the whole of Bucharest with his trademark golden loaves, Franzisca entwined her fingers with his and led him to the bed. They lay down on their sides facing each other, catching their breaths, measuring their burning desire.

Franzisca inched closer to him. Her lips touched his when she spoke. "What I said to you the day I left the tunnel, I meant every word. You hold the other half of my heart. The key, it is yours. Alex, there has never been another, nor will there ever be."

Alex could not form any coherent thoughts. There would be time for words later. He hovered over her and kissed her deeply with tenderness and yes, love. Then, he slid his hands under her round bottom and brought her hips to meet his, to meet his need that now throbbed against the gates of her moist, warm opening.

Franzisca locked eyes with his and ran her fingers through his hair. With one quick thrust, he entered her hard. Pain shot down her toes and it was gone as soon as it had come.

Startled, Alex paused and stared at her. "You never said—" She pulled him down to her lips. His words were drowned in her kiss, his soul lost to hers.

Their lovemaking created an unbreakable pact of love the moment their joined bodies had found the safe haven they had sought from the moment of their separation. Franzisca's words, *you hold the other half of my heart,* became their truth. Franzisca knew those would be the last words she would say when death claimed her.

For the next few hours, reality eluded them and they grabbed this rare moment to laugh like children and love with the abandon of new lovers. But as the day waned, the ghosts of things unsaid made their unannounced entrance.

"Tell me." Alex entwined his fingers in Franzisca's hair.

Franzisca peeled her body from Alex's, sat on the bed and covered her naked breasts with the rumpled bed-sheet.

He couldn't take his eyes of her. Never before had he seen such beauty. Her mouth swollen from his kisses, her soft skin a radiant gold, her eyes filled with love only for him. His first impulse was to draw her to his chest and tell her to forget about it, that he didn't want to know. No, it was a lie. He was sick with jealousy. She was his and he had to know everything.

Franzisca weighed in on his demand. Tell me, he had said. She did not know where to start. Did it really matter? So she started with her mother's last farewell. She told him about the murder of her grandparents. About her association with Lucien, the plans Vasile drew and their trip to Switzerland. She showed Alex the signed document that made her a baroness. And then, because all that mattered to her at that moment was his love, she told him the story of Asil, Anna and the keys.

Alex followed the events of her life as though he walked through a maze. One thing was very clear to him. Franzisca's story started and ended on the two most pivotal points of her life, which happened on the same day. The loss of her mother and the moment she met him.

It was his turn. Their beginnings were similar, although her mother and father had not share the love Asil and Anna had. With anger, he told her about his father and of his fear of becoming a monster like him. "I would rather die," he said.

Franzisca reached for his hands and kissed them. "You are not like him."

Alex put his arms around her and pressed her to his chest.

"When we were in the tunnel, you spoke of Old Nicu." Franzisca sat back. Their bodies had responded immediately to their touch and she meant to finish their talk. She still had one more thing to say to Alex before surrendering to him one more time. That was if he still wanted her after she was finished talking.

Franzisca listened to Alex describe the character of the old baker and she wished she had known him. He confided in her his golden find, and then he told her about Jakub and his brothers.

The story of the brother's ordeal and survival pulled her out of the momentary bliss she had allowed herself. Franzisca grew somber with the weight of her guilt. She left the bed and faced the window. The light was completely gone and the evening had turned unseasonably cold for summer. An icy ripple crept up her spine. She knew it to be shame, not cold.

Alex jumped off the bed, stood behind her and wrapped his arms around her naked body. She pushed him away.

"I don't deserve this, any of this. I don't deserve you. I don't deserve to be alive. But I couldn't get you off my mind. I know it's selfish, but I had to experience love if only this once."

Alex went to her again and tightened his arms around her when she tried to escape his hold. "Tell me," he said–for the second time that day.

"I'm as good as a murderer. I knew of the pogrom by the Iron Guard and did nothing to stop it. I'm as good as any of them, Alex. But I want to change that. You have to believe me." She turned to face him. "Whatever I did afterward, the transfer of the fortune, marrying Lupescu…I stood and watched before. I can't do that anymore." Franzisca shrugged. "I have plenty of money now. I have a noble title and a name good in the eyes of both the Nazis and Antonescu. I know it's late, but I'll do whatever it takes to bring any of the survivors to freedom." She stood tall. "Walk out of my life now, or stay and help me."

He held her at arms' length and spoke calmly, meaning every word. "I believe you, Franzisca. You're mine to hold now, and I mean to hold you forever."

Chapter Thirty-Four

Walking out on Franzisca was not an option for Alex, not then, not ever and he told her as much. When she calmed down, he tried to make her understand her precarious position in a country that had not objected to the murderous industry the Nazis had spread throughout Europe.

"The stories that Jakub told me, Franzisca, the things that he lived through..." Alex closed his eyes as if he could erase the horrible images in his mind. "It will only get worse and I will not lose you to this war."

Franzisca shook her head, "I'll be of no use to you if I sit and wait for the war to end. You know that, Alex. You are doing what you can to keep Jakub and his brothers safe. I have the means now to do it, Alex. If what Vasile said it's true, I believe I can get people out of Europe and into South America."

By the time Franzisca told Alex about the passports and her wish to use all of them to get Jews out of Europe, night had filtered through the windows. When they had drawn up a plan for their immediate future and for the rest of their lives, they reached for one another and in the darkness, they made love again.

Lucien was standing by the front door when Alex and Franzisca walked out of the bedroom. The big man fixed Alex with a warning look, one he had adopted solely to address him.

"Have you eaten dinner, Lucien?" Franzisca asked in a way he had not heard her speak before. She sounded happier.

"Not yet, Baroness."

"Please join us. I'm famished and there's something I'd like to discuss with you."

The table was set for one, as it was every night. At the sight of the lady's guardian and the young man who had eyes only for the lady, the maid added two extra settings.

After they sat down, a veal stew with vegetables served over polenta was brought to the table. During the meal Lucien kept a watchful eye on his baroness; the young lady was actually enjoying her food and was very close to finishing her plate. He had been so worried about her. The young baroness barely ate anything and was growing thinner by the day. He had blamed the cook for the baroness' unhealthy pallor and ordered her to prepare an array of dishes daily to tempt her appetite. It seemed that nothing worked, not until today. To Lucien's palate, the food tasted as good as any other day, the only difference at the table was Alex Alcaly.

The meal finished with cooked fruit, walnut cookies, and tea. Franzisca thanked the maid and dismissed her until the next day, but the maid would not hear of it.

"If the gentlemen wish for more tea or dessert I'm very capable of taking care of it," Franzisca explained. The maid bowed respectfully and turned to leave when Franzisca spoke again. "Do you think you could bake a fruit pie for breakfast? I really loved the one you made on Monday. Oh, and a cup of that Turkish coffee you brought me yesterday instead of tea."

The maid beamed at her. "Whatever you wish, *doamna mea*, as long as you eat." The maid took her leave.

Franzisca fretted over her decision. Convincing Alex to agree to her plan had been challenging. Lucien, was another story altogether. The man was overly protective. One look at him and it was plain to see the way he measured each of Alex's attentions toward her. With or without Lucien's approval Franzisca had to put her plan into motion

"Lucien," Franzisca started.

"Yes, Baroness?" Lucien stood up ready to take orders.

"Please." She motioned her hand. "Sit down, and please, call me Franzisca. The title is a sham; we all know it. And if I'm going to confide my deepest secrets to you it is because I consider you a friend."

Lucien was shocked at her words and looked quickly away to hide his emotions.

"The thing is, Lucien, I'm going underground. I'm going to defy the Nazis."

"We," Alex stated.

Lucien sprang from his chair with such speed that Alex had no warning when the giant pulled him off his seat and closed his hand around Alex's throat. "You filthy piece of shit! I should kill you right now."

"Lucien, stop!" Franzisca leapt from her chair, grabbed a knife from the table, and jumped on Lucien's back, trying her best to pull him off Alex. "Alex has nothing to do with it."

Alex fought back and at Franzisca's words, Lucien loosened his hold. Franzisca stumbled back, then quickly stepped in between the two men, arms spread wide to keep them apart, knife aimed at both of them in turns. "I promise you, I will kill you both in your sleep if you as much as take one step forward."

The two men knew Franzisca would not make good on her promise. They stood staring at each other with loathing. Lucien and Alex had many things in common. They were hot headed and they were both fervently protective of Franzisca. The blows would come later; it was clear in the tension that emanated from both of them. For now, they would abide her orders.

The first one to laugh was Alex. Lucien glanced at the baker and an instant later, the big man's body trembled with suppressed laughter.

"What?" Franzisca could not find the humor in the situation. "What?" She was edgier than the two of them.

Alex pointed at the knife in her hand. "What were you about to do with a flat dessert knife, *inima mea*? Spread jam over us?"

Franzisca stared at the knife in her hand. The tension ebbed in the room and all three of them shared a laugh.

"Lucien." She turned to him, "I don't expect you to be part of what I must do. In fact, I would rather have you gone and be safe with your family."

Lucien looked solemn. "With all due respect, Baroness, I'll be the judge of that"

They made their way back to the table. The two men avoided eye contact.

"My main focus is Ploesti. After the uprising hundreds of people, mostly Jews, were taken into forced labor camps at the refineries in the city. Many of them children. Some escape and live off the streets until they die of hunger or they sell themselves in exchange for scraps of food." Franzisca swallowed the knot in her throat before continuing. "The children roaming the streets must be rescued before Nazi troops can get to them or Russian soldiers can enlist them as bait."

Lucien hesitated before he spoke out loud. "I have debts of my own to pay, Franzisca." It was the first time he had addressed her by her given name. "I would be honored if you would allow me to be a part of your operation. How do you plan on doing it?"

His question was met by silence. Franzisca looked around the table. A chauffer, a baker, and a housemaid up against Hitler, Antonescu, and their followers. Ridiculous, impossible, a suicide mission, but something she and Alex could tell their grandchildren one day, if they lived to tell the tale. In the meantime, all she could do was try.

"Things have changed since my marriage to Lupescu." Franzisca glanced toward Alex and saw his eyes harden. "Not only do I have diplomatic immunity as Baroness Lupescu, but among my *late husband's* properties there is a title to the biggest refinery in Ploesti."

"And what are you planning to do with that? As far as I know all those refineries are now under government control," Alex contested.

Franzisca brushed off his challenge with a smile. "Tour the premises with the excuse of surveying the current work and living situations of my countrymen. Get on the good side of the guards by praising their impeccable ethics and their patriotism for subduing Jews, the worst enemies of the nation, into forced labor." Franzisca paused and looked from Alex to Lucien. "Romanians love their nobles and since the abdication of King Karol last year they crave for anything close to a monarch. Do you think a guard would turn away a young baroness? Furthermore, do any of you think a lower ranked guard would refuse a sizable extra income for a few prisoners a month?"

Lucien sat in silence. Alex sighed. Both their faces were contorted with worry.

"You have given this a lot of thought, *inima mea*. I don't like it. I don't want you to take any chances. I won't allow you to go through with it," Alex said.

"I agree with Alcaly, Baroness," Lucien added.

"I'll go ahead with these plans with or without you," she stated putting an end to the constant nagging of the two men at the table. Franzisca reached for the teapot and served a second round of tea. They all sipped in silence while Franzisca's plan sank into their minds.

Franzisca set her cup down in its saucer. "There's more," she resumed. "While my mother was bedridden, I took her place serving tea to Lupescu and the many officials that met with him at the palace. I overheard valuable information. Lupescu didn't know that I'm fluent in German, so they were careless in discussing their business. Some of their main concerns were the resistance groups disrupting Nazi operations and feeding intelligence to the allies, and the unpredictable actions of neutral countries."

Alex nodded. He had gathered priceless information through his dealings on the black market for supplies. Since Jakub and his brothers had come into his life, he had seriously considered joining a resistance group. He had brought it up in conversation with Jakub after he witnessed the brothers' cabin fever, but Jakub had dismissed the idea as too dangerous. "The resistance groups that have spread throughout Europe are the biggest thorn in the Nazis behinds, if you excuse my language, especially since the German invasion of Russia in June," Alex contributed his knowledge. "One of the advantages of dealing in the black market, like I do, is identifying the highest paid commodities. Human cargo is the most profitable industry along the border with Yugoslavia today."

"I have a cousin that works the border between Romania and Yugoslavia. That thug's only loyalty lies with coin. The man is a pig." Lucien snarled.

Franzisca frowned and bit her upper lip. "But what of their fate after their passage to Yugoslavia?" She turned to Alex, "We must set up a meeting with members of the local resistance group, Alex."

Alex dueled with the situation in front of him. Franzisca's position as a Romanian baroness and Nazi sympathizer would be an asset the resistance could not refuse. "I'll arrange that," he finally agreed.

Regardless of the men's misgivings, they agreed that Franzisca as Baroness Lupescu was the key to the operation and gradually their plan took form. The prisoners would have to be smuggled out of the camps in the dead of the night, and from there, Alex would take them into hiding to one of the many tunnels across the city. Lucien's cousin and the passage into Yugoslavia would come next.

The country had entered a recession. Big businesses had closed their doors and their owners had left their homes and taken their fortunes to Switzerland, Spain, Portugal or Canada. Massive unemployment had given way to distrust in the current government, and corruption—a newly acquired way to make a living—overshadowed national pride. With that important factor to consider, all three agreed that they would undoubtedly find willing participants along the way.

Alex turned his head to look out the nearest window. The dark sky was slowly shifting to cobalt blue; a new day was soon to begin.

"I must go back to my bakery." He stood up and stretched his back. "My absence will raise suspicions and there's Jakub and his brothers to consider."

"I'm going with you." Franzisca rushed into her room and came out wearing her white coat.

Lucien held the front door open for her, "After you, Baroness."

***

When they arrived at the bakery, Alex knew something had gone awfully wrong when he saw the makeshift door of the bakery torn down. He stepped over the rubble and ran to the back of the store. The trapdoor to the basement was wide open and a quick inspection was enough to see that it was empty. There were no signs of struggle. The bedding the brothers used was neatly folded and piled up against a wall. The dishes were clean and set on the table right next to a note addressed to Jakub.

Alex scanned the note, frustrated with his scant knowledge of the Polish language.

"Damn kids. Here." He handed the note to Franzisca. "You seem to know every language spoken across Europe."

Franzisca took the note and read it. "Not every language, but I can manage Polish."

Franzisca confirmed what Alex feared. Jakub had gone out to find out what had happened to Alex. The brothers had run away to join the Russian army. They begged Jakub to forget about them and about the promise he had made to their parents. He deserved happiness, they wrote, and that he must find his own way out of the war. They vowed to look for him after the war was over so that they could be together again.

Was there no end to the guilt and grief? Franzisca thought as she lowered herself down onto a stool by one of the stone ovens. There were so many *ifs* swirling around in her head. *If* she had not have asked Lucien to look for Alex. *If* she did not need him so much, *if* she did not love him with every ounce of her being, Jakub would not have left the bakery to find Alex, and his brothers would have still been safe down in the basement.

"It is my fault." Franzisca rubbed her face and hunched in dismay.

"No, *inima mea.*" Alex knelt down by her side and looked into her eyes. "You must learn to stop blaming yourself for things that happen, things you have no control over. The pogrom, Jakub's brothers… It is not your fault, my heart, it is *this* horrible war's fault."

***

Sirens blared loudly across the city, a reminder of the nightly curfew. Soon, patrol cars would roam the streets in search for fugitives. Even though Jakub had lived as a captive for the past months, he was familiar with the geography of the city. Before the pogrom had assaulted the streets of Bucharest back in January of that year, when Jews still enjoyed a rare freedom while the rest of the European Jewry didn't, Jakub and his brothers spent their days hopping from corner to corner, doing their best to divert attention from themselves and fine tuning their skills necessary to survive as street rats. But things had changed since then. Antonescu's alliance with Hitler condemned those without Aryan or Romanian blood to work as forced labor in prison camps.

The loud tromping of boots and a stifled scream along with a nearby gunshot froze Jakub in his tracks. He hadn't wandered far from the bakery, but his legs would not obey him, either to go back to the safety of the room beneath the bakery or move forward in search of Alex. A round of gunshots and laughter followed by profanities shouted at a murdered Jew on the streets swept a wave of panic over him. He could not recall such a feeling when his parents were murdered, or when he was taken into the work camp with his brothers. It was pure survival instinct that drove him to escape the camp and to travel for months until they reached Romania. From the moment of his parents' murder, Jakub took on his brothers as his driving force, his reason for living, fighting. Now, separated for the first time in over a year, he felt raw, exposed. His body shook uncontrollably and he knew this was not a battle he could face alone, he needed the reassurance of his brothers' love to fulfill the promise he made to his dead parents.

Jakub hunched down behind a pile of trash that had been ransacked earlier that night by vagrant dogs. He waited until the murderous activity on the streets was out of earshot. When the first rays of the new day scratched the sky, he made a run for the bakery shop.

He slowed at the sight of a Rolls Royce parked a few meters from the bakery. The car flew two flags on the front bumper. One bearing a family crest, the other one with the swastika. Cold sweat bathed him when his eyes caught sight of the bakery's main entrance. The wooden plank that served as a door to the bakery, which he had left chained, was smashed. Jakub's heart jumped in his throat. His brothers had been caught, killed!

Frantic, Jakub stepped over the splintered wood and was met with a tower of a man who grasped him by both arms restraining him as if he were no more than a puppy.

"Let him be, Lucien," he heard a woman say.

Jakub's breath had slowed momentarily when he recognized Alex. But his heart stopped when he tripped over the opened trap door and reached for the note Alex gave him.

His brothers had left on their own accord. Jakub wailed a cry of despair. He had broken his promise and with that his will to live was gone. In front of Alex, standing over an empty basement, Jakub felt his soul leave him.

It was his fault. He should have never left them alone, especially not after the heated argument they had. The bitter cold would kill his beloved brothers before a bullet could. Shame washed all over him, an unwelcome feeling. He had gone out to find Alex out of fear for his own life. A moment of weakness had cost him what he loved the most. How could he let that happen?

Rare violet-blue eyes pierced his blurry vision, his thoughts suddenly interrupted. "I'm sorry about your brothers, Jakub."

Jakub pushed her away from him and was rewarded with a slap from the giant Lucien that sent him sprawling against the nearest wall.

"You will show respect to the baroness," Lucien growled.

Alex went to Jakub's aid. "Tell your guard dog to stay away from Jakub," he spat at the so called baroness.

Jakub lifted his eyes and caught the brief silent exchange between the baroness and Alex. She wore a snowy white, knee length coat, the kind his mother would have worn over an elegant dress when attending one of the many functions his parents went to frequently. He noticed the unique brass key she wore around her neck. Nearly identical to the one Alex wore around his. There was a history behind those perfectly matching keys. They were not just casual acquaintances.

"Lucien," the baroness said. "Jakub is Alex's friend, a brother, and should be treated as such."

The word brother stung Jakub's gut. The almighty baroness had replaced Jakub's loss in a few short minutes with a new brother strange to his blood.

While he stood in front of the baroness, stripped of his dignity and in despair, Jakub's mind flew to one of the stories of the bible that had always puzzled him; the story of Job. The baroness had done to him the same thing God had done to Job, he thought. He had shredded Job's heart to pieces with unbearable pain to later trick him into gleefully accepting replacements for what he had torn away from him. Jakub was not Job. God had been the reason for Job's pain, and in that moment, Jakub decided that this so-called baroness, the person that had taken his brothers from him, was the reason for his own pain. He did not feel guilty anymore. He had become the victim of her actions.

"As you wish, Baroness," the servant replied, keeping a wary eye on Jakub.

A glimmer of light illuminated Jakub's handsome and grief stricken face. Even a blind man could see that the full extent of his hatred was directed toward her.

"It was you who came for Alex," Jakub said to Franzisca.

"In a way. Yes," Franzisca replied.

"It was because of you that I went out to find him," he continued, measuring his words.

Franzisca did not reply; she just stared at him.

"Then it is because of *you* that my brothers left." Jakub pointed his finger at Franzisca. "Every day my brothers suffer of cold and hunger, every day they are faced with death, if they die, if they never come back to me, know that you are the *only* one to blame." He handed down his judgment.

It was a showdown.

In Jakub Berkowitz Franzisca saw the face of her first enemy and her heart cooled toward any sympathy she had felt for his predicament. Faced with Jakub, Franzisca reached a few decisions in lightning speed. For Alex's sake, she would do everything in her power to see Jakub safe out of Romania. But she did not trust him.

Jakub studied her features. She was about his age, with lustrous, raven hair, rare ocean colored eyes and golden skin. In his roughish days, before the war, he would have sweetened her ears with verses of romantic poetry to gain access to the buttons of her blouse. Now, in the back room of the bakery, with a life of darkness ahead of him, he could only feel hate.

Everything in time, he thought after he memorized each one of her features. Everything in time.

Chapter Thirty-Five

Bucharest, August 1941

A few weeks after their first meeting, *Operation Baroness* was ready to start. A meeting between the newly formed organization and two senior resistance fighters was set up at Franzisca's secluded country house. Franzisca was introduced solely as *Baroness*. Underground routes throughout Europe were already established and refugees were being smuggled day and night across hostile borders. After forming an alliance with the resistance fighters, Franzisca detailed her plan to hide the refugees in her manor in England until they could escape Europe for good.

"Our arms stretch throughout the globe," the younger fighter assured Franzisca. "We use hideouts all over Europe."

The opportunity to free prisoners from camps with the baroness' influence was dangerously tempting for the fighters. "Do you understand the risks involved? There are resistance fighters impersonating Nazi officials and Nazi spies amongst our own. This is a no mercy game, Baroness. We are at war. An eye for an eye," the older of the two fighters said to Franzisca.

"An eye for an eye," Franzisca echoed. Her heart filled with resolve.

The resistance leaders left the meeting with the precise location of the Schultzes manors in England, France, and Austria and with a substantial influx of cash for firearms and supplies.

In the following days, the duplicity of the Romanian people was put to the test. In exchange for a weeklong supply of food, blind eyes were turned toward the activities of the resistance in different areas of the city.

The Rolls Royce became a regular sighting around the refineries in Ploesti. A short time later, reports of the first *cargo that* arrived safely in England reached the headquarters of Operation Baroness. During the same time, Baroness Irina Lupescu received a string of invitations to black tie affairs in the Spanish and Portuguese embassies.

Escorted by Lucien, Franzisca shook hands with allies and Nazis alike. From one side of her mouth, she expressed her admiration for the Fuehrer and for the service her husband the baron, who had gone missing in action, had provided for the Nazi cause. From the other side, she arranged safe passage and visas for the refugees with the help of some daring Spanish and Portuguese diplomats.

What was supposed to be a short-term operation reached its first year in the blink of an eye. At that time, the three founding members of Operation Baroness met to regroup and go over the latest news and developments over a late night dinner at Franzisca's country manor.

"Seven hundred and twenty-one," Alex informed his partners, having kept an accurate tally of the prisoners and refugees that had been transported.

"It is not enough," Franzisca responded sharply.

"It might have to do for now, Franzisca," Lucien said, avoiding her piercing stare and looking to Alex for support.

Lucien's and Alex's concern for Franzisca's safety heightened when her regular visits to Lupescu's refineries in Ploesti had become the talk of the town. The young baroness represented the beauty and national pride the Romanians strived to be known for. They longed for the days when the country was a monarchy. In Baroness Lupescu the people of Ploesti saw the closest thing to a queen.

The operation had run swiftly since its inception. They had lost twenty-two refugees during their runs from the camps to the tunnels or when crossing over borders. Disease and malnourishment were the two main factors in the loss of life, Franzisca tried to convince herself of that, when in reality many of the rescued prisoners had lost the will to live. Every death was a dagger in her heart and reminded her of the debt she had yet to pay. She did not voice her feelings in front of Alex or Lucien anymore, only because they could not see it through her eyes and she didn't expect them to. Men, as she came to realize, functioned on objectivity, the here and the now. She feigned the same attitude, especially in front of resistance fighters, but that was only at the beginning.

A year into the operation, Franzisca could barely recognize herself. She had become a hard, ruthless woman. To get whatever useful information from her enemies' lips, she partied with them, flirted with them and in more than one occasion, she had allowed them to cozy up to her, to let their filthy fingers feel the contours of her body while they rubbed their hard cocks against her. She would never reveal this side of herself to Alex. It would devastate him. It would devastate them.

Alex was seldom around. He kept the doors of the bakery open under the care of some trusted old neighbors to run it during the day, while at night it became a drop off and pick up point for refugees. His main focus was on the tunnel network in which he worked hand in hand with resistance fighters.

Every time they parted, it was an emotional farewell, for they were uncertain if they would ever be together again. Every reunion felt like finding an oasis after years of wandering lost in the dessert. It was in Alex's arms where Franzisca became alive. He would pronounce her name over and over again until a glimmer of her own self would peek through the body armor she wore in this war.

She slowly melted at his touch. She would view his key as a constant reminder that he would forever be her beacon.

"This is far from what we wanted, Baroness," Lucien cut into her thoughts bringing her back to reality. He turned to Alex, "Alcaly, they worship her. Only last week a young mother with three brats at her feet stood with her mouth hanging open like a dog at the sight of Franzisca in the back seat of the car. The woman made all three children bow low when we drove by."

Franzisca sat silent. She had overstayed her welcome in Romania. SS officers buzzed around her prodding into her affairs. Questions being asked, especially about her marriage to the baron and her own origins. So far, she had been able to manage them without incurring their suspicions.

Not for the first time Franzisca wondered if her mother had tutored her as if she could foresee the tools Franzisca might need in the future. The story of the Dobos, as well as her patrician education served Franzisca well, enabling her to navigate the murky waters of power, politics, and lies. She had also developed a sixth sense in order to read people. The eyes of her enemies upon her had felt heavier recently. The guards at the camps had grown greedier. She too knew it was time to leave. At least for the time being.

"We'll do our last run in Ploesti tomorrow. We can leave the next day," Franzisca informed the two men in the room.

The next afternoon, they drove away from the refinery where a preposterous sum had been demanded for the release of four prisoners. Even though it was hard to stop Operation Baroness, she had to think of the many lives that would be endangered if she got caught. She was not alone in this fight. A community of fighters had joined her cause.

"Your children are very lucky, Lucien," she said. Lucien turned and looked at her and she smiled at him. "To have you as their father. They are very lucky."

Franzisca thought she heard the big man swallow a sob but her attention was caught by a flash of a movement in the mouth of a giant pipe that lead to an abandoned aqueduct. "Lucien, stop!"

The man stepped on the brakes and surveyed the desolated road. "What, what is it?"

"There." She pointed at the pipe. Franzisca jumped out of the car with Lucien at her heels. He outran her and reached the pipe before she did. Lucien and Franzisca knelt at the opening and found three pairs of frightened eyes staring at them.

"We cannot, Baroness." His protest even weak to his own ears.

Franzisca smiled at him. She had caught sight of a little girl. She looked no older than four. Her eyes were huge with fear and hunger.

"Don't be scared." Franzisca reached out her hand for her.

The little girl took refuge behind one of the older children and did not look up when Lucien bundled them into the back seat of the car.

That night, after the delivery of the children into the hands of the network that would see them safely out of the country, Alex, Franzisca and Lucien sat at the dinner table in Franzisca's cottage for one last time.

"Operation Baroness is over," Alex declared.

Lucien nodded.

"For now," Franzisca contested.

"All your papers are in order. You and the baroness will leave on the first train tomorrow morning. The exchange with the guards at the camp earlier today was unpleasant. I wanted nothing more than to crack that son of a bitch's skull. The way he sneered at her... Franzisca must disappear from Romania," Lucien spoke directly to Alex.

"For now," Franzisca challenged them again. The two men in the room chose to ignore her.

Franzisca bit her lip, looked at Lucien. "The little girl, the one we found in Ploesti with the other children, did she tell you her name?"

Lucien shook his head troubled. "The poor thing is mute, maybe deaf, too. The other children said they've never heard her say a word."

"Little Margaret," Franzisca muttered. "In the meantime we shall call her Little Margaret."

Saying goodbye to Lucien the next morning was harder than Franzisca had imagined. She clung to the big man and sobbed. "I wish you and your family would come with us now, Lucien. What am I to do without you?"

The big man was as emotional as a new mother and could not contain his tears. "We will be there to celebrate your birthday, Franzisca. I promise, and you know Lucien never breaks a promise."

"If you're not in England by January twenty-first, I'll come for you." Franzisca gave him one last hug.

"Thank you, Lucien," Alex said in earnest.

"Thank you, Alcaly," Lucien replied.

Alex and Lucien shook on a firm and warm handshake. "We'll see you soon, big man."

"Take care of her, will you?" said Lucien, fixing Alex with that hard stare of his.

Alex clapped him on the shoulder. "I wouldn't worry if I were you. I learned from the best."

With one hand, Alex picked up two small valises from the ground, and helped Franzisca onto the train with the other.

Franzisca turned around and waved at Lucien. A blast of steam from the train muted Franzisca last words to him. Had she said *I love you*? Lucien shook his head and smiled feebly. They had formed a bond, they had become friends and he loved that young girl as if she were his own. Lucien stood watching the train pull away until he lost sight of it in the fog of the early morning.

Lucien wanted to shed the emptiness Franzisca's departure had caused in him before going back home to his family. He drove slowly assessing the turn of events in his life over the past year. As a man, for once in his life, he felt proud of his actions. As a result, he had gotten his family back. Mariah loved the life in the country and had laughed when Lucien taught her to milk a cow. The kids were growing happy and strong and jumped all over him whenever he walked through the door. He had Franzisca to thank for it. Being dismissed from the Lupescu's services turned out to be the biggest blessing of his life.

Lucien drove up the long driveway to his home. He was already savoring the meal that he knew awaited him. Mariah had taken to gardening, since the move to the country, she had treated Lucien to new dishes every time he spent the night at the house. The food was not the only thing on his mind, though. The kids, of course, he wanted to hug them and play with them, but today more than any other day, he had a pressing need to thrust his cock between his wife's meaty thighs. With that thought in mind, he was resolved to tire out the kids with some rough play and send them to sleep early.

When he pulled up to the house, it was midday and he was met with an unusual quietness, instead of the excited welcome he had expected from the flurry of energy his twins had become. On any other day, the kids would be seated by the hearth playing with blocks, or perusing the many picture books Franzisca sent to them, pretending they could read.

When he stepped into the parlor, he saw the books and blocks lying by the cold hearth. As he moved through the kitchen, dining room and living room he could not find signs of his family.

"Mariah." His voice echoed as the only response.

The weather was bitterly cold outside and he knew that Mariah would not take the children out for a walk and a picnic as she had done during the long summer days. But he could be wrong; Lucien shrugged and smiled. Mariah was a changed woman since they moved out of the city and he bet all his gold that she had bundled up the twins with heavy coats so that they could enjoy a bit of fresh air. Frigid air, he corrected himself.

Lucien stoked the fire up to a bright flame to warm up the house upon their return and made his way to his bedroom.

The door to the room was closed. Lucien thought that strange since Mariah insisted on keeping all doors open to let the country air flow continuously from room to room. Another crazy, new habit, Lucien shook his head with humor.

Pine and tobacco scent and the unmistakably stench of blood penetrated his nostrils the moment he opened the door. He found his children lying on the floor, a bloody splitting axe inches from them. He looked again. Where those broken bloody dolls his children? Lucien could not tell. There were body parts. Hands and legs and feet scattered around the room. He knew those parts to belong to his children, because they were imprinted in his memory. He was so confused. The twins were sturdy little kids, not parts... He tore his eyes from the carnage at his feet and saw Mariah on the bed spread eagle tied to the bedposts. Her face was beaten beyond recognition. There was blood between her beautiful legs, raw flesh where her breast should have been, a deep slit across her throat.

"She was a good fuck, Lucien. Rather loud. You always had an eye for the best whores, my friend."

Lucien turned to find Baron Mihail Lupescu leaning against a wall, calmly smoking, bathed in the blood of his family.

The baron took a step toward Lucien, who stood in shock. "I came to claim what's mine, my dear Lucien." Before his stunned mind could react, Lupescu dug a knife deep in Lucien's gut. The big man gasped, his eyes fixed on the baron. "Where is my wife?"

Chapter Thirty-Six

Buenos Aires, April 2013

Lukas Blau had exhausted the last of his energy and had fallen silent. Pain shot down the fingers in my right hand, they felt stiff, numb. Only when Daniel moved slightly, I noticed that my fist closed tightly around his wrist.

"I'm sorry," I muttered, and used the same fingers that until now had kept him hostage by my side to bring back some blood flow to the rest of his arm.

Daniel smiled tenderly at me and patted my hand. "Are you all right?"

I shook my head. I didn't dare utter a response; my tears were too close to the surface. Daniel read me like a book from the first day he saw me, and captured my hands in his.

"Señor Blau." Daniel was not about to let the old man cool off and regain his cocky attitude. "Were you in England when Alex and Franzisca arrived?"

The old man, sat shriveled on the white sofa and fixed Daniel with suspicion as if seeing him for the first time. I could hear the machinations of Blau's brain. So many years of having a personal vendetta against my abuela left him hovering between truth and fiction. Whatever he would say next would forever shatter the hatred that had driven him for the past seven decades. It was risky, I thought, he could very well die if he let go of all his anger.

"The baroness did not want me anywhere near her," Blau spoke directly to me. "I don't blame her. She was a smart, smart woman and had sensed my feelings toward her from that first day when I unjustly blamed her for the death of my brothers. Still, I was at the manor in Derbyshire, when they both arrived. I heard them argue when she saw me, but always the picture of decorum; she composed herself and walked past me as if I did not exist. They stayed at the house for over a week. Without her knowledge, and per Alex's request, I had become the administrator of the manor. To conceal the true purpose for the house, nuns— the most admirable resistance fighters—had taken up residence and turned it into an orphanage."

"Where did adults go when they arrived in England?" Daniel asked.

"England and France," Blau replied. "The baroness had everything arranged with the Spanish and Portuguese diplomats. They continued on to either country with government issued visas." Blau stopped to look at both of us. We must have looked perplexed and transparent at the same time. "You must be asking yourself why I didn't leave for Portugal or Spain." Like two bobble heads we nodded at the same time. "Believe it or not Sofia, I wanted to help. The house was filled with children... I could not save my parents, my brothers, but if I could do anything to make a child smile, then I felt like I could stand living for another day."

"I do believe you and I don't judge you." The knot in my throat was finally dissolving. "What pains me is that you did not get the chance to know the real Franzisca, my abuela. She was a formidable woman."

"That she was," Blau agreed." But I did not find out the truth until it was too late. You see," words rushed out of his mouth as to not be interrupted. "The baroness was a woman of steel around others. She showed no emotion. She chose her words carefully and never had a smile to spare. She even treated Alex in the same cold demeanor. Even though I knew they were lovers, I thought he suffered for her ill treatment of him, and I could not stand the idea of seeing another person I loved suffer."

"What happened, Blau?" Daniel pressed, cutting to the chase. He had had his fill of Blau's personal feelings. He wanted to get to the core of the story, the part where Blau would confess why he thought he had wrecked all our lives.

"Alex left the manor right away, he was still involved with the resistance, and the baroness stayed until a little girl, she called *Little Margaret*, arrived with five other children."

"Margaret," I exclaimed.

"Yes, Margaret," Blau confirmed. "Your abuela travelled constantly to Spain and Portugal, this is information Alex let slip accidentally, and I believe she had a place in London she called home. On occasion she made unannounced visits at the manor, to check on the children, but especially on little Margaret."

"Of course, she did," I said to myself. What the hell, I finally let tears slide down my face.

"It must have been three, perhaps four months after Alex and the baroness arrived in England when one of the nuns received an urgent message from the resistance. Our cover had been blown. The baroness' guard dog in Romania, Lucien, had been murdered and so had others who had collaborated with her. No one knew who was behind it, but it was time to disappear."

"Where was my grandfather?" Daniel asked.

"He arrived alone at the manor that same day. The man was a complete mess. He did not know where the baroness was. The resistance had lost her trail. He thought she was dead, too. Later that night he received a message. It was from her. She couldn't disclose her location. The message said that it was urgent that he transferred thirty-four of the thirty-five children at the manor to Argentina. The thirty-five blank passports issued by the Argentinean government to Nazi officers were hidden under the floorboards of the room she slept in when she visited the children."

"What about my grandfather?"

"He had his own passport. His papers were legitimate. Remember in those days Alex did not live as a Jew," Blau remarked

"Why not Margaret? Why was she left behind?" I asked him. I could already guess the reason, but I wanted him to admit it out loud.

He looked somber, guilty. "The baroness, she never broke a promise, and she had promised Alex I would be safe." His words cracked with emotion. "You had to be there to see what I saw. *I* witnessed the way she conducted herself around the government officials on the occasions they made formal visits to the manor. She radiated greed and power. I always felt she used the Holocaust to make a mark for herself in the history books. To be worshipped as a Goddess. She had the way of a lioness, seductive, fierce. She had only to look at men to have them fall down at her feet. My blood boiled when I thought about Alex. I had no doubts she slept with other men to get what she wanted."

"What she wanted?" I hissed. "*If,* and only if she slept with other men it had nothing to do with her wants, Señor Blau. My grandmother, Franzisca, was a fighter, not a whore. You did not know her. You did not know Franzisca. I did. I grew up with her. I lived through her battles; I felt her joy, her fears, her pain." I was on my feet, screaming. "You have no idea who my abuela was because you have never seen anything through her eyes."

I felt winded. I couldn't get another word out. It had suddenly dawned on me. What I had thought to be a ludicrous request, her last wish, not to bury her until *I could see it through her eyes*, had been part of me ever since I could remember. I had always seen it through her eyes. And through her eyes now, I finally understood the words Franzisca wrote in her last note to Alex.

You hold the other half of my heart.

From the moment Abuela got separated from Alex she became half a woman. It had always been about the boy she found, or about the boy that found her, and it would always be.

"No, I did not know her," Blau's remorseful voice intruded in my thoughts. "And it is because of that reason that I destroyed her. All those years I chose to blame her for the fate of my brothers, when I actually blamed myself," he admitted, overwhelmed with shame.

Lukas Blau stood up from his immaculate white sofa. His eyes stared at something behind us and smiled.

In my dazed state, I had lost sight of any activity going on around the room. I turned around, curious to see who had entered, but there was no one behind me.

The next thing I heard made me think of a sack of rattling bones. It was almost musical. One bone collapsing against the other. A domino effect, until the frame that had held Lukas Blau erect for the past seven decades was nothing but a puddle on the white marble floor.

Daniel rushed to him, felt his pulse. He shook his head. Lukas Blau was dead.

Part III

Chapter Thirty-Seven

San Rafael, Mendoza, April 2013

Marcela put the phone down and pressed the heels of her palms against her closed eyelids. Undertaker was the word that came to her mind, she felt like an undertaker.

She was not fond of Lukas Blau, but when she talked him into helping her—coerced him, being a more fitting word—she did not wish for the man to die of it. He had lived with guilt for most of his life and by purging his sins he had finally found a way to freedom. To death. If only…

She had lived with guilt since the age of fifteen and had attempted to take her own life three times. Every time she had woken up hooked to an IV in a hospital room with either Margaret or her mother hovering over her blanched face, she understood that she did not have the right to die. Death, as she saw it, was not for cowards and she was a coward.

"Sofia was hysterical. My poor girl," Margaret said over the phone. "The man dropped dead at her feet. I thank God she wasn't alone."

Then Margaret had gone on and on about details Blau had revealed to Sofia. Marcela allowed Margaret to talk as much as she needed to. Dear Margaret was in shock. A vast portion of Blau's accounts explained Margaret's early life, especially the one thing that had eaten her heart out for years. She had finally come to the knowledge about the circumstances surrounding her fate. Why she had been left behind when all the other kids at the English manor were put aboard a ship to South America.

The death of Blau did not come as a real shock to Marcela. The man had nearly fulfilled his end of the bargain, and had dropped the ball, literally, when Claudia Lazar's story was about to start.

Marcela stood up from the bed in her former room at the finca, and stared at the window. Fall was upon them and there had been an early snow only two days ago. She loved this place. She had from the first day her mother, holding the tiny Sofia in the crook of her arms, had opened the doors to the house.

The finca held a rare kind of magic. It was very easy to wander around the orchards or walk down to the creek at the bottom of the property and forget about what lay between mother and daughter before they had arrived there.

"Everything will be all right, Marcelita," her mother had said to her while stealing a glance at the baby in her arms. "All three of us we'll be all right."

Marcela wanted to believe her, but she couldn't. The last time she had believed in anything, Marcela had been twelve-years-old.

When the truth came out, it was far from what Marcela had fantasized. Like any other child, her own included, the mystery behind the man who had fathered her haunted her. She knew that her father was not dead, her mother had disclosed as much, but that was the pivotal point where the conversation always reached a dead end.

According to a therapist, who had spent half a million dollars on the many diplomas on his wall, the absence of a father in her life, the unanswered questions about his anonymity had turned Marcela into an insecure child, a reckless teenager, and a suicidal adult. Such a cliché verdict. Stupid, inept therapist, Marcela thought. She had been the happiest of girls during her childhood. What had turned her into a vengeful teenager and later a suicidal adult had nothing to do with her father's anonymity and everything to do with his identity. But that had been a secret she had sworn to take with her to the grave.

Her steely determination wavered the day her mother paid an impromptu visit to her studio in Florence exactly a year before her death. She had gone to her looking for reconciliation. She had gone to her looking for help. He mother had spoken to her of love and of bonds that could never be severed, not even with distance, not even with silence. How could she make her *mamá* understand that she had never held her responsible for the predicament in her life? That she was the one who carried poison in her blood. Leaving was the only option that had seemed rational to her at that moment. She needed to keep her mother safe from her and give Sofia a chance for a somewhat normal life. For years, she had rehearsed her speech for when the time would come to explain her side of the story.

But her mother had robbed her of words when she pulled her into her embrace. It had been a fleeting moment, but long enough to remind Marcela how much she longed for her mamá's scent, for the safety of her arms, and yes, for one last chance to say, *I'm so sorry, Mamá.*

After the door to her studio closed blocking Claudia's retreating footsteps, Marcela stood in the center of the room wondering if Claudia had actually been there or if her sudden presence had been an apparition. Italy and all its religious superstitions were getting to her head, she thought, feeling silly. Her mother had been there and that was a fact. Her scent still floated in the air and the tears they had both shed during their embrace still clung to Marcela's face. How long had her mother said she had left? Six months? A year? "All right," she said, when she gained back the command of her voice. It was time to stiffen her spine and open up her box of secrets to Sofia. It was her golden opportunity to do something for her mother even if it meant to ease her path into death. Filled with resolved she called Margaret. "It's time she finds peace," she blurted out as soon as Margaret picked up the phone. No more words were needed. A plan was already in motion.

A year had gone by and not without complications. The plan she had engineered with Margaret had gradually reached its pinnacle and it was nearing its conclusion. Marcela hadn't counted on Blau dropping dead without disclosing his sins, or on Daniel Alcaly entering the picture and romancing Sofia senseless. Even though Margaret swore that Alcaly's feelings for Sofia were genuine, Marcela had her serious doubts. She couldn't image the man to be driven by anything else other than revenge. She was familiar with the boundless actions a maddened person could take when driven by bitterness. But this time, she would take the bullet. Once again, she would do anything to safeguard Sofia. It was a promise she had made the day Sofia was born and a promise she had pledged again the day her mother died.

According to Margaret, Sofia and Daniel Alcaly would be arriving in Mendoza that afternoon. Marcela had begged Margaret to be with her when she would reveal the truth to Sofia, especially now that Daniel Alcaly had become part of the mix. Her actions had gotten him involved and Alcaly, friend or foe, deserved answers as much as Sofia did.

"I've held your hand all these years, *luvie*," Margaret had said, using that pet name reserved just for her, which always made Marcela feel loved. "You're ready."

True to her cowardly nature, Marcela had tried to prevent this moment from happening. She had met with Sofia at the house in Solvang for that specific reason and what a painful episode it had turn out to be for Marcela. The realization that her daughter no longer hated her had wounded her deeply. Sofia had desensitized the blood that ran through their veins and had finally broken the last string of feelings that had connected them. All the more reason to come clean now, more than ever, Marcela mused. How much worse could it get?

It was still early morning. She had most of the day to organize her thoughts, perhaps even stage the story. "*You haven't become a world-renowned painter for nothing*;" Margaret's words of encouragement rang in her ears.

"If you say so," Marcela said out loud as if Margaret were in the room.

She walked back to her bed, kneeled, and looked under it. The box she had left the day she moved out the finca for good was still there. Marcela was not surprised to find it exactly where and how she had left it. Her mother would not come near it. Claudia Lazar had sworn by the privacy of boxes.

In the beginning, the box had started out as a way to keep their living space clean. After her mother had enough of stepping on Marcela's drawings or finding little rocks, pins and on more than one occasion dead insects in between the sheets, Claudia had presented the idea of a box to her four-year-old daughter, *Marcelita*.

As time went by, Marcela had narrowed her collection down to penciled sketches she drew on pads and little mementos, like paper napkins with messages from this or that boy she liked, or cinema tickets from her favorite movies.

Until the day a man gave her the newspaper clipping.

Marcela pulled the rectangular wooden box from under the bed. A veil of dust covered the lid of what had once contained a priceless Chinese vase. The size had seemed big at the time, but Marcela had no doubt she would soon fill it with whatever her new curiosity might be.

Life was good for Marcela in the days preceding *the man with the newspaper article*. There was the issue of her father, of course, but back then, Marcela still believed in fairytales. Frustrated from the lack of responses from her mother, Marcela took matters in her own hands and gave her father the title of a prince. She envisioned him to be a great warrior that was busy fighting and defeating enemies, a capital enterprise that kept him from her. But wars end, she was sure of that, and at that point, he would gallop home to her, astride his magnificent horse, and would claim her as the child of his heart.

With the help of the innumerable colored pencils and watercolors her mother kept her stocked with, Marcela put a face to the father of her dreams: A brawny, blonde prince with pale blue eyes, exactly like her. Satisfied with her work, she hid the painting in the box and never showed it to her mother. The story had to be kept a secret. If word got out about the identity of her father the prince, then his life would be in danger, and he might never come for her.

Shortly after, the man gave her the newspaper clipping with the picture in it.

Marcela opened the box and rummaged among its contents until she found the faded newspaper article.

The man had stood waiting for her at the main gate of the private English School she attended in Buenos Aires a day after her mother left for another business trip. The trip had involved some new artistic venture. In all honesty, she hadn't paid much attention. All of her attention was on the plans she had for when Margaret arrived to stay with her during her mother's absence. Margaret was all the family they had and Marcela cherished the time they spent together.

Marcela remembered waiting at the gates of the school for her mother's driver to come for her. Traffic, she thought, it must be traffic that had him delayed. Lately, the streets were swarmed with people screaming with unhappiness. It had something to do with Peron, the dead President, and Isabelita, his widow and current president.

To ten-year-old Marcela this or that president did not make a difference to the amazing life she shared with her mother. She did think Isabelita looked a little like a bat, with hair stiff like an army helmet, though.

And then the man walked up to her.

"Marcela Lazar."

Marcela raised her eyes to see a man as old as her mother, fifty or so, tall, with light brown hair.

"I'm waiting for my driver and Margaret will be in the car, too," she said, braver than she felt. Her mother had warned her never to step out of the school's gate until she or an adult of their trust walked up to the school to get her.

"Margaret," the man muttered. "Little Margaret."

"She's not little." Marcela chastised him. "Nor is the driver."

"Of course not... big as Lucien, I imagine. The baroness likes her guard dogs big," the man muttered under his breath.

Marcela did not like the man and was truly frightened; she pivoted and made a run for the school gate.

"Wait," the man yelled. "I have something for you from your father."

Marcela stopped dead in her tracks. The man came over to her and handed her a yellowed newspaper clipping.

"My father sends this for me?" she asked, staring at the picture. Marcela was entranced by the image of a stoic soldier, with medals and colorful badges covering both planes of his chest. The man had his face slightly turned to the right, displaying a straight nose very much like hers.

"The soldier in the picture *is* your father, Marcelita." The man pointed his finger at the picture.

The caption under the photograph read *General Armendariz back from diplomatic appointment in Switzerland.* The date at the top of the newspaper was about a year before her birthdate.

"General Armendariz," she whispered. "Does he ride a horse?"

The man barked out a laugh, "Oh, child. Ask your mother. She surely knows of his riding habits."

There was something macabre in the way the man spoke of her mother, and what was that thing he had said about a baroness? Marcela's ride approached the curb by the school. "There's my car," Marcela exclaimed.

"It was a pleasure meeting you, Honorable Marcela Lupescu. Tell your mother Jakub Berkowitz sends his regards."

Macabre indeed, Marcela thought back at the way Blau had planned his revenge. Jakub Berkowitz or Lukas Blau walked into her life to set her onto a path of destruction, to use her innocence to drop the hammer of judgment over her mother.

Marcela emptied out the objects from her box into a pile at her feet. The clipping Blau had given her the day she met him, more clippings about General Armendariz and his appointment as ambassador in Germany months after his return from Switzerland, the pale yellow handkerchief her mother used to dry up her tears the night she told her the truth, a torn dirty shirt with blood stains on it from the night Armendariz died, and wrapped in pink tissue paper–Sofia's first undershirt.

Marcela picked up the tiny undershirt and walked out of her room. She pressed the garment up to her nose and inhaled deeply. Sofia had been so small that Marcela had feared she would die in between breaths. Her mother had fallen in love with baby Sofia right away. She had walked around the private clinic in Buenos Aires with a smile on her face. The last time she had seen her mother smile like that was before the party she held for Marcela and her friends for the inauguration of the Soccer World Cup in 1978.

Sofia. There was no end to the damage Marcela had caused. In her heart, when she walked out of Sofia's life after her tenth birthday, she thought she was doing the best for her daughter. She had never intended to scar the child's life, to pass a legacy of misery onto her daughter. But she did.

There wasn't any room left for more regret. What was done was done. Holding the little garment, Marcela continued on to the living room to organize the rest of the elements she needed for her dramatic show and tell.

A few days ago, Marcela had contacted her studio in Florence and had her assistant ship to the finca selected pieces of her work. There were from her early days, paintings she had never put on the market.

Art critics fell head over heels over her work. The images spoke of war and death. Of the dismemberment of a society through violence, of loss, of exile, the write-ups claimed.

She had to agree with the critics, yet her artwork did not paint the story of Argentina during the military regime that extended from 1976 to 1983. Her artwork spoke of her life. When the coup struck the country, she had been too young and sheltered to notice its dramatic effects. During the military regime's later years she had become too involved in a war of her own.

She picked up the first painting. War and death, it was her mother's story. Marcela placed it against the wall and removed the linen that covered the next painting. The fingers of her right hand traced the scar on the inside of her left wrist. After she had finished that painting, she had reached for the box cutter she used to open everything from art supply boxes to pantyhose packages and slashed her wrists. In front of her eyes lay the dismemberment of her pretty little fantasy world the moment she learned about the murderous nature of her father. The next painting was also tainted with violence and it depicted the death of the man that fathered her. Loss was all over the painting she unveiled next. This one was for Daniel Alcaly. It was about the senseless loss of his family and her role in it. Exile, was the last of the paintings; her uncertain place in the world.

And what was she to say to her daughter? Would Sofia believe her if she told her that ever since she was born, Marcela had painted in her head a world where she would never get hurt, a world where she would find only happiness? Probably not, but all she could do was try.

With all the objects and paintings arranged in the manner of an art exhibit, Marcela had nothing else to do but wait for Sofia and Alcaly to arrive. She chose to sit in the middle of her makeshift gallery. In one way or another, she was deeply connected to each one of them as the author or the protagonist of the events so vividly portrayed.

Surrounded by her paintings, Marcela retraced her steps to the day when she ceased to be a happy child. She hadn't meant to bring the subject of her father up, ever. She had buried the picture Blau gave her that day after school with the other treasures in her box. She only looked at it on occasion, when she caught mention of her father *The General* in newspaper articles. Claudia, her mother, had been humored by the sudden interest her *Marcelita* showed in the news. An interest Marcela justified due to the rather obvious social upheaval in the country.

Blame it on the *Mundial del 78*, Marcela thought. The country had come to a halt to watch the highly anticipated opening ceremony of the 1978 Soccer World Cup. She had begged her mother to buy tickets for the opening ceremony and first game, but Claudia preferred to stay home and watch it on television.

"How about a party?" Claudia suggested.

Before Claudia's last word was out of her mouth, Marcela had already phoned and invited ten of her closest friends over for the *Mundial* party.

When the day arrived, the house looked as if the ceremony was about to be held there and not at the River Plate Stadium. The familiar *Mundial* theme song played in the background, and flags of all the participating countries adorned the walls of their penthouse in Buenos Aires. A long buffet table held Argentinean specialties as well as from other countries. On every chair that surrounded the new color television, there was a *Gauchito* doll, a reproduction of the Argentinean mascot dressed in the team's striped jersey, accessorized with gaucho garb.

They girls ate, gossiped, and danced before the ceremony began. Marcela was the happiest girl on earth and had ran numerous times to the kitchen where her mother kept busy making sure food and drinks flowed uninterruptedly into the party, to hug her, kiss her and thank her.

Silence took over the T.V. room at the start of the ceremony. The cameras narrowed their lenses on President General Jorge Rafael Videla, the first of a string of military dictators, while the national anthem was played by a military band. Right behind the President, among the highest dignitaries of the nation was General Armendariz, standing proud, intoning the words to the anthem with passion.

Marcela was shocked to see him as a living, breathing being for the first time. She remembered pointing at the screen and the look of horror on her mother's face when from somewhere in the room she heard the echo of her own voice say, "that's my father."

Their whole life had spiraled down from there.

Chapter Thirty-Eight

Buenos Aires, April 2013

Daniel insisted we stay in Buenos Aires for a few days and then head to his *estancia,* the cattle ranch he grew up in, which was located one hundred kilometers away from the city. After Blau had literally dropped dead at our feet, I welcomed the respite of few days of sleep, good food, and plenty of reflection.

Through revelation after revelation, Blau had validated each story I knew about Franzisca. One could have said my mission was accomplished and I could go back home and make the necessary arrangements to have Abuela shipped, *ugh*, the term made me shiver, but yes, shipped as *cargo*, to be buried next to the love of her life, Alex Alcaly, in Buenos Aires.

The weeklong stay at Daniel's estancia proved to be just what the doctor ordered. For a few days, I was able to let Franzisca and all her ghosts remain in the past for a while longer and decided to explore my present, which came in the delicious form of Daniel Alcaly.

The main house at the ranch was nothing like I had imagined. It was a mansion, from the early nineteenth century, Daniel pointed out. The manor, a combination of French, English and Colonial architecture, sat overlooking vast expanses of countryside where cattle, sheep, goats, and horses grazed.

Besides the breathtaking beauty of the place, the estancia was a real working ranch. On our first day, we visited the grounds on horseback. One of the horse trainers treated us to a jaw-dropping exhibition, the taming of a reluctant white *Argentine Criollo*. When night fell, the cattle herdsmen set up a *real gaucho* fire outdoors and officially welcomed us with traditional beef empanadas and the best cuts of the meats the ranch had to offer. I had never seen Daniel so carefree before, he ate with abandon, drank his fill of red wine, and when all his inhibitions were down, he took hold of a guitar and sang some folksongs I had long forgotten. This man loved his land, his people, he needed all but to wear a pair of *bombachas*, gaucho pants, to be one of them.

Rested, well fed, and clearly besotted with each other, we set out to the finca in Mendoza. There were some documents that needed notarized signatures in order to complete the transfer of the title to my name, but mostly I wanted to show Daniel the place I once called home.

During the drive from the estancia to the airport, all the issues I had left dormant while at Daniel's place began to surface again. Since the incident at Blau's I felt further from the truth than when I first began to nose into Abuela's past. I wasn't the only one. Daniel had also retreated to his thoughts. I couldn't help but resent Blau. Regardless of his heartfelt apology, I felt he had the last laugh on us.

Once we took our seats on the plane, I broke the silence. "What do you think Blau meant with his full on *mea culpa* confession? He admitted to have done his best to keep our grandparents apart; he got what he wanted there. But, how does that affect me, you... I don't know, and the mention of my mother..." I sensed Daniel stiffen next to me as our flight to Mendoza took off. The man was not afraid of airplanes. With his former James Bond job the man must have spent more hours flying than an overworked stewardess. As part of his Mossad training it wouldn't surprise me if he could fly a plane too.

"What is it, Daniel?" He had become unreadable since we left the estancia.

He turned to me and reached for my hands right when the flight hit a patch of turbulence. "What"? I asked again, this time a bit worried.

"I haven't been completely honest with you," he said.

Great, I thought, what a better place than a closed cabin where I couldn't scream and run, at I don't know how many gazillions feet in altitude, to come clean about wife, children and why not, a dog or two while at it. I pulled my hands from him. "Say what you have to say."

"There was more than Alex's and Franzisca's story when I set out to find you. It has to do with your mother," he spoke slowly as if he were addressing a mental patient.

"So you lied to me then, and I was right. There's history between you and my mother." I felt tears burn the back of my eyes. He would not see me cry. I looked away. "Did you sleep with her?"

"Sofia..."

I crossed my arms and stared at the front of the plane.

"I did not sleep with your mother, Sofia. I said it once and I'll say it again. I was supposed to meet with her, but I couldn't." I heard him swallow hard as if in pain.

My mood had softened enough to realize the panic in the cabin. The plane was doing everything but summersaults. "Spit it out, Bond. We might not make it to Mendoza in one piece."

"It has to do with my father." Before I could blurt out a smart comment, he cut me off. "And no, she did not sleep with my father, either."

I raised my hands in capitulation, "Okay, okay, I'm listening."

"My father was involved with a group, an intellectual faction, if you will, opposed to the military during the Dirty War. He was not, however, the type to set bombs in foreign dignitaries' homes or fire at passing military envoys. My dad was a pacifist at heart and loved his country. He loved freedom. His activities were subtle. He was all about telling the truth to his students. He was a high school history teacher, a great writer also. I have his books, which of course were banned in the country during the time of the *Junta*."

The words came out of him with some difficulty. I suspected this to be the first time Daniel had spoken about it. He was pulling them from a place deep inside of him, from his own little box. I reached for his hands.

The plane had steadied and the passengers sighed in relief. A stewardess, with penciled eyebrows and a grave expression on her face, paced up and down the aisle making sure no one needed hospitalization upon arrival. She paused when she reached our seats.

"You can continue on your search and recovery mission, we're good here," I assured her with a bright smile. She looked at me in disbelief and moved on to the next passengers. That got a laugh out of Daniel, breaking the tension, "You're crazy, you know?" He slid a hand out of my grasp and cupped my cheek. "But you're good for me."

I rubbed my face on his hand and smiled, "Don't get ahead of yourself, Bond. I might still kill you after you finish with your story."

"Right... my story." He sobered. "My father was your mother's history teacher, talk about a small world, and she was pretty captivated by him."

"How do you know this?" I frowned. I didn't know a single detail about Marcela let alone who her high school history teacher was.

"I looked up some of your mother's old schoolmates. Everyone remembered that for the most part Marcela Lazar was a happy-go-lucky girl." I had to laugh at the foreign description of Marcela, but Daniel's seriousness sobered me up. "They all described the relationship she and

305 • Franzisca's Box

your grandmother shared as tight, loving." He paused to make sure that I was taking his story seriously.

I nodded.

He continued. "But they all agreed that something shifted after a party she held at her house the day of the opening ceremony of the Soccer World Cup of 1978. My father became her teacher the year after the *Mundial*. I believe it was your mother's first year in high school. Apparently, she had become a regular, the younger among a group of other students who stayed after hours with the excuse of a homework club, but in reality they were there to get the unofficial story of the true events going on in the country."

"I cannot imagine my mother interested in anything other than herself, but if I learned anything over these past few weeks is that nothing is what it appears to be."

"I was shocked to learn about my father, too," Daniel admitted, "but most of all, it made me feel proud of him. My father spoke freely and tried to answer all his students' questions. According to one of my father's former students, Marcela Lazar was obsessed with a particular General that spent most of his career abroad on diplomatic assignments. His name was General Miguel Armendariz and there is weak proof, but proof all the same, that your mother killed him."

That was too much information to take in at once. Marcela a happy girl with a loving relationship with Abuela, interested in the state of affairs of the country back in the day and also a presumed murderer. No, he was wrong. The Marcela I knew was a miserable person who hated my grandmother and was too much of a Narcissist to care about the events happening around her. And the murder allegations? As questionable as Daniel's story was, I needed to have the whole picture.

"How old was she when she…?"

"Fifteen."

"Gunshot?" I had the need to create a mental visual of the events.

"A grenade. Thrown into his house."

Why would fifteen-year-old Marcela storm into General Armendariz's home gripping a grenade with murder in her mind? It just didn't add up. If she committed the action Daniel suspected her of, *no*, accused her of, there had to be a good reason behind it. Marcela was far from being my cup of tea, but within her selfishness, I could always find reason.

"What's the connection with your father?" I knew I was shaking and had probably blanched in a matter of seconds because Daniel asked the flight attendant for a glass of wine.

"Drink," he said, as he shoved the glass under my nose.

I took a sip. "Your father?"

"He was blamed for Armendariz's murder, even though there is a witness that saw your mother running out of the General's house seconds before the explosion."

I closed my eyes to collect my thoughts. My mother killed an army General and his father was blamed for it, "You must have been a baby when this happened."

"Six months old," Daniel replied.

"Your family went into exile, you didn't." Following the logic, Daniel stood out as a lonely, angry boy amongst the rubble of the story. "You blame us, all of us. You probably hate us." Realization hit me. "You wanted answers to solve your own riddle, *that* is why you got close to me, it had nothing to do with Alex," I accused him. "You used me, but it backfired on you, didn't it, Bond. You thought I could hold some answers to your pitiful life. That my *mamita* and I were thick as thieves and you could get anything you wanted out of me in bed." I stared at him daring him to respond. Bile rose up my throat.

Daniel sucked in a rugged breath, stared at me blankly. "Yes," he responded softly. "Like you said Sofia, it backfired on me. I couldn't be more thankful for the turn of events. Bear in mind I did not have to disclose any of this to you, but can't and won't lie to you. When I first saw you I had set out to crush you, instead I fell in love with you."

Daniel searched into my eyes desperate for acceptance, desperate for an answer. I stayed silent until the plane landed.

"Sofia, please. Say something," he pleaded.

I smiled at him sarcastically. "I would have preferred that you'd slept with my mother."

Chapter Thirty-Nine

San Rafael, Mendoza, March 2013

During the car ride from, *El Plumerillo,* the Mendoza airport, to the finca I went back and forth with my decision to break it off with Daniel. In all honesty, I couldn't. He had said he loved me, a fact I left unacknowledged until I knew what to do with his blunt declaration. The thing was, I believed him. I believed his hatred for us, *me*, as part of the past, and I believed he loved me. I felt his love on every inch of my skin, and I loved him back. My body screamed for me to surrender to my primal instincts and forget the reason why Daniel came into my life. Could it be that simple?

I thought about Franzisca and Alex and what might have broken them. Blau could have been a contributing factor, but there had to be something bigger than a resentful war survivor to come between them.

The word *war* flashed in front of my eyes as a warning sign. War was the one constant that kept folding all three generations involved into the same tangle. We were all huddled in our own bunkers careful to step outside for fear of getting hurt. In the meantime we kept plotting new strategies to win a war to only give birth to a new one. It had to end.

"We should declare a pact," I said to Daniel, breaking the silence. "A peace treaty of some sort. I'm exhausted, Daniel. I don't want to fight this war anymore, and I can't be with you unless you commit your heart and mind to it."

The car made its way up the familiar road to the finca. I opened the window and inhaled the cool, clean air of the Andes. The peaks of the mountain popped at every turn already wearing their white winter bonnets. If my memory served me right, the night would bring freezing temperatures. Oh! How much I had love those nights. The scents of winter were what I remembered the most about my life with Abuela in Mendoza. The aroma of pine in the air, the smoky smell of fire in the hearth when the evening cooled down, the pies in the oven promising a mouthwatering late night snack, and the scent of her when we snuggled close at night for story time.

I wanted to go back to those fond memories at the finca and it was with Daniel I wanted to create new ones. I had come to that decision when the house came into view. But there was a very important *if* in the equation. We could only move on together *if* he let go of the past.

Daniel must have sensed my anxiety for an answer and finally spoke. "Do you know why I couldn't get close to your mother and turned around the day we were supposed to meet?" It was a rhetorical question. He did not wait for me to ask why.

"When I saw her standing at the spot we had agreed on for our meeting, I wasn't sure what I would do to her if I had her within my grasp, Sofia." He turned to me, looked into my eyes. "I know you want me to forgive and forget, but if I am to do that I need to know."

"And then what, Daniel? Then what will you do?"

"I don't know. I really don't." He looked away.

The need for answers to his past weighed heavier on him than any possibility of a future with me. As much as I wanted to live in utopia and call for a cease-fire, I knew I was being unrealistic. As a filmmaker and as of late—with Franzisca's story filling every page of my notebook—a writer, I understood the need for conflict to move a story forward. Conflict created story. War created history.

I did not have to look very far to see firsthand the devastating effects of war fought on a battlefield or throughout the years. Franzisca's story was one, Jakub Berkowitz's was another, Marcela had her share of wars to fight, and right next to me sat the most amazing man, but a wounded warrior at heart.

I kept my eyes closed as much to evade Daniel's gaze as to remember the sounds of the land I had once called home. The change of terrain under the car's tires from smooth pavement to rough gravel indicated the gradual ascent on to the property. I opened my eyes and looked out the window to my right. The creek where I had spent endless childhood hours plotting fantastic stories came into view. And my last warm afternoon skipping along the trail up to the house, the afternoon I met Alex Alcaly, knocked on the gates of my memory.

"Stop," I ordered the driver. "Right here. I'd like to walk."

The diligent driver stopped at my command and regarded me questioningly. "Please, deliver the luggage to the caretakers. I'll be up shortly."

I stepped out of the car, grounded my shoes in the soil of my childhood, and filled my lungs with the morning's crisp air. I hadn't looked back to see what Daniel was doing. I didn't have to. The slam of the car's door and his approaching footsteps said it all.

We walked in silence, a few feet apart, but kept up the same pace. Daniel knew better than to disrupt the moment. With the information we had gathered since Abuela's death and the force of Franzisca's tales breaking down the barriers of fiction and turning into real life stories, I needed time to tie up loose ends.

At close range, the creek glinted as if it was made of silver coins. When we reached its edge I stooped down and swished my hand through its frigid water. "I believed this creek to be magical when I was little." I stood up and walked to a mound of large rocks immersed in the water. "Here." I ran my fingers along their sharp, slippery angles.

"In the crevices of these rocks is where I used to find encrypted messages." I breathed out a laugh.

Daniel didn't laugh. He stood next to me and reached for my hand. "What did the rocks say?"

I pulled away softly and walked further up the stream. "Just stupid girl's dreams. You know, the knight in shining armor, a father, a mother that would love me."

Daniel's ragged intake of breath was his only answer. He had wished for some of those things, too. A pang of guilt hit me. What if he was right? What if Marcela had been responsible for his misfortune? If I said yes, if I said I loved him back, would he be able to look at me and wave the ghosts of the past that came along with my name, with the features of my face?

"Was it here where you met him?" Daniel stood behind me close enough to feel the warmth of his body.

I turned to him. He wanted to know about his grandfather Alex. He wanted me to walk him through that afternoon. I pointed up the dusty path up to the property. "Further up." I led the way up road. "On the way to the house."

We walked up to the house in the same silent fashion as the walk down to the creek. I had told Daniel about the afternoon I had met Alex several times over. As if by memory, he stopped at the exact spot I had stumbled into Alex. He kneeled down and brushed the dirt on the road with his fingers as if he could salvage a piece of the past and change its outcome. "Do you think they still loved each other then?" He looked at me with watery caramel eyes.

His eyes, although lighter in color, held the same intensity I had seen in Alex's that afternoon when he looked at Abuela. Filled with passion, need, and love. Roused from my memory I answered. "Yes," I said. "Then and always."

I hurried to the house where I was enveloped in the loving arms of the two housekeepers, a couple which had been in the family's employ since the earth was created. Daniel followed after me and I introduced him to them as a friend of the family and asked for his luggage to be sent to one of the guest rooms, while I'd be staying in my old bedroom.

"Guest room," Daniel repeated.

"It's for the best," I replied. "I need some space. I'm not used to things moving this fast in my life. And you might need some space of your own, Daniel. Remember why you came searching for me. It wasn't for curiosity or attraction, it was for revenge." An uneasy feeling washed over me as I spoke those words. He had disclosed the truth to me, that his first instinct was to hurt me. "Yes," I said, more sure than ever. "We need space. We need to let go of the past if we intend to have anything between us."

"I said I love you, isn't that enough?" His tone was rising. I was having none of it and took a step away from him. He grabbed my shoulder and turned me to him. "Am I to be penalized for wanting to know the truth?" he shouted.

"I'll tell you everything you want to know, Daniel Alcaly." It was Marcela's voice. "For now, keep your hands off my daughter."

Our heads spun toward her direction. She stood under the shade of an arch, which led to the bedrooms. She moved slightly but not enough to show herself fully.

"I won't stay here long, I promise. But there are things I *must* tell you both."

"Make it quick." I crossed my arms and jutted my chin toward her.

Marcela took a step into the light, "Please, I know I don't deserve anything from you... I..."

I knew Daniel wanted to hold my hand, but I did not want to be touched. I felt attacked from every corner and I needed to protect myself. "Speak."

"Follow me," she said, as she moved past us toward the direction of the living room.

Daniel pulled me back. This time his touch was softer. "I know you're disappointed, but know this: I could never bear to find out the truth, if there's any truth to the story connecting my father to your mother, without you by my side." His eyes were intent on me. "I need you."

Hypocrite. The word described me perfectly. Moments ago, I had cornered Daniel with a speech about war and peace that was worthy of a Nobel Prize. Yet at the first opportunity to prove my philosophy right, I acted like the resentful person I was. I filled my lungs with enough air to propel me forward and entwined my fingers with his.

"I've got your back, Bond."

And we took our first experimental steps toward my yet to be proven theory.

Marcela was a magnificent artist, as much as it pained me to admit it. Her work was as magnetic as her persona. Enigmatic. As a spectator, I wouldn't leave any of her exhibits before I knew her story. I stood in the middle of the living room hands akimbo admiring the obscene spectacle, randomly, yet deliberately displayed around the room. I eyed Daniel and saw him become prey of the same effects. He paused in front of every object and squinted at the subliminal meanings behind them.

"I'm glad you chose to walk away from our meeting, Daniel," Marcela said. I was relieved, because I would have lied to you then."

Marcela seemed to have gained confidence since she walked into the living room. Her body language was relaxed; her voice did not waver. Between the objects of her creation she seemed at home, safe.

My Dalai Lama moment of peace and love to all reached its abrupt end. Knowing Marcela, I couldn't help but feel that this exhibit was yet another *all about me* stint. "It's showtime, Marcela. I'm all eyes and ears."

She nodded slightly. It was obvious words did not come as easily to her as the language of shapes and colors on a canvas. She bit her upper lip and eyed the first of the paintings.

"That's Mamá," she said, before I realized the show had begun. "Mamá," she repeated and looked at Daniel. "She loved your grandfather so very much. When I found out the truth. When I found out what had kept them apart..." Marcela got lost in her thoughts. "My mother cried herself to sleep at night, most nights. She was careful about it, but I heard her. The truth came out, because sooner or later it always does. I was the reason her heart had been broken. I am what came between them and I swore to fix it. I swore to break my mother free from her pain and bring Alex back into her life. I swore to see that key." She pointed at Daniel's key, "joined with my mother's. I swore to bring them together."

I looked from Daniel to her. There was something in her sick exhibit that had caught his eye.

Daniel looked up from a faded newspaper photograph to Marcela. "Did you kill him?"

"Yes," she replied. A blunt declaration of guilt.

Chapter Forty

Bucharest, March 1943

The months after their passage to England, Franzisca worked hand in hand with the Portuguese Ambassador at Hungary, Carlos de Sampayo Garrido, and José Rojas Moreno, the Spanish Ambassador at Bucharest. The diplomats contributed actively to the rescue of Jews by providing safe houses and false documents for the refugees' transport out of Nazi infested territories and into Portugal and Spain. Through the underground network, Franzisca fed the diplomats with those seeking asylum and supported their efforts financially. Alerted by the suspicions surrounding Swiss banks and their ambivalent policies regarding Jewish money, Franzisca emptied her accounts at the Swiss National Bank and transferred her fortune to banks in Spain, Portugal, Canada, and the Dominican Republic. Her new partners in crime, the diplomats that fought the Nazis from their highly appointed positions, had suggested she create iron clad trusts and sell her properties to them as the best way to protect her assets while the war still raged through Europe, especially now with the Red Army marching firmly into Nazi territories.

After her financial transactions were finalized, she held a secret meeting with the senior member of the underground fighters she had originally initiated Operation Baroness. The man was as stoic as ever, but now she glimpsed respect toward her where there had been none two years before.

"It's the Russians people are afraid of now," the senior fighter said. "Stalin is no better than Hitler; the bastard loves power and those who step in his way do not live to tell the tale. He showed what he was made of in the Battle of Stalingrad. The Reds are not going away, Baroness." He shook his head. "I see more of them of them on the streets now. It won't be long before we fall under their hammer next."

Franzisca had to agree. The Red Army led by Stalin had fought an industrious and gruesome war against Hitler and on February of that year, they had finally defeated him. Stalin had the same demented edge as Hitler did. Blood and destruction were the means to accomplish their dreams of world domination.

Their meeting was interrupted when an out of breath resistance fighter broke in unannounced.

"How many?" the senior resistance fighter asked. He did not need a full disclosure to know the news were bad. His knuckles gripping his pistol until they stood up like a row of bullets.

"The cargo to Yugoslavia," the messenger responded between gasps. "The baroness," he said, avoiding Franzisca. "It's her they're after."

From then on it was a real war for Franzisca. A vital part of the resistance had been exposed and publicly executed hours before. Among other loses, Franzisca was briefed about the murder of Lucien and his family five months before and of sightings of Lupescu in and around the palace. There was a price placed on the head of the baroness. She was wanted alive.

Franzisca had to escape Romania. Money and contacts were no match for the sadistic baron who had risen from the dead declaring treason at the hands of a woman who claimed to be his wife and had emptied his coffers. The laughter of his peers and former allies fueled his anger. Lupescu had been bested by a house servant. The daughter of the woman he had punished to death. The granddaughter of the man his father had robbed, and a Jew.

Franzisca's defiant nature screamed to stand face to face with Lupescu and see the expression on his face. She finally had him where she wanted him. The man was on his knees desperate to capture her and was doing his best to corner her. The baron's frenzy to get his hands around her neck had resonated throughout the many branches of the resistance across Bucharest, identifying her as a high-risk fugitive to harbor.

"There're many lives at risk, Baroness." Those were the parting words every time she was transferred from one safe house to the other.

Lupescu had ordered troops to strip and search every corner of Bucharest. Except for one place, Franzisca thought as she weighed the risks the resistance was taking in order to protect her. "The palace,' she said. "He would never look for me there."

Two weeks after Baron Lupescu had launched his bloodiest hunt since the war started, on a moonless night, Franzisca slipped into his house through the servant's entrance. Marietta, the main housekeeper, had only to hear three consecutive knocks on the door, Franzisca's childhood password when playing hide and seek with the rest of the staff, to know it was her knocking.

"Have you lost your wits, child?" Marietta hushed as she led her to her room. "He'll kill you, he will. I've never seen him in such a rage."

Franzisca laughed, hugged, and kissed the housekeeper. "That man has never set foot in this wing of the house. And as smart as he thinks he is, he would never suspect that I'm hiding under his roof." The fleeting smile on Franzisca's face vanished. "It was a gamble I risked coming here. The question is, why are you still here? I sent enough gold for you to leave the country. I don't want you around this madman and I don't want you to take the fall for me."

Marietta, a humble old lady, stood hiding her embarrassment. "Where am I to go, child. All I know is this house. I was born into service." She opened up her palms. "I saved the money, that I did. We buried it under my sister's house. When I see you safe, when the war is over, I'll move to the country with her." The housekeeper wrinkled her nose and sniffed the air around her as if looking for the origin of something foul.

For the past two weeks, Franzisca had gotten a taste of what the resistance fighters endured with pride and without complaints. She hadn't slept more than an hour a day, food was scarce, and a bath completely out of the question.

Franzisca smelled her armpits. "It's me," she said, without shame. "Would a bath be too much to ask?"

Thirty minutes later Franzisca sat stark naked in the small tub the housekeeper brought to the room. She moaned as she slowly dipped her head under the water reveling in the pleasure of clean water soaking her scalp.

"How am I to explain you to the other servants?" Marietta groaned as she scrubbed Franzisca's back with the devotion of a mother.

"Tell them I'm the new help in the kitchen. You know I can bake a good pie." Franzisca was running a huge risk. But the palace was the best strategic point to monitor Lupescu's moves. Eventually, he would move his hunting party out of the city, at that time Franzisca intended to make contact with the resistance and flee Romania.

The housekeeper agreed to help Franzisca and to keep her abreast of Lupescu's action. However, she steadfastly refused to let Franzisca out and around the kitchen in open view of the other servants.

"Times are tough, child. I don't trust nobody." Marietta hid Franzisca in a storeroom located off the kitchen.

The door to the storeroom remained locked at all times, unless supplies were needed for the kitchen. Marietta kept the only key that opened its door and no one went into that room unless accompanied by her. She kept a tight tally of the food going in and out of the storage room. Food was scarce in the city, and many of the new help hired after the baron's return to the residence six months ago, had taken the job based solely on the two meals a day it offered.

"Bear with me, child," Marietta said, as she supplied Franzisca with blankets, a chamber pot, and enough food and water for a few days. "I'll be back on Friday."

The door to the storeroom closed and Franzisca was left in complete darkness. Friday, she thought, six days to Friday. She would surely drive herself mad in that tiny space. Franzisca was wary of dark, tight spaces. "Breathe," Alex had whispered in her ear the first night they spent in the tunnel, the day her mother had died in the explosion. So she breathed, slowly, calming the pace of her racing heart. One by one the tears came. Tears that had stung her chest, but could not find release when she was informed of the carnage her dear Lucien and his family had befallen at the hands of Lupescu. Tears for her uncertain future. Tears for Alex.

By now, Alex would be well on his way to South America. The possibility of something going awfully wrong was always discussed before any plans were put into action. Alex knew of the passports, of her wishes to have Jakub transported with the rest of the children, of the gold coins all children were to carry stuffed in the Norah Wellings dolls, and of the arrangements she had made for little Margaret's safekeeping. Tears spent, she made peace with her efforts of the last two years and finally dozed off.

Whenever Marietta popped into the storeroom, with a clean chamber pot and supplies, she informed Franzisca of the latest news.

The baron had doubled the number of men needed for his hunt. Homes and businesses of suspected Jewish sympathizers were raided and their owners beaten to no avail. He could be heard screaming through the length of the palace with vitriol in his every word, *the Jewish bastard*, his name of choice for Franzisca, was as good as dead. Lupescu was as violent as ever and many of the new servants had fled the palace without pay to avoid his fist. There wasn't a single wall around the palace without a fracture or a hole, the results of his furious punches and kicks for every day of fruitless search.

On the third week of his pursuit, Lupescu received a report from the officials working the border with Yugoslavia of a priceless cargo—the so called baroness—expected in five days' time.

Smelling blood and vengeance, his fingers tingling in anticipation for every bone he would break in her body, Lupescu left Bucharest that very same night en route to intercept Franzisca.

"Hurry, child," Marietta hushed when she opened the door of the storeroom. "A car is waiting for you outside the gates of the palace with its lights off."

Marietta gave her a bundle with clothes and food and gathered her into the warm embrace of her ample bosom. "Your mother would be very proud, child." Overwhelmed with emotion, Franzisca could only nod, kiss the sweet woman for one last time, and break into a run to her freedom.

Having reorganized some of the routes that had been ambushed by Lupescu and having opened new ones; Franzisca was smuggled out of Romania through Bechet and into Bulgaria. Once in Bulgaria, she was under the protection of Bishop Kyril of Plodvdiv.

The Bishop had made a defiant stand in an act of civil disobedience against his king by allowing local Jews to take refuge in his church and in his own home. He had also prevented the deportation of nearly sixteen hundred Jews, who had been ordered to assemble at Plovdiv's train station during the night of March 9, 1943, by vowing to lie across the railroad tracks and made a promise to the Jews, words that would echo for generations to come: "Wherever you go, I'll go with you."

The Bishop welcomed Franzisca with open arms. A fervent opponent to the Holocaust, Bishop Kyril had kept a close ear to the activities of Operation Baroness in Bucharest and across Europe. He had imagined her to be older, sturdier, not the nineteen-year-old, hollow eyed child, standing in front of him, shivering with cold and hunger. But looks were deceiving; he came to understand not a day after the baroness arrived in his church. The young lady cared nothing for her safety; her only concern was to transport as many refugees out of the scope of the Nazis as possible.

It was the spirit of the Bulgarian people that renewed hope in Franzisca. A melting pot of minorities; Bulgaria rose against its monarch and refused to comply with its deportation policies. The Patriarch of the Bulgarian Orthodox Church, Archbishop Stefan, issued fake baptism certificates in an attempt to save Jews from further deportations to Nazis extermination camps. He harbored leaders of the Bulgarian Jewish community in his home despite of the continuous threats that the government made on his life, Stephan declared the doors of every Orthodox Church and monastery open to Jews.

Franzisca worked tirelessly with both Bishop Kyril and Archbishop Stephan. Through diplomatic channels, she had been able to move funds from her various accounts to buy passage for fugitives. In and around the churches that were flooded with persecuted Jews, Franzisca had taken over the care of the children who had been separated from their families.

"I have a certificate of baptism for you, Baroness," Bishop Kyril announced to Franzisca one morning while she inventoried the food supplies the church kept for the refugees. "What name should I write on it?"

***

It took Franzisca until January of 1944 to arrive to Spain. Her ally and friend, Ambassador José Rojas Moreno, nearly fell off his chair when she walked into his office. Franzisca wore her white coat, the only garment that had survived her long ordeal, and a smug smile on her face.

"Baroness," he cried out, after pulling her into an impulsive embrace to insure himself that it was her and not a specter what had walked in his office. "They said you were dead. Lupescu…" Rojas held her arms tightly. "We had word that you were shot at the border with Yugoslavia." He shook his head and led her to a chair. "Alcaly thinks you're dead."

Franzisca recounted her activities from the moment she had disappeared underground, her stay at Lupescu's, her experience in Bulgaria, the death of the baroness and the birth of the woman who now sat in his office.

"You stayed under his roof…" Rojas shook his head bewildered. "Romanian officials deny the evidence of Lupescu's return from the dead. They had declared him dead in battle, serving his country. They turned him into a national hero." Rojas raised his eyebrows in disbelief. "His house went up in flames sometime after reports of your death reached our ears. The servants that survived swore it was the baron who set the palace on fire. No one has seen him since."

Franzisca said a silent prayer hoping that Marietta was among the survivors. "I need to get to Argentina," she said. "I must find Alcaly." Franzisca handed Rojas her new identification card.

Rojas burst out laughing. The name in the card, Claudia Lazar, belonged to the woman that had robbed young Rojas of sleep during his teenage years. In a bout of confidence, while still in Romania, he had confessed to Franzisca his secret love for a neighbor, a young woman, from a known *Converso* family that had not lived to see her seventeenth year. "Oh, Baroness." He chuckled. "You're trouble."

On April 14, 1944, Ambassador José Rojas Moreno, made an impromptu visit to Buenos Aires, Argentina, with his mistress, a beautiful young lady in a white coat, with olive skin, raven hair and violet-blue eyes. Her identity was concealed, to protect Rojas' impeccable reputation as a family man, and her entrance to the country was never recorded.

Rojas returned to Spain alone.

The moment Franzisca set foot on Argentinean soil she exhausted every resource she had to find Alex. Not a day went by that she did not start a new trail to go back to him. People had heard of him and of his successful endeavors as a cattle rancher in Buenos Aires, but all leads were severed every time she felt he was within her reach. It was as if he did not want to be found.

Chapter Forty-One

Buenos Aires, July 1963

Alex had escaped the snowstorm in time. For the past twelve years he had made Cipolletti, a city located in the High Valley of the Rio Negro province, down in the Argentinean Patagonia, his home. The beauty of the area, the crystalline lakes, the mountains, the thick forests, and the ever-changing colors throughout the seasons, left him breathless on his first visit when he was scouting for land and it had put a smile on little Isaac's face.

Rio Negro was famous for its juicy red apples and Alex needed a change of pace from the strenuous life of a cattle rancher in the Pampas and wanted free time to raise his son Isaac. The gold Old Nicu had left for him, whatever was left after the war, had been plenty to let him live comfortably and purchase land in the Buenos Aires province, when he single-mindedly decided to become a *gaucho*.

Cattle ranching proved to be a profitable business. Alex's growing wealth was a testament to his talent for the trade, and had encouraged him to invest in other farmland ventures. Besides his ambition for growth and his desire to build a solid empire for Isaac, Alex had the constant need to keep busy. He did not want to think. Thinking always led him to Franzisca.

During his first years in Argentina he concentrated on working hard. It was the only way his body could numb the pain of losing Franzisca. Over and over again, he had read the telegram he had received from Rojas upon his arrival in Argentina and he still did not believe Franzisca was dead. Not his Franzisca. She was a fighter, smarter than Lupescu. She was out there in the world; he felt it in his gut. She would come back to him.

But Franzisca did not return to him. In a matter of two years, Alex turned into a brute, hairy like a wolf, living in the wilderness on his own ranch. He talked only to cows, horses, and to Jakub, who now called himself Lukas Blau—a successful investment banker—when he came around for a visit.

Having had enough of his friend's sulking, Jakub decided to take matters in his own hands. The community of Polish Jews had grown rapidly after the war. Some made it into the country legally, while many, rejected by President Peron's anti-Semitic policies, were denied entrance and diverted to Brazil. Jews eventually found their way into Argentina, illegally, through Pasos de Los Libres, a northeastern border crossing between the two countries.

Jakub had been introduced to a handful of beautiful young Polish beauties who wanted nothing more than to marry and settle, but he remained skeptical about love and marriage. Some of his old roguish-self resurfaced in his new life. Jakub loved women in his bed at night and out of it in the morning.

There was one girl in particular, Clara, he had abstained from luring between his sheets. She was beautiful, with blonde hair and green eyes, smart, and too good for the likes him. I would spoil her, he thought, the night he met her at the Polish Jewish Center in Buenos Aires. Clara was a nice woman, a woman for Alex.

"Take a bath, Alcaly, you reek of shit," Jakub said as he walked unannounced into Alex's house.

Alex had a three-week-old beard; his skin was brown from the sun and splotches of cow manure stained the front of his shirt. "I like it," he responded, "the cows like it, too."

"I don't mind," came a female voice.

Alex raised his eyes and met Clara's green stare. She was beautiful and his groin tightened at the sight of her. He threw an odious glance at Jakub, who shrugged innocently.

"Alex meet Clara. Clara meet Alex."

Two months later, Clara moved onto the ranch. A year and half later they celebrated the arrival of Isaac Alcaly, their baby boy. Four years after that, Clara left the ranch, Alex and their son, never to return.

"I can't compete with the ghost of your Franzisca," she had said to Alex. "You will never love another woman the way you love her."

Alex did not fight her nor did he try to convince her to stay. He had his son and the memory of the only woman he had ever loved. That was all he needed.

For thirteen years, Alex and Isaac lived in Rio Negro, with Alex dividing his time between his two properties. Isaac had the sheltered childhood Alex wanted him to have and had grown into a sensible young man, in love with books, history, and social justice. Alex encouraged his son's intellectual inclinations. When Isaac was a young child, Alex spent hours watching his son's behavior, dreading that in a blink of an eye his father's violent character would emerge in his good-natured child.

As Isaac's University years approached, Alex decided Buenos Aires to be the land of opportunities for his son. So, they packed up, Isaac finished high school in a private boarding school for boys, and for Alex, it was back to the cattle ranch.

Alex had just finished cleaning the horse stalls, and had checked on the newborn calves that by now were already growing into promising strong cattle. The previous week Jakub had mentioned he might stop by after he returned from a business trip, so Alex did not turn around when he heard footsteps on the dirt floor of the barn.

"I was thinking dinner in the city, I want to stay over tonight and visit Isaac in the morning, what do you think?" Alex had his face close to a cow's butt.

"Dinner sounds good."

Alex froze. The cow mooed.

He heard soft footsteps approach him, but he was afraid to turn around. No, he did not want to hope. How long had it been? He didn't have to think. Every day without her had left a mark in his heart. Twenty years.

She kneeled beside him. "I've been looking for you for the past eighteen years."

Alex turned to her with eyes closed. His dirty hands found her face. He traced the bones that made up the face he dreamt of every night, the lips he had longed to kiss, the shape of those rare violet-blue eyes he never lost hope to see his reflection in again.

"Franzisca," he whispered, "*inima mea.*"

***

Alex kept the news of Franzisca's return from Jakub. He wanted her to himself. For six months they hid from the world. They travelled from Rio Negro to Buenos Aires. Laughed, cried, and made love every time as if it were the last time. The war was over; the nightmare was over, they could finally be together.

"Marry me." Alex bent down on one knee and produced a most dazzling diamond ring. "Marry me," he said again and again, grinning like a boy.

Franzisca bent down in front of him and kissed him tenderly. "You hold the other half of my heart."

Franzisca did not want to marry until she could do it under her rightful name, Franzisca Schultz. Under the name Claudia Lazar, and with the help of her Spanish friend, Franzisca had led a normal life since her arrival in Argentina. She got an identification card, a passport, bought properties, and ran businesses. But to start a life with Alex, she wanted to shed all remnants from the war years. She wanted life to be normal for once.

Scratching his head Alex looked at Franzisca. "I understand, *inima mea*. I would still marry you even if you had a man's name. But I understand. The problem here is that I don't trust the Department of Immigration, they are not the most efficient, you know?" True to Alex's words Franzisca's paperwork had gotten lost in the system and the wedding got delayed.

"It's all right," Franzisca said to a furious Alex. "We have the rest of our lives ahead of us, what would a couple of more months of waiting do?"

***

Jakub did not take the news of Alex's impending marriage to the *baroness*, as he still called her, gracefully. "You lied to me." He scowled like a little boy. "Aren't I your brother?"

"You are my brother, Jakub." Alex grasped Jakub's shoulders with crushing strength. "I want you to be by my side under the *Chuppah*. I want you to be our witness."

Jakub nodded and smiled, but the smile did not reach his eyes. He would never stand witness to the union of the man that had become his only family and the woman that had played a major role in the loss of his brothers. The wedding would never take place, not if Jakub played his cards right. Jakub's arms folded around Alex with deep emotion. For Alex, it was a congratulatory gesture. For Jakub, it was farewell.

***

Jakub recognized the General from a picture in the newspaper and had monitored him ever since. General Armendariz enjoyed his afternoon tea at the Alvear Palace Hotel, located in *Recoleta*, the most luxurious neighborhood in Buenos Aires, every day at five o'clock sharp.

Jakub stood on the sidewalk and saw the General walk into the hotel. He counted to ten before he followed him inside.

***

Franzisca hadn't been back to her flat in Recoleta since the day she walked into Alex's barn seven months before.

"But, I need clothes and my plants will die," she argued, not too convincingly, the morning after their first night back together.

Alex held her to him possessively. "You're not going anywhere out of my sight ever again, we'll buy you everything new." He started nibbling on her neck and she knew what the result of his exploration would be.

So, they did. Franzisca allowed Alex to choose things for her, even though his taste in clothes was somewhat earthy. But, she did not mind, she was finally happy and the clothes... did not stay on for long, anyway.

Since they had reunited, it was the first time Franzisca had flatly denied accompanying Alex to Rio Negro. There was nothing she loved more than to spend every moment with him, but she had neglected her obligations at the many artistic and humanitarian foundations she chaired far too long. "You'll be back in a week, Alex, and I'll be exactly where you left me. You'll see."

The memory of the look on Alex's face made her regret her decision the moment she walked into her empty flat. The shutters were closed allowing only slivers of light to filter through. The place reeked of decay and abandonment, the dead plants Franzisca thought, as she walked toward a window to let some fresh air in. A whiff of another smell made her freeze halfway. Her skin prickled, her heart stopped. Pine and tobacco.

The first blow to her head left her stunned, unable to process what was happening. The second blow threw her down on her back on the hardwood floors. Her head hit the floor leaving her dazed. A face loomed above her. The right side was disfigured with burn scars. It was the face of the man she had defied, tricked, and humiliated. It was Baron Mihail Lupescu.

"I have come to claim what's mine, wife. I will not kill you, bitch, but you'll wish I would."

The beating was endless and so was the rape. The sadist held her at his mercy for six days and five nights.

During that time, Franzisca wove in and out of consciousness praying silently for death, only to find him inches from her, ready to break her, torture her, rape her.

When she came to consciousness at the end of the sixth day, her limbs were no longer bound and Lupescu was gone.

The morning Alex was due back in town, Franzisca packed her bags and left.

Chapter Forty-Two

San Rafael, Mendoza, April 2013

Even the flies had stopped their annoying buzz to listen to Marcela. Abuela had told her this story. It had come from her. Not from Franzisca in a way of a nighttime story. It was real.

By now, Marcela was standing by the faded newspaper picture.

"So that is…" I couldn't bring myself to mention his name.

"Baron Mihail Lupescu," Marcela finished for me. "My father."

"How old were you?" I suddenly felt sick. Thinking of Abuela at the hands of Lupescu, my mother the product of his rape. Me with his blood in my veins.

"She did not tell me the whole story until I was fifteen. But by then, I already knew about the character of my father." Marcela looked at Daniel. "Isaac, your dad, he helped me find the truth behind Armendariz and the Lupescu name. He had access to records no one else had. I never told your father why I wanted to know about Lupescu and he never asked."

"I didn't know my father, but I have the feeling he must have known why." Daniel smiled weakly. "Some things run in the family."

"Mossad agent," I added as way of information.

Marcela nodded and moved on to her next exhibit, the torn and bloody shirt.

"Alex did not rest until he found Mamá." It was so strange to hear Marcela speak of Abuela with such affection. "When he found us, I was barely three months old. She begged him to leave her alone. She lied to him. Told him she had a lover and that the baby was his. Mamá told Alex she did not love him anymore. I was the spitting image of Lupescu and with Jakub's sudden disappearance, it didn't take long for Alex to piece the story together. Still, she told him she didn't want to see him again and asked him for his key back."

"Franzisca always loved him, till her last breath," I said. In my mind, I could read the last note she sent to him, *you hold the other half of my heart.*

Marcela smiled. "Of course he never gave the key back to her. It was his to keep. He knew her like the palm of his own hand. If you ask me, Alex had no doubts he was the only man she ever loved, even if Mamá learned to hide her emotions. She had the ability to turn into someone she was not. It was at night when the walls came down. She cried, and cried. She held her key in her hand and cried. Throughout the years, Alex had begged her to come back to him to forget about Lupescu. But Mamá couldn't. Lupescu had done things to her, horrible things… and the things he had forced her to do. Mamá was broken, she felt unworthy of Alex. She felt dirty." Marcela closed her eyes and swallowed her tears. "I couldn't bear it, when I found out… Lupescu had to die, and I was going to bring Mamá and Alex back together."

"The grenade," Daniel said.

"I had enough money at my disposal," Marcela replied.

"Did my father put you in contact with a supplier?" Daniel demanded straight answers.

"Yes." Marcela shook her head, "Daniel, your father was the most wonderful man. He would've never… it was me. It was all me."

"But he helped you," Daniel expounded as if conducting an interrogation.

A heavy silence fell over the room. Marcela turned her back to us and stared at the artwork and artifacts that spoke on her behalf.

"Yes," Marcela answered. She sucked in a labored breath and turned to face Daniel. "He also wanted Lupescu dead. He knew my mother and he loved your grandfather. Isaac had seen your abuelo Alex suffer. So, we talked about it. As young as I was, I knew that it had to be me the one to look at Lupescu in the eye. It had to be me carrying the grenade. Isaac did not want to hear of it, but after I told him everything he had done to my mother, he consented to my request. He drove me to Lupescu's house, stood behind me when I faced him. And so I did… I killed him, I killed my father." Marcela looked from me to Daniel and waved at the remaining paintings. "You know the rest of the story."

Fifteen years old, I thought. What was I doing when I was fifteen? Stressing out about my frizzy hair and hating my mother. Mulling over which boy to go to Winter Formal Dance with, and hating my mother. Travelling around the world with Abuela and hating my mother some more.

At fifteen, Marcela fought to save her own mother. At fifteen, Marcela drew a well thought out strategy and went to war against the one man that had engendered her and destroyed her mother. At fifteen, Marcela acted out of selflessness to give her mother what she had taken from her the moment she was conceived. Marcela Lazar was a victim, a fighter, a survivor.

"When I understood the repercussions of my actions," Marcela went on, "Isaac had to leave the country right away. And then you were left behind, Daniel." Marcela looked down, gathered strength and fixed her eyes on his. "I *am* sorry."

Daniel studied her in detail. Her confession had been truthful. She had answered all his questions. Still, he regarded her with a hard stare.

"I would've have done the same thing you did, Marcela," he admitted. "In fact, I did when I joined the *Tza'al*. It doesn't ease the pain, though." He raked his fingers through his hair. "It doesn't help to understand, but you already know that." Daniel looked at me then at Marcela, "To know that my father fought for abuelo Alex, does help. Thanks for telling me the truth."

The Marcela I knew had been a selfish, arrogant person and never showed any regard for Abuela or me. I couldn't look at her and reconcile the old Marcela with the one I just had been introduced to.

"I don't expect you to love me, Sofia, or approve of my actions or even understand the why of the decisions. Please know that after what I've done, as much as I loved you from the moment you were born I had to give you up. And then, when I watched Mamá coming out of her shell and become Franzisca again, even if only through stories, I knew I had done the right thing for you both. "

"You could've been part of it. You could've started all over again... with me." I was close to tears.

"No, I couldn't. I didn't know how and I had no right to do to you what I had already done to all of them." Marcela's hands fanned out. "I couldn't be a mother to you as much as I ached to have you."

I saw Marcela do something I did not imagine her capable of, she cried. I stood paralyzed at the display of emotion. She was crying for me and for herself, for abuela and Alex, for Daniel and his family. I inched toward her without realizing that my feet were moving. My arms came around her shoulders and I held her close to me. Her heartbeat resonated on my chest and shook my body into a kind of feeling I didn't know was possible. Marcela was my mother. Love her or hate her, I couldn't deny her.

After a very long time, we disengaged from each other. Light blue eyes stared into brown eyes, a new beginning.

All three of us stood in silence in the living room, licking our wounds, tracing our scars. Daniel walked over to me and reached for my hand. I looked from our entwined hands to Marcela who had once again retreated to a dark corner of the room. What would Abuela do?

The response came to me in the way of stories and pie dough. I disengaged my fingers from Daniel's and headed out of the room. "Aren't you two coming?"

"Where are you going? Daniel asked, startled. I saw Marcela move in the darkness. She turned in my direction.

"Where else? To the kitchen," I said. "It's about time we bake a pie."

***

Later that night, when the house was asleep, I slid out of my bed and rummaged into the depths of my suitcase until my hands came in contact with Franzisca's box. The stories I had penned and stashed there in the last couple of months, made up my history, the history of the ones that came before me, I glanced toward the bed and smiled at the peaceful, sleeping form of Daniel, and perhaps the history of the ones that would come after us.

Abuela was right; stories don't have a beginning or an end. There are continuous, they repeat themselves, they sneak up on us, and they are played out in front of us, to be relived over and over again.

I heard Daniel whisper something in his sleep; my heart filled with love for him. I knew what I had to do next.

I opened my battered notebook and biting my lower lip, I wrote the unfinished chapter of Franzisca's Story.

Chapter Forty-Three

San Rafael, Mendoza 1987

Little Sofia stood on a low stool and playfully kneaded some left over dough from the pie that was already baking in the oven.

"And then he called out her name." Sofia's brows furrowed in the way she did when she was serious.

"Who called out whose name, Sofia?" Abuela asked.

Sofia turned to Claudia Lazar and frowned at her in disbelief. "Well, who else, Abuela? The boy she found, of course."

"Are you talking about Franzisca?" Sofia had her Abuela's full attention. "But, that is not part of the story, Sofia."

"Yes it is. It is part of *my* story. You said I could make up whatever I wanted." The little girl pressed her doughy hands on her hips and Claudia had to stifle a laugh.

"Tell me, then," Claudia said.

Little Sofia stepped down from the stool and climbed on Claudia's lap. "He will call out her name, but only Franzisca will hear him. She will know then that it is time for her to stop fighting the ogres and live happily ever after with him, the boy she found."

"Do you think that is what will happen to them?" Claudia's eyes filled with tears.

Sofia lifted her little hand to Claudia's face and stroked her softly. "Of course, Abuela. I will make it happen."

About the Author:

Sandra was born and raised in Argentina, and immigrated to the U.S in her mid-twenties. While her academic background is in psychoanalysis, anthropology, Judaic studies and Hebrew language, her interests ultimately turned to writing. Through the years, Sandra worked as a freelance writer. She is also a screenwriter and screenplay consultant.

Franzisca's Box is her second novel.

Acknowledgements:

In this my second novel I want to express my infinite thanks to my dear friends Author Brenda Mckoy and Producer/writer/director Christine Fry for sticking with me every word of the way. To Michael Mejias for his mentoring during the early stages of Franzisca's Box. And last but not least, to my husband, children, parents, brother, and my friend Lucy for their love and encouragement.

I'm so fortunate to have your relentless support.

Social Media Links:

Website: www.palabrasandstories.com

Facebook:
https://www.facebook.com/Sandra-Perez-Gluschankoff-1960339320857070/?ref=aymt_homepage_panel

Twitter: https://twitter.com/SandraGluschank
@SandraGluschank

Goodreads:
https://www.goodreads.com/author/show/6451518.Sandra_Perez_Gluschankoff

Amazon author page: http://www.amazon.com/Sandra-Perez-Gluschankoff/e/B009TDKBNU/ref=sr_ntt_srch_lnk_1?qid=1448303472&sr=8-1

IMdB:
http://www.imdb.com/name/nm5295886/?ref_=rvi_nm

www.ingramcontent.com/pod-product-compliance
Lightning Source LLC
Chambersburg PA
CBHW060943030726
47503CB00003B/710